small stations fiction

Teresa Moure

Black Nightshade

Published in 2018 by
SMALL STATIONS PRESS
20 Dimitar Manov Street, 1408 Sofia, Bulgaria
You can order books and contact the publisher at
www.smallstations.com

This book was first published in the Galician language as *Herba moura*
by Ediciòns Xerais de Galicia (Vigo, 2005). A list of our fiction titles
can be found at www.smallstations.com/fiction

ISBN 978-954-384-085-4

Teresa Moure

Black Nightshade

WINNER OF THE XERAIS PRIZE FOR NOVELS

Translated from Galician by **Philip Krummrich**

Small
Stations
Press

Contents

I

Christina of Sweden

1

This spring Stockholm seems not to have awakened from its winter's lethargy. The birds have not shown up yet, much less the flowers or the butterflies. The trees continue gleaming naked: one might even say these days it's too much of an effort for them to bud out after a raw winter like the one that descended on these blessed northern lands. Night is falling on Stortorget Square, right in the middle of the city. Although it is no more than five in the afternoon, the yellowish ocher color of the whole neighborhood is already fading in intensity; in a few minutes, it will look as washed out as the water that eddies under the bridges, as gray as the water that has just passed by, as cold as the water that at this very second is flowing towards the sea and in a moment will be swallowed up in it. With a stage consisting of such a dreary landscape, and with the cold air lashing the faces of the passersby, thoughts are inevitably going to be on the sad side. "Never again will we see the waters of the same river passing by." For Stortorget is a square between bridges, and moreover a sad square, linked to the violence of life. Even if there is no monument to bear witness to the event, in another time Stortorget was the scene of a crime, which the people of Stockholm called "The Bloodbath." In November 1520 the Danish king Christian II besieged the Swedish ruler Sten Sture the Younger, until he made him surrender and the Swedes had to accept Christian as king. The latter promised amnesty and organized an incredible three-day celebration in the fortress of Tre Kronor. After laughing and drinking, dancing, moaning, toasting, swearing; after loving and falling asleep, and drinking and eating again, and hugging each other, after enjoying, in short, the good fortune of being alive, on the third day, when the end of the festivities was drawing near, all the participants were arrested, accused of heresy. On the following morning, more than eighty citizens, the majority of them nobles, were decapitated in this square, now and forever a square of pain and wounded pride. But today blood does not run in the canals of Stockholm, even though the incident has left its mark in the suspicion with which the Swedes regard foreigners. "We will never bathe in these same waters again, because they have passed us by, once and for all." The thoughts are not in the landscape; they come from a human head that projects an elongated shadow over the water. No, to tell the truth, it is the whole body, tall, slender, that projects that elongated silhouette; the head is a small part of that shadow-figure, the least representative part of it, perhaps, because just as the light strikes it right now, it is the lower part of the body that is outlined and widened by the effect of the twilight. It is a human figure, resting its hands on the railing of one of the bridges, it does not matter which one now. The hands, slender, with extremely long fingers, cannot be seen, for they are encased in gloves. Without the clues that the hands could offer, it turns out to be hard to tell whether it is a man or a woman. It is wearing loose-fitting outer clothing, rich and well-cut although not ostentatious. There are no hems or ruffles on the lower edge of the outfit that would reveal a lady. Nor is there a moustache or beard, nor breeches over boots, nor a hat with a feather, to give away a gentleman. It could be a young man or a young woman, not an old woman, nor a face from another country, with a different skin color. The person who is leaning on the bridge and looking at the water thinks: "Why is it that we do not realize that the water is passing until we see it murmuring on the rocks, one step below the level where we are standing, when we are no longer able to grasp it?" With such thoughts, one would say that it is a man, for the head of a woman, as is well known, is better suited to adornments than to thoughts, especially if they are serious and profound like these. The human figure that leans on the railing of the bridge is a sad person. Or, if you like, it is a person and, in addition, it is sad. This is as much as can be said about it. Besides, of course, that it is wearing a black cape down to its feet with a hood pulled over its head. Like a friar, exactly. And, at the same time, any observer who looked at it would know that it is not a friar: the clothing does not suggest poverty, the look is too rebellious to accept obedience, and... well, regarding chastity it is better not to speak, in these times when there are so many naughty people with outwardly exemplary lives... and chaste people who have been hoodwinked, of course. In any case, those lips, the ones belonging to this human figure leaning on the railing of the bridge in Stortorget, are quite arrogant, and seem not to be made for the worms to devour without first having been a storm, a nest, a grave, without having sought and received. In other respects the face is balanced, not exactly beautiful or ugly: either adjective could be applied to it without going too far wrong, pure conflict, with strong cheekbones and a rather long nose. There is no way to judge the eyes, because the hood of the cape, without actually covering them, does not allow them to be seen clearly and gives them a mysterious appearance. This human figure, alone like this on the bridge, could be that of a Knight Templar just returned from Jerusalem and in possession of the most precious of secrets. It could also be a convict just escaped from prison. Or, why not?, an artist who was seeking inspiration in these waters that circulate and pursue each other without ever catching up. It could be, this human figure on the bridge, many different characters, and it is precisely that difficulty in assigning it attributes that would perturb an observer. For whoever sees, for example, a young woman with two children clinging to her skirts knows at once that she is a mother who is crossing the square quickly so as to get to shelter in her house before she catches cold. But a figure like this one that is to be seen today in Stortorget is indefinable, independent, and that makes it disturbing. This figure, as if it felt that it was not well accepted by the passersby, scarce at this hour, turns and begins to walk. The movement lends authority to its bearing. The elegant and stylized figure is not going to leave Stadsholmen, the largest island of Gamla Stan, and after a short walk through its narrow streets, suddenly, as though pulled by a spring, it turns on its heel and heads with a confident stride towards the castle of Tre Kronor, currently the residence of the Swedish monarchs. For the figure that was watching the sad ebbing of the water was not a man, but a woman; not old, but young; not merely a human figure, but the genuine queen of Sweden. What could she have been doing there on her own? And at this hour? Could she be mad? She could. Her name is Christina.

2

From the *Book of Women by Hélène Jans*
The herb called milfoil, yarrow or woundwort
(*Achillea millefolium*)

A modest plant, topped by flower heads of white, purple
or pink which you may encounter in pastures, knolls and
woodlands. Collect the parts of the stem that have not yet
become woody up to the flowers, and dry the bunch in the
dark. Some crush them and press out a bluish oil, but I prefer
to use them in an infusion. They may be given to children
to control diarrhea and, in larger quantities, to women to
ease the pains of menstruation. Prepare an infusion with
two tablespoons of milfoil for each cup of water; it must
be drunk the same day, for it will not retain its curative
properties any longer, since the rays of the sun corrupt it,
as they do all things. Be careful not to take it in large doses
or for long periods of time, for in that case whoever has
drunk it may begin to dream of freedom and feel constant
desires to fly. You can also make compresses with it, to treat
suppurating wounds or cleanse the private parts of women.
Twice I have attempted to use such compresses to wash
hands furrowed by the labors of life. Wounds are healed
quickly, even though, since the true source of the malady is
not attacked, but rather the symptom, they will recur again
and again. All in all, that use can be recommended, without
great enthusiasm, for no one should be made to believe in
improvements that will never happen.

3

Why did everybody keep telling her that life goes on? Why did they insist on consoling her, when she did not wish for any consolation? That pain would never end, nor did she want it to end, for death was not some insignificant episode from which one should remain sheltered, in safety. On the contrary, like a skiff tossed by the waters, she found herself at sea in death, even though it was his death and not hers. Still, no matter how much she rejected consolation from others, it was just as well that spring was late this year! For if there was anything she did not want to see, it was the beautiful crocuses, yellow and pink, violet, red, orange, emerging slowly until the earth was all clad in colors, that same earth that was devouring his body, and would go on implacably doing so until there was not a single trace of him left, until there did not remain any footprint of his passage through the world except for the memories of those who knew him or a stack of papers with his thoughts written on them. "In his own hand," she thought. That is why she was busy writing today, to leave a memory of his presence. Or not for that reason, but rather because she, Christina, could do nothing else but write. As she had always done. And more so now when the pain did not even let her fall asleep at night, much less speak, govern, or laugh. She liked to write, of course, although it was not so much a question of likings as a natural inclination she could not even dream of changing. Of course, when someone likes to cook, no one asks if she is cooking to improve the diet of her family, to show off at social gatherings or to satisfy her own greed. She likes it and she does it. Simply. Without giving it another thought. Well, the same things happens to her with writing, exactly the same: she cannot stand against a blind force that drags her to the pen, just as others are drawn to other pleasures. However, writing... writing was something different. Especially being a woman. And, over and above that, being a queen. And, even worse, being a young and marriageable queen. "*Mais vous écrivez, c'est mervilleux, ça!*" the courtiers would say to her, and immediately she knew that so much enthusiasm could come only from a powerful, open and absolute disapproval. And so, didn't the queen have anything better to do than write? Christina smiled bitterly when she thought of the disapproval of others, for she, seemingly distant, would have wished for all of them to applaud her, as they did when she appeared on the balcony of Tre Kronor, but that they would applaud her, the true Christina, not the symbol of power that she hauled laboriously around with her... Christina longed for sincerity... And sincerity was not a plant that flourished in her vicinity. Her people respected her, perhaps loved her after their fashion, but it was cool and distant, and she had learned to behave according to the precepts of the five senators to whom her education had been entrusted. The country was not going through the best of times. When, in 1611, her father, King Gustavus Adolphus, may he be in glory, had risen to power, Sweden was defending itself in war against Russia, Poland and Denmark. In the intervening time, during that reign, the country had gained influence in the Baltic, and Stockholm had become the beautiful city that it was today. "Beautiful... and political," thought Christina. But in 1630, twenty years ago now, the

magnanimous and never sufficiently praised Gustavus
Adolphus decided to take part in the accursed Thirty
Years War on the side of the Protestants, using religion
as a pretext. Sweden achieved several military successes
in the battles that followed, but also paid a heavy price,
carrying on an expensive and draining conflict. In 1632,
in the bloody battle of Lützen, the king himself lost his
life, and she, his six-year-old child, sat on a throne from
which her little royal doll's feet did not even reach the
floor. Perhaps for that reason, she had never been able to
touch the floor as queen; always lost amid papers, always
avoiding the intrigues of the court, for all those dogs that
were running loose in the palace could bite her hands at
any moment. She ruled by getting up early, learning, and
studying. Nevertheless, even though many esteemed her
as the ablest of those who had held the reins of Sweden, at
least in matters of the cabinet, the criticisms were constant.
Over trifles or over important issues. A couple of years
earlier she had been acclaimed as the mastermind who had
promoted and signed the peace treaty; in recent months,
on the other hand, general opinion had condemned her for
spending such vast sums as the Imperial Circles had to pay
to control the troops after Westphalia. And on what had she
spent such vast sums? Well, not on dances, nor parades,
nor palaces, nor parties, nor jewels, nor brocades, nor on
anything that would attest to the greatness of Sweden. She
had been the supreme figure in the kingdom for seventeen
years and ruled for six, which are a good many years, when
she held her first celebration after acceding to the throne.
No, no, she only squandered it on buying rare books and
inviting scholars to the court. Well, of all things! Of all the
misfortunes that could threaten a country, not the least is

having its queen turn out to be a bookworm! She did not much care for being talked about by everyone. She would much rather that they would leave her in peace, free, to throw herself off the bridge and let the waters, which are never the same, bathe her, cleanse her soul, caress her hair. The waters, which come down joyously and which she was watching from the bridges of Stortorget, could wash her clean and wash her away... No, for she was not a fool. She did not want to die. Even though he would never come back. Even though once again it was so hard to distinguish the cold from the heat. Even though pleasure did not seem attractive, nor pain stifling, for pain ended up putting one to sleep like a drug... even though no one anywhere could understand a young queen, in love with a philosopher who was neither handsome, nor young, nor wealthy, nor considerate, nor courtly, nor graceful, nor Swedish, nor Protestant... who was dead, and, in addition, whom she had never touched in her life, not so much as a thread of his clothing.

4

From the *Book of Women by Hélène Jans*
The herb called lion's foot *(Alchemilla xanthochloris)*

What they call lion's foot is a herb, rather than a plant, with strong roots, which support a little rosette of ground-hugging leaves where a drop of rainwater or dew tends to collect. If you should happen to come across it, you must make the most of it, for that droplet has genuinely magical properties: with no more than five drops the strength needed to recover after the loss of a loved one can be restored. Likewise, any people who drink these drops with regularity will be vehement, resolute, sure of themselves in speech and action, and tremendously vigorous. Even in the event that you do not find the magical drop, do not despise the lion's foot, which is a good plant with many healthful effects, some of which I will tell of here, but not all, so as to keep something in reserve, for it is never a good idea to be left without resources and with nothing to say, like those who reveal everything that crosses their mind, for one also learns by keeping quiet. The leaves of the lion's foot should be collected during fair weather and dried in the dark, although complete darkness is not necessary. Afterwards, infusions are made with four tablespoons for each cup of boiling water; after it is left to steep for a little while, it is used to relieve cramps or to stimulate the kidneys. Also, pregnant women should take as many as three cups a day during the four weeks before giving birth to make it easier, for the lion's foot softens the flesh and makes things a bit less troublesome at the time of birth. And, as the extract of lion's foot, dried and ground, encourages sweating and the changes of humors, I am going to try using it for the apathetic, the indecisive or the not very vigorous, these being conditions that occur with greater frequency in men than in women, for the former do not alternate their humors naturally as the latter do every month. Of course, for the apathetic one could try mixing in one part of wild rose, two of hibiscus, a pinch of grated peel of bitter orange, a few elderberries, and also a handful of mint. This infusion should be taken readily, sweetened with honey, and one should try to breathe in its aroma as much as its taste, because the desire to love life and face up to affliction comes to us through all of our senses.

5

Eija-Liisa entered the personal chambers of the queen. They consisted of two adjoining rooms, a bedroom and a small study, decorated very plainly, almost neglected. "It looks like a monk's cell. Oh! If this were mine...!" And Eija-Liisa, no matter how accustomed she is to passing through that private part of the palace, never stops imagining how it would look if she were the queen. She would not worry about expenditures or efforts in her quest to fill it all with beauty, with purples and brocades and embroidery and figurines and rich curtains and ruffles and cabinets and paintings and tapestries and coffee tables covered with knick-knacks, and fans, and feathers, and musical instruments, and elegance, and colors, and shapes, which everywhere would show the pleasure it gives to enjoy beauty, in addition to demonstrating the natural discernment of the one who spends and arranges in such a way. Here there is not to be seen anywhere a single detail to indicate that the queen has good taste... or bad. Not even the old king, as the older servants tell it, paid less attention to his home than does his daughter, who was educated like a boy and who behaves like a boy. Eija-Liisa sighed. The queen was looking at her, so she decided to anticipate any rebuke:

"Do you want anything, my lady?"

"No, I didn't send for you."

"I know that, but... as I was aware that you had returned... I saw you walking across the square from the upper balcony, and I thought that perhaps you might want company tonight."

"No, Eija-Liisa, I don't need anything." Christina's voice has just delayed spring a little longer. It will be hard for Stockholm to bloom again after this coating of ice.

"Very well, I can stay here, and later…"

"I will not be needing you later either." If the conversation goes on, the flowers will make up their minds never to emerge into the light again.

"My lady… I would like to talk with you. In the past…"

"In the past the world was different. Do you know something? We will never again bathe in the waters of the same river." Christina raises her hand in a commanding gesture that cuts off Eija-Liisa's futile protest. "Don't go on talking. I will send for you if I need anything. I'm trying to write, and I will thank you for not presuming on the relationship we once had. I don't like to be bothered when I'm writing." Her eyes go back to watching the hand that, in turn, guides the pen…

"Yes, my lady." Eija-Liisa bends her knees slightly, as if making a genuflection. Something passes through her head and, impetuously, she approaches the queen and kisses her ardently on the lips. Christina scarcely responds. The kiss does not affect her, does not touch her: one would say that it leaves her indifferent and, while her friend goes away, she once again becomes engrossed in her writing.

6

From the *Book of Women by Hélène Jans*
A recipe for not miscarrying

If you should wish to make a remedy for a woman who
tends to have miscarriages, make it in this way: when there
is reason to suspect that she is pregnant, anoint the dimples
in the back over the kidneys with pine resin, which should
be very fine. And have made up some powders of fat and
mastic, and dragon's blood, and red coral, which stanch the
menstrual flow and that of the sperm, and control the white
purgations of women. You must add all these things in equal
parts. And, after you have anointed with the pine resin, you
must grind it to a very fine powder. And keep working it
until it falls off by itself. And, when the time comes when
she tends to have a miscarriage, give another dose fifteen
or twenty days beforehand, which is very beneficial; be
aware that with this remedy I have attended at the birth
of babies who could have had as many as fifteen brothers
and sisters, their mothers had miscarried so many times.
And even though mastic and dragon's blood may be used
by witches, do not be frightened, for this is only one of the
many things that can be known about the body. And many
of those who are called witches are nothing but women
who have been unfortunate in finances or in abandonment,
most of them old, who dedicate themselves to easing the
pain of other women and for that are persecuted or executed
by those who refuse to understand that pain, no matter how
natural it may be, is not a good thing, for it turns human
beings into beasts, and to mitigate it is an art, and a science;

and indeed didn't the religion of Jesus command us to take pity on the hungry and the thirsty, the poor, the naked? Well then, how much more should one take pity on those who suffer pain. And I will say nothing further, for I want to keep myself free of suspicion, and healthy.

7

Walking through the narrow streets of Gamla Stan, one quickly gathers the opinion that the Swedes have of their queen: "Boys and girls are all the same to her," with a raucous belly-laugh. And the opinion is not right, for it is not a matter of what suits her nature, but rather, more precisely, what she likes and what she doesn't. And in this respect there would be a great many fine points, because she doesn't like them equally, the boys and the girls, she likes them in different ways. Just as similarly she likes some of the boys in different ways, and some of the girls. The queen leads a somewhat licentious life. If you like, the life of a poor little rich girl, for rich girls treat the ailments that wealth must cause by becoming libertines. But none of that matters now. It doesn't matter that the people love her and hate her at the same time; it is the job of monarchs to be the target of these opposing emotions, and they must get used to them. In fact, there are very few things that can matter now, when she is overcome with that tepid sense of longing. First she wept about the death of her friend; then for days she maintained a tense calm, as if nothing had happened. Perhaps she was hoping to see him arrive in the room where they used to converse, and she even sometimes included her session with him in her agenda for the following day. She refused to admit to herself that it was a pure wish for power, that death could win the game from her on the opening deal. No, not this time, this time it was important. But as the days went by without him, she had to resign herself and accept the fact that nothing would ever be the same again. From that point on Christina went off to live in a remote place called melancholy, probably several leagues from Stockholm, for it could be said that she is not present in body or in spirit when she is spoken to. And she lets herself be carried along by the waters of fate, desperate about not being desperate, about the fact that her character and the royal upbringing she has had do not allow her to pull out her hair, pluck out her eyes, tear her flesh, pull up trees by the roots and other marvelous acts that would make her pain known. And so she settled down to live in sadness, and almost nothing is left of that exuberant Christina, who entertained her subjects with racy stories concerning the many and varied visitors that her canopied bed welcomed. Not now. Now her womb is a cold field and no sun will ever again make her quiver with desire. Thus it is best that the Swedes stop jabbering, because now it's neither boys nor girls: is that perhaps what they were aiming for? And, of course, the truth of the matter, as in all matters, branched out along multiple pathways, because the story was not superficial and had its own certain something. It's said that when Christina was still a girl, the ladies of her court played a bold game with her, one of those games that are customary in palaces like hers, palaces of monarchs who are all-powerful and driven by adolescence. Taking advantage of the fact that some gypsies were passing through Stockholm, they hired them for some rather special services. They, he and she, so young and lovely that it was glorious to look at them, were to lie in one of the chambers of the palace, while the little ladies, also young and pretty, although less experienced, destined to preserve intact the gateway of their flesh for the husband who would purchase them, watched from the neighboring room through a number of peepholes, naturally not tiny ones, which had been drilled in the wall, probably for other purposes, if not better ones, then more easily justified ones. And the gypsies agreed. And the little ladies, including Christina, could see, or glimpse, for under such circumstances it is understandable for there to be a lot of shoving, "Hey, move, it's my turn," and courtly courtesy is put aside for a few moments, they could see, as I was saying, how the man mounted his companion: the taut muscles, the inflamed mouth, the dark shadow of the pubic hair, the desire shown on the face, the aggressive jut of the member. "What's that?" "Hush, you sound like a ninny too." Meanwhile, the naked man was seven times naked, as many as the little ladies who were watching him; the lad could very well have answered, if he had been asked, that he had been with seven different women that night, after a fashion, at least; meanwhile... Christina was obsessed with the gypsy woman. The girl's black mane flowed over the pillow, her face had a roguish, provocative look, her breasts round and big as cannonballs, inviting caresses. A few moments later, when the man reaches climax, it looks as though someone has just struck him with a whip; he collapses in defeat and the game comes to an end. The little ladies hurry to hide their observatory, all except for Christina, who cannot forget her, the hot dark gypsy girl, she who is blonde and cool... the gypsy girl, pure provocation, who shook her anklets in a rhythmic beat, turned into music, and emitted savage cries from between her full lips: the image of her noisy, laughing pleasure drives Christina crazy.

Indeed, walking through the streets of Gamla Stan we could get a very mistaken sense of Christina, the queen. Her subjects like to tell stories, and who knows if they ever happened. And that serious, studious, profound, imaginative woman has problems much more weighty than the one of deciding with whom to roll around. The first is the death of the philosopher who, as the story is told, never went to bed with her and nonetheless, or perhaps just because of that, fascinated her. Yes, something like intellectually fascinated, for in these matters of human attractions there is much variety, and there are those who, after blowing through half of Stockholm, go and fall in love platonically, with a dry dike, if you will pardon the expression. Christina's second problem, and not a lesser one, is one that is impending. The best-informed sources in the palace affirm that the General State Assembly, the highest governmental body of Sweden, is going to request, as they put it, although in a case like this requesting is the same as demanding, that the queen, our lady, Christina, daughter of Gustavus Adolphus tragically slain in battle, our queen since 1633, get married. That she get married, that simply, that she get married, for God's sake, that she get married already, that she get married, to see if once she is married her uterine furors will be extinguished and, above all, to provide better security and unity for the Crown in the future. Because it is all well and good to amuse oneself, but the business of a queen has to be to rule, which includes giving birth to new kings, and not to amuse herself, or experience forbidden sensations, and much less study or write. There is sin in writing too...! Eh? Therefore Christina cannot rest today. Her friend died on her just three months ago, that friend who was not as intimate as she would have wished, and for his sake she would like to give herself up to melancholy. But she cannot. She cannot allow herself sadness. It's very hard to be queen... Christina is horrified. Because they want to force her to belong to a man, her, to be a possession: to be a womb to produce whelps. And, if there is anything she cannot do, it is this. Not for the crown of Sweden, not for the memory of her father, not for anything whatsoever; she has been swearing to herself for ten years now that she will never be a mother. She will not change her mind. And, when she asks herself what he would say if he were alive, it strikes her that the philosopher would have to say she was right. She does not want to be a mother and she thinks that there is a reason she is strange, well supplied with lovers and not as well behaved as the queen of a Lutheran nation ought to be. She believes that she doesn't want to be a mother because she is different. If someone were to study her closely, however, if there were psychologists in charge of royal therapy in the court at Stockholm, it would be discovered that she still sobs and cries and mourns about what happened ten years ago, The problem is that psychologists haven't been invented yet, of course. And if this episode is recounted here, it is not so as to go spreading nasty stories about people's lives, for everyone in this vale of tears gets along as best he can, and, because you ought never to say "I would never do any such thing," nor should you get all wrapped up in the woes of others, or go around spreading evil gossip with "I heard this" and "she said that." For if this little matter is recounted here, this *affaire* as the hoity-toity would say, for there are plenty of those in the court of Stockholm, it is because many believe that the incident had something to do with Christina's vehement determination not to be a mother, even though her eyes were drawn to every passing child, an extreme reaction that was likewise never confirmed, although it would be very natural.

The story goes that Christina's mother, Maria Eleonora of Brandenburg, born Hohenzollern, had made the decision in that spring of 1640 to flee from Sweden. She had nothing to keep her there. And it might be said in her defense that it is quite true that the life of a widow with no role in the court is not, shall we say, very exciting, what with having nothing to do—she didn't even have needlework, or a viol, or harp, or a romance of chivalry, or an aptitude for political issues. With a prayer book all the livelong day one doesn't get anywhere, much less if one is a young widowed queen, and the oafs of your court keep on refusing to flatter your ears with amorous insinuations on account of the respect owed to the dead king. For, if while he was alive he was no great shakes as a lover, dead he even scared off the flies, which was exactly the opposite of what she desired. She would definitely escape, she would sneak away. It could even happen that she might turn into smoke from a chimney or steam from the soup kettle, or into morning dew and evaporate into the air, as in an authentic Scandinavian saga, so intense was her desire to escape, if not for the fact that the vicissitudes of history had come to assign her a role, albeit secondary and second-rate, in the chronicles of Sweden. What the poor queen didn't know was that she had turned into a piece of candy, that that story of courtly love, reserved for the nobility and perforce adulterous so as to be pure and disinterested, must have been an invention of men to seduce as married women those whom they had not managed to seduce while they were maidens. Eleonora had been flirting for some time, not so much with a man as with some letters, which had arrived to her with the most absolute secrecy from the neighboring and rival country of Denmark. And she noticed how each letter kept renewing her hopes, each line rejuvenated her, and she thought that her figure, still rather more than merely presentable, and her reputation as an intelligent conversationalist had made King Christian IV of Denmark prefer her over any of the girls that would be on offer to him in Copenhagen, without considering that that little king might have annexationist intent, for men always seem to be thinking about the same thing and they aren't—they always surprise her with that business of power and glory. She began to dream about a way of escaping from her cage to fall into the king's arms. "I wonder if he's handsome?" "Oh, my lady, how can he not be handsome if he's the king…" "I wonder if he's kind and affectionate?" "How could he be anything else, saying what he does about you in those letters…" And she and her ladies-in-waiting, savoring the secret, enjoyed the excellent qualities of the unknown Denmark, a true lovers' paradise, according to the story told by the passionate royal correspondence. They ended up lowering their lashes, decorous, abashed by the things that came into their minds when they were alone—oh, those ladies!—things all having to do with what lovers in Denmark must get up to. And, while they were waiting for the moment to escape, Eleonora and her ladies-in-waiting believed it best that her daughter should know nothing. "Well, considering how rigid she is, and that look…!" "On top of that, she wouldn't understand, she's still very young…" "And a bit mannish, my lady." "Anne! You're talking about your queen." I beg your pardon, my lady, but that's how it seems to me." "Yes, she really is a bit mannish." When the opportune moment arrived, the widowed queen, feeling at last like an unmarried queen, for during all those years the shade of the dead man had followed her relentlessly through the hallways of the palace, giving her tearful nights and tumultuous dreams, asked permission to move to a different wing with a few of her ladies-in-waiting, on the pretext of spending a few days fasting. Permission granted, for even if the guardians of honor realized at the time that there was direct access to the garden from that wing, no one would have imagined that there could be anything wrong with taking the air. And one night, Eleonora crosses the garden at a run, like a butterfly; on the other side, there is a carriage waiting for her with the Danish coat of arms concealed behind the curtains. Without anyone's seeing a thing, it carries her to Nyköping Road. There she embarks for the island of Gotland, where two warships—for in Denmark they spare no trouble to show the world the value of the honor of a woman—serve as her escorts to conduct her to freedom. Needless to say, freedom is called Copenhagen.

Christina, self-contained, icy, sober, well brought up, calm, Christina the queen in pigtails, without breasts, with a short dress that shows her legs, Christina, the daughter of the fugitive, cries, shrieks, threatens, spits, shouts, bellows and for several nights in a row wets the bed. Christina does not understand, she does not ask questions, she does not forgive. When she learned about what had happened, called by many an *affaire*, Christina was playing with her rag doll and dreaming of being the mother of thirty children, because, "Oh, my God, who can teach a queen anything?" she didn't know how they were made, much less that, in order to have thirty children, she would have to be split open, and cry, and wish she had never been born thirty times, besides seeing her graceful shape turned into a bulging belly for two hundred seventy months. When she learned about what had happened, what the most gossipy called an *affaire*, Christina threw down the doll and, immediately, those who saw her realized that she had been left withered, stunned, bewildered, stupefied, exhausted. Because, being the queen, whom could Christina ask about what her mother was missing, the young widowed queen? How could a queen in fuzzy slippers imagine that her mother was seeking ardent words that are not supplied in the court of the hero slain in battle? And Christina, finished, suffering, furious, vengeful, spends three years trying to convince the great men, the five senators, the State Assembly, which is the highest power in the country that she only symbolizes, for she is still too young to rule, besides looking mannish, that the queen and her lover must be punished. And in 1643, at last, Christina's eyes stare red with the heat of revenge, because she has succeeded, with all due solemnity, in having Sweden declare war on Denmark because of the offense given to the memory of Gustavus the Great, contrary to the respect owed to the queen, his daughter, and to the illustrious body of Senators of the Realm and likewise to the entire Royal House of Brandenburg. And, if she did this, it was not because she was straitlaced, or pious, or out of family pride, or ambition. If she did it, it was because she could not accept the fact that her mother would not share the secret with her.

Needless to say, Christina's anger had to be controlled; a year later she would manage to free herself from the regents when she came of age, and take on fully the part that history had surprised her with. And, in order to do things properly, she had to end up signing that Treaty of Brömsebro, by the terms of which Sweden and Denmark became so friendly, and moreover Sweden extracted all the benefit possible from the royal ire, for in order to placate monarchs, as with the gods, it is required to pay in gold for what was done in bed. But it is not fitting to stray from history; they say that from 1643 onwards the queen, who no longer wears fuzzy slippers or short dresses, who has breasts and knows how to glance sidelong, decides that she is not going to obey any of the rules of monarchical life. And she takes advantage of her familiarity with her little ladies-in-waiting to initiate herself into forbidden games… although her mother had supposed that she would not enjoy the games of the bedroom. And she also enjoys, of course, the fact that in the palace there are chamberlains, accountants, officials, fiscal agents, scribes, secretaries, counselors, dance masters, French masters, masters of every art that is practiced, players, if you will excuse the expression, of viol and harp, for in this matter of playing there are some true artists, all gentlemen, in order to see what gentlemen have that makes them so interesting. And that is without even mentioning that the palace is also inhabited by servants, gardeners, grooms, cooks, who, not having the elegance or the somewhat over-refined manners of the other men, have the same attributes that make them so interesting, for democracy was never so well served as in these matters. To put it briefly, Christina takes advantage of the fact that a queen is also, when all is said and done, a woman like all the rest… No, not like all the rest, for Cristina has sworn not to have children, so as not to fail them, so as not to fall short for them, so as not to forget them, deny them, so as not to do to them what her mother had done to her on the day when she decided not to open her heart to her with the secret.

8

From the *Book of Women by Hélène Jans*
The plant called motherwort (*Leonurus cardiaca*)

A plant with a wrinkled stem, oval leaves and pink flowers. It is a plant of fields and woodlands, not fond of associating with crops, like so many people who, on account of having suffered a severe blow in childhood, never bring themselves to trust those around them. It is harvested whole and should be dried in the dark. The infusion, which is made with a tablespoon per cup, is taken twice daily to ease a woman's nervous upsets: headaches, excessive cravings and the feeling of anxiety, palpitations when they are powerful, presentiments when they are not fulfilled, and bad dreams. It is quite bitter but, if the acidity is eliminated by the addition of honey, as I have seen done, it no longer prevents bad dreams, although it can be effective against other ailments. Nevertheless, for those other ailments there may perhaps be better remedies.

9

When the philosopher arrived in Stockholm he did not come there by chance, for she herself, the queen in person, was the one who had invited him. First she learned of his works, for he was not exactly a nobody of forgettable bearing. And the works that reached her royal hands pleased her and made her mutter to herself, very quietly: "I wonder why he says that? How could he dare to go so far?" And that was quite sufficient, for it is known to everyone that curiosity is the first raiment of Love. And in fact the queen had never read anyone so convinced that he could change the course of the universe with words, defy the authorities, anyone who did not cite other famous names. And she liked him. She liked him because he was daring, solid, assured. She liked the *Dioptrics*, and even more the *Meteors*, and the *Geometry*, and she even liked the introduction. Except, perhaps, for that mess of a Book IV, which it seems to her did not fit well with the rest of the discourse, which was all so scientific, especially there where it said that since he, the philosopher, could think of perfections that he did not find within himself, as they were foreign to human nature, and since those perfections had to come from somewhere, ergo God existed. For, so it seemed to Christina, such forced reasoning about the existence of a supreme being could stem only from an intention of staying on good terms with the very illustrious doctors of theology of the University of Paris... Unless, of course, and here she let out a mischievous snicker, the author were waiting for someone in his audience to say to him: "What do you mean by perfections that you do not have, when you have all of them?" And no such blessed innocent had ever been made in the world, or, if it had been, it could only have been for the purpose of stimulating the curiosity of a queen. And curiosity, a garment of Love, is treacherous, because immediately she decided to find out what one who expressed himself in that way could teach her. She felt an urge to experience the tone of his voice, and how he would escape from a verbal assault in one of those disputes that everyone in her court liked so much. And she wanted to learn the color of his eyes, and the nobility of his spirit, and the shape of his hands, and his tolerance for suffering, because, unfortunately for the philosopher, Christina, like everyone else, was not especially good at separating what the spirit makes from what the body dreams, or it is the other way around? Well, be that as it may, Christina could not hold out any longer, for patience was not one of her virtues, and the upbringing she had received, while austere and puritanical, was the upbringing of a queen, and she had not been given much training in hesitating before satisfying her whims. So then: among her courtiers was the French diplomat Monsieur Chanut, known to be a correspondent of the philosopher, and for her it was enough to do what was typically done in her time, no more and no less. As was the custom, ladies or gentlemen of the upper crust could make contact with any other person, even with someone to whom they had never been introduced, if they did so through a mutually trusted intermediary. In this way, all the correct forms were preserved. That was not the strange thing about this case. When, during the next reception in the palace, Chanut was summoned for a private conversation by Her Majesty, the fact that she would ask him to serve as an intermediary in her correspondence so that she could articulate to the famous philosopher certain questions of interest to her did not cause, in the coteries, circles and cliques in which this confidential action was commented on, the slightest surprise. It surprised no one that the queen, so erudite, might wish to be instructed by one best capable of instructing her. It surprised no one that she would use that guffin Chanut as an intermediary: he was quite ugly enough to dispel any suspicion that he might be the object of desire. Nor did it surprise anyone that from that moment on the queen appeared animated and cheerful, and greeted Chanut with the same hand signal that hunters use with their falcons: "Chin up, my dear friend, you'll bring me the prey." No. What surprised everyone was the look on Chanut's face when Christina, Queen of Sweden, sprang her little question on him, which, as they tell it, was something like: "What causes incite us sometimes to love one person and not another, even before we become familiar with that person's merits?" And there he goes, poor old Chanut, with that hangdog look on his face, all set to transmit that little question to the fashionable thinker, and even a "let's see what you can get out of there," keeping quiet about what he thinks is the pure and only reality, which is that the said thinker has made the queen rather hot, and has done it just by way of the ears. Christina didn't hesitate for a moment. She learned through her spies, for that's why she had them, everything that was muttered in the coteries, circles and various cliques of the court. She learned what Monsieur Chanut thought of her. She learned what all Stockholm thought of her, for Madame Chanut let her know it with that way of controlling her gaze that women reserve to punish each other, and, delighted to have sown so much scandal, she sat down to wait for the answering letter, happy, serene, sparkling, sure of her own élan, although she would not have expressed herself in that way. And, despite the fact that nobody would have bet a farthing on her getting an answer, the answer came. It was, in keeping with all the international conventions governing mail between exceedingly respectable persons of very high lineage and great power and, on top of that, of the opposite sex, a moderate letter, addressed to Chanut but couched in a double language, so as to make quite clear to whom so much thinking was being devoted. As is preferred in these cases... So that Christina could savor it... So that it might be sampled in the court and its coteries... So that everyone could enjoy it, except poor old Chanut, who had to play carrier pigeon again... The answer arrived, and gave pleasure; it said:

I was once in love with a girl of my own age who had a bit of a squint. The impression that she made through my vision on my brain, when I would look at her errant eyes, combined in such a way with the one that she made to arouse in me the passion of love that, much later, whenever I saw people with a squint, I felt more inclined to love those persons than others, only because they had that defect, and I was not aware that it was for that reason. On the contrary, ever since I have reflected about this, and after recognizing that it is a defect, it no longer moves me.

Examining it closely, if Christina felt so contented, it must have been because he, the famous philosopher, had deigned to answer a question posed by a woman, and not by another sage, and moreover by a woman with a bad reputation, whom everyone regarded as the greatest public hussy in history. Because, if it had been something else, I mean, if Christina's question had been an ambush or snare to conquer the gentleman in question, she should not have been happy about it. And I say this because Christina did not have a squint, she had eyes with a straight and deep look, although somewhat bulging. And furthermore, I say as well, because the philosopher was telling her: "Look here, girl, this business of falling in love is not chosen, mostly or at all; rather it seems that the heart slips out through the ears instead of staying busy beating and pumping blood, which is what pertains to it by its nature. But, if you want advice, never stop examining the merits of those with whom you fall in love." Well then, the reserve is that of the one who is telling about this; Christina was very determined and very self-possessed. She, of whom the people said that she liked men as much as women and yet, no matter how much she had cavorted with her body, kept her heart virginal, perhaps ought to have said: "Well, given that I should pay attention to merit, you are not lacking in merits." And in the following weeks she took to writing letters a great deal. She was deeply preoccupied with the mail.

10

From the *Book of Women by Hélène Jans*
Lotions for the hands

The hands of women suffer a great deal in their daily chores, the majority of which are not the kinds that keep the skin delicate and smooth, what with the many things they do every day. Thus, if you want to protect yourself from these troubles, you can make some lotions, as I will explain now. Take a bowlful of juice from grapes that are not yet ripe, and another of cow's bile, and half a bowl of soap, chopped very fine, and three ounces of pumpkinseed oil, and three more of poppy seeds, and also half an ounce of oil of bitter almonds, and an ounce of vegetable oil, and a little sulfur ground very fine, and a little bit of mercury diluted with saliva. Combine all this in a beaker and set it on the heat until the soap melts; once it has melted, pour the mixture into a glass container and let it cure in the sun for nine days, stirring it two or three times every morning so that it does not settle at the bottom. When it is cured, put it on your hands. The longer you leave it without washing, the better, for your hands will look as if they had never done any work or been worn by the labors of life. Take note, when you do wash, you are taking life away when you slough a part of it into the water; nothing should be washed except what is dirty; the human body has its own aroma, different in each individual, so that, just as we can be recognized by our shape through sight, we may also be recognized by the nose owing to the scent we emit. I have never seen a mother who didn't recognize her child through her sense of smell, or a lover who was not driven crazy by the smell of his beloved. Those who cover up what seems unpleasant to them with perfumes are killing a way of being themselves. However, hand lotions do not hide anything, but rather provide protection so that there is no pain in the fingers or the palms; those who see you looking in bad shape must not be allowed to think that you only move your fingers and never do any work with your mind.

11

Letter from Monsieur Descartes to Queen
Christina of Sweden
Late 1645

My Lady,

If it should happen that a letter was sent to me from the sky, and I personally saw it descend from the clouds, I would not be more surprised, and I could not receive it with more respect and veneration than that with which I received the one that Your Majesty was pleased to write to me. However, I realize that I am so little worthy of the kindnesses it contains that I cannot accept it save as a favor and a boon, for which I feel particularly obliged because I shall never be able to repay it. The honor that I received upon being consulted by Monsieur Chanut on behalf of Your Majesty repays me lavishly for the answer I gave you, and, when I was informed by him that my words had been favorably received, that made me feel so thankful to you that I could not hope for or desire anything further for such a small thing, especially from a Princess whom God has placed in so high a position, surrounded by so many important matters as you have responsibility for, and whose least actions can have such an impact on the common good of the entire earth. All those who love Virtue ought to judge themselves as happy indeed whenever they can have an opportunity to do you any service. And because I in particular profess to belong to that company, I venture to promise Your Majesty that you could not request anything so difficult that I would not always be ready to do everything possible to carry it out, and that, if I had been born Swedish or Finnish, I would not do it with more zeal or more perfectly...

12

From the *Book of Women by Hélène Jans*
A remedy for asthma

A remedy to promote good breathing can be made by cooking eggs with the fat of a cat, for the cat, just as it causes sneezing and itching, is capable of curing them, and its blood eases the respiratory troubles of anyone who suffers from them. Not only these eggs mixed with cat grease should be served to anyone who is suffering from asthma, but everything that must be cooked in butter can be cooked with the said grease for that sick person, for it is a very good remedy. But one must not always assume that a person who is having trouble breathing is asthmatic. I have seen a man stop breathing when Love grips him tightly, just in that moment when words offer no help to the mind, this being a problem that is often seen among those newly in love, for with love the blood does not flow as it ought to, and therefore they are confused, and prefer daydreaming to working and, when they want to tell about anything, especially in the presence of the loved one, they keep repeating "I can't think of the word, it's not coming to me." One can also stop breathing because of a fright; however, the sensation is not so pleasant: some even die when they receive an unexpected letter, or one that reveals something startling, which they could not even have imagined before having read it.

13

This time the letter that the philosopher addressed to the queen was not talked about by the gossip circles. That's natural, for the gossip circles were formed to spread bad news: rendezvous to which he never showed up, improper caresses that she permitted, and even enjoyed, people putting their foot in it and similar incidents that offended against good taste; there never was seen a coterie in a court where people told about everything going smoothly: that the queen read a philosopher and asked him a mischievous little question by way of a third party, and the former, that is to say the philosopher, answered with great pleasure and from that point on, he said she said, one of them going one of them coming. So that after several months there was no subject on which they had not disputed. But what did end up becoming obvious is that, once the time for questions had passed, she made up her mind, because if curiosity is the first, boldness is the second garment of Love, and she invited the philosopher to come to her, and even to take up a post as a sage in the court. As Christina was aware that he was always a bit lax, indecisive and languid, she even arranged transportation for him, informing him that, in case he made up his mind, he had at any place he might name a ship of the Swedish navy at his disposal. Christina must have been quite fiercely attacked by the little winged god with the bow and the pointy arrows, since she did not recognize that she was doing exactly, although in reverse, the same thing that King Christian of Denmark had done with her mother, and which had seemed so wrong to her, for when Love drives us on, all ships are nothing much. But the warships were never so happy, or ever so justified, as when they were dedicated, as occurred in these episodes of the Swedish crown, to serving as the means of transport for idle lovers. Especially because this new use required some preparations which improved them: take that ammunition out of there and put me in some rose petals for when he boards, get that cannon out of the way, or no, better not, you'll be using it for salutes to welcome him. And, instead of salt pork, serve him wild strawberries with orange juice. And instead of scale-model war mock-ups, let the tables hold bowls heaped with exotic fruits, and put up some curtains, and wax that floor, and scatter some books around, and forget all about troop movements, and make up his bed with clean sheets, for no matter how little Christina cared about her own dwelling, at least in Eija-Liisa's opinion, she was not going to be so silly as not to have the stage set so as best to facilitate seduction. For Love sweetens all, and, in everything having to do with these matters, the Scandinavian peoples are as attentive and meticulous as in all others. The story is even told of a Swedish admiral, who signed on with a Dutch ship for a certain overseas mission, nothing that matters here, and had to wait around for three months in the Antilles. Waiting, waiting, he did nothing but drink coconut wine and deflower native girls. Boom, just like that, any girl who passed, he was after her, for with the change in temperature he noticed that his body was getting a little slack and, not having anything to do, he saw no harm in doing what he enjoyed so much. He was doing quite splendidly until one day he accosted the most attractive mulatto woman on the whole island: it was a real treat to watch her shaking her hips in front of the admiral, and the poor man, who knew so well how to keep body and soul separate, even though he had never read the philosopher, even though—since he didn't read—he hadn't even read the mail, I was saying that the poor admiral must have left his soul trapped with his body during his invasion of the gorgeous mulatto, because what is certain is that he fell in love, in that savage and headlong way that those feel who have done a lot and not felt very much. And when he snuggled up next to her every night, he, so accustomed to thrashing about and to the attack, heard her, speaking slowly and rhythmically, "not like that, loooove, you're hurting me," and, even though he didn't understand anything, for he had never spoken anything but his own rude native dialect, one day put aside his gun, and the next, "not like that, loooove, be gentle," his gun and his cartridge belt, and the next day, "not like that, loooove, you're killing me," his gun, his cartridge belt, his sword, his leggings, and his spurs, because what did he want all those toys for on these occasions, and little by little, "not like that, looove, I don't like it like that" little by little, "not like that, looove, it's better like this," receiving his lessons in Caribbean fun, "yes, yes, keep going like that, oh, that's good, my looove," he ended up the way his mother brought him into the world, wrapped in softness and given over, with all the meticulousness of the Nordic peoples, to the not very warlike task of loving as well as possible. Needless to say, the Swedish navy had to discharge its high-ranking officer because the blond crude galoot, who by then was known all over the island, had decided to settle down with the mulatto to raise half-castes in a hut under three coconut trees. But we must not digress, for the point is that when Christina offered the philosopher a warship for the voyage, she was doing the same thing as the king of Denmark whom she had cursed so much: using official vehicles for seduction, and putting her personal desires above the respect owed to the interests of the State. Note that at this point Christina, our majesty, was somewhat dopey, no matter how queenly she felt, since anyone who might analyze her behavior could see that she was taking the lead in the dance. And that is the place of the man, not the lady: from all the fooling around that Christina had done she had picked up, naturally, some of the ways of men. If I insist on this detail, it is because her offer was in all respects excessive, and even a blind man could see that, let alone a philosopher who had just given to the press a manuscript entitled *Passions of the Soul*. And moreover, a philosopher who did not much care for these sinecures as a kept sage, for he had never been a courtier and, according to what they say, not only because he was ugly, but also because he was affable towards everyone and disinterested, for he took pride in having no refinements except not having any refinements, and with that, of course, one goes to no courts at all. So that's how things went. It's said that at first he acted lazy and, not saying yes or no, kept putting off giving an answer. It's said that next he wrote to his friends about the queen's invitation, telling them something of his scruples about making the voyage, for if he had enemies everywhere in his role as author of a new philosophy, if he was a Roman Catholic and that perhaps for that reason he should not settle down in a Protestant country, if this and if that, so that all of his correspondents came to realize that the philosopher was protesting too much and bringing up problems in writing while, at the same time, he was packing his bags. And so it was that in October of 1649 he arrived in Stockholm, and perhaps he stood for a good long while on the bridge of Stortorget, for it's remarkable how life is full of coincidences, for he happened to lean on the very same railing that his beloved would use a few months later to keep herself on her feet when grief was battering her most. Looking at the water, he felt himself filled with sadness, but not with a concrete pain attributable to a problem or to an event, but rather just sadness. He did not feel afflicted by an aversion, or think that life was not smiling on him; that wasn't it. He was not living in poverty, nor was he confronted with a vexing situation, nor did he think of himself as insignificant, or that existence was meaningless. He was not bored, or grumpy, or drained, or homesick; he felt lively, renewed and confident about his future. Simply, on the bridge of Stortorget he felt as though all the sadness of the universe was falling on him: the sadness of the waters that flow by, knowing that their passage, once and for all, has already happened; the sadness of the lifeless planets condemned to wander eternally through an endless space; the sadness of the flies that would stop flying forever that evening. Because, in some way, on seeing his reflection as a Breton gentleman mirrored in the water, he realized that he was going to Stockholm to die... and that he would die there.

14

From the *Book of Women by Hélène Jans*
Recipes for perfumes

Despite what I have said about preserving the personal
aroma of the body, it is typical of a woman to adorn herself,
primp, comb out her hair, put on scents and anoint herself
as if she were a goddess so as to forget that one day her
precious body will be food for worms. And, since men are
used to encountering well-groomed lovers, I myself have
fallen into the bad habit of wanting to please and to stir up
passions, as if we women could improve ourselves with
ointments. And, although it is not a good idea to abuse
them, nature does offer pleasant aromas of which we can
take advantage. To make a musky perfume that can be
quite helpful in love-spells, take one part orange flower
water, two of rose water, and a little red clover, a dash of
myrtle and a splash of essence from that spiny rosebush
they call moss rose. Then, with all these liquids mixed in
a flask, put in a bit of amber and another of ground musk,
and finally, another little pinch of musk. Cover the mouth
of the flask and set it out to cure in the sun; check it every
morning for nine days, and then you can use it, taking good
care whom you allow to smell you when you are wearing
such a perfume, so as not to produce pointless disturbances
and passions you cannot satisfy. Also very strong-smelling
and pleasant is the perfume that is made by mixing a pound
of red roses and another of orange blossoms, another of
laurel buds, and another of lily roots with two ounces of
clove pinks and half an ounce of lavender. Once all these

things have been mixed, one has to distill them over low heat. The perfume that results is exceedingly fine, and allows one to have agreeable sensations when life offers no passion but that of the sense of smell. For although all the senses feed pleasure and promote contentment and well-being, they do not work in the same way: sight feeds lust, hearing tenderness, touch love, taste fullness and smell homesickness, which does not seem like a passion to the theologians, being nothing more than the coal that feeds the fire.

15

It cannot be said for certain if the first time they saw each other it was just as each of them had dreamed it would be, for they had become so fond and exchanged so many opinions and letters that in many different ways they were deeply familiar with each other, and the only thing lacking for them was that face-to-face meeting, crucial, from which each would come to know the expressions, the gestures, the charms of the other. And, most likely, they had not been impressed, not at the first glance, which is so deceptive. Not he with her, nor she with him, of course. Not by a long shot. It was a clear fresh morning in the month of October. He was eager to settle down in the surroundings to which he had just arrived so as to start writing, which was what he did, besides which he could not even imagine himself as an ornament of the court: the very idea, when it passed through his head, caused him pain. But before beginning any new work, he thought it would be advisable to pay his respects to the queen who had invited him. At least that was what he told himself, even though the act was not the pure courtesy of a guest, for if truth be told, his heart harbored a warm, stimulating, lively curiosity to meet the woman with whom he had exchanged so many words. We have already said earlier that curiosity is anything but innocence. That means that he, who thought of himself as a man of mature age, who had seen all there was to see, reasonably sensible, able to control his instincts—he, that man who thought of himself as if he were an automaton, that man, the philosopher who knew how to separate the soul from the body, was feeling all hot and bothered about seeing the woman who was naked under the label she wore as queen.

Her Majesty, for her part, felt nothing, for women are taught early on to control their emotions, and Christina, with that fondness of hers for writing, which everyone knows makes women pedantic and shriveled before their time, was more than a bit advanced in age. Likewise, if women are taught early on to control their emotions, so that by the time they are twelve or thirteen they already have them under lock and key, this is even more the case with the refined women of the Nordic courts. And much more so with queens. And much more so with marriageable queens. Therefore Christina felt absolutely nothing that morning. Except perhaps a viscous, heavy substance that settled in her stomach, producing something that resembled nausea, without being that. And except perhaps a vague, fluctuating and dull queasiness—nothing!—which passed quickly. Thus we can state honestly, as scrupulous chroniclers of this story, that Christina felt absolutely nothing that morning, except perhaps the sensation that her body was too large, and that she would like to curl up, make herself short, tiny, so as not to tower over the philosopher... but as far as feelings were concerned, nothing. She heard a singing blackbird when she awoke in her royal bed, and took it as a sign that everything would go well, but that is not feeling something, it's just interpreting life. She brushed her hair three times, because her hair did not look the way she wanted: loose and clean, which is indicative of freedom of spirit, and curly, which represents tenderness and care for others. In the mirror she realized, damn it!, that her eyes and eye sockets were swollen, but I don't know the point of including that in this truthful account, for it has nothing to do with how she was feeling on the inside, and it is in any case quite natural that any woman, most certainly a queen, would be concerned about how she presents herself to others. When she got up to walk across the few meters that separated her personal bedchamber from the room where she had decided to receive the philosopher, she felt nothing, just a touch of cramp in her right leg, a chill up and down her spine, a dampness on her palms, a cold antsy sensation on her scalp, a trembling of her lashes, heat in her face, and her nipples as if two almonds had just bloomed: hard and pushing outwards. But feeling, what you would call feeling... nothing. She made him wait long enough so that he would not notice that she was the one who was waiting for his arrival. She finished writing what she was writing, cleared her throat, and crossed the corridor. That morning the carpets kept clinging to her shoes, and would not let her move forward. Her skirts, three layers of cloth over a couple of golden-haired legs, kept getting tangled up in a strange way. As if she had never received anyone before! She cursed women's clothing, for she would have liked to go around in riding breeches, more flexible, or, on second thought, better not, for it would be quite awkward to have to appear in front of anyone, even worse a man, with her body outlined by trousers. That morning, the objects arranged in the corridors, the clocks, the figurines, the tapestries that Eija-Liisa had ordered to be placed in strategic locations, all seemed so absurd to Christina that she could not stop looking at them, as if her mind were being scattered into the forgotten corners of Tre Kronor. Halfway there she felt afraid, and thought about going back, and was turning to retreat when the royal arms of the houses of Vasa and Brandenburg appeared before her eyes, and she had to go on. Before raising the latch she saw Magnus, one of her trusted aides, with whom she scarcely exchanged two words, for she was in no mood for subtleties; while it pained her that everyone in the palace thought that that rustic and loutish count was her lover, they shouldn't come running to him with tales of the madcap loves of the queen. And before she fled, before she turned to dust, before she went up in smoke like straw, before she evaporated, before she was swallowed up by the sea, before she vanished, she opened the door. A bow. There he was. A greeting. There he was. The usual courtesies. There he was. Formulas. There he was, himself, in fact, the philosopher, her longed-for companion of the intellect, soul and pure spirit, there he was, soul and body. Yes, also in body. And she, who was not feeling anything that morning, letting herself be overwhelmed by her royalty and the pure blood that ran, blue, through her veins, began to issue orders: light the fireplaces in the guests' apartments, arrange things this way and that, for the best time for conversation is early in the morning, when my head is clear of all the many affairs of state, and so on and so forth. She barely let him say anything. She finished in just a moment, turned, and went back to her chamber, distant and glamorous as befits a correspondent queen. Nevertheless, when she closed the door, some kind of dampness slid along the tough wood so that, if not for the fact that it would have been very odd in someone who is not feeling anything, one would have said that Christina was crying, that her nerves had not let her be herself, not this time either. They had not let her say: "How glad I am that you're here! At last! Thanks for coming! I was so eager to meet you and talk with you and I'd like for you to tell me that not everything I'm doing is futile, that despite the fact that I'm surrounded by a gaggle of clowns, I have still not become entirely vulgar, I don't know how to say it, the words just don't come when you're there in front of me, the daily issues of government used to preoccupy me until your works arrived and stirred me up, and set the gears of my brain in motion, drawing me away from this stupid business of being a princess, making me see that there were important things and that happiness in life was to be found in coming to understand the little that it is given to us to know and so many things that I would say to you… if it weren't for the fact that I have made a firm resolve never to feel anything."

16

From the *Book of Women by Hélène Jans*
Horehound (*Marrubium vulgare*)

I'm interrupting the recipes here, excellent though they seem to me, because at times in life it's a good idea to pause and put one's ideas in order before one carries on with living. Just now I remembered the enormous value of horehound, a magical plant, which grows in thickets and produces small white flowers. Its virtues are many because it is capable of being something different from what it seems to be and, like many people who can't control themselves when they are facing a situation of which they have high hopes, the horehound bush fools us with its humble appearance as a rustic forest plant, rarely seen in ornamental gardens, only to astonish us by emitting a powerful scent of apples. For in nature, as in life, nothing is what it seems: the flowers of horehound are not apples, nor are there apple trees that smell as powerfully and intensely as horehound. You will come across the plant especially in sunny areas, and for that reason I suppose it stimulates the appetite and improves digestive processes when it is taken in an infusion, which you prepare by boiling a cup of water and adding two tablespoons of finely-ground flowers. It will ease stomach-ache, cleanse the liver and relieve the kidneys. I also use it externally, applying it as a medicine to heal wounds, for it deadens the skin and soothes pangs, and thereby makes certain days less painful for women. For many of them, who bleed not only from their uterus but also from their soul, a wound difficult to cure, this medicine turns out to be as magical as its aroma promises, for apples and women get along well together and at times have contrived great remedies against boredom.

17

Really he wasn't doing very well. Perhaps he had already considered the trip from another angle, as something outrageous and, after preaching so much that he shouldn't have gone, had ended up believing it. But everyone knows how a pair of carts can pull, especially royal carts... And the philosopher ended up getting on board, for Christina had sent him a ship, with an admiral and everything, all the way to Egmond. Christina paid no attention to the cost; to carry a man to her she sent a ship with two or three masts, a magnificent ship which did not pass unnoticed by those who were knowledgeable regarding the nautical arts. The rear mast had a square sail, most effective for sailing with a following wind, whereas the foremast held a lateen sail, the best one for sailing when the wind is coming from the prow. To put it briefly, let the wind blow from any direction it liked, the precious cargo of the ship would land in the arms of the queen. Quite unaware of all this preparation, the philosopher came on board with a great deal of luggage. The sailors understood at once that a man of learning was never going to travel without plenty of clothes, for although the habit doesn't make the monk, no monastery is going to take in a monk if he's not wearing a habit. Nor was a man of learning going to travel without his writings, those he was still cooking up and the ones that were useful for showing off, or without the writings of others, to which he can always turn for irrigation when there's a dry spell, and a number of books, and pens, and an inkwell, and a blotter, and even a lectern. While the sailors were lugging all those loads, however, the philosopher took a notion to tease the crew, saying that he had so much luggage because his daughter Francine was traveling with him. And the sailors believed it, for there was no reason to doubt it, because he might very well be traveling with a companion, and that would explain all the stuff, for it's well known that girls are always dolling themselves up. No matter how poor they may be, they all work hard on their hope chest; there never yet was a girl who couldn't get married because of a lack of cloth. Thus it's to be expected that, in the event that they are traveling, they would bring along more clothes than would fit into any suitcase. But, since human beings are always longing to talk, the sailors were dying to see the philosopher's daughter: it's well known to everybody that there's no such thing as an ugly Frenchwoman, and since he was French, they assumed that the supposed daughter was French. Then they all lurked and spied and watched from hiding to see if they could catch a glimpse of the girl with the thousand petticoats. And nothing. And look here, it's got to be interesting to make love with a woman with so much clothing; they even say that nowadays rich women wear a kind of pantaloons under their petticoats, no way, yes way, that's impossible, pantaloons are for men, no way, they say that women love the way their legs look with that garment. No way, yes way, just the way I'm telling you. Hell, if women are wearing pantaloons under their petticoats it'll be the end of the world, there won't be any children born anymore. Yes there will, man; if they wear pantaloons it's probably to get rid of the men they don't want, but they can always pull them down, the pantaloons, I mean. So then why put them on? Well, I don't know...

just because. Well, I don't get it. I don't believe it. And one of them, who had been a servant of Monsignor Batin, concluded that these times in which they were living were the last times, and the end had to be drawing near, for women, according to his master, who was a dean, a genuine saint, don't put on those pantaloons to cover themselves, they put them on to disturb the minds of chaste men with scabrous thoughts; it's amazing to see the subtlety they employ for evil. And although this was totally true, nobody paid him any attention when he spoke, for they all considered him worthless and a bit of a fool. While they were debating a point of such high importance as the decency and necessity of the intimate feminine garment, the philosopher was doing quite odd things: he went up to the gunwale with strange devices, just as if he wanted to pilot the ship. And the admiral, right before the eyes of the bewildered crew, began to treat him like a valued guest, to kneel when he passed by, mentally and not with his body, of course, for military ranks did not allow him to engage in such gymnastics with civilians. And all because the philosopher was walking around with new devices for measuring space, which he pointed directly towards the stars, and then took various notes and disappeared once again into his cabin. That seemed like matchless wisdom to the admiral, who was very eager to know what the philosopher was doing. Finally, on one occasion, when the admiral was using the astrolabe, the philosopher, humbly and calmly, offered him his own calculations, more precise, arrived at with a curious device, made of a frame with two branches separated at an angle and a movable sight that slid along a graduated arc. How? Well, it was as simple as this: with this sight that covers a sixth of the circle, it is possible to find geographic coordinates rapidly, especially the latitude where the ship is located, by measuring the height of the stars or the sun itself. This was quite enough to fascinate the admiral, for all children make friends with new toys. Since the philosopher had given him a sextant of a new design, something never before seen, the admiral thought it was fair to pay him back by showing him how to use the astrolabe and the armillary sphere, and the philosopher, caught up in that excitement that a writer feels who wants to surprise a friend by inserting a fragment of his story in the tale, went down to his cabin and returned with an exact replica of Galileo's telescope, a true piece of modernity. And back and forth, there were those who saw them looking at the same angle, with a silly grin on their faces and a friendly hand on each other's shoulder. And so on, time after time—that must have been the voyage most thoroughly marked by new inventions in history, for some were obsessed with figuring out what panties were good for, while others were applying themselves to the latest things in navigation, for although all may have been born free and equal, it's well known that society was tabbing some for destinies that would be unthinkable for others. The thing is that, in the middle of the reading of a lunar calendar of tides, they interrupted the admiral, which is just not done, asking him about the philosopher's daughter. The admiral wanted to know what time the tide would be in on the 10th of November, and something wasn't going quite right with the measurements, confound the devices, they couldn't do it even if they were alive, because the tides are so complicated... and you come and interrupt me now, when I have to work out the fixed point for a reading? You ignoramuses, by any chance do you not know that there is a certain lag in each point that has to be anticipated and calculated? And you come talking to me about some daughter? Get out, get out, I give up, for the admiral was bewildered; he didn't know whether the man had a daughter or not, but what he was sure of was that nobody else had boarded his ship. And the sailors, more and more intrigued, decided to take advantage of one of those incursions of the philosopher into the ether, during which he measured the interstellar voids, and, wrapped up as they were in the question of the pantaloons, they slipped into his cabin; it's anyone's guess what they had in mind to do. There inside, books, clothes, all a bit jumbled together, nothing to startle them, they found a large chest, and there's no telling what was going on in the mind of Pieter, the most eager, so that he couldn't think of a better idea than breaking it open. No, just a little, right here, and the lid finally gave way with a phantasmagorical noise and let its macabre contents be seen. A woman made out of wood, real-looking, life-sized, with joints, looking like a young girl, with hair and everything, like the female saints in the churches. God help us. Or no, better say the devil take us. This fellow is a pervert, I always thought he was strange. No, no, it's not like that, it's a doll with joints, he must have had a daughter, and she died on him, and he made a… a… A wooden daughter? Well, yes, something like an imitation of a daughter, a replica, a fake daughter. The men, who had sailed the seven seas, lived through mutinies and nor'easters, revolutions and punishments both military and civilian, and rough work, for they were not some softies of the court or palaces, were horrified by that soulless body. Francine was a machine. The men wanted to throw it into the sea, but at this point the admiral intervened and denied that it was an object of black magic, responsible for the cloudburst they had just endured and other calamities still to come; he said that his distinguished guest could bring along whatever he liked, and he could call things his daughter or whatever he wished, for he himself, who was perfectly sane and not a sorcerer, loved his ship like a son and also attributed feelings to it—sometimes the poor little ship just couldn't manage, and other times it was full of pep, and tackled the waves fiercely, and even did a little sweet-talking when a lady got on board. All of us, even if it doesn't look that way, do the same thing. So that's that, because wherever there's an admiral no sailor is giving the orders. The crew just had to accept it and disperse all over the ship, which wasn't all that far, and the voyage continued, with the sailors singing obscenities and other nasty stuff below decks. The philosopher said nothing, even though the incident had been one of the saddest in his life, since in the end it just went to show that everything, everything, absolutely everything that is looked at by a human being can have a soul. That didn't cheer him up at all, for it quite contradicted what he had written. Francine, sad to say, was dead, quite dead. He knew that. And since he had never known how to be a father, since he had not known how to arrive in time to say goodbye to the child, since he had not known how to deal with the memory of the child without Hélène, who disappeared as soon as she buried her, he made a Francine out of wood. In the five years that Francine had lived, he had felt enlivened by a second youth; he wrote the work that made him famous, and everything he undertook came to a successful conclusion; and he used to repeat to anyone who cared to listen that he was going to live to be a hundred. When the clock stopped for Francine, it also stopped for his longings for eternity. No! He believed in the superior life of the soul; the only thing Francine was missing was a body, a shining strong body, flexible, perfect, a far cry from the miserable, frightened body, eaten up by the sickness, which they had returned to the earth. And, if this body of Francine the automaton were to manage to speak, it would say to him: "I don't think, Papa, I don't think, I can only repeat the messages that you dictate to me on that disc that you insert in the middle of my back," and with that in mind, he would have had to finish the lapidary phrase, and acknowledge that, not thinking, perhaps the child had ceased, once and for all, to be. Although it's not certain, for the negation of the first part does not necessarily imply the negation of the second, right?

18

From the *Book of Women by Hélène Jans*
Powders to dry up tears and clear the vision

I have read in the writings of Arab physicians that burnt
shells are a good remedy for the eyesight. With several
of those recipes of the ancients I have prepared one very
much my own, which I present below. Collect burnt shells
and also unpierced pearls, which dry up the humors of the
eyes because they strengthen the nerves, and mix them in
quantities of two ounces per ingredient. Then add starch
and alcohol, the weight of a silver coin for each ingredient.
Then add rose water, three dashes, and three more of a
gum called camphor, which is produced in India from a
tree so large that more than two hundred men can be in its
shade, but don't ask me if they're comfortable or in what
position; I would say that they must be a bit crowded, but
this is what the wise men say in order to underline the great
size of that tree, and let's not waste any more time on that.
It's said that, mixed into eye-drops, this camphor gum is a
sovereign remedy for any hot ailment of the eyes. Together
with the camphor, also put in refined sugar, which is the
most prized variety, obtained via a slow evaporation, as
all important things are obtained, slowly and without
hurry, and it is used to make cataracts disappear. Put in
the weight of half a silver coin each of the camphor and
refined sugar. To this lore of the ancients, I add that you
should also put into the recipe a pinch of dates and another
of mirabelles, which are fruits similar to plums, which
come from the East Indies, and which are cultivated around

here nowadays; when gently applied to the eyes, they cure inflammations, clear up the eyesight and dry up untimely tears. When all these ingredients have been ground and thoroughly sieved, put the mixture into a box and cover it at once with a taffeta cloth with some weights on top. Those who suffer from awkward fits of crying should have their eyes bathed with the mixture, and they will not cry anymore. Sometimes a cold wind, or dust, or smoke will make everybody's pupils water, but there are those whose eyes, for no apparent reason, are sad and apt to cry, and in this way that can be well remedied. There are also people who have stronger emotions than others, for although they are all human, emotions are not given equally to all, and there are those who spend their whole lives with overflowing emotions. I have always liked these sensitive and emotional people, and it really annoys me when others criticize them for laughing so much and so loudly, or crying so much and so regularly. Therefore, if you happen to be part of that group that hard-hearted people call crybabies, whimperers, bawlers, snivelers, don't stop being what you are. But, when you get tired of their taunting, control your tears with this unguent which, I assure you and promise you, prevents the visible manifestation of the feeling while leaving the emotion itself intact, which is what matters.

19

Letter from Descartes to Monsieur Des Tûilles
December 3, 1649

My dear friend,
I begin this letter by wishing God's blessing on you,
your family and your household. My voyage was as hard
as expected. After a crossing full of incidents that left a bad
taste in my mouth, I finally arrived at my destination.
Stockholm is impressive: as beautiful as can be; I do not
encounter in it the noise of Amsterdam, or its feverish
activity, but it is clearly a powerful city. The Swedes live
well. There are no indications of poverty to be seen, or
abandoned children running around in the streets, or
beggars such as are regularly seen in the places I have
visited. This city is not built, like yours, protected from the
sea, but rather built on top of it. The first buildings were
put up on a little island in the narrow Strömmen Channel,
between the Baltic Sea and Lake Mälaren, and from there,
the city grew, occupying a dozen islands on both sides of
the Strömmen. This watery view surprised me: in the
Netherlands you all contain the water with strong dykes so
that they will not trouble people, whereas here, on the other
hand, everything seems to float on top of the waters. I
suppose that this must influence the character of the people
of these two countries. Nevertheless, I can't spend a great
deal of time on the analysis, for I still haven't had time to
get to know these new surroundings in much depth, and
thus I will go on telling you about my experience as the
trip gives me new themes. I have formed another quite

different opinion regarding the people of the land. The queen of Sweden, Christina, has amazed me with demonstrations of her clear and noteworthy intelligence; the profundity of her thinking had made me imagine her court as an idyllic place. If at any point I showed any reluctance to accept the invitation she was extending, my doubts had nothing to do with the predisposition of my mind to consider the Swedish surroundings in a positive light. Truly I was mistaken. The country is cold, and the beauty of the capital can't hide the fact that the people of these latitudes are quite reserved, not very disposed to show affection. The court, like all those with which I am acquainted, is a nest of vipers, thinly disguised with courtesy. A crowd of schemers has taken over the palace. A certain Dr. Boudelot, a countryman of mine, but no friend, dominates a circle of crown parasites who show all the qualities natural to courtiers: they're hypocritical, idle and repugnant. Moreover, the queen, interested in communicating with all the peoples of the world, speaks Latin, French, German, Flemish, and of course Swedish, besides studying Greek with determined dedication; with all this Babel she needs, clearly, dozens of grammarians. Alas! If there is any job or profession I detest, it's a grammarian's. They repeat what little they know like parrots from the Indies; they are fonder of exceptions than regularity, and, masters over the school, they settle into a knowledge that never explores. But God spare us the fury of a grammarian if you confuse a preposition with an adverb! No, there is nothing to stimulate our understanding in Grammar. Well then, I don't know how to convey to you my surprise when I saw that the queen is surrounded by grammarians: they dictate her letters and inform her about everything, like actual counselors. As if that weren't bad enough, I didn't relish being invited to courtly gatherings where I'm looked at as the foreigner that I am, where everyone expects of me a grace, a gentlemanly flair that never shows up… for, as you know well, a talent for coming up with sharp witticisms is not one I can boast, and they want nothing less than for me to treat them to ingenious learning and playful diatribes. After attending one of those masquerades I wrote to Her Majesty's secretary to say that I would not go again, and that I requested that they not bother me with this kind of social obligation, which I didn't know how to meet. Despite my having made an effort to hide my exasperation, with the greatest courtesy of which I am capable, that secretary looked up at me incredulously after reading the letter I handed him. I'm sorry to disappoint them, and far be it from me to assume rights that do not belong to me, but I was not born for the amusement of the damsels of the court. After publishing my essay on the passions, my goal is, more than ever, to develop a total vision of the essence of man, and I need a concentration that I can't achieve among oafs. Therefore I have to be miserly with my time, whatever the cost. This is another of the problems that afflict me. Consider: my whole life I have been working in a peculiar way, perhaps not very normal for a scholar. I usually sleep ten hours, wake up late and get up even later, because I really like to meditate in bed, in the warmth of the blankets, a habit I acquired during my childhood as a sickly boy, and which I would very much regret having to give up. At noon I dine, and then I potter around in the garden, ride my horse, or entertain friends. Only at nightfall do I start to work, sometimes extending my labors into the wee hours. I won't be allowed anything of the sort now. In her first interview with me the queen decided that five in the morning was the best time for us to see each other, with the pretext that, before she turned her attention to the political issues that keep her busy, she would have her head unclouded for the meditations that I might suggest to her. She set the appointment so naturally, as if no one lived in a way different from hers, with such respect for my knowledge, which demanded a clear head from her, that I was not able to offer any objections. So we see each other around five in the morning, in an impressive salon, as cold as iron. In order to meet with her, I have to come over to the palace from a nearby building and, now that the frosts have made their appearance, I don't know what I fear more, whether it's slipping and breaking a leg in this uncongenial land, or becoming ill in the lungs from the cold. I think I didn't do the right thing coming here. As you know, I am carrying on a correspondence with other important ladies. Elizabeth of Bohemia, for example, a woman of brilliant intelligence and a tranquil disposition, has been writing to me for many years, and has never troubled me like this Swedish princess... Probably I should have stayed in the Netherlands, where I was so well received for twenty years. As soon as I can, I'll reverse this bad decision, and convey to the queen my longing for those lands. I'll do it gently. I perceive a double nature in her: either she is very active or she is indecisive and melancholy; she is unstable, and something is boiling inside her: she seems to have been forced into a position of authority that she would have liked to avoid. But I don't know if I will be able to get out of her power; something in her puts a spell on me, and I don't carry out what I want to do. I didn't want to come here, and I came; I didn't want to get up early, and I got up early; I'm very much afraid that this woman may have deprived me of my free will. She even gave me the task, after the first interview, of writing verses in French for a ballet, and I agreed cheerfully! It's certainly true that I've always liked music, and maybe the moment has arrived for me to devote some time to it; ever since my youth I've been gradually abandoning this noble art. You can't deny that I've sunk pretty low: troubadour and pedagogue for a queen, and, at the same time, incapable of rebelling against her wishes! I am subjugated, and it's no small matter, for the scarce time I spend with her, when her obligations and her court full of grammarians allow her a moment for herself, is genuinely glorious. Truly it's only for the sake of these brief moments that I still remain in this country full of bears, where everything is rocks and ice! I can assure you that no one has ever perturbed me the way she does. She turns around all my arguments and, even though she respects me, she in no way follows the philosophy that I impart. Whereas Elizabeth of Bohemia often complains about lacking the necessary time for the introspection that the method of which I am author prescribes, Christina puts a teasing smile on her face and adduces that her thinking is rather that of an ascetic. And her affection for grammarians has yet another twist: the curious and immoderate inclination she professes for the Greeks. The queen has shown herself to be an expert on obscure and little-known texts of the ancients, from the Pre-Socratics to the Epicureans, texts with which the majority of men of letters are not familiar, and among which she gets along easily. I have nothing against this fondness of hers, but I don't want it to influence me, or for her to demand that I should operate according to a tradition I have always rejected. As you know, in my works I have meticulously avoided citing this or that sage, because scientific knowledge should never submit itself to the opinions of authorities, people who are dead, who can't judge the current stage of development. Neither Aristotle nor Galen, to give an example, was familiar with the works of Harvey, so that one will not find a single word in their writings that matches what we know today about the circulation of the blood. Well, Her Majesty now importunes me in my early-morning disquisitions, which I deliver half asleep and frozen stiff, saying to me: "This 'certain astronomer' you refer to in this text, is it Copernicus?? "And this one you allude to in this other fragment... it's Galileo, isn't it?" Sometimes I don't know whether she wants to listen to what I can teach her, or show me the boundaries of the territories where I will never get in my explorations. They've told me that ever since she was a little girl, she has insisted that the learned people in her service should entertain her during her leisure hours with the most curious sciences, and her spirit, eager to know everything, demands information continually. Not a day goes by without her reading something from Tacitus's history, which she calls "a game of chess." To my surprise, this author, who makes the most learned stop and think, is intelligible to her even in his most obscure passages; where others stop, wondering about the meaning of the words, she comes up with the right expression with marvelous ease. Finally, she has an extreme liking for taking on problematic questions with agile minds that maintain opposing positions, and she never gives her opinion until all those present have spoken; then she speaks in so few words, and so well reasoned, that her opinion seems rather like a formal and positive argument. That stems from the fact that she takes on any question with intelligence and without haste, and when she speaks about something, she reflects a great deal before she makes up her mind. I never expected to meet anyone like her, and I tell you this, because these feelings surprise me: as you who know me and whom I have the honor to call my friend are well aware, I'm not a man given to concupiscence or frivolous love affairs. In spite of this attraction, or precisely owing to it, I feel sad here in Stockholm, rubbing shoulders with this magnetic, intelligent woman, in this cold and beautiful space, when everything to all appearances is smiling on me… I don't know any reason for the idea of death to come to my mind again and again, an idea which is also magnetic and cold, like the queen whom I am always desiring to see… And, if I never liked having sad thoughts, now death repels me more than ever; one might say that my perturbation resembles fear too closely not to be given such an evil name… I will not weary you further with my little troubles: I just want to add one more thing. Before I left the Low Countries, I heard the queen's loose behavior spoken of at great length. But, after two interviews with her, I already believe that I know her well enough to venture to say that she is adorned with more virtues than her reputation gives her credit for. In these past few weeks I have had occasion to defend her several times, aligning myself spontaneously against the poison tongues who, even here, in her own home, attack her. I can attest to the most high and excellent virtue of this admirable queen, so far removed from the weaknesses of her sex and so absolutely in control of her passions. She is, quite certainly, the most attractive woman I have met in my entire life. That is why I'm afraid of not knowing how to control and guide this feeling, do you understand me? If so, all the credit is yours, for I myself don't understand me. Receive with this letter the wholehearted friendship of your most loyal,

R.D.

From the *Book of Women by Hélène Jans*
Caraway (*Carum carvi*)

A plant with very deep roots, crowned with a rosette of serrated leaves and a branching stem, ending in tiny white or pink flowers. The entire plant emits a delicious aroma. The little flowers have seed-heads that can be ground to a fine powder or chewed whole, half a tablespoon per day. It sweetens the breath and eliminates intestinal gases. Its principal virtue, however, is that it stimulates the production of milk in women, which must be why it is administered generously to the underfed, who are the majority. I say this because in our time beauty dictates that a woman, to be beautiful, ought to appear quite well fleshed and I am very much afraid that if fat women are well liked, it is on account of their rarity. Women eat only what is left over from the rest; they serve at the table and are the last ones to sit down. I have always heard it said that a mother never dies of a surfeit. And that is true. Therefore, when the period of nursing demands of a woman that she release nutrients that she needs to keep her health, nature can help her with substances like caraway. I'll take the opportunity offered by this dissertation to affirm that women shouldn't try to get fat so as to be better liked, for their bodies are the way they are, and whoever loves them should do so because of what they are, not for what others would like for them to be. If I say this it's because many times women come to me to cover up their true nature; one would even say that it's shocking to think of a woman who has tastes of her own.

Letter from Queen Christina
to her friend the Baroness, Madame Dupont
December 3, 1649
[Madame Dupont, before her marriage, was
a lady-in-waiting to the queen and one of the little ladies
who looked through a certain peephole in the wall. E.A.]

My dear,

How much I regret that the gout that afflicts your husband prevents you from traveling to Stockholm this winter! You're going to miss out on a genuine festival, for the city is like never before: excessive and profligate. You may ask the reason for such a tempest. Well, very simply, it's that I am preparing a serious celebration, and it's high time for it. As you know, when my father died, the senators decreed a very prolonged period of mourning, as befitted the length of his reign, and afterwards they didn't want to show the public the image of weakness that an adolescent queen would convey. Next came the *"affaire"* of my mother, and after that, a certain lethargy came over me; life is quite complicated enough without getting mixed up in big celebrations, where you're forced to stand around all day talking with people who don't understand you, leaving the country ungoverned and your spirit neglected. Thus time kept passing without my making up my mind, and one day after another the years kept slipping by. But now I've realized that I want to put on a really lavish celebration, before it's too late. Don't go thinking that I'm ill or afflicted by some misfortune. Nor do I believe that there are more lunatics inclined to assassinate me than might reasonably be expected, given the post that I occupy. In short, there is nothing going on that should alarm you... Still, I suspect that I'll startle all of you with a certain decision that I plan to make without delay. I will not tell you anything beforehand, because fruits must come in at their proper time, as they are green if too early and later they're rotten, and neither in the first state nor in the other are they agreeable to us. Probably you're noticing something different about me. I myself feel different. In part it must be on account of the presence of that great mind that, as you know, is among us. I have already spoken to you about him in my last letter, but I must do it again. The intellectual challenge that his presence implies for me has an effect like that of a tonic: it makes me feel alive. It's as simple as that. Still, I'm afraid that it's not going to be possible for me to keep him here for long. He can't get comfortable anywhere. He traveled all over in his youth, and developed a taste for changing his surroundings. And, though he remained in the Low Countries for twenty years, don't assume that he was settled. They tell me that he changed his address eleven times, eleven times! He stayed a long while in Amsterdam, but he also spent time in Franeker, in Egmond, in Deventer, in I don't know how many places... Probably this palace routine doesn't appeal to him. Indeed, I notice that he seems gloomy, perhaps bored. I look for the truth in what he says, but it's not so easy. I believe that, on the one hand, he wants to go away, and on the other, he wants to stay. Certainly I don't speak to him the way I ought to either, not asking him according to how my mother taught me, but rather by giving orders, and unfortunately, I neither want to nor can demand of him that he stay here for the rest of his life. Moreover, he is terribly diplomatic. You already know that when he writes, he tries to stay on good terms with everyone: he wants to please equally the scientists persecuted by the Inquisition and the Pope and the Paris theologians. Many people, of course, consider him fickle and a fence-sitter because he has reversed his views several times, and he himself has confessed to me that at some moments in his life he has felt frightened, thinking about how his writings would be received, especially around the time of the trial and punishment of Galileo. I don't know, however, if perhaps people might not be running their mouths too much about this episode, as they have so many other times, because changing one's opinion doesn't necessarily mean knuckling under to those in power: prudence is a virtue of great value, recommended by the Church Fathers as well as by the sages of Antiquity. As you see, I have informed myself thoroughly regarding his life. I'm certainly not short on details! He has always liked to live in good lodgings with good servants, enjoying a comfortable standard of living provided by the wealth of his father, a gentleman from the north of France who served as a judge for many years, just like his older son, for in this respect he's a bit of a black sheep of the family. In the Low Countries he followed a very orderly routine: he would get up late, dine at midday, take some light exercise outdoors and work until the wee hours of the night. I arranged for no one to alter this rhythm, for it is very pleasant when one can keep up the habits that one finds congenial. I only broke in on his routine by asking him to explain his works to me in the morning. I suppose that this won't bother him, since it's the only time when he wasn't doing anything interesting, just sleeping, and so I gave him to understand the importance for me of listening to the lessons he chose to give to me spoken out loud. No, I don't think that could disturb him, could it?... If you ask me what he looks like, I will tell you that he's attractive, even though his features are not regular. His dignified carriage and soft way of speaking stand out particularly. He's quite shy, you know—so much so that it turns out to be a challenge to get him to talk about anything other than his philosophy. He's always impeccably dressed, not the way we typically go about in these parts, more protected from the cold than elegant, and it surprises me that he always wears a sword. You didn't expect that, did you? I didn't either, just as I was equally surprised that he came across as extremely pious, maybe a little sanctimonious... I knew that he was Catholic, but not that he practiced it so assiduously... And nevertheless, I don't know why it seems to me that, no matter how much he prays, he's lacking in spirituality. I need to reflect on this so as to explain it to you better... it seems to me that he's more concerned with observing the forms of the rituals than with cultivating the sensitivity that true religion requires. I don't know... Moreover, according to my informants, he works very few hours and reads almost nothing. Perhaps he wrote all his works in short spasms of intense concentration. Amazing, isn't it? I don't know why I'm going on and on so much about these details, because after all he's just one more guest, like so many that we have lodged in this Stockholm that awaits you, my dear, anxiously... And when we host these illustrious guests it is a demonstration of the natural tendency of the Swedish people towards study and meditation, for we are not, as it is said elsewhere, a tribe of stupid bear hunters in frozen caves. It could be that government business, which is always so wearisome, has me a little agitated, and I'm attaching too much importance to details like these; I don't know why it should matter to me whether the agenda of daily activities of the philosopher is amusing or not, since he came here to teach me and that gets done when I can, as I am occupied with more matters than I would wish... and, as I was telling you earlier, soon there will be something very important to announce to all of you. Take care of your husband and, with or without him, come here. Don't forget to bring little Louis-André, I'd love to pamper him. With lots of kisses, my little pigeon, looking forward to seeing you, I am

Christina

Q. S.

22

From the *Book of Women by Hélène Jans*
A recipe for making sublimate, which is a recipe that fits
well here, towards the end of the book, as a tribute to all
the wet-nurses there have ever been in this world

Sublimate is an ointment that women have been
using since ancient times to beautify themselves, and its
excellence is such that many physicians have spoken out
against it, for men fear that women who are thus anointed
may appear to be what they are not, and that their parents
will palm them off and the men will end up married to
old hags who look, owing to sublimate, like very lovely
maidens. But the principal merit of this recipe that I use is
that it not only acts on the beauty of the face, on wrinkles
or crow's feet, but also goes deeper, and brings laughter to
the face, and makes one feel happy, and look at life with
delight, and it makes all the small beauties that every day
brings lift up the spirit. I'll give you my recipe with only
one condition: that you will use it to improve from the
inside out, and not just on the surface. To obtain an ounce
of this substance, you must take two eighths of mercury,
and soak the mercury with a hunk of bread until the bread
turns white. Then take it in your hand, kneading it with
the milk of a woman with child, for mother's milk was
used by the ancients in many remedies. The milk is more
potent if it comes from the mother of a male child, only
surpassed by that of the mother of male twins. They even
say that mother's milk is widely used in France to cure
consumptives, for which purpose they look for a woman

who is beautiful, young, light-skinned, clean, healthy, cheerful and graceful, who will put her breast in their mouths and, both with sweet conversations and also with her delicious milk, will reinvigorate and restore them. What can I say, when I read this in Pliny the Elder: the consumptive, if he doesn't get well, at least will spend the last period of his life quite agreeably. But in our remedy there is not so much madness, for, once the mercury is kneaded with the milk, it must be covered with a clean cloth and left to rise like dough. Once it has consolidated, work it in your hands again until it takes on a color that is neither black nor white. Knead it again and shape it and leave it to rest one more day, taking care not to get in too much of a hurry, for it's best to wait as many days as needed until it begins losing its color. Once it becomes white, tie up this dough in a linen cloth, which should be new and well folded. Take a hen, which should be black, and take out the crop and the innards. Put the cloth inside the hen and place it in a pot and fill the pot with rainwater, and let it heat over a strong fire until the hen falls apart. Then take out the cloth, put it on a plate, and make little balls with the contents, and there you have your sublimate.

23

On the second of February of 1650, as he was heading for his early-morning meeting with Christina, Queen of Sweden, of the most noble house of Vasa, the philosopher felt a sudden chill. He decided to ease it by drinking off a good glassful of brandy. The remedy, though manly and to the purpose, must not have been effective, for the next day he had to stay in bed. And rumors started running like hares through the palace. According to some, the illness stemmed from the efforts he had to make to organize his philosophy so as to explain it to the queen, who, being a woman, was not very well suited for understanding, not very well provided with intellect by nature, not particularly well educated. How understandable that it must cost him a great effort to come up with a synthesis in such a case! He couldn't say: "Your Majesty, copy this out for me a thousand times," or stick donkey's ears on her, or hit her with a ruler, or… in short, a pedagogical effort like this one could very well bring about fevers in someone as enfeebled as the philosopher. According to others, it was the inclemency of the weather during the voyage, along with certain wounds that some events during the crossing had reopened, that had left him sickly and morose, for no man in love was ever so wan: they all assumed that he was in love, definitely. Nor were there lacking those who affirmed that his passing indisposition was attributable to the excess of Spanish wines with which the physicians of the Low Countries had treated his gout. He had never

suffered from gout, which was a common ailment, true…
and it occurred in the most elevated figures, true… but
he did not suffer from it. Finally, the sharpest tongues in
Stockholm spread to the four winds that the philosopher
was confined to his bed because of the poison that the
grammarians had administered to him, envious of his
growing influence over the queen. And, along with the
grammarians, there must have been the most numerous
group of malcontents. It is well know that, as evidence
of their general animosity towards him, what the
Englishman Gideon Harvey published in his *Vanities of
Philosophy*, that the dubious Frenchman, with his pleasant
conversation, with that cordial tone and resonant baritone
voice, could not help enthralling those who listened to
him, especially if they were women, for the daughters
of Eve are superficial and vain, and let themselves be
influenced by these things, and even more let themselves
be carried away by the natural impulses that tend to place
them in a horizontal position. But the sure thing is that the
possession of a deep voice and seductive manners served
to mix his insignificant discourses on the direction taken
by bursts of light with really important questions, such
as religion. So that, what with professorial explanation
and example, it was a sure thing that he was slipping in
for all who listened to him the insinuation that they ought
to convert to Catholicism. Thus it had turned out with
Elizabeth, Princess of the Palatinate, and Prince Philip
of England, and with Christina herself, and, if he lived
a long life, he would seduce a great number of notable
and distinguished persons, for the philosopher was
actually a Jesuit in disguise, a genuine preacher from the
Society of Jesus behind the mask of a gentleman, a sage,

a philosopher, and fancy that, even a mathematician. Nevertheless, all of them agreed, those who thought of the effort of synthesizing rationalism, those who blamed the voyage, the wine or the poison, all were convinced that the philosopher had come to Stockholm to die, and that he would die there.

And so he was for nine days, feverish, weak, weary, nervous. At first he refused to let them bleed him, for he had little confidence in Swedes or in physicians: so much the less was he going to trust, logical and methodical as he was, in Swedish physicians. He continued drained, delirious, drenched with perspiration, with the disquieting feeling of having lost his sense of time. At times he thought fondly of Hélène, who would have imagined it so long afterwards?, and smiled at the memory of how she used to look at him, with those eyes that read him to his depths, and he thought how good it would have been to have her there, dedicated to curing him with her plants that smelled like paradise, with her hands, with her words, for Hélène knew how to cure in every known way, along with some new ones of her own invention, and he lamented that he didn't know anything about her, not having learned anything about her for all those years... And he lamented not having loved her as she deserved, without any doubt, as much love as could be given to anyone on this earth. Then he ordered that they should do the bleeding at once, because he didn't recognize himself, getting so sentimental. And they bled him. And they waited. They waited to see if it was God's will that he should recover, because in his state there was little that men could do. They waited while he plunged deeper into delirium, like one who was hurling himself into the water off the bridge of Stortorget, and he remembered Hélène's laughter, and he associated it with Christina's body, and his mind came up with distorted mixtures: he must have had a poltergeist or an evil spirit loose in his head, and in these delicate moments that mysterious entity was giving him a hell of a time. In a lucid interval, he rummaged through his papers and left a few of them in very good order for the queen; although he had to experience the shame of having a person like her, whom he admired so much, see him in the nakedness of dying, which is always a grotesque garb, she might thus retain at least some good memory and some evidence of what he felt towards her. Together with this declaration of love, the only one he had ever written, he put into the packet, mysteriously, a few parchments labeled "H.J.," expecting that the queen would understand what she had to do with them, for one does not give instructions to the beloved, since lovers' hearts intuit with extraordinary precision what the other desires. And he fell asleep, and woke up, and remembered the caresses, the smell of damp earth, the warmth of the smiles, the embrace with his companion at the end of a fencing match, Francine's little voice, childhood play, the feeling of cold water on diving into a river, he no longer knew which one. He mixed everything together because nothing was clear and distinct anymore, as he liked for it to be. He requested, one last time, a pen, and began to write to his brothers, but he had to give it up and continue with dictation, because all the strength of his body was abandoning him. In the letter, now a testament, he implored his family, especially Pierre, his older brother and the head of the family, to continue supporting Madeleine Brun, the woman who had been his wet-nurse in his infancy and who was going to outlive him. My treasure, my dear little boy, so pretty, who sucked so strongly, so eager to live... and now dead! If it had not been for her I would not have enjoyed this mortal life, of which so little remains to me. I've been supporting her, Madeleine, all my life, for you can't repay so much care, don't let that skinflint Pierre leave her neglected as an old woman. And, as his strength declined, and he coughed, and he noticed his growing difficulty in breathing, the philosopher began to experience what it was truly like to have the soul separated from the body.

24

From the *Book of Women by Hélène Jans*
And now for the conclusion of the recipe book

I have regaled you with a collection of remedies, all very good and all of them tested by me, with which you have at your disposal a real manual for women. I do not promise you that the ointments are magical or the recoveries miraculous, but instead a true knowledge of the art of preparing potions, tonics, perfumes, balms, and even foods, for we are dealing not only with hygiene and cosmetics: our mothers knew a great deal, and never gave sick people or children the same dishes as the other members of the family. I have taught you to concoct syrups and preserves, to mix plants, to collect, dry and apply medicinal herbs, and many other things. Everything you have found written here was not in the jargon of medicine or in obscure words, but rather expressed in ordinary language, so that any person could understand it. Frankly, I believe that this work of mine is quite good: I know only one other previous book that is similar, by a Portuguese man who was regarded with suspicion by the authorities. However, even if there were more of this kind, since I wrote it with so much care and enthusiasm, I don't believe that others could surpass it, but at best match it. I bring together everything I know, what I have seen done, regarding how to cure those whom I saw to be weakened, so that women can resolve their problems without calling in Hippocrates or Avicenna, even though I, if I have invoked them at times, may at my pleasure combine what the great sages say with what can be read in the household notebooks of those women whom I have often heard called witches. If this does anyone any good, more power to him, and anyone who doesn't want to try, let him not read and remain eaten up by fear, for honey was not made for timid fools: one must know how to steal it from the bees, and everything that is pleasurable in life must be sucked in by overcoming fears and doubts. So, this book contains:

Firstly, many remedies for various sicknesses of the body and the soul, which I do not believe are separate things, for when an injury is hurting a person, that person immediately becomes sad and, the other way around, when one is irritated, one's stomach often hurts, or one doesn't breathe well.

Recipes for aromatic products.

Waters, exfoliants, softeners and other products for the face.

Many products for washing and others for the teeth.

Useful remedies to soothe mistreated hands.

Preserves, soups and foodstuffs to revive a person who is dying.

Bleaches and conditioners for the hair and the skin.

With all of this the ladies should be satisfied. Still, those remedies which will bring you the greatest benefits are, according to my way of thinking, the recipes that are devoted to the sicknesses and troubles specific to women, and this is for several reasons. In the first place, pregnancy, birth and the period after birth with all of their complications are everyday things. At the same time, physicians give little attention to learning about these matters, and when they do know something, they insist on hiding their knowledge or pretending not to have it, and they rarely treat women, even when they are needed by them, so as not to examine some parts that other men might think they shouldn't have seen. It's a poor excuse for a physician who lets himself be pushed around in such a way over trifles and allows a patient to die without visiting her because "oh dear, they mustn't say that I saw and touched what I shouldn't even have imagined." Another reason moved me to devote myself to women's matters, which is as I explain below. The sages affirm that women are characterized by darkness, weakness, cold and dampness; a fellow named Hippocrates, with quite a reputation, says that the character of a woman depends on her womb. And from that there comes a whole series of tales, which the sages pass off as science and modern knowledge, although in fact it is as old as the hills and spread about by the malice of the most worthless men and those least well disposed towards women, who declare that the womb is controlled by the moon and the imagination, which is true, but from that they conclude that this promotes the growth of the passions of hatred, vengefulness and lust, and they keep quiet about the fact that, according to the old lore, the moon and the imagination that operate on the womb, although they do provoke those wild passions, also increase tenderness and compassion, of which the best kind of love is made up. And it can't be surprising that, with such contrary physicians, women don't want, when they are being racked by both spasms or bleeding, to be examined by someone who thinks so badly of them, and prefer to be looked over by other women. That's why I placed so much emphasis in my book of recipes on remedies that women need and would like to know about, and if the male reader feels uncomfortable, let him put aside this little work he is holding in his hands for later on, when he matures and realizes that one can't hush up what must be spoken of. I also am fond, among the remedies dealt with in this book, of the making of pills and potions, which succeed in preventing contagion with delicious aromas, because scented oils, when the body is anointed with them, cure wounds, besides infusing clothing and pleasing the nose. Many are afraid of these substances, which theologians condemn as contrary to chastity. The Church Fathers, according to what I have heard said in my youth, say that women who use cosmetics are sinners, which alone has always made me feel inclined to use them, because they are wrong when they declare that in this way women are committing the extremely serious mistake of correcting the image that the Creator has given them, and with this new appearance they are collaborating with the devil. But exfoliants do not undo the image of God, nor do they modify what He designed, for it would be great arrogance to try to amend what He made. So then, all one has to do is look at the faces that some people carry around to realize that, if God is perfect in his works, sometimes he must slip up a bit or, on the other hand, if God is perfection itself, it must not be in his works, for sometimes they turn out to be quite defective. In any case, it is not a known fact that He said: "Thus I made you, and thus you must remain." In other respects, so far as I know, moralists have always valued the paths to self-improvement, so that someone who had a proclivity for lying and for whom, therefore, it was twice as hard as for someone else not to lie, by not lying would offer a gift more welcome to divine eyes than that other person who did not have that inclination to start with. Following this line of reasoning, if you are born beautiful and allow life to spoil you, I believe that you're not putting your talents to good use, or not as much as when you're born ugly and manage not to look that way to others, by dint of making improvements, for a glowing look, a skin without wrinkles, or a pleasant aroma are beauties that neither provoke lust nor amend the divine work. And I declare, finally, that with there being a God who created beauty, beauty must not be a bad thing in his eyes, for he must have created it for a reason, which can't be to lead to everyone's perdition. But I won't continue in that vein, for if I had been born a man, I would surely be a theologian, such is my eagerness to correct the nonsense that moralists have written. And I will say, and end with this, that of all the things you may need to prepare my recipes, I think you can find all of them in a well-stocked shop: I am not suggesting that you convert your house into an alchemist's den. Almost all the substances are among those mentioned by the sages Pliny, Hippocrates, Galen, Avicenna, Rhazes and others. But I have also experimented with the ones used by the grandmothers, the old-fashioned apothecaries, the friars in monasteries, the midwives and some healers, white witches, bonesetters and other trades associated with magic. Don't be surprised, then, by the use of burnt shells, lizard's bile, cat's fat, the patient's urine, or bull's horn, all things that are said to be connected with witches and which, nonetheless, if they help to remedy our ailments, I don't see why they shouldn't be used, for at times they make very good remedies. In this respect I would ask the moralists, in case they had a child of their own whom they loved very much who was dying before their eyes, if they would hesitate to have recourse to any one of these potions on account of their bad reputation, thereby risking the patient's health and chances of recovery. I would like to ask the very religious men who trot out their story that life and death come from God, and are only in his hands, whether applying one remedy or another to the sufferer can really go against the divine will, which is supreme and acts on a higher plane than our humble efforts as healers. But, as long as God leaves us the body on this side of life and doesn't move it to the other, it must be so that we may do with it as much as is in our control, not so that we can be hindered by vain scruples regarding whether or not it is proper to apply this remedy, for my practice is to try every last one before giving up, and I have never felt tainted by the use of a witch's recipe. You don't have to give me any response out of your reflections, for all of us have our own cares and worries. As far as anything else is concerned I can't promise anything. I have seen someone I loved very much abandon this world, no matter how my arts tried to keep her body on this side, and I could do nothing... And so, beautify yourselves, get well, recover from coughs and weeping fits, fix what can be fixed, and enjoy what each day brings, for the other, the black one, the unnamable is waiting impatiently for you, and it will come, for certain, without any recipe, potion or wash being able to free you from its coming. And goodbye. H.J.

25

The queen, having recognized the capacity of the philosopher's spirit, which extended to matters quite different from philosophy, did not delay in including him in her Privy Council, and the confidence she placed in him served to regulate her personal conduct a little, which had been somewhat lacking in rules, and to orient her on various points relating to the governing of her states, queen as she was of the Swedes, the Goths and the Vandals. This esteem that the philosopher enjoyed, almost without deserving it, as it came to him very prematurely, alarmed the grammarians and other pundits of the palace, who studied closely how to deal with him and how to lessen the ardor that the queen appeared to feel for the new philosophy that was causing such a fuss in Europe. In the first place they tried to persuade the lords of the court concerning the strange power that this recently-arrived foreign guest had acquired over the confidence of the queen, our lady Christina, and how dangerous it would be if he had a part in matters other than those related to philosophy and the sciences. Confronted with these and other similar arguments, Monsieur Baillet found himself obliged to intercede on behalf of his dear Descartes, although all of this, in my opinion, only goes to show how easily we often exaggerate the merits of our friends. For, judging by the letters of Descartes to Princess Elizabeth, all the interest of this great man was limited to finding a way to make his philosophy to the taste of the queen, but it is certain that such an objective could very well have been attained without becoming part of her Privy Council. Regarding the intervention of the sage in government affairs, our opinion is skeptical. Christina had been educated in the best school for politics that existed in Europe, to wit, the Swedish Senate, where there were a great many gentlemen who were experts in the most important issues of war and peace; with that in mind, what new thing and of what kind could she learn from Descartes, who was emerging from the most absolute seclusion, from the most definite and stifling aloofness? Moreover, she, who well before the arrival of the philosopher in Sweden was acclaimed as the possessor of all the qualities required to govern vast states, why would she let herself go down in history as the queen who allowed herself to be instructed by the sage in vogue at the time? Monsieur Baillet—we must not skip over this—affirms that the queen had asked him to plan out an academy, in which she would enjoy the roles of head and protectress and of which Descartes would be the director. It is quite true that we have reliable information that Christina did want to establish an academy, but not of philosophy, rather of theology and in support of evangelical religion, though intended to work towards the unification of the Protestant churches. The celebrated doctor Johannes Gezelius, we are told, would be named to preside over it. I have no doubt that she may have thought at some point about founding an Academy of Philosophy, and that she would have wished for her very dear friend Descartes to be its leader, but it should be kept in mind that these influences must have been exaggerated, since the philosophical interviews of the queen with Descartes lasted only a couple of months. And, whether because of the change in Descartes' habits, or because of the climate and the season, around the beginning of February he suffered a sudden inflammation of the lungs along with a high fever, which carried him away in a week. It is true, as Monsieur Baillet, said, that the queen was moved by his death and that she wished to dedicate a marble monument to him so that posterity might judge the esteem she had for his merits. However, the tomb in the end was very simple, as was advised by his friend Chanut, who was given the task of composing the beautiful inscriptions that appear on it. Madame de Motteville said, on the death of the philosopher: "Queen Christina, instead of making men die for love, makes them die of shame and disappointment, and in this way it can be explained that the philosopher Descartes lost his life because she did not give her approval to his strange way of philosophizing." Jokes of this kind were spread around again and again in the court by Descartes' enemies, but, so that we may judge the great esteem that the queen felt for the philosopher, we must simply bear in mind the fact that she had chosen to spend with him a period of time so precious as that of her nightly repose. Monsieur Sorbière relates, in two of his letters, that in the illness of Descartes there were observed some symptoms of his having ingested poison, but he adds: "I absolutely do not believe it. It is not customary in the northern countries to employ such instruments of vengeance, and above all with a person of beautiful spirit, which the grammarians of the queen did not think anyone possessed in such a high degree as Descartes." The best thing about the death of Descartes having occurred in Sweden was that he left some disciples there who applied themselves to delving deeper into the principles of his philosophy, and who made up a veritable Cartesian sect.

[Arckenholtz: *Memoirs concerning Christina Queen of Sweden, intended for the elucidation of the history of her reign, and primarily of her private life, and the events of the history of her time, civil and literary, followed by two works of this learned princess which have never before been printed.* Amsterdam, P. Mortier bookseller, 1751, on some page or other]

26

Now he was dead. And Christina had not known how to make the most of the time. Time that slips through the fingers of our hands and, when we think we have it, is already gone, just like the waters of Stortorget. Because it is spring in Stockholm, and, just as the rebirth of life triumphs over the lethargy of winter, just as the lakes thaw out, the days become longer, the buds appear on the naked trees of Stockholm, just as the glaciers hurl themselves in an eternal fall down the mountainsides, and the first flowers solace the sight with their colors, just as what was sleeping begins to awaken, as desires are born anew in souls, she would like for his body to feel the rays of the sun again, and the aroma of the forest, and the urge to dive into the water and make a splash.

27

It was during the month of October, 1651, when Queen Christina, Her Majesty, who had always been a bit different, but lately had seemed determined to show her subjects that she had all at once become strange, called together the Senate. She wished to speak. She wished to say something. Could she have decided whom to marry? The fancy men of the court, and the military men of the court, and the learned men of the court, and the political men of the court, and the ordinary men of the court, all stroked their moustaches and said: "It's all the same to me, the queen is very much her own woman." She wants to speak, she who has been silent for so long, who has been living like a recluse in Tre Kronor for the past few months writing moral maxims, which is enough to make a person laugh when it's told. And in that immense room, all red velvet and golden glitter, Christina, regal, imposing, defiant, with a stare that cuts like ice, with a face so devoid of expression that it even seems as though she has been robbed of her spirit, Christina stands up. She's wearing black, with no ornament other than a white neckpiece as dictated by fashion, which is nothing but an inner garment pulled up to the face to indicate that the one wearing it is as clean on the inside as on the outside. The dress has a strange look: it could look like a floor-length garment if not for the fact that it's belted up at the front so as to spread out behind in an extremely long train; seen from the front she looks like a woman, of course, but from behind she resembles a man, perhaps a friar, even though the carriage of the figure does not exactly speak of poverty, obedience and chastity, which are unquestionable attributes of the monastic life and unthinkable in Christina. And, once her image has been seen and seen again, Christina for the final time allows the Swedish senate to say all that it has to say, for her, the heiress to the throne, ruler by the grace of God, to follow up by taking her turn to speak and, very softly, she lets it flow between her lips: "After having reflected time and again on a matter of such importance as this one..."and still nobody knows what the matter is, "I have found no better measure that the one I am about to propose to contribute to the unity of the State and the peace of its people than to ensure the succession to the throne by causing heirs to the Crown to be born..." The listeners eagerly seize on the matter and, knowing what she is like, decide that she's having a child with every one of the Swedish men. The murmurs do not allow for distinct hearing of her clear, cold voice, distant like a glacier that awaits, with the spring, its time to crash down, to fall, to carry away all in its path. "And since I am completely resolved not to marry," here, one can well imagine that there will be scarcely-stifled titters rising among the listeners, "neither now nor ever, because I feel no inclination whatsoever for matrimony," there's no lack of rude commentators reminding the audience in whispers that boys and girls are all the same for her, "so as to satisfy in some way my people and to ensure the necessary succession, I have decided, then, to abdicate, to abandon my position and ensure the continuity of the state by naming a new king, in the person of my most dear German cousin, Prince Carl Gustav." No matter how well-mannered the attendees at this Assembly may be, they cannot control themselves, and the room, turned into a beehive, is a chaos of buzzing and flapping. "The prince will immediately be declared heir to the throne, and, as soon as he is crowned king, he will be obliged to take a wife. And the male children who may be born of that union…" How strange! Why only the males if she, who is not a male, as least so far as anyone believes, inherited the crown of her father? Well, say what you like, the matter of her not being male has never really been cleared up. "The male children who may be born of that union will be declared heirs to the crown, according to the order established by their birth. In this way, the line of Carl Gustav will secure our nation from the fear of the evils that often accompany the election of kings." And the queen, as she does when she walks alone through the square of Stortorget, turns, and all can see in that moment the train of the dress, imposing, of a lady who will never marry, who will never carry behind her a throng of maids-of-honor bearing her long train and also her veil to hand herself over to a handsome suitor from another royal house. In that precise instant they all realize that that mysterious queen is going to go away, magnanimously, out of history, where she could have figured as the splendid, authentic model queen, who made her court into a temple of learning. But no. Christina had decided to disappear… the time had come for her, at least, to become herself at last.

The philosophy of René Descartes has a preeminent place in the history of gender. Even though he, of course, did not concern himself with the question in his own writings, he has been heavily criticized for formulating metaphysical and epistemological perspectives that consolidated a construction of gender that privileges males. The mind/ body dualism, it has been said again and again, confirmed a view of the lives of women as lacking in importance, and Rationalism, by requiring objectivity, would tend to eliminate from consideration the knowledge derived from experience that women accumulated in their daily lives.

[Class notes of university student Einés Andrade. Subject: *Feminist Keys to Understanding Philosophy*]

When she was leaving Stockholm en route to Rome she wasn't feeling anything, for she was quite well trained for keeping things inside. The carriage that was taking her to the port was not exactly filled up with packages. Next to her a few items of clothing were bouncing around in the suitcases, a few assorted knick-knacks, some family jewels, not much, because none of these kinds of things interested her. It's true that she was taking along several bags of gold coins, for she did not consider poverty or even simple need to be suitable for her. She also took along books, lots of books, and a few of her ladies-in-waiting with their belongings, and also a silly parrot that had been given to her as a pet and who endured the cold patiently, even though the change of air had left his beak silent and his brain primed for malice... And there were, to be sure, other things, but they had been sent to the ship in the preceding weeks, so that there would be no delay in weighing anchor. Of all the things that Christina was taking along on that morning, when she left Tre Kronor, never to return, deciding of her own free will to leave behind the good life that fortune had offered her, with her little bit of power, and glory, and wealth, and adventure, and Fame, of all that she was taking along, as I was saying, the only thing that mattered to her was her jewelry box: a leather case, precious, very finely crafted, with several compartments, and tiny hidden drawers, and trays that could be lifted out, lined with velvet so that the jewels would feel at home, snuggled there in great comfort. And in that case she was not carrying diadems, or necklaces, or rings, or bracelets, or elegant courtly adornments; what she was carrying in it, sealed, tied and tied again with red ribbon, was a certain document that had been entrusted to her. Therefore, while Stockholm was receding in the distance, homesickness was not taking hold in her heart, which was now changed by the urgency of meeting the woman who had written such a document. About her she knew, first and foremost, that she signed her writings with two initials: "H.J."

II

Hélène Jans

1

Anyone who might be looking at her through a chink in the wall would think she was asleep. Her body is scarcely moving. Only the rise and fall of her breathing gives away the animal that rests quietly, is waiting, perhaps in ambush. A lovely animal, anyone who might observe the scene would see that, since, even now when the sorrows of life have etched deep lines in her face, those lines do no more than extend the power of her stare up her face and to the sides. She is not sleeping. Flies walk around on her fingers, settle on her nose, buzz as they explore the tepid dampness of her lips and make her swat at the air and snort, but they don't manage to pull her out of the state of profound concentration in which she is submerged. Her furrowed brow, her fixed stare, her quiescent limbs: one would call her a tranquil and warm animal, a cat by the fireplace, a dog or a tortoise, it makes no difference, if not for that mouth that never stops forming words, as if it were pronouncing a prayer. She's reading.

She holds in her hands a thick volume of yellowed leaves that emits a humid, moldy smell. A smell not to be expected in a house where everything has a scent, and a pleasant one. She turns the pages slowly; one notes that she enjoys caressing the book. One would say that reading is a task that she does with her entire body, made languid today by the heat. The book is probably old; it's been gnawed by mice, and the pages have swollen with long use. The moldiness is hardly a distinguishing detail:

in Amsterdam everything smells moldy—bread kept in a kneading trough, bleached clothing laid out to dry in the pale sunshine, gutters, houses and the bodies of lovers all smell of mold. Much more so a book... Now that she is moving, on the front cover of the volume there can be read, printed in block letters, the name of a man, "Jean Liébault," and, below this, a title in French: *Thrésor des rémedes secrets pour les maladies des femmes* (*Treasury of Secret Remedies for the Ailments of Women*) and a date, 1585. It's quite true, the book is not new, for it is now the spring of 1655. The person who's reading it is a woman, no doubt about it: the twilight coming through the window casts the shadow of her body on the wall and makes visible some feminine curves, generous curves, rounded, which seem to be made for one to sink into them.

It's a woman, no doubt about it. And nevertheless, she's reading. And she's not reading a love story or naughty verses, she's reading a medical work. She must be wanting to learn something wicked by reading the book. Or she may have done something wicked and she's seeing how to cover it up. Definitely it's a woman. How strange that she's not heading off to the fountain to chatter, or to the market to gossip with her cronies. She's a woman, reading. Peacefully reading. And so... could she be a witch? She could. Her name's Hélène.

From the *Thrésor des rémedes secrets*
pour les maladies des femmes
[A fragment, most probably from the preface]

The ancients carried on a lively polemic regarding this matter which, still today, attracts our attention. The majority view, following the teachings of Aristotle, defines the gestating female as the passive receptacle for the embryo. However, the followers of Hippocrates considered that the body of the woman played a more active role in the formation of the child: in addition to housing it, it must also give it shape, combining, to this end, the power of the masculine seed with the strength of the foodstuffs that she would consume during the course of gestation. It is not our purpose here to take part in a quarrel that would earn us more detractors than friends, from the very moment when we declared our preference for one or the other of the viewpoints. It would be strange if a good judge did not feel sympathy in this dispute (as in any other that could be carried on) with one of the two opposing parties, before they had even set forth their arguments in support of their opinion. And, granted that the defense of the viewpoint that might be adopted on the jousting field is not based so much on the reasons that could support it as on the level of respect that might be felt towards the one who proposes it, any attempt to arrive at a fair judgment is futile. It would be completely impossible for a philosopher versed in the texts of the Stagirite to give way before Hippocrates, and it would be equally strange if physicians did not band together to say that their distinguished master was right, and to look with a jaundiced eye on the speculative philosophers who, unlike them, had never stained their hands with the blood of a fellow being. That's how human affairs are, and thus is explained the behavior of men, who tend to turn into a *casus belli* what is really nothing but a hidden sympathy. And because of my suspicion of the impossibility of discerning solutions to any polemic, I do not aspire in this treatise which, o reader, you hold in your hands, to deprive you, or to provoke you, or to dispossess you of your own ideas so as to lead you through mine, but instead to warn you that rather than being yours because they match up with your judgment, they are yours because of your intent that they should be so. Instead, rather than wearying the intellect with reasons with which some would be annoyed while others would be delighted, I prefer to begin by proposing a compromise that presupposes a certain change of attitude towards my distinguished predecessors. And, since for human generation there must be, in addition to the prolific masculine seed, a female body to house the fruit of the joining of both of the bodies, it does not seem useless to me to study the anatomy of the woman. We will dedicate ourselves to this study in the present book, even though, according to the master Galen from whom all of us physicians have learned so much, that body of Eve may be no more than an inversion of the male body, provided with entryways where the latter has projections, caves where it has mountains, and cold ice where he is all heat and abundance.

3

Someone's knocking at the door. The reading woman barely stirs. The knocking is repeated, nerve-racking, insistent. "I'm coming, I'm coming already." The reading woman stops being a lovely seated statue, reluctantly leaves her reading, and goes to open the door.

"All you had to do was push, I always leave it open."

"Hélène, good day to you, could you help me?"

"Come in, Camille, relax for a while. What do you want from me?

"I need… Don't laugh, all right? I need a spell to attract men."

"And you think that if I had a remedy like that I'd be living alone?"

"Hélène," the voice gets all confidential, nudge nudge wink wink, we're friends here, "if you're on your own it's because you feel like it…!"

"Don't doubt that for a minute." Hands on her hips, Hélène tosses her hair away from her face with an abrupt, defiant movement. "I want to be as alone as a person can be in this world, without all of you interrupting me all day, taking me away from my studies."

The woman who has just come in asking for help could feel intimidated by Hélène's complaint, but she doesn't… She doesn't seem to. She knows very well that the whiny, victimized tone makes up part of the ritual. It's the same way at home: sisters, neighbors, old women readily drop what they are doing when someone else asks them for help, but not in silence: they'll say that they are so busy, but no one gives them a hand when they want something, that no one ever notices what they do. Saying this is just part of the game, never let anyone think they aren't hard-working or that they're wanting to exchange work for distraction. Hélène continues explaining herself:

"But what do you expect? On winter nights the warmth of a man makes flowers grow out of the ice, and the sweat that comes from huffing and puffing under the blankets is a lot sweeter than the sweat from slaving away at the river or in the kitchen…"

"Hush, Hélène, you nut… what if someone heard you!"

"So what? What would she say to me? Is there any woman who doesn't like trembling at the feel of someone's breath on the back of her neck?"

"My God, Hélène, I'm blessed if I understand you… only you, the way you like men!"

"It's not men that I like…"

"So, do you like women?"

Hélène laughs a wild laugh, frankly amused.

"It's not that. I believe that I don't go crazy for men… not just any man, anyhow… there are some that I wouldn't take even if they were all gift-wrapped in gold. I was going to tell you that what I like is for them to love me more… now that you mention women, and if I have to be honest, it's not just a matter of loving, because I also like for them to have projections where we have entryways, mountains where we have caves, and for them to be abundant and hot…"

Now it's both of them sharing a good laugh.

"The way you talk makes a person blush… and tremble. I don't want that much. I'm not looking for forbidden pleasures, or miracles, or help from the Evil One." Camille crosses herself as she speaks. "I just want to look pretty tomorrow night. I'm going to meet Johannes at the mill. Do you understand, Hélène? I want it to be so there's nobody else for him.

Hélène listens closely and the rummages in a chest.

"Take this," she says, handing her a bunch of herbs tied with a string.

"What is it?

"Are you doubting me?"

"Not at all! But it mustn't be anything wicked… You're so bold today…!"

"One part bergamot, two parts lime-tree blossoms, one part all-heal, which is also called valerian." Hélène chants the recipe as if she were in front of a tribunal of the Holy Inquisition: sure of herself, a little pretentious, like one who has mastered her field. "A touch of millefoil, two parts motherwort, a tiny pinch of restharrow and belladonna, and… finally, some herbs I can't tell you… They don't grow in this area and they're nothing like anything you might know… Besides, what difference does it make what it is: the point is that… with all of this your colors improve, your skin gets smoother, your eyes get brighter and your pupils dilate as they never have before… You'll be the apple of his eye, there's no man who can resist a good long stare. I'm telling you, he won't even see anyone else."

"Should I wash with them?

"Nooo, are you a ninny? Boil them when you get home and let them rest all night. Early tomorrow morning drink the liquid without eating anything: he'll fall in love with you by nightfall, unless there's a greater force at work or your love goes against the natural order that all things follow and which is written since the beginning of time…"

"So will I get him to fall in love with me or not?"

"My science can't make promises—it can only help. And… for sure, Camille, never wash your face. Water is the worst enemy of women's faces: it ruins the eyesight, causes toothache… and colds, and it dulls the skin, which becomes too pale in the winter and dark as a wolf's maw in the summer. Leave water to the frogs and take good care of yourself: rub your head vigorously with a scented towel, brush your hair, scratch your ears and rinse out your mouth… And take what I gave you. He won't even look at anyone else… What's more, what problem could you have, when you've got twenty-nine out of the thirty perfections of beautiful women?"

"What are those?"

Hélène looks around on the bookshelf. She takes one out, a small and old one, for treasures multiply in value with the passage of time. On the cover can be read: "Morpurgo, *The Ways of Women*," although for Camille the letters are just odd squiggles, drawings, arabesques, nothing worth the trouble. Excited again, Hélène interprets the strange symbols of the letters for her visitor:

"'A woman, to look beautiful, must achieve thirty perfections. She should have three long parts, which will be her hair, her hands and her legs; three short ones, to wit, teeth, ears and breasts; three wide ones: forehead, chest and hips; three narrow ones: waist, knees and there where nature has placed all sweetness…'"

"Do you mean…"

"Hush and listen, you must pay attention to learn! I continue: 'three large ones, which are height, arms and thighs; three fine ones: eyelashes, fingers and lips; three round ones: neck, arms and buttocks; three white ones:

throat, teeth and hands; three red ones: cheeks, lips and nipples; three black ones: the pupils of the eyes, the eyelashes and the one you know about already.'" And, with a wide smile on her face, Hélène's roguish look fills the room while her hands snap the book shut.

"And which is the one I'm missing," Camille asks, very seriously.

"You ought to know, since you're so sure about the other twenty-nine…"

Camille and Hélène look, smiling, at each other without saying a word. Camille takes a half-dozen eggs from her basket and leaves them on the chest. It would be hard to know whether it was a payment or a present. "He won't even look at another woman," the phrase floats in the air like the humidity of the canals. Hélène goes with her to the door, tidies the hairs that have escaped from under the cloth that covers her head, and puts the basket, now empty, on her arm. The two of them kiss each other on the cheeks. Their bodies intertwine, and each of them can sense the smell of the other, the touch, the warmth. The embrace lasts for an instant. Hélène gently shuts the door and returns eagerly to her book.

4

From the *Thrésor des rémedes secrets*
pour les maladies des femmes
[Fragment from Book IV, perhaps]

I write in words that will not give away my status as
a surgeon, for I was surgeon to the king, and I attended
Her Majesty the Queen in her two confinements, besides
the miscarriages and some other illnesses for which
my art is useful. I do not wish to boast about my status
because I believe that the post should not bring with
it any privileges except what comes from providing
genuine remedies and assistance for the ills that can
be remedied, not including the one that God sends us
when the time comes for each of us and which can no
longer be put off, for definitely it is a matter of the
natural reunion with the dust of which we are formed,
and also with His omnipotent mantle. And I write in
simple words, because I am not only addressing my
colleagues who, like me, practice this noble art. I aspire
also to reach the simple midwives, who often aid us in
toxicological and obstetric tasks and ensure that the
profession is always practiced with the proper decorum.
And I am also addressing all women who, save for rare
exceptions, value others and come to their aid in the
difficult moments of giving birth, even when they are
not suffering the like in their own flesh. And finally, I
am addressing all persons of good and healthy judgment
who may wish to learn something in this respect, at least
that part of the truth that it is given to us to know.

And given that many times the art of surgery must be applied to the private parts of women, I think it would be ridiculous for modesty to hinder us from undertaking a detailed description of them, being as they are the inverse of the male body. But perhaps it may not suffice to describe the hidden anatomy of women; it is also needful to explain the being called woman. Of what does this creature consist, who in the form of mother, sister, lover, wife or daughter accompanies us throughout life? Why do her organs exist, so opposite to ours and so causative of perdition? Why her humors? Why do some go mad to enjoy her beauty, which is made up only of adipose sacks disposed in places where they can attract the attention of the man?

To begin, woman is defined as the being who gives us life. Well then, such a definition must be carefully interpreted, since it is God, and only He, who grants us the breath of life, the woman being no more than the physical body which the divine mover employs for this purpose. Thus it is that many authors, and not only Aristotle, have emphasized the negligible role that women play in the conception of children, being mere receptacles for gestation. I believe, nevertheless, that women do also possess spermatic organs but, since they are of cold and damp temperament, these organs must be colder and damper than those of the male. And, given that cold contracts and compresses, the feminine organs hide in the interior of the body, just like a flower which, for lack of sunshine, cannot bloom. I affirm, therefore, that the woman's body is impotence and weakness, whereas the man's is potency and strength and, consequently, even though later on I may praise some virtues of the feminine soul, such as endurance of pain or temperance, which the practice of my profession has allowed me to observe on numerous occasions, I will never therefore attempt to disturb the natural hierarchical view of beings, in which the female alone occupies the empty space that God has left between beasts and men. For this reason, besides anatomy, the present treatise explains primarily the peculiarities of the feminine essence: that everything in her functions opposite to men, the daughter of Eve not possessing anything that is worthy of interest considered for its own sake, for Adam was made in the likeness of God, according to what the sacred books tell us, whereas she was taken from the man's side, bone of his bone, flesh of his flesh.

So then, the woman being, as she is without any doubt, a damp and cold field, she readily spoils the prolific seed of the man. Perhaps God wished to subject women particularly to the shame of sterility to humble their pride and make them understand that they are less perfect than men. My distinguished colleagues at the School of Paris add that beautiful women are sterile more frequently than the others. But I fear very much that in this, as in so many other things, can be easily perceived the excessive influence of the theologians who, as they see the influence of their discourses lessening as opposed to the power that the new sciences are gaining both in educated minds and among the simpler ones, wish to quibble and seek out moral explanations for facts that can only be proven materialistically. I, however, am of the opinion that sterility, as it stems from a defect in the constitution, must occur more often among ugly women, because a coarse character corrupts the humors, so that the female seed, with which the woman makes a modest contribution to gestation, becomes acidic and cannot lend itself to conceiving the child, which is its only objective. But, whether it comes from acidification or lack of warmth, or from some moral disorder, sterility is, according to all men of science and without room for the slightest of doubts, a feminine disorder and only the woman can be blamed for not fulfilling the commandment that God gave to everyone in the holy book of Genesis: "Be fruitful and multiply, populate the earth and subdue it."

And, in order that woman may be the way she is, it is needful for her to bleed each month, shedding from her private parts a symbolic payment for the sacrifice that Our Lord God made when He allowed the blood of His only Son, Jesus Christ, to be shed on the Cross. For my distinguished colleague from the Low Countries, Levin Lemne, has noted that the formidable malefic power of women comes to them from the emanations of this menstrual flow, which was cursed by God for reminding Him always of the death of the Innocent who had committed no sin. And, nonetheless, I would not venture to say that much, for God sought out the body of a woman to become flesh, and He would not do such a thing if that body of Eve were solely a sink of vice. I affirm, on the contrary, that the blood which the body of the woman sends forth is made up of three necessary elements. The first is a substance rich in nutrients, with which the child in the womb is fed throughout the forty weeks which human gestation ordinarily lasts. The second is a viscous fluid in which those nutrients float and which, after circulating through the interior channels of the body, wells up in the breasts, turning into the milk with which the infants, once born, will be suckled. Finally, a third element, acidic and vitreous, comes from the female body in emanations that contaminate everything. This third element is highly poisonous for the man, a reason for which he should avoid coming into contact with it, refusing to lie with a woman who is bleeding, under the penalty of being seriously harmed, for the control of the appetites makes man man, and distinguishes him from the beasts, who cannot control them, and from woman, who is herself pure appetite. And many of the medical treatises that I have consulted attest to the existence of cases in which a man ended up deprived by nature of the part of his body that he loved the most, because of not controlling his desire and sinning with a bleeding woman. According to Pierre Laphont, an Alsatian physician, a certain careless fellow who thus went against medical advice struggled for at least a week amid terrible pains, shouting and cursing, in unendurable suffering, and saw his member, formerly vigorous, become putrid as rotten meat and detach itself from his body, bloodied and stinking because of the woman's poison. For this same reason the man should abstain from entering the room where the birth is taking place, unless professional activity, as a physician, or moral, as a priest, obliges the man to despise this mortal life, and with the assumption that in such cases the contact with the body of the woman giving birth is minimal, since the poison can reach the man only through aerial emanations, which are the least dangerous. This same vitreous humor is the one that sours wine in the cellar, curdles milk, separates the yolk of the egg from the white, and surely causes many other ill effects that have as yet been little investigated. In the hundreds of births that I have attended I never saw, on the other hand, as the distinguished doctors of the School of Paris claim, that a woman can manage to poison her own child, in case it is male, solely through the contacts that the infant may have during the birth with this *humor terribilis* of the maternal blood, and I am inclined to think that the cases that are described in this way are true abortions in which the midwife, in complicity with the mother, gets rid of the infant and then tries to excuse her guilt with such a lame pretext. If my opinion is asked, I should add that I do not know whether or not the woman is at fault for the production of these harmful substances, although I am inclined to consider this flux, rather, as an excess provoked by the dampness and also the cold inherent in the feminine constitution, which must be incapable of converting all the foodstuffs that her body ingests into useful and clean blood.

5

Hélène, as she is reading, smiles. Her eyes crinkle mischievously at the same time as she declares out loud: "How very many things learned men see in a little blood!" While the subject is on her mind she goes over to the clothes chest. Now she can almost consider herself rich. She has, as she examines the contents, two... no! three camisoles, a slip, a pair of ribbons to tie back her hair, along with several long pieces of colored cloth which she can use for the same purpose, and a pair of nightdresses, and also a girdle. Everything in white, clean, gleaming. Who would have told her when she was young, when misfortune had taken its toll on her family, that she was going to own such rich possessions? It's true that there are not fine garments in the chest, garments of a fine lady. There are pieces made of hemp that smell of the apples with which she perfumes the wardrobe. But a camisole of hemp costs four days' earnings. A small fortune! In the chest she also stores two dozen small cloths, softened by repeated laundering, which she keeps for her monthly period. "With such clean cloths, the blood can't contaminate. They would have done better to wash their underwear instead of writing nonsense..." she thinks. She continues rummaging in the chest a little while longer. She doesn't quite know what she's looking for. Or rather she does know: she wants to take something to Zachariah's daughter, although she hasn't decided what. She'll spend the night helping her bring a child into the world. She doesn't know Zachariah's daughter. Not anymore. She wasn't sure what she looked like even when she was still a little girl. "How time flies! And tomorrow she'll be a mother too," she thinks. "Another mother." She keeps on rummaging. Zachariah is poor, and surely his daughter won't have sheets in the house to change the bed, old rags to soak up the blood, soft rags to wash the baby… "How did it go? The blood with which women pay God for the shedding of Christ's on the Cross. Well… that's one hell of a divine way of squaring accounts! In installments, the way usurers get paid! And with all this, there must be a hundred Christs all paid for by now!" In spite of the outrageousness of the thought, she doesn't cross herself: Hélène is irreverent, and believes in her own fashion… and in what she likes. She goes on rummaging. Yes, this one… not this one. This other one, yes… no, this one's no good. Cloths to change the bed, cloths to soak up the blood. Yes, this one. It doesn't matter whether it's nutrient blood, blood that turns into mother's milk, or contaminating blood, it still always has to be cleaned up. Not this one. Cloths to wrap up the mother, poor thing, with the trembling fit that comes on as soon as the birth is over. Yes, this one. In case Zachariah's daughter doesn't have plenty of cloths in her house, she's looking for some cloths. Not this one. Yes, she's going to take something along; not much, because Zachariah might get offended when he finds out… Yes, this one. Not much, because if there's anything that Hélène still enjoys in this life, it's having her house well supplied with cloths: cloths for cleaning, for bundling up, for scrubbing, for wrapping a present, cloths to give warmth, cloths perfumed with lavender to keep termites away, cloths to swaddle newborns, cloths to wrap up the bodies of loved ones when they lie ill, cloths for bandaging, belting, covering, jumbling, shrouding, wrapping, decorating, cloths to celebrate life and disguise death, cloths to admire in their finishing touches, in their stitching, in their embroidery, in their weave, clean cloths, very white, soft, cloths to be caressed with the fingertips but don't get them dirty, cloths cherished so that with their soft touch Hélène can experience the illusion that they are touching her, one more time.

6

From the poetical diary of Einés Andrade

Poem I

I didn't remember that it was all illusion:
love, the grass,
friendship, humor and the landscape;
it was all illusion.
The broken promises,
the future and the mountains were illusions.
Everything I had
—I, who was dreaming—
was also illusion.
And from that mythic kingdom
after the apocalypse
nothing remained but the word.

7

"Is it going to be a long time yet?"

The time spent giving birth is time that is not broken up into minutes, time identical to itself like the time of the angels in heaven, or worse, the time of torment in hell.

"It'll be as long as it needs to be."

Hélène takes no chances: she gives time to time for it to do its work. Tonight its work is birth.

"It's just that I don't know how long it takes other women... A whole night?"

"The first time it can take quite a bit longer."

"It's just that my pains already started at noon, or in the morning." The woman giving birth speaks with all the anguish that the universe will hold concentrated in her gaze, her hands clutching the blanket that covers her like claws. "I can handle the pain well enough... I kept working as long as I could; that's why I didn't send for you until late afternoon... Will it be born tonight, maybe?"

"Could be."

Hélène takes no chances. The silence in the room can be cut with a knife. The room was lent to her for the effort of giving birth; in this hovel everything is done in the kitchen; people talk, eat, and even conceive babies next to the hearth.

"Hélène..."

"Hush... conserve your strength."

Hélène doesn't want to talk today. Not tonight. She's seen too many births to be offering hope or weaving bad omens.

Sometimes a short hour, as women wish for themselves at the end of pregnancy, tears open the belly and carries off the life of the mother, and what seemed as though it ought to pass quickly, the fearful present, was all the time that the woman had, the whole life that, in the opinion of others, "she had in front of her." Sometimes the cries of the mother brought tears to the eyes of the midwife, who couldn't remove the child from her insides, as it was stuck in her pelvis; she could neither look away, not console her by praying to a God who had given life at such a high price. The slow and painful wait doesn't guarantee that in the end she'll be able to hand a baby to this suffering animal. There's nothing to do but wait. Not say anything. What point was there in consolation if it could turn out that she had been dealt very bad cards?

"Hélène... don't you have children?"

"No." Hélène gives an answer so cutting, so cold that it doesn't sound at all like Hélène. But one of the effects of fear is to keep a person to the point: the woman giving birth would chat with the devil himself, on the condition that he would be the one to visit her, since she's not about to move from the cot. So she soon tries again.

"Well, it's strange that you don't have children... you're still pretty young... you must not want to."

"The pains must not be bothering you much; all your strength is escaping through your mouth... Hush, and wait a little while, and stay calm."

In some houses the time of giving birth has something of the feel of a party and public meeting. The women of the family, along with maybe one from outside, as long as she's good friends with the protagonist, cluster around the bed and talk. They talk about the births of children who are now over twenty years old; they talk about recent births, which are still kept in memory without too many tall tales; they talk ironically about the woman who had seven sons in a row, without any girls in between, and the one who had seven daughters without a single boy, and they talk, of course, about what a laugh it was when Sara's fourth son turned out looking just like Paul, like a picture, and the look on Mark's face, Sara's husband, when he saw him; he was playing cards with Paul and some other men out on the patio and he got up to see the son, and he came back saying in a very loud voice for anyone who cared to listen: "He's so much like my family that it looks like he doesn't take after anyone in it…" Long live badmouthing. There's nothing of the sort today, when Zachariah's daughter is giving birth; when Hélène attends a birth there aren't any stories or parties; she likes to be alone with the woman and use her secret knowledge to soothe the pain, without any spectators present who might go around later talking about what she did and offering their views on whether it's good or bad to ease the pain that God has sent as a punishment.

At this moment the woman who is giving birth closes her eyes and groans: an intense pain convulses her belly. Hélène looks at her with compassion.

"You see? Up to now they were just warnings. From now on it's going to be like that. Every time it'll hurt more and last longer. Do you understand?… So don't get tired. You have to get to the end and… it'll be a while yet."

The woman giving birth is no woman, she's barely an adolescent. All frightened animals look the same. Hélène feels an urge to save her, to rock her in her arms, and she remembers the book she was reading a little while earlier. She remembers the natural hierarchy of creatures.

"So, couldn't we be closer than they are to the animals? It wouldn't surprise me. And I certainly would rather be like a bitch or a cow that gives birth, and not that mystic God who collects for the blood of His Son and goes around handing out curses…" Hélène is bitter when she thinks and, nevertheless, when she speaks she becomes all crystalline water, flowing musically, tenderly:

"You need to stay very quiet now, and save your strength, understand?" And, as if to entertain the poor patient, to cheer her up, she goes on talking in a softer tone. "I had a precious little girl. Her name was Francine." And Hélène's eyes shine as if she were taking one of her own drugs. "She was pretty as a rose…"

"Did you lose her?"

"I did."

"And you didn't have another one? It's not good to stop with just one child."

"Nobody could fill the void she left… and besides, I had neither a husband nor means to live…"

The girl was surprised. She had always heard the older folks speak of Hélène with deep respect, and that didn't match up with the opinion that they would have had of a girl who'd been seduced. Hélène, a fallen woman? Who would have thought it? Such a wise woman! It was very strange. Everybody knew that Hélène, just as she attended at births, also brought about abortions with pessaries based on parsley and artemisia, or that she gave away mint for free to prevent pregnancy, or water lily to bring on menstruation after a little affair that had come to a bad end. Why wouldn't she have applied that knowledge for her own sake? The fact that her people spoke ill of a woman who had been seduced had nothing to do with

Jewish doctrine. Three streets down, in the Catholic part of Amsterdam, she had a friend who spoke in the same terms about the sins of women, and punishments. But Ann, her friend, was more sure of herself with regard to her religion, since she maintained that anything a priest preached in the Church was a result of his own ignorance about women, since, according to what Ann insisted on explaining to her, the rabbi of the Catholics, whom they call a priest, has no dealings with women. Nothing very decent, of course, because although they might be different religions, no divine being was going to accept that they reject with so much revulsion half of what he had created. The Catholics also believed that the Messiah, who had already arrived, had been made flesh in the body of a virgin, Mary, and let's hope He will know how to pardon all of us for our wicked thoughts, because this woman who conceived without a man would be considered of very dubious morals by her neighbors. In any case, if she had been forewarned about seduced women, it was for more practical reasons. A while back her aunts had talked to her about a certain painter's model; Amsterdam had been full of painters for some time now. The artist had asked her to pose for him and had made her drink wine every night, on the pretext that the girl would have her best coloring for the painting. And so it was: every night she drank and he looked at her slowly, with her quite still for several hours in front of his painter's eyes. Until her belly began to grow... The poor lovestruck girl had no other chances; the child remained in the painter's house, and she eventually had to prostitute herself in order to eat, for the pleasures of man were called sins in women. On Sunday the priest in the church and also the rabbi in the synagogue, much the same thing, would preach against fallen women, lustful bellies, who deprive men of their fortune and also their health: "Woman is the enemy of friendship, the unavoidable pain, the necessary evil, natural temptation, domestic peril..." All the same. Any one of them, one woman just like the rest, like so many... Like Hélène? No, because Hélène must have been working as a herbalist for some ten years now, as a healer, a midwife, as the wise woman that she was. No one had ever spoken of her as a fallen woman. The respect with which her father Zachariah mentioned Hélène made one think of something quite different. Finally her curiosity won out over her pain, and she ventured to say:

"Hélène... why don't you tell me your story?"

"Because you have to concentrate on what you're doing; you don't want the baby to come out all frightened by the silly story of my loves..."

And both of them realized that that way of refusing to tell the story was the "once upon a time" of the tale. They had just initiated together the magical time of confidences.

8

From the poetical diary of Einés Andrade

Poem II

He came, that's very clear, in Springtime;
the longer days around St. Blaise,
 the festivals of lights and candles,
with the scents of the fields at night,
with the almonds.
He came.
It could have not been him, was all the same.
These days I have my doubts about his merits.
It was the broth that we were cooking in
that made him an ingredient in my recipe:
putrid dreams served up with rice.
He came.
That much was true.
With a big smile, open, luminous,
with all his grace fixed in his hands,
with an edge of sadness in his look,
and Springtime settled in to do its work.

9

It was in the spring… no, a little before, right when the days start to get longer, around Candlemas or the feast of St. Blaise, when I saw him for the first time. It's not strange that I ended up falling in love. As you know, with the spring the body's temperature rises and the humors, held in the glands during the cold months, begin to circulate freely and, just as the muscles wake up after the night's long rest, stretching and coming back to life, the spring calls to us to give to the body what is the body's.

I was working as a maid in the house of a well-known bookseller; I won't tell you who just now, because he's still in business in Amsterdam. It was not a luxurious house, but it was comfortable. After the death of my two older sisters, in the plague of the previous autumn, I had to go into service. Before that my family never thought that the daughters would have to work for others. We were well educated. For example, we had learned to read in Dutch and in the French spoken by our mother, who had come here from Gascony twenty years earlier. We all learned, the two boys and the three girls: my father used to say that knowledge, like error, should be shared between men and women, for if Eve had known how to read, she would have read the sign under the apple tree that said: "Forbidden Fruit," and would not have sinned. My father enjoyed telling stories like that one to everyone who came to visit him in his shop, whether to buy plants, drugs or dyes, or just to chat for a while in his company. As a result his shop was always full. While the grown-ups were talking and laughing, I was poking around in the chests, keeping my eyes open and paying attention to whatever my father was doing. He noticed my interest with amusement, and sometimes, when the clients had left, he would perch me on his lap and slowly go through the inventory: "Look, Hélène, this is angelica... it's used to calm the nerves, to ease headaches and cramps... This is leopard's bane, which heals wounds and makes them scab over. Put these on Shelf A... Take this one away and put it in its place. It's hops, which stimulate secretions and regulate the digestive processes. With this you can treat irritability and insomnia, and, if you're good at the trade, you can discover more secrets in it, which will be revealed to you when the time comes." "Tell me, father, what else does the hops plant do? What is it?" "You'll find out when you grow up; it's not fit knowledge for a little girl like you." "Tell me, father." And he didn't tell me; it was enough for him to plant the seed of curiosity, so that when the time came I would do my research and learn that hops, administered in the right dosage, let lovers enjoy each other several times without feeling weariness in their muscles or being able to control such a voracious appetite...

Honestly, even today I don't know what my father had in mind with those lessons. I never knew whether, if things had not gone the way they did later, I could have continued the trade because, of course, that had always been men's work. Still, all through my childhood my only game was playing around among my father's pots and mixing up nasty brews. I was born, besides, gifted with curiosity and a good memory, indispensable qualities for a herbalist, and it never seemed to annoy my father to share the secrets of alchemy with me. In any case, it's no use now wondering what might have been... The winter of 1628 turned out to be especially harsh. Some lung-fevers came in through the door of my house and didn't leave until they had changed the course of our lives... But I'm getting away from the story that you want to hear... The fact is that Misfortune made me a servant in that big and well-appointed house on Westermarkt Square. She could very easily have made me a princess, a shepherdess or a camp follower, for in any position Fortune would have smiled on me more than she ended up smiling on me there. A servant! Fancy that! I, who knew how to read and write, who was acquainted with arithmetic and geometry, who could apply remedies to cure more than three dozen ailments... a servant! And I knew very well, on top of all that, that I had nothing to complain about. I had become part of a good household, with decent and hardworking people, and moreover a family like that one would always need a maid because of the many children that the couple already had by that time. If I was quick and diligent, I could be set for life. Just as well that it didn't go that way: I wouldn't have wanted to see myself a slave when I could be free! But in those hungry times, it wasn't inclination or personal preference that brought security, only wealth. And on that score I could feel at ease, for I wasn't even the only person in service. My work consisted especially of caring for the clothing of the household, a hard job, which had as its only advantage that it left my mind free to fly, and dream about the past, and imagine better times... In well-to-do houses in Amsterdam, well away from public washing-places, this job can also be done without going out or carrying heavy loads. I used to work in three-day rotations. On the first day I would sort the clothing and leave the dirtiest to soak while I scrubbed the whole load to get out the stains. On the following day I would wash it with soap, rinse it, boil it and wring it out before spreading it out to dry in the midday sun, making sure to save the brightest places for the precious white clothing. Only on the third day would come the time to gather it up and build up the fire so as to iron it carefully. Then, with everything nicely folded, it would go into the wardrobes. If you take into account that there were four young kids in the house (with a fifth on the way), along with the father and mother, my masters, and the maternal grandmother, plus an unmarried daughter of hers, the cook and Seraphim, the boy who helped the master, you can imagine that I wasn't short of work. No, honestly, I was never loafing; they also called on me to go to the market or the greengrocer, or to lend a hand with the meals. Besides, after eating I had to wash the dishes and, once that was done, I could consider myself lucky because I had a little while to rest or sit in the patio doorway and sew. The last chore of the day was to scrub the floor so it would be clean and fresh in the morning. So it was, one day after another, in a monotonous rhythm, working, cleaning, polishing, sewing, my hands pushing and my soul withering away for lack of the commotion of the shop.

At the beginning of 1629 he came. He was a learned man. You won't understand me if I tell you, but he was the author of a new philosophy that challenged everything that other scientists had thought about the world up to that time, and proposed unheard-of notions. "Monsieur the philosopher has arrived," that's how they told me about his coming. And I thought, naturally, that a philosopher had to be somebody important. He was going to stay in the house for a while, as the very esteemed guest, which he was, of my master. Very little was said to me about him. When I saw him I was impressed by his bearing: elegant, discreet in his trappings, even though he was probably a bit too fancy for our tastes in these northern lands. Don't get me wrong, his outfit wasn't at all womanish, he was a man... and a real man! And brave. I liked his courteous gestures, his soft tone when he talked. As he himself used to say, frankness was his main virtue: "My greatest refinement is precisely not having any," as he always used to say. Don't go thinking, however, that I had many chances to see him; my work kept me busy from morning to night. I had just turned seventeen, and I had just about halfway learned my job: I had not been brought up to serve any master but a husband that I'd never had. The philosopher, without my aiming at it, and much less his wanting it, was going to be my true lord and master... Still, I really didn't have to see him, for it's not through the eyes that passions enter us women, but rather through the skin, and the desire to touch, isn't that so? And if not, tell me, what do you feel when you see a pretty little thing? Or a child? Or a cat? An urge to hug it around the neck, wrap your arms around it, caress it... Isn't that right? Well, that desire to touch is what betrays us, because it doesn't come over you only when you're confronted with beautiful things: tiny little things also provoke it, anything that looks delicate, or dear, or precious, or that seems out of reach. And I had never seen such a delicate spirit, such a sincere smile, such sweet manners. How can I tell you how he looked to me? He lived a frugal life: he was austere in his habits without going overboard, moderate without affectation, and calm; he soon won the affection of everybody in the household. I never saw him demand anything. Everything was just fine with him, except for the crying of the kids, which drove him to distraction, because he loved silence above everything, and his only request was to avoid awkward visits with effective excuses, so that he wouldn't have to show up personally to apologize. He was a good man... In fact, even though he valued his study time so much, he had the idea of organizing a weekly meeting in the back room of the bookstore to converse on various subjects with the friends and clients of my master. And he himself requested the attendance of all the people in the household, including the servants. It was a treat to see ourselves on Thursday evenings, all dressed up to chatter and chatter. All because he showed himself to be sincerely concerned that even the humblest of us should have access to knowledge, just like the most high-ranking lords. Because for him there didn't seem to be poor or rich, man or woman, worthy or unworthy: the only measure for anyone was that person's impulse for self-improvement. He was a good man... Along the same lines, Antoine, the servant who accompanied him in those days, who had been at his side since he was twelve, had received as much instruction in mathematics from him as if the poor fellow were going to teach classes in Leiden. To be sure, some time afterwards, when he went to Stockholm, he had him called, for at the time he was no longer in his service, and asked him as a favor to accompany him, as he was feeling weak, and nobody like good old Antoine knew about the organization of his affairs, how to keep the books and the domestic accounts...

But the fact is that on Thursday evenings we all used to get together in a room at the back of the shop. A sturdy pine table with a few books—the philosopher always brought with him new publications or manuscripts—made up our setting. Sometimes he offered for our consideration collections of his own thoughts, well set out on parchment, such as a *Compendium of Music*, which we had the chance to comment on there, or the letters sent to the philosopher by Mersenne, Beeckman and other scholars who were famous in those years. I never saw anything like it, nor attended in all my life a festival or pilgrimage that gladdened my heart like those Thursday meetings. I learned there that he wrote in French to allow any reader who happened to get hold of his books to develop his Reason. He never thought of addressing himself exclusively to his friends, educated in Latin, but rather also to humble folk, those who hadn't had opportunities, to women, many times to people who had not even set foot in a school and who, nonetheless, were gifted with common sense, the only quality that is so evenly distributed that everyone is confident of having plenty of it. There was even a cobbler from the neighborhood whom he steered towards the highest realms of mathematics!

He was vigorous and enthusiastic, and so sure of himself that at times he seemed to despise those who didn't accept his interpretations. He was a bit abrupt. But he was also patient... He always proved capable of getting past the differences that might arise in a dispute if the others showed him their good will. He was welcoming towards everyone, warm with his friends, to whom he was often linked with strong bonds, standoffish with annoying people, malicious with nosy people, and contemptuous of humdrum conversations. He was so sincere, so noble, so ready to help, like no one I had ever known. In short, no sooner had I seen him than I knew that unless I built a huge dyke, the tide would drown me, because my land had very low defenses.

10

From the poetical diary of Einés Andrade

Poem III

I'm playing go, chess, checkers,
Chinese checkers, rock-paper-scissors,
doing crossword puzzles.
I'm always playing the same old game:
I see myself as separate,
I bet on myself,
believe,
enjoy believing myself.
A second, a doubt, a freak of chance
defeat me.
And strategy, brilliant test of humbled intelligence,
is nothing.
I'll play Parcheesi, play Monopoly,
I'll play with dolls.
or better, I will play no more, I'm fed up.
I'll sit on a bench, at the end, and watch as life goes by;
the life of others: mine will be the hand I'm dealt.

11

I used to go to those gatherings, of course... like everyone in the household. Well, not like everyone, no... maybe a bit more skeptical. I couldn't understand how someone so meticulous in the details of all the subjects he dealt with in his studies could neglect the most important issues of life. In any case, the very name of philosopher was too fancy for the arrogance of my young age not to find defects in him. It's true that from the beginning I liked the frankness with which he expounded his ideas, with which he explained himself. If I could never put up with philosophers again it was because I never ever met with such an honest disposition among them. On the contrary, philosophical treatises are offensive because of how excessively some authors cite others: one has the impression of being at a ball where all the dances are promised beforehand. Superfluous, vain, excessive with their Latin and their erudition, they never reflect about anything that could be of interest to another human being, unless it were one like them, another victim of the echo. Did you ever listen to the reverberations of your own voice, repeated by the mountains? It's an interesting phenomenon, and very amusing... if not for the fact that some people remain attached to those mountain fastnesses, waiting, until, again and again, Echo sends them back the resonance of their own voice. Echo, surely you don't know this, was for the ancient Greeks a beautiful and talkative nymph. And precisely because she dared to talk too much, Hera, the wife of all-powerful Zeus, punished her by taking away the speech she loved so much. She would not be mute, however; worse than that, she could only repeat to the point of deathly boredom what other people said. Well, just like poor Echo, that's what philosophers are like… The majority, at least: people with pompous ways of speaking who only know how to cackle out the same things they've heard. Just as the echo in the mountains sends back the voice that is given to it… But not him, he was different. He spoke for himself. He would tell about his experiences as a man, not very different from those of other men, even if they weren't brilliant and famous as he was. He talked about his mother who had died giving birth to another child when he was scarcely a year old, and how everyone in the family hid the truth from him, making him believe that she'd died during his own birth. That's cruelty, for sure! Now I believe that explains his reserve with women: perhaps he felt hesitant because of the fear that other women would condemn him for having brought about the death of a member of their sex. Or, I would say, maybe the lack of a mother turned into a sense of guilt that he dragged around with him painfully, and the absence of such a beloved being might have made him perceive the feminine universe as a violent world, one it would be tremendously dangerous for him to enter… He always spoke slowly, of this and that. He used to talk about simple things: childhood games, the tenderness of his sister, his jealousy of Pierre, the oldest. He enjoyed very much remembering La Flèche Academy where he studied, and where his fondness for poetry, ball games and fencing began. And, like everyone, he had something to hide. His face would change whenever he referred to his rebelliousness towards his father, who expected of him that he would study law and become a gentleman of authentic nobility. Just to contradict him, as he told it, he had joined the army, which had made possible his wanderings around the world. He never implied that his knowledge came from any privileges: neither his lineage, nor his teachers, nor any refinements had made him what he was; his curiosity and the relentless eagerness to learn that he stimulated so much in all of us were the only things that moved him. Thus there, in that back room of a bookseller's in this damp and noisy city, talk went on just like in the most refined court, and the only authority recognized by all of us was the strength of the arguments. That was a lovely time: we studied geometry, optics, cartography, metaphysics… yes, a bit too much metaphysics for my taste, the master had a weakness for it… There seemed to be no subject that was foreign to us. And don't go thinking that he, the philosopher, was lecturing to us: he simply guided us when we needed some piece of information about recent discoveries in the sciences.

Looking back on it, all that camaraderie may seem strange to you; those were magical times. Maybe all of us say that about our own youth, but… what can I say if it really was magical? I don't know how to explain it to you… In those days Amsterdam was boiling. In the end, the impetus of engineering in those years of my youth gave shape to the great works of the struggle against the sea, and we all felt like fellow soldiers in that great battle to win a plot of land where we could settle and live… And, if you kicked any place, money would come spurting out like a jet from a fountain: the trading voyages coming back from the colonies made people unbelievably wealthy, and the sailors, chock-full of experience, were making strides in map-making and navigation. Of course they also brought unknown customs to the city, exquisite products that had never been seen before. Markets sprang up overnight, full of potatoes, tomatoes, cacao, tobacco, pineapples... and you'll never believe what happened: instead of mistrusting the novelties, people flocked to the port. In just a few years it became synonymous with distinction to acquire the merchandise that came from beyond the sea. The organization of the trade unions and guilds also helped the arts to enjoy high esteem: houses, which had been austere and grim until then, were built with triangular façades decorated according to the whims of the *nouveaux riches*, all adorned with the little rose-colored bricks that we all like so much now, and there was no respectable family that didn't commission a painter to do a portrait, if at all possible very flattering, which would show the decoration of the house and the refinement of the people who lived in it. Ideas were bubbling up like never before: the printing press encouraged more and more people to learn to read and become aware of the usefulness of culture. The Jews, the exiles from Antwerp and the Huguenots settled in this damp and tolerant city, renewed and tolerant, rich and tolerant... and indeed, even my good friend, the philosopher, had come to carry on his work here without interference, seeking peace and quiet. The curious, the enterprising, those interested in everything, everyone I knew in those days saved his greatest enthusiasm for study. A blessed time, I tell you in all seriousness... even if everybody answers me back: "The springtime of life is always blessed..."

There was one aspect, however, that caused me uneasiness and doubt, and hindered me from trusting the select group of studious people in which I had ended up. The philosopher, attentive as he was to new fields of knowledge, appeared excessively dubious regarding any interest in tradition. That went unnoticed by the others… or perhaps it pleased them. Someone like me, however, trained by my father in the art of recognizing poisons and substances in plants, could not be indifferent to the catalogue of knowledge accumulated in the monasteries by the herbalists, or in the lonely woods by those misanthropic wise men that people call wizards… Why did traditional knowledge repel him? He liked to make inventories of the stars in the sky; I liked the plants in the ground. He longed for wings to learn what caused the movements of the celestial bodies; I preferred to keep my feet firmly on the earth that nourished me and to which I would return. Two passions, two longings… However, don't go thinking that he considered that our interests might be of equal value: his own, it seemed to him, were transparent, clear and scientific; mine, it seemed to him, were occult, false and improbable. I accepted his word as an honest and learned man, but… why all the speculation about these things that he knew nothing about? He gave no respect at all to alchemists, or herbalists, or healers. They were cheating hucksters, sellers of illusions… so it seemed to him. On one occasion he told me, however, that when he was very young he had taken an interest in the occult sciences, and, when he realized that it was a barren field, as it seemed to him, predisposed to falsehood, he had locked it away in his mind behind an iron gate. For he was like that: absolute conviction and firmness under the fragility of his feeble appearance. Once he had made a decision, he imposed as much discipline as necessary on himself to stay with it.

His knowledge, though it amazed me with its variety... and also its depth, disoriented me. I never missed a single one of the Thursday gatherings, even if I had to get up from my pallet at five in the morning to do my chores so as to have the necessary time, for no matter how well the philosopher's democratic impulse was accepted in the bookseller's house, the daily work had to be attended to with the greatest punctuality. I didn't miss a single one of the gatherings, I tell you, even when they started taking on a metaphysical slant. Metaphysics—have I told you?— didn't interest me. It was like thinking about nothing, about why beginnings and ends exist, about what fits into the mind of God and other folderol of the sort. To tell you the truth, metaphysics bored me profoundly. Now I know that, if the subject didn't matter to me, it was because I wasn't listening: most of the time I was just watching him talk. Thus I was looking for something essential in his words, something that would explain to me once and for all... I don't know, the truth is that I don't know what he had to explain to me... But it was his fault: he had planted the seed of curiosity in me and it couldn't be stopped anymore.

One August night, darkness caught us unawares in the middle of an animated discussion: we were all going round and round with the idea of dualism, which was to make him so famous. The philosopher, in response to the questions of Dijkstra, one of my master's friends, had been definite in affirming that the human body is a machine that operates according to mechanical laws. Life itself, he explained to us, is pure mechanism. The philosopher became vehement in declaring that in our times it was no longer feasible, as in the dark ages that preceded us, to speak of the soul, unless it were pure Reason. It's as if I could still hear him, his cadenced voice and inflamed air: "Examining attentively what I am, I see that I am perfectly capable of pretending that I have no body, and even that the world does not exist. From all of this I can only conclude that the nature of this substance is characterized by thought, and, finally, that in order to exist I have no need of any place at all, nor do I depend on anything material."

It made me laugh. Even at that tender age it surprised me that the philosopher should consider himself an angelic substance who depended on nothing external to his mightily powerful mind to define himself. What a dreamer! How sure of himself and how childish he seemed to me at those moments. His own body, it seemed to him, was something accidental, a shell in which his blessed God had carefully deposited the glory of a good mind. Either this man was insufferably presumptuous, or someone ought to help him get his unruly imagination back into his poor body. So much insistence on contemplating the body as something superfluous did nothing but increase the attraction that I felt towards him, even though, inexperienced as I was, I hid it under an intellectual cover, much to the taste of the philosopher. In short, I may have been inexperienced in amorous contentions, but I wasn't stupid. After listening for a good long while, I couldn't restrain myself and I blurted at him: "That may be for you, sir, but many of us who are here wouldn't be anything without what our forebears taught us, without the activities that we share every day, which give us the security of being alive or which, at least, make it possible for us to do without the required exercise of introspection that your method prescribes. The majority of people like us, sir, can't even think that they're thinking, and I believe that they don't cease to exist for that reason." My voice was trembling as if I were hiding a secret; my throat was dry. "Moreover, if you will allow me, I just can't see why I have to do without my body. It doesn't make sense to me that being Hélène should be anything other than hauling around Hélène's limbs, putting up with the aches and pains that afflict her or treating her injuries. These hands that the worms of the earth will eat," I said, raising my arms, "are just as much Hélène as the brain that thinks so." The rest were staring at me, and I can assure you that my body felt, at least as clearly and distinctly as my soul, the weight of general disapproval. He looked at me gently. Most of the time he was a calm, courteous man. He spoke without losing his temper: "Yes, Hélène, but can you imagine if an unfortunate accident were to take the life from your limbs? Lying in the bed you would continue being Hélène as long as you preserved the necessary lucidity of mind. Death, the disappearance of Hélène, does not come through the deterioration of the body, which we often see damaged among old people or the sick, but rather through the nullification of the mental faculties caused by the lack of clean air from the lungs." "Thank you, sir, for your explanation, but I'm so slow-witted that I'm still confused. Do you mean that I would still be myself without feeling emotions in my body?" Twenty pairs of eyes fixed themselves on the philosopher. A blush, which would only have been expected in me, rose to his face, and a slight, barely perceptible trembling of his upper lip made him seem human while he continued his explanation. I didn't interrupt him again. We couldn't stop looking at each other.

12

From the poetical diary of Einés Andrade

Poem IV

Now I regret having talked
so much,
having pushed the situation,
provoked misunderstanding,
analyzed
the conscience of the other with such care
when he just wanted to get there.
I regret having talked, pushed, provoked.
I regret
not having, simply, been there.

13

We couldn't stop looking at each other. Maybe what we were feeling, or the very fact of feeling, of desiring each other so much, was not a mental reality and, ergo, it wouldn't have been something human, properly speaking.

14

Since the body keeps us linked to an animal world that we must learn to control and master, the image of humans as civilized beings depends on a supposed superiority over the natural world, the world of animal needs and desires. Human beings can be guaranteed their freedom only if they persist in identifying with their rational faculty and, since there are more men than women who achieve this identification, the opposition of reason and passion functions in the Middle Ages as a discriminating factor that excludes women from full rationality, because of their imperfect control over their passions.

[Class notes of Einés Andrade, university student. Subject: *The Philosophy of the Modern Age*]

15

"Nature," the philosopher said to me on that Sunday in October, "has nothing about it that can be admired. Whenever it lacks its own purpose, it lends itself to any manipulations that the human being may consider fitting." We were strolling along the Plantage Middenlaan one afternoon when I was free of my duties, and he had invited me to meditate on the role of nature as the setting for existence. There couldn't have been any place in the world better suited for what was going to happen. The Plantage Middenlaan included—and had done for some years by then—my beloved Hortus Botanicus. Do you know what I'm talking about? When, in 1578, our land, which everyone insists on calling Low Countries, as if we had all we could do to be at sea level, let alone admiring the sea, when our land, as I was saying, rejected Spanish sovereignty and the northern provinces rebelled, the pretext that the princes used to justify our disaffection was that we had become adherents of the Protestant religion. From that moment on the guilds of physicians and herbalists, so strong in those days in Amsterdam, decided to take advantage of the rich store of medicinal herbs of the monasteries, suddenly closed. The way that was chosen to do it was to build this delectable Hortus Botanicus, visited every day by a multitude of travelers and full of the great variety of plants that the trading ships had transported from the Orient. I was in the habit of going there to seek relaxation and a peculiar excitement, the one produced in my mind and senses by breathing in those rich, rich aromatic herbs. That was where I decided to start my own herbarium, which would prove so useful to me once I had to make my living in a different way... The point is that, knowing my fondness, he had sought out the appropriate place for such a difficult conversation... and for other things, of course. I was riled by his interest in establishing absolute control over nature as the goal of all science. It angered me that plants and animals for him were an extension of the general mechanism of the universe. "Perhaps you judge that everything we're looking at right now, the gorgeous palms and the other rare trees that surround us, the insects that we crush accidentally as we walk along, the sunlight or the rainbow colors of the water are there only to serve us, without anything that can alter that subordination?" He assented quietly, and even affirmed that beauty was a subjective property, a value that I (showing thereby, he added, great sensitivity) gave to the landscape, but absolutely not a quality that it exhibited in itself. "I must conclude, then, that for you nothing exists outside of your exquisite working mind." "Outside of my humble working mind," he corrected with a smile. Of course! Stupid me! How did I not see it, when I had already read declarations of this kind in his manuscripts! Nothing else existed and there he was, walking along, calm, arrogant, walking on the earth that held him up, and not stepping softly on it. I was enthusiastic and stubborn and... I was so convinced of his error... of his errors, for I had spotted several in the words he had just spoken! It hurt me very deeply that someone like him, with an extraordinary sensitivity, should be caught in the spider-web that he was doing so much to construct. On the other hand, his way of speaking was so intense! He believed so much in what he was asserting! And that coldness, that rejection of the senses that he was preaching, was contrary—and quite contrary, for certain—to everything I knew about men. With no desire to perturb him or vice to corrupt him, he wanted to pass through life without getting stained. And he was wrong. He was wrong like a fool, I was sure of it, in trying to distance sensations from himself… While he was continuing to explain to me of what, in his opinion, the true nature of the mind consisted, I carved my name in the bark of a birch tree, H-É-L-È-N-E, softly, persistently, focused on the very bodily task of writing. H-É-L-È-N-E, with nice even letters, simple, not very fancy. Why should writing be an activity regulated by the mind if it's the body that does the work? H-É-L-È-N-E, with its two accent marks that seemed to project the image of the roof of Hélène's house, the roof of my house. Why should loving be a mental activity if it's the body that does the work? And why should the body do such ill-considered work if the one to blame for getting obsessed with the beloved is the mind, which never stops? Hélène is written with three Es; six letters, and only three with different sounds: E, L and N. "The mind is…" fine, that's how it seemed to him. As if moved by a spring, I loosened my bodice and lay down on the damp grass of the garden. When he traced with his lips the shape of my breasts I closed my eyes. I don't know if I intended to demonstrate to him the sensory component of the soul… however, I can swear that there was a bit more than ideas in his angelic mind that afternoon.

16

From the poetical diary of Einés Andrade

Poem V

Everything I say's too much.
Too many words.
They're already spoken.
Others have wept, have vomited phrases,
lamented before I did.
Everything I say's too much.
A drone, a proverb, fractured song, cliché, garment
        made of rags
of others, of what all of them share,
like a dish from which they all of them have eaten.
You already get my meaning without my speaking.
You understand me and what is just implicit.
You know already whom these verses are about.
And while I keep mum,
do not mention,
and omit,
keep silent,
no one—not even the poem, María—
will know about me.

17

That October afternoon the philosopher found out that the sex of women tastes like water and sea-breeze, and that it contains the same dark crannies that he had seen in the seashells on the beaches. That October afternoon the philosopher found out that one can miss places where one has never been, bodies never before visited. That October afternoon the philosopher found out, with no room for doubt, as he liked to say, that the emotions felt by the body are so subtle, so delicate, so dangerous, so intimate and so fascinating that the soul would sell itself to the devil, with all the eternities promised to it since the beginning of creation, in exchange for having a skin with which to experience what the body is living through. The soul, so pure and rational, so feeble, so self-controlled, would sell itself to the devil in exchange for becoming an earlobe, a breast, an armpit, a tongue, a lip… any one of those secret places that the philosopher got acquainted with on that October afternoon.

18

October, November, December. The trees lose their leaves and the wind moans, while the rain, falling constantly, tirelessly, comes to remind me of the existence of time. In his arms I could think that there do not exist days different from others, if it weren't for the rain, which drums, toc-toc-toc, sequences on the window. Amsterdam is beautiful and gray. He strokes my cat. It doesn't annoy him anymore when she meows asking for petting and weaves her way through our interlocked legs. I laugh a belly-laugh, a loud one, I laugh softly, I smile, and I laugh hard and cover my mouth with a pillow so as not to laugh loudly. I ask him what laughter is. He says he doesn't know; I'm discovering that there also exist matters of which he is ignorant. This question of laughter concerns me, for ever since I've been enjoying his love, laughter has invaded me, as if my body were a field and laughter had pitched camp on me. Gretel, the old cook, pinches my cheeks and asks what's gotten into me to make me walk around the house with my face all shining. She knows perfectly well. I don't answer her; I laugh quietly, with a rascally little laugh, and go to work. I do the same chores as ever in the blink of an eye; love makes me grow, makes me better, turns me into a different person, more beautiful, better. I, who had never let a stray hair appear from under my headscarf, now enjoy brushing it, so that it will shine, and caressing with it the body of my beloved. I laugh and enjoy, savoring every instant, and in some way I'm more myself than ever before; maybe the pleasure of my body is escaping through the windows of my soul… He continues to be pure contradiction: he loves me and suffers, he reads and suffers, he works and suffers… he suffers and suffers. Good grief! None of the pleasures that I provide for my beloved is sufficient to mitigate the sadness in his eyes, and even when he kisses me I see that he's a shipwrecked man who, no matter how much he swims, never gets to where he wants to go. But why hide it? My skin is hot with caresses, my eyes moist, my mouth ready for kisses. How can this emotion be so complicated, so that I cry because I can't make him feel that way, and I'm happy even seeing that he—the one I love most—doesn't have what I have to overflowing? Truly he's acting strangely: today he searches through the house for me to embrace me furtively, and tomorrow he avoids me and goes out engaged in animated conversation with any one of the many who flock to him. Even if it embarrasses me, I can't avoid it: I enjoy love. Maybe he can't avoid it either: he suffers from love. I'm a windmill, and this wild force makes my vanes move; he sows the grain that bursts with its seed inside me. It's fine by me: I have more than enough strength to cope with him. Or rather, I must be the dyke that holds back the waves: I can't let the open sea swallow him up.

[From a personal diary, of unknown authorship, which was found among the papers that, just before his death, the philosopher handed over to Queen Christina of Sweden]

19

Why we devoted that autumn to devising a secret language is for me, even today, a mystery, a chance occurrence, a joke of fate. Mersenne, his Jesuit friend, whom I was fortunate enough not to meet, had sent him a strange prospectus, written by a certain Delaunay, probably a lunatic who aspired to win fame and fortune with the dubious notion of freeing people from their languages. Somewhat later he sent him an essay by an Englishman, Beecroft, if I remember correctly, who was also trying to design a new way of writing, independent of the spoken language. Both of them were businessmen and, plainly, were eager to communicate with as many buyers as they could. Therefore they both wanted to come up with a set of letters, short and easy to manage, with which to represent the primary concepts without having to give them any of the names that known languages had capriciously set aside for them. The philosopher rejected very swiftly the very idea of considering such projects; a passing fad, it seemed to him, promoted by those who saw that their interests would be better served if there were no borders between countries. He just grumbled, while he was reading Mersenne's letter, something like: "Gang of merchants! They go crazy looking for better ways of making sales. They'd pay to have their wares hawked at the same time in every market in the world." The letter ended up in my hands to be disposed of, since the philosopher didn't like distractions that might interfere with his attention. I stopped and read part of it. It wasn't nosiness, eh? His letters rarely contained anything personal, and he let them circulate among his friends without embarrassment, especially if they contained reflections by his correspondents that he considered worthy of dissemination. Delaunay's scheme turned out to be excessively difficult to learn and use, but not Beecroft's. I don't want to bore you, and this is not the time to go into detail, but I liked the idea, definitely… It was a quite ingenious idea and, it seemed to me, practicable. I felt caught up in the desire to construct a language. I wasn't thinking, however, like these authors, about a code that would represent the real world, but rather an image of the world, a secret image. I had done something similar when, as a child, I had played at passing the rainy afternoons by concealing the secrets of my father's shop from prying eyes. Many of the substances of a herbarium—if you don't know this you ought to know it—are extremely dangerous. Although in tiny doses they can remedy hair loss, women's pains, male impotence, scurvy or scabies, if they fall into careless hands they can cause great pains, if not the worst evil, which I won't name right now so as not to attract its shadow to us or to the baby that will be with us soon… A magical language would protect the secrets of the sciences better than chests keep treasures. It goes without saying that I had never achieved in my games anything as elaborate as what I was looking at. Nor had I been trying to. I thought constantly about what Beecroft had written in the following days. Delaunay wore a person out with beautifully drawn signs that, nevertheless, were hard to remember: a little curlicue, according to whether it was inscribed face up or face down, facing left or facing right, with a dot above it or at the bottom, denoted the different ways in which a body in motion changes place: rolling inadvertently, or moving of its own volition, walking or running, climbing or flying. One would have to be a well-trained miniaturist to do the calligraphy for so many different signs. Beecroft's, because it was austere and rigorous, turned out to be much closer to what I had in mind. Still, it also committed the memory to an intolerable burden. It would be better, I thought, if instead of enumerating the entities of the world, they could be arranged according to some criterion of organization, My passion grew as I gradually realized that a *lingua nova et universalis*, as the prospecti that the philosopher had told me to throw away expressed it, could be a lovely way of making a compendium of the totality of human knowledge. I forgot about my former goal of hiding secrets and began to think about leaving for those who would come afterwards the knowledge of medicinal substances that others had transmitted to me.

20

Fragment of a letter from René Descartes
to Monsieur Chanut
January 30, 1629

I see nothing in these projects of which I am speaking to you except pure nonsense. It's not languages that we lack, but rather clear and distinct concepts which can be communicated through them. I'm not going to allow the fad of emulating Adam and renaming the creatures to occupy my mind more than is necessary, that is, to attend to the propositions that some persons of agile and vigorous mind may be able to present to me, in case there may be some interest in them for the science that I wish and ought to profess. And, since it is an interest of merchants to find real characters with which to convey meanings independently of the languages that we use, let them deal with their merchandise, and let's not turn the attention of philosophy towards treatises on the most vulgar topics. Right now, when I am occupied with giving final form to an idea that has been nagging at me since my youth, any distraction is odious to me, and, most especially, one that makes no sense, like the illusion of universal communication.

21

From the poetical diary of Einés Andrade

Poem VI

If someone were to put a belt beneath our feet,
a rolling belt,
like in the factories of modern times,
we, the merchandise, could be
conveniently displayed,
manipulated,
offered up to the gaze of others,
shamelessly.
And, on top of the belt, we'd spin
in concentric circles, eternal spiral
snail ensnailed
and we would pass again, along the roads already traveled.
And we'd regain our innocence.

22

From *Lingua nova et universalis*,
a fragment from the preface
[An anonymous work included among the manuscripts
that the philosopher handed over on his deathbed
to Queen Christina of Sweden. At the end of the sheets
of parchment can be seen, in letters that are not
very clear, only the initials "H.J."]

Of all the institutions with which human beings surround themselves, that of language has always seemed to me the most capricious and vain. It is sufficient to walk from one town to another to notice differences of expression that can confuse us or leave us baffled. The language of Frisia, without venturing further afield, is quite different from the Netherlandish dialect we tend to speak in Amsterdam, or the Middle Netherlandish that our forefathers spoke, and the forms of speech of Paris and its court, so widespread in all the great capitals, likewise turn out to be unknown in many parts of the world. The great ultramarine expeditions remind us that wherever human beings are settled, no matter how primitive their customs may be, they always possess a language of their own, which seems to meet their everyday needs. Thus I find it interesting that the new philosophy should endeavor to construct a *lingua universalis*, valid for all lands and inhabited places, which would allow knowledge to be carried from one place to another, recently discovered lands to be civilized and whatever they may have to offer to be brought here, for I believe that other peoples must know some things that we could learn as well. It must be a logical language, clear and rational, flexible, rich and harmonious, one that doesn't get bogged down in unnecessary refinements, or affected by the forms of purity such as we generally hear spoken of, for being a woman as I am I never had occasion to learn Latin, and it surprises me at times to witness how two learned men can get lost in an important debate, bitterly contradicting each other regarding whether a certain word comes from a particular root or not, or whether it's possible to find this or that grammatical construction in the writings of Cicero. In recent years, as we have learned, many renowned thinkers have devised various artifices with which to express as many concepts as will fit in the human mind, without feeling obliged to work through languages, which have as their greatest defect that they do not coincide in naming the same things in the same ways. These authors seek universal communication among persons and countries in order to carry out mercantile transactions, or for the world of politics and diplomacy. But the artifices that we have been able to review are impracticable, especially because they require a prodigious memory of their users. This limitation, however, can be overcome by following strict philosophical principles in the construction of the language, which would impose on the ideas a similar order to the one that rules among numbers, for if the arithmetical system was built on just a few figures, it must be possible to emulate it and also exhaustively symbolize thought using a few symbols. The *lingua nova et universalis* that I propose requires first that philosophical truth be obtained, that is, a correct and precise knowledge of the world, of its categories and relationships. I do not aspire thereby to imitate the languages we ordinarily use, but rather to improve upon them with a system as logical and rational as possible, free of irregularities and ambiguity, concise and clear, which will not lead to confusion or allow misunderstandings. And for that it is not sufficient, as in the efforts with which we are acquainted, to elaborate a system of real characters and a set of rules that function as a grammar: we must organize the notions that human thought employs into a perfect catalogue so that the relationships that we generally observe among the entities of the world will be quite plain in the composition of the language. To this end I propose that all ideas be divided into six degrees, because six is the most suitable number, as all methods are divided into six parts, including the one of my master in philosophical reflection. The samples gathered in each of these six degrees would be designated with a Roman numeral: I for abstract entities, II for motionless concrete entities, III for living concrete entities, IV for anything relating to human beings, V for matters of knowledge, and finally, VI for everything concerning nature. Next, within each degree there are new divisions or classes, which I will make correspond with an Arabic numeral. And finally, inside each grouping, just as in families each child has a name that identifies it as a particular and unique individual, even though all the individuals of the household have many features in common, each sample will have a letter of the alphabet which, making it distinctive, will serve as its name. In this way I intend to obtain an authentic catalogue of reality which, although it must be subjected to review by the most critical eyes, I venture to propose as follows:

DEGREES

I. ABSTRACT ENTITIES

Classes:

1. Unrestricted: A=God.

2. Restricted & true: A=time, B=devil, C=poltergeists and malignant spirits of all sorts, D=good spirits and ghosts of predecessors etc.

3. Restricted & imaginary: A=illusion, B=phantoms, C=monsters etc.

4. Mathematics: A=numbers, B=signs, C=calculus, D=geometry, E=algebra etc.

5. Codified: A=classical languages, B=modern languages, C=music etc.

6. Grammatical: A=noun, B=verb, C=adjective, D=adverb, E=particle.

II. MOTIONLESS CONCRETE ENTITIES

Classes:

1. Celestial bodies: A=planets, B=satellites, C=stars, D=rainbow etc.

2. Materials and substances: A=wood, B=stone, C=textiles, D=clay and mud etc.

3. Gems and precious metals: A=gold, B=silver, C=diamond, D=ruby etc.

4. Aromas and essences: A=scents of flowers, B=scents of the forest and its animals, C=humid and marine scents, D=chocolate, E=vanilla etc.

5. Utensils and tools: A=house and shelter, B=plough, C=cultivating tools etc.

6. Various objects, not apprehensible though of defined limits: A=road, B=mountain, C=river etc.

III. LIVING CONCRETE ENTITIES
Ordo vegetalis
Classes:

1. Wild and medicinal plants: A=gentian, B=fennel, C=chamomile, D=linden etc.

2. Cultivated plants, garden plants and edible herbaceous plants: A=wheat, B=millet, C=rye, D=barley, E=lentil etc.

3. Woody and shrubby plants: A=blackberry, B=pea etc.

4. Large trees: A=oak, B=chestnut, C=willow etc.

5. Fruits: A=apple, B=pear, C=cherry etc.

6. Parts of plants: A=roots, B=stem or trunk, C=leaf, D=fruit.

Ordo animalis (an apostrophe was added to the corresponding number to distinguish each class from the corresponding one in the *ordo vegetalis*):

1'. Wild animals: A=wolf, B=bear, C=snake etc.

2'. Domestic animals: A=dog, B=cat, C=cow, D=sheep etc.

3'. Flying animals: A=sparrow, B=finch, C=thrush, D=kite, E=gull etc.

4'. Animals of the waters and wetlands: A=fish, B=frog, C=clam, D=salamander etc.

5'. Animal products: A=milk, B=egg, C=honey, D=feathers etc.

6'. Parts of animals: A=head, B=paws, C=teeth and jaws, D=tail, E=wings or fins etc.

IV. HUMAN BEINGS

Classes:

1. Types and characteristics: A=male, B=female, C=sanguine, D=phlegmatic, E=Ethiopian etc.

2. Parts of the body: A=head, B=chest, C=abdomen, D=arms and hands, E=legs and feet etc.

3. States of mind: A=joy, B=love, C=sadness, D=anger and excitement etc.

4. Health and hygienic habits: A=washing, B=rest, C=food, D=bloodlettings, E=enemas etc.

5. Happiness and aspirations of the soul (including matters of religion, faith and sacramental confession): A=love of others, B=obedience, C=honesty and good conduct etc.

6. Organization of institutions and public affairs, also called Politics: A=government of nations, B=laws and norms, C=administrators of the law and judges, D=infractions and misdemeanors etc.

V. KNOWLEDGE

Classes:

1. Practical knowledge: A=crafts, B=domestic matters etc.

2. Sciences: A=arithmetic, B=astronomy, C=cartography etc.

3. Arts: A=architecture, B=painting, C=sculpture etc.

4. Letters: A=philosophy, B=literature and old books, C=theology etc.

5. Metaphysics.

6. *Terrae ignotae*: for the many unknown things that will appear as we increase our knowledge.

VI. FORCES OF NATURE

Classes:

1. Elements: A=water, B=earth, C=fire, D=air.

2. States: A=solid, B=humid and liquid, C=hot etc.

3. Feelings: A=love, B=friendship, C=lust etc.

4. Feelings of the cosmos: A=phases of the moon, B=tides etc.

5. Landscape: A=winds and storm-winds, B=waterfalls, C=capes, D=rivers and bays etc.

6. Occult and mysterious forces: as with unknown lands, except that instead of relating to human knowledge, these have to do with nature in its pure state.

The *lingua nova et universalis* that I present in this treatise is not finished. Thus, in degree I, class 1, I can include only the divine power as a sample; no other substance that has these characteristics (being an abstract and unrestricted entity) comes to my mind. On the other hand, in degree I, class 2, abstract, restricted and true entities, I have infinite samples available and I provide only a few by way of example. We shall have to see what we can do in the cases in which the number of samples outstrips the letters we have to list them. For now, I am trying only to sketch a project that will occupy me for the next few years and with which I hope to achieve an instrument for the service of Reason, which will allow the cataloguing of the knowledge that has already been obtained and open up new ways of understanding the world and, especially, that will stimulate people of good judgment not to get lost among the adornments that their languages offer them, and instead to dedicate themselves to pure and simple concepts, which those languages do nothing except disguise.

23

Letter from the philosopher to Monsieur Mersenne
November 26, 1629
[Where a noteworthy change of opinion on the part
of the philosopher occurs, by contrast with the
beginning of that same year, which has troubled
his biographers considerably]

There is a way of inventing a language, or at least
one written with characters and primitive words made
for the purpose that can be taught in a very short time,
and this is through order, that is to say, by establishing
an order among all the thoughts that can enter into the
human spirit, just as there is a naturally established
one among numbers. And just as one can learn in a day
to name and write all the numbers up to infinity in an
unknown language (there being, as there are, an infinity
of different numbers), it can be done in the same way
with all the other things comprised by the human spirit.
If we did that, I am sure that language would spread
all over the world, because there are many people who
would gladly devote five or six days in order to be able
to make themselves understood by all of humanity. The
invention of this language, my friend, depends on true
Philosophy, since otherwise it would be impossible to
name all the thoughts of men and arrange them in order,
or even to distinguish them so that they might be clear
and simple (which is, in my opinion, the greatest secret
for acquiring good science). If anyone had explained
what the simple ideas are in men's imagination, what that

which they think is composed of, and if this were known by everyone, I would venture to hope for a universal language, easy to learn, to pronounce, to write, and, the main thing, that would aid the judgment, presenting things to it so distinctly that it would be impossible for it to get confused. [...] I believe that such a language is possible and that the science requisite for it can be discovered, through which common folk will judge the truth of things better than philosophers do now.

24

From the poetical diary of Einés Andrade

Poem VII

She would like not to have any words,
not anymore.
Not know how to say: snow, today, poem, dine, sock,
afterwards, cravings, porgy, desire, waterfall.
No.
She would like to have just a single word:
Silence!
Even so, for sure they'd take it from her.

25

I don't know how to tell you what it was like, I just know it was like that. He was with me for five years... Or I was the one who was with him. Or, in some way, I played at life and love, while he was living and loving with pain, sadder and sadder, more and more distant. It was easy to see that he didn't love me. Most likely he had never loved anyone... That was probably the way of it. Even if once or twice he had fought a duel over a lady, as they told me, for the actions of men are not always motivated by their heart: it might well have been boyish bravado that pushed him into a dramatic gesture in that case. I believe that he could only have accepted a love that came from the head, from the soul as he used to say: it was the love of the body that seemed to him something dishonest and inferior. And he was very busy with his work: the time had come for him to write. I prolonged as much as I could the fondling, the caresses, and, when they started to become scarce, I realized that he would soon go out of my life, and I began to make preparations.

I was still living on my pallet in the basement of the house on the Westermarkt, where everything I owned fit into a wooden hutch that I'd brought from my father's shop and which I still keep in my house. There, among my treasures, I kept the herbarium that I had started in the Hortus Botanicus five years earlier. It was a parchment tied with a red cord... I've still got it, of course... There I had catalogued as many herbs as I knew, with their name, a detailed description of their appearance and many indications as to where they could be found, their properties and effects, the way they should be administered and the minor side effects that, during a long course of treatment, their toxic qualities could produce—side effects that are minor for a person who is gravely ill, but sufficient to warn us against their use on a patient of weak or weakened constitution. In short, that was everything that I knew. Or rather, it was everything that only I knew. Because after seeing during that time with him how the sacred ideas of the most intelligent men of Europe were circulating, I realized that not all the lanterns were lit in the learned men's houses; on the contrary, they all had their minds very full of dark regions. When I was a little girl, my mother told me that in her mountainous country, different from the one where I was growing up, they kept kids from getting lost in the hills by scaring them with magnificent tales about the witch's den, the little cave, or the mountain man who carried little children away in a sack. I was always struck by the certainty with which they assumed that any child would avoid a dark place. I saw the same fearful attitude in the learned men of those days: when any notion called their knowledge into question, they invented a dark cave and resolved never again to walk that way. Those years did a great deal for me. Now I was familiar with the classics and the thinkers of my times; I knew how to read, reflect and discuss, and these were, and still are, rare skills in a woman... But above everything else, in those years I learned to give everything its right value. Therefore, when I was looking over my manuscript, I was thinking about the things I had learned to do in my life: knead bread, wash, sew, and also stitch up clothes without the patch being visible, make baskets, carry water for drinking and watering plants, decorate with flowers, shop for the freshest produce, fetch drinking water, take care of children and tend to sick and old people, listen, fetch water, realize when people are lying to me, fetch water, cut grass and dry it so that animals will have fodder in the winter, gather blackberries from the roadsides to feed the rabbits, fetch water because thirst comes back quickly, listen, milk cows and sheep, hoe, fetch water for watering plants, gather wild fruits and medicinal herbs, listen, fetch water, gather dried animal dung and store it so it doesn't stink and can be used to warm up the hearth in the winter, fetch water… I knew as much as other women did, with their little invisible bits of knowledge, and yet, he said it himself, I knew how to read and think and, by thinking, I could do as much as the most famous men of my times. And I swore that a day would come when I would dedicate my time to knowledge, to learning what can be read in books and what can be read in the eyes of others. I wanted to devote myself to providing care and devising theories and never again to be the daughter of a herbalist, or the maid of a bookseller, or the lover of a philosopher. The time had come for him to write; well, for me the time had come to be Hélène. Bless my innocent heart, I didn't know the price one pays in life for independence!

During the following days, I sketched out my plan: every morning, before starting work, I set aside time to add new entries to my herbarium, with plants that I didn't know well or notes that I had in my head but had never written down. The important thing was for him not to know about it, for if he knew, he would ask me for it to read at his leisure and he would lose sight of it, tucked away among other writings, or he'd lend it to one of his friends and I wouldn't know what had become of my work. Throughout the day I would do my work with a very particular routine: I gradually lessened my attachment to the children of the house, for I already knew that I wouldn't finish bringing them up; I wrapped up the things I valued in a bundle so as to be able to leave quickly if necessary, I made excuses to go to the Dam and buy pieces of cloth… I bought sheets and a nightdress, and towels, and I bought a piece of cotton of the kind that only exists in Holland to make tiny little shirts. Slowly, little by little, I kept on buying, washing, ironing and folding clothes. When the hutch was full of the items of my hope chest, all complete and tidy, I made a date with him for another October afternoon, like that first one, in the Hortus Botanicus. Before leaving the house, I crossed myself three times over my belly: once to keep death away, once to ward off bad omens, and once to satisfy a hidden desire. I dosed myself with sea thrift, the herb of love, *Armeria pubigera*, which grows near the sea and tones the skin. When taken in a single gulp, without breathing, under a waxing moon, there's no one who can resist it… Don't laugh, eh? I don't know whether, if it were taken properly, you might not even need a male to get pregnant.

From the poetical diary of Einés Andrade

Poem VIII

First there was the era of caresses
sweet, ever so gentle.
Then came the century of waiting,
broken only by the headsman sharpening his axe:
they sentenced me to spend a year in silence.
Behind the grillwork I'd await my prince,
the handsome prince named Nevercame.
I spent a whole month licking spat-out words
unmentioned,
a whole week bawling out my seven bawls,
a day of headache,
from all those tranquilizers, uppers, feeble remedies
taken to see if I could get to be not myself.
I spent an hour with the sense that he might come back
          any minute.
One minute, one, was ample for me to look in the mirror
and recognize myself.
One second to see that the spider-web was gobbling me,
          all sticky,
slow-
ly
like quicksand,
like mud beneath my feet,
no chance to stick my head above and live.

It all went very quickly. When I told him, he accepted his responsibility. No emotion, no joy. No love. He talked with my master so that everything might be handled discreetly. He looked for a house where I could retire to have the baby. It's evident from that he was a good man... And I can tell you that the day my Francine was born there was nobody in the world more contented than he was. Also, of course, it was the happiest of my life. The only thing lacking in happiness is lasting for a while, because, if it lasted, who would want any paradise different from the one of being alive? And on top of that, it was a girl...! For the third time I crossed myself over my belly, though I didn't tell you, was to get myself pregnant with a girl and not a boy; since we were going to be alone in the world, it would go better for us if we were the same sex... The girl was born on the 16th of July of 1635; now she'd be... I'm an idiot! What difference does it make how old she'd be now, if she never got to that age? The philosopher acknowledged her so that my honor wouldn't be affected. Ha, ha, he thought there was still some way of saving my honor... But I must say that it never once crossed his mind to give her his last name. Still, I'm grateful to him for looking for a family so that I could have my daughter in peace, in the solitude of Deventer, far from the hubbub of Amsterdam, where everybody was probably gossiping about the maid seduced by the philosopher. Some time later, when the baby and I were both fully recovered, he had us go to the home of his current patroness, whom he asked to shelter "Hélène, a maid, and also my niece." That hurt me, of course, although I knew very well what could be expected from him in the realm of feelings, for those were not the forces of nature that interested him; I never saw anyone who was so thrilled about knowing the courses followed by the stars and who cared so little about the courses of his own inner self... not to mention the inner courses of others! In case you're curious, we never resumed our relations. He forgot the nights of love and the days of work. He forgot who I was and what my name was. It hurts just to remember it, and how many times must I have remembered! The way he used to say "Hélène" made my throat close up, and I would get a knot in my stomach. Whenever he called to me, that way he used to do it, like this: "Hélène, Hélène," I felt the way the soil in the forest must feel when it's soaked by spring rainstorms. I used to feel dizzy, and hot in my cheeks, and cold in my feet, and I felt as though I was falling and rolling through a meadow full of daffodils. However, he never called to me again. Even though in the next five years we would live together at times, and between 1637 and 1640 we wrote each other often, he never again called me "Hélène." I was just the maid who took care of his daughter.

28

From the poetical diary of Einés Andrade

Poem IX

Never
said the poet, weeping.
Then farewell, replied his shadow.

29

He boasted publicly about not having relationships with women. Nevertheless, no matter how he tried to hide it, some of his critics learned of the existence of Francine and, especially by the sectors closest to the Catholic Church, he was accused of being a libertine. He reacted like the frank person he was. He wrote letter after letter to anyone willing to listen to him stating that his daughter had been conceived on Sunday, October 15, 1634. It was extremely clear, for those of good understanding, that like Adam in Paradise he had sinned... just one single time. These oddities of his made me laugh a lot, even if they weren't among the best laughs he had provoked in me. I say this because, even though the classical authors mistrusted laughter as a depravity that turns the face into a buffoon's, I consider that laughter is good, for it improves the circulation of the blood and favors the elimination of the toxic substances we produce during digestion. I even believe that it may have curative effects but, to be really good, laughter must be innocent and come from the belly, like the giggles of lovers after sex or the chuckles evoked by stallholders on the streets; bad laughter is the kind that comes from the brain, which makes us feel superior to others, and makes its appearance only to reassure us that we're a long way apart from their stupidity. Haven't you noticed that there is laughter that makes a person part of a group? You laugh and look at another person, and you build more bridges than there are in Rotterdam... Isn't that so? That laughter comes from the belly and frees its heat. That other laughter does not, the kind where you laugh just to yourself, thinking: "Ha, how stupid," that kind is as destructive as a plague… To be sure, I know some herbs that, when burned and inhaled, cause laughter… Blessed herb with seven-pointed leaves, which makes people affectionate and prone to laugh! But let's get back to my story; you made a mistake when you tugged on my tongue, for there's nothing that any woman in the world likes better than clearing out her heart and leaving it without sorrows. Let's get back to my friend. What a strange thing to take pride in, not lying with women! I can understand that someone might get puffed up about having done a lot of loving, but… to be ashamed of having been with another person! I don't know… I just can't understand it. I was never proud about not having lovers. On the contrary, it's not so big a thing nor so bad as to despise it, on top of everything, right? One day a letter came into my hands indirectly, in which he confessed to being the father of our little girl and justified himself in mighty silly words: "Not long ago I was still young, I'm a man and I've never taken a vow of chastity, and I never tried to pass myself off as better than others." Well goodness, if all of his sins amounted to one, and such a little one, the gates of heaven must be wide open and waiting for him, and I say that I sure hope there's another life set aside for him he can adequately enjoy so as to make up for what he deprived himself of here.

His patroness managed a large house where she looked after several families, which came to have no fewer than eight children scampering around the rooms. Next to the main building, after crossing a well-tended garden, one came to a little hut, also part of the property, and that's where the philosopher stayed so as to preserve his precious independence, separate from the group, accompanied only by a servant. He enjoyed getting together with Francine in the garden. There was, I remember it well, an echo in one corner of the garden that the child found very amusing. I liked seeing her in the summer, when she wasn't yet even two years old, with her wobbling walk, laughing her head off at the echo, just like me when I used to laugh with her father back in the time of caresses, and I liked discovering that the philosopher was looking at her as well... This whole image is imprinted on my mind: I remember watching both of them, but from a little distance, trying to show him the proper respect, as servants always do with masters... because we weren't equals. It made no difference to me. I knew that he loved the little girl and, by loving her, who was flesh of my flesh, he was also loving me a little. He was thriving at the time: he was studying medicine and metaphysics, and he used to tell anyone who cared to listen to him that he was planning to live to be more than a hundred. Quite a statement for someone who was always fussy and sickly, very worried about his health. How did he not realize that it was happiness he was experiencing, and that I had something to do with it?

With what I've been telling you, don't go thinking that I was idle. I had never lived such a pampered life as that one and, even though I kept myself fully occupied with the child, I had time to learn secret arts. Certainly I wasn't old, or ugly, or wicked, but for that very reason I took advantage of being above suspicion from the tribunals to learn, from all the sources I could, which I mustn't reveal to you now, the arts that learned men like my friend despised. No, don't be afraid. Men can't dominate nature; therefore there's no way to cause plagues, or floods, or bad harvests. That's an invention of the Jesuits and Dominicans, devil take them; if they devoted to working for others what they waste in spit, they'd put an end to the evils of the world. If they haven't been burned at the stake yet it's because people, especially in isolated villages, forgotten by gods and men, want scapegoats for their misfortunes, and witches are very handy for that. I know that in 1595 a decree of Philip II for the Low Countries mentioned old women as particularly suspect for crimes of witchcraft. And similar warnings were circulating among the authorities cautioning against ugly women or widows, especially those who knew how to read. What claptrap! The ugly ones were not dangerous because they were readers, nor was there any woman who could save herself from the calamity of making formidable enemies. I knew plenty of married women or girls in those days who practiced their arts, and I'll tell you that, even with some of them being of very good families, and despite having piled up money with the craft, they couldn't avoid being accused and condemned. I learned in those days to cure using my body, my hands and my eyes, which was just extending a little what I had done in caring for the children of the house: massages for spasms brought on by fever, or rubbing the temples to calm the nerves. I learned to cure with symbols, and to seek in the patient the cause of the illness that was afflicting him, because I believe that many people are poisoned by substances produced by their own bodies, and they end up growing genuine tumors from which they can't recover because they don't relax. I learned to set broken bones and twisted joints, to ease the pains of women in childbirth, and I even spent time experimenting with my knowledge of herbs to soothe the illnesses that afflict children. But I also learned how to drive away the evil eye, how to make a straying lover come back, how to make the bellies of women inhospitable so that the seed of men won't thrive there if they don't want it to. I learned in which phase of the moon it's best to cut hair, get pregnant or undertake a project; I learned why seasons change our moods and tides perturb the female cycle, which explains why women on the coast have more children than the ones inland. I learned as much as could be learned in so little time of an art as old as that one, and above all I wrote down everything I was learning: if they were going to accuse me of anything, I preferred that it be necromancy and not witchcraft, because there are categories in everything, and necromancers are considered studious and cultivated, and witches ignorant and sloppy... don't laugh, it's true... I was getting myself ready for the final separation. In the spring of 1640 I realized, by the way my heart was beating, by the way the buds in the fruit trees were looking, and above all by the way the birds arrived after having migrated to warm countries in the winter, I realized, I was saying, that he was planning on separating me from the child once and for all.

The pain almost drove me mad. Understand this: Francine was my whole life. Francine, my little girl, such a pretty little thing. You know? She had a tiny little mouth like holly flowers, and I had never felt silk as soft as her hands... What was he thinking, that she was his because he had made me a gift of his seed? No, the child was mine: those eyes that looked for me were mine, "Momma, Mommy... where are you?" that hair that I brushed every morning and arranged in two big coils around her ears was mine, the games were mine: "This one's the little boy, this one is his nephew, this one's everybody's father..." her crying was mine, her sicknesses, her first times, what she learned... And he was planning to take her away from me and have her live with a relative of his and give her what he called a good education. What did he mean by that? Maybe a bunch of pedants stultifying my little girl with Latin...? Or with the distinctions of Aristotle, perhaps? But who did he think he was? I, who had dreamed of her, who had longed for her before she existed, who had carried her in my belly, who had given birth to her, who had taken care of her, I who had held her up so she could walk, who had washed the nasty stuff off her body, who had been there with her the whole time... I, who had laughed with her... and laughed so much and so well, with a laugh that came from the belly, seeing her little mouth all a mess with food, seeing her fall down like a little duckling... I, who told her stories, holding her in my lap as she played with my breasts... I, her mamma, her tit, her lullaby... I there forever without her, for she was Monsieur's daughter, and Monsieur, like his father back then with him, wanted to make a lady of her. I was beside myself, believe me... I was about to go crazy. But I had no way out. What could I offer Francine beyond myself? Maybe I was being selfish, one of those women who expect their children to look after them when they get old? No, all I asked of life was to enjoy watching my little girl grow up...

One afternoon the two of us went to take a walk. We walked as fast as we could; Francine was having trouble keeping up with the savage rhythm of my gait: I was trying to use the exercise to stimulate my muscles so as to invigorate my mind and find a solution to my problems. We went out, as always, with a little burlap bag where I put the plants that I saw and that caught my interest. This was a good game for Francine, who was beginning to learn in my company to distinguish the beautiful herbs for adorning her wheat-colored hair from the useful fruits that serve as food or the fantastical curative herbs. That day we got somewhat farther away than was usual for our walks. I've already told you that I was nervous and moving fast. While the child was playing, I had the thought that recently I hadn't seen as many plants as could be seen in my childhood. No, there weren't as many, neither in quantity nor in variety. Maybe there just weren't as many plants as previously. I realized that my country was dying from so much wealth: we had won land from the sea but we had torn the belly of the mother who protected us. All those grand works were destroying the woods and the meadows. They were serious challenges, of confident men who wanted to control nature… While I was gathering a few blackberries here, and herbs there, I didn't stop thinking… I was thinking about the earth, and also about him and his knowledge. The philosopher was, like my country, gaining fame and prestige. In those years he had written as much as could be written… and he was traveling a lot, they were calling him from various places, such was his fame as a learned man. He was rich, rich in his own way, and rich in knowledge, which makes a man just as secure in this world as money… But he had plowed my mother belly and now he wanted to leave it dry, as barren as the fields washed by the river Ij, by the Amstel, by the Zaan, sad waters that no longer gave life to plants, but only turned mills, were held back by dams, lapped against dykes, respected polders, waters tamed in silence, not the surging waters of a waterfall. That afternoon I made a decision: the two of us would go to Amsterdam; we would settle down in the Jewish quarter, where any new business that was started flourished. I would escape him. I had enough knowledge to make a living, to support my daughter; I didn't want more wealth than was necessary for our upkeep, and I preferred, to the extent possible, to provide my knowledge free of charge to anyone who needed it. If I hadn't fled up until then, it was so as not to deprive Francine of such a first-class father, to whom she also had a right. I had been thinking it over for a long time… and definitely the time had come to be Hélène.

30

The whole Dutch coastline, from the mouth of the Scheldt to that of the Ems, underwent profound transformations in the course of the preceding centuries. The broad estuaries, which spread out sheltered by the chains of coastal sand dunes (some of them more than thirty meters high), have been partially filled in with their own marine sediments, transported to this area by the tides, or by the alluvial soils deposited in the mouth of the rivers. Still, the sea forced its way between the dunes again and again, easily winning back control over the lands built up by the high waters. In these places, which nature persists in leaving unprotected, there may have been human settlements from prehistoric times, even though, logically, until the thirteenth century no effective defense for the population through works of containment could be completed. The sea must often have destroyed the dwellings and flooded the planted fields after violent and unforeseen downpours in which everything that breathed, everything that had life in it would be soaked. Even in more recent times, after the first human interventions, the sea has attacked fiercely. The chronicles attest that on November 18, 1421, the sea wiped out thirty-five settlements and carried off some hundred thousand souls in the Delta zone in the area around Biesbosch. With these episodes in memory it is not strange that the dykes, which had already begun being built in the thirteenth century, reached a real apogee in the seventeenth century, the time of great scientific discoveries, the years in which windmills were also built and the first lands won from the sea were dried out, christened forever as "polders." Gradually the capricious level of the water was regulated and the excess was drained off towards the open sea by means of substantial canals with locks. The capital necessary for carrying out such an enterprise in the provinces of Holland, Zealand, Flanders and Frisia came from the extensive commercial activities and overseas trade. At that time the sale of slaves and the exploitation of the metals and exotic fruits of New Holland, New Zealand, New Flanders and New Frisia would have sufficed to build silver bridges even to the moon, if some intrepid sailor were to dare to tame its seas.

The vegetation of the Netherlands almost completely lost its original character, owing both to the drying up of several districts and the radical transformations of the landscape. The forested zones represent less than nine percent of the land area of the country. At present (and probably in the seventeenth century this was already the case), broad-leaved species predominate, such as oak, beech and linden, alternating with scrub. In the coastal and low-lying zones salt-tolerant species are widespread, native to saline soils, and psammophytes, which grow on the dunes and sandy areas of the coastline, helping to stabilize the soil. One of the plants is in fact given the name of Dutch cane. On the shores of the Ijsselmeer there also grow marine algae and reeds. Besides the small forested zones and wastelands inland, the most interesting, from the point of view of the conservation of native flora, are the coastal dunes, the marshes and swamps where wild herbs can still be gathered, such as a small creeper, invasive in cultivated fields, persistent in spreading, beautiful, with round black fruits that look like a woman's eyes. Experts call it *Solanum nigrum* and attribute calmative powers to it. The healers and witches of the Netherlands gathered it avidly and considered its effects in reality to be little short of magical. To conceal the name *nigrum*, which could have alerted the Inquisition during the period when so many witches were being burned in this region, they opted for the very ingenuous measure of translating into Dutch, and they called it *zwarte nachtschade*, which we could say as *black nightshade*.

[From the research notes of Einés Andrade, typed. True enough, on the back, handwritten, there are ten poems, bad ones, immature and not worked on much; I don't know what she's trying to accomplish with that; I'll have to ask her. M.V.]

31

And now that we are acquainted with all the passions of the soul, we have fewer causes than before to fear them, since we see that they are all good in their nature and that the only thing we must avoid is misuse or excess, against which the remedies I have explained could suffice, if everyone were to take good care to put them into practice. But, as among those remedies I have included thinking ahead and diligence in correcting our natural defects, striving to separate in ourselves the motions of the blood and those of the spirits of thought to which they tend to be joined, I must confess that there are few persons sufficiently prepared in this respect for all kinds of situations, and that these motions stirred up in the blood by the objects of the passions are produced so immediately and suddenly as a consequence of the impression that the brain receives, and of the disposition of the organs (even if the soul does not contribute to this in any way) that there is no human good sense capable of putting up resistance to them when it is not thoroughly prepared. Thus, for example, there are many who cannot refrain from laughing when they are tickled, even if this does not produce any pleasure whatsoever in them; for, aligned in their fancy the impression of pleasure and the surprise that previously has made them laugh for the same reason, their lungs inflate without their volition, owing to the blood that the heart sends to them. Thus also, those who by their nature are very inclined to the emotions of joy and piety, or fear, or anger, cannot avoid fainting, or weeping, or trembling or having their blood roil as if they had a fever, when the object of one of these passions moves their fancy. However, something can always be done in such a case, and I believe I can list it here as the most general and easily practiced remedy against all the excesses of the passions: when we feel our blood agitated in such a way, we must be on the alert and remember that everything that presents itself to the imagination tends to deceive the soul and make it consider the reasons put forward by the object of its passion, in order to persuade, to be much stronger than they really are, and much weaker those that tend to dissuade. And when passion only persuades regarding the things whose execution can tolerate some delay, one must abstain from passing any judgment at all at the moment, and distract oneself with other thoughts until time and tranquility fully calm the agitation of the blood. [...] For the rest, the soul can keep its pleasures separate, but those that are in common with the body depend entirely on the passions, so that the men they can affect the most are capable of deriving the sweetest satisfactions from this life. It is true that they can also encounter in it the greatest bitterness, when they do not know how to manage their passions well and fortune is against them; but in this respect is where good sense has its primary usefulness, for it teaches us to control the passions in such a way and to manage them with such skill that the evils they cause are very endurable, and pleasure may be derived from all of them.

[Fragment from *Passions of the Soul*, a text of the authorship of the philosopher, art. 211]

32

When I arrived at the house the child was ill. That was the worst night of my life. Like all mothers, rich or poor, city or country, I was always, from the moment my daughter was born, very aware of death. Death, Madame Death, the Lady in Mourning, also showed up more than one night in my dreams... I knew well that the majority of women, even if they gave birth every summer, didn't want to get too fond of their children until they were six or seven years old, because it was so easy to lose them! That night when it was getting started, I knew it, I was going to have to fight fiercely against it. That's why I allowed the patroness, Catholic as she was, to put a scapular around Francine's neck to protect her. It wouldn't do her any harm... But I wouldn't rest; I was ready to fight Death for that treasure of mine. In a few hours I distilled all the best of my knowledge: I cast a spell over the little girl's bed, and gave her sage and horse's hoof for her cough, milk thistle for her fever, primrose and elderberry to improve her breathing, thyme and egg-yolk candies for her listlessness and her diphtheria. I scoured my old parchments, looked for the very best in the herbarium, "child, open your mouth, you'll see..." and I even forgot to make notes about the remedies I was trying for the first time, because I had stopped seeing the future and I couldn't even think about anything except Francine. The day dawned gray and raw. I would keep on trying one potion after another, in a frenzy: "Take this, just a few drops under your tongue, you'll see..." I gave her gentian for her sores, goose grease to make her chest sweat, chamomile to soothe her eyes. I gave her broth to warm her blood, and eucalyptus to ease her breathing. And another day dawned. When I had no more herbs left, I gave her massages, did ritual circuits around her bed, put in her hand the seven-sided bell that protects against evil spirits, cast blessings, burned essences in the incense burner, muttered the prayers of the Lutheran church that I'd been taught in my father's house, then the Catholic prayers I'd learned from him, and then the Jewish ones, the conjurations of the wise women, the spells of the witches, the ones of the living and the ones of the dead… And another day dawned. When I realized that there was nothing to be done, I sat down to stay with her through the crisis, to keep her company: I caressed her as always with my eyes, with my hands; we were holding each other close, I soaked up her little face so that the memory would never be erased, I cursed my blood and my lot, I soothed her with stories that she couldn't hear, I brushed her little hair and finally, I had René called. On the 7th of September, scarlet fever, and not he, took Francine away from me forever… I would never hear again her little giggle, or feel her soft little body reaching out her arms to me under the covers, or hear her sweet little voice. The two of us would never play again, sitting in the yard in the sunshine; we would never have snow in our hands, or wash together, or wrestle, her smooth feet against my feet, our legs up high and our hands on the ground, to see who was stronger. I would never teach her what herbs are good for. Damned herbs: the ones that were supposed to make people fall in love didn't make them fall in love, and the ones that were supposed to cure didn't cure!

Nothing in the world worked right. And as far as I was concerned, let nothing work. I hoped it rained blood and the crops rotted and succubi terrorized the towns, and the land was flooded by high tides... There was nothing else that could be done to me. They had to give me sedatives so that I wouldn't lose control, mysterious potions that cured muteness and made the sufferer who was crying out continue to have a voice when she didn't have words anymore. They had to raise and lower my chest so that I would keep breathing, for even the air I inhaled weighed like lead from the shame of my being on the earth and Francine being under it. They had to encourage me to go on supporting my head on my shoulders, to put up with the weight of my skin, because black damned fortune had taken my little girl away from me, as it had taken my beloved earlier, as it would take my beauty one day, because, damn it all, everything goes away and nothing remains... My despair would not have been so great, I think, if I could have felt innocent, but how could that be when all my knowledge and all the drugs I had at my disposal had not allowed me to save my little girl from the claws of the Lady in Mourning? Damn death!... I left the house without saying goodbye to anyone. I never wanted to know anything else about him: ignoramus! who declared that the rational mind could control the forces of nature... I settled down here and I live here. And, my dear, I do not want any more children... would you like to tell me what for? I don't know what's wrong with me, nothing seems to me the way it used to. She never left my head... and after all, you never have two children who are the same... No, don't say anything to me, I don't want my burdens to weigh you down. But no, I don't want any more children. I study, I study and, you know what? I haven't satisfied my urge to know, because even if I lived two lifetimes I wouldn't be full of everything I want to learn. Sometimes, when I feel like laughing, I take a man to my bed and springtime makes my cheeks rosy again. Nevertheless I have my heart closed behind seven doors… I have everything I need in my house. What I wrote back then remained in the philosopher's satchel and, you know what? I don't care. After Francine, they can't take anything more away from me… Now, since I'm not Francine's mother, what else can I be except Hélène? I wanted so much to be myself and here you have me, sentenced to be myself and not the caregiver for the ones I love… And now, stay quiet for a while, with all this talking the moment is still going to come for us, and I'm going to make a few signs of the cross over the bed, and burn rosemary and lavender, which protect against infection; this is going to go quickly, your little cub is in a hurry… Come on, wait a second, hold on, hold on, it's coming, and when you see your baby it'll make up for all of this… all right, there she comes.

III

*Those women
who are talked about
so much*

1

There are moments in life when people feel, in an obvious way, that something important is going to happen to them. Somebody ought to study that feeling, which probably is caused by the diet, owing to a deficient intake of vitamins, or proteins, although it may also be attributable to the action of some confounded amino acid, a wretched trace element, or an erratic base; it doesn't matter, the fact is that somebody ought to study the chemistry of that feeling so that we can avoid it or control it if it happens. Nonetheless, in my opinion the most likely thing is that it's the fault of the hormones. Yes, those same clever substances that allow hairs to sprout on the faces of men and, at the same time, ensure that women don't have beards, without even mentioning other skills of these substances, for they might even seem gifted with intelligence, they act with such purposeful resolve. If you think about it a little, it's surprising, the perfect way the world functions. The thing is that it might also have to do with the humidity of the environment, or the temperature, or it could have something to do with the conjunction of the planets, or divine will, or fortune, which is capricious, or the waves that are emitted by the aura that each person radiates, or who the hell knows what, but through a strange alliance of hidden or obvious forces, which may or may not be subject to universal gravitation, there are moments in life when we all feel that something important is about to happen to us. The feeling can be smelled in the air. There's a scent of vanilla, cinnamon, damp earth, freshly-brewed coffee, dust floating in a sunbeam, roasted chestnuts, friendly dog, baby's piss, rose-petal tea, the skin of arms on a hot day, a page of an old book; a scent, as can be observed from the preceding list, quite characteristic, which doesn't resemble anything else. And whoever has the feeling that something important is about to happen in her life goes around with a smile of premonition, hair flopping over her face, the insecurity of adolescence in her hands, and walking on eggshells, for it's not the most graceful figure that can be viewed, this one of someone who knows that something important is about to happen to her. And of course, there are always thickheaded and oafish people, pessimistic, wan, beaten down, shut up inside themselves, who believe at every moment that the life they lead, regardless of whether it's happy or pinched, orderly or exciting, that life they inhabit every day is a stoutly-constructed building that's going to stand without changing until the very day of their death. Dimwits! Numskulls! Inconsistent fools! They forget that they're building it every moment and that at every moment they're setting the stones that raise the wall. An intense look at a stranger, a letter that never reached its destination, an unexpected accident, an invisible microbe, a fleeting idea passing through the head can ruin everything, absolutely everything. All the more so if that something so important that's about to happen is objectively something important, not something that shakes you up, you who are an easily shaken being, but rather something that would shake the very foundations on which Atlas rests the ball we live on. And if I say all of this it's because Hélène, when she was leaving Zachariah's house, covered with blessings, for everything went well, you have a precious granddaughter, give your daughter chicken soup and an infusion of water-pepper and silverweed, she knows how to prepare it, I left her a little sackful with a big enough bunch for three days, she should drink it all, yes, let me have a taste of your cheese whenever you like, there's no hurry, I'm not hungry, take care of yourself, Zachariah, you're a grandpa now and you still have a roguish look and roving hands, at the time when she was leaving, Hélène, I never saw a woman like that, if only I were ten years younger, felt something in the air and had to stop to catch her breath. She hid it by fussing with her headdress; she was wearing one of the kind she preferred, a white headdress, cone-shaped and with two big points on the sides that she folded upwards and managed to keep stiff the way she wanted by ironing them with potato water, as Gretel had taught her back in the time when the two of them were servants in the house of a certain well-known bookseller. While she was making sure that her hair was well tucked under the headdress, so that passersby wouldn't notice her sensuality, for it's in the hair that one sees in women the urges to be touched, really she was sniffing the air. Because the air smelled of vanilla, and cinnamon, damp earth, freshly-brewed coffee, dust floating in a sunbeam filtered through a window, roasted chestnuts, friendly dog, baby's piss, rose-petal tea, the skin of arms on a hot day, a page of an old book; a quite characteristic aroma, which didn't resemble anything else. And all the muscles of Hélène's body tensed, like the wily cat that she was, because at that very moment she realized that someone was trying to unravel the threads of her destiny and divert the path that she had carefully prepared for herself, and, a little less confidently than usual, sensitive, attentive to the particles that remained suspended in the air, she walked slowly towards her house.

2

From the authentic *Moral Maxims*
of Christina of Sweden
[which, at times, Einés Andrade copies out and comments
on, as if she had nothing else to do]
Selection from the First Hundred

1. One must forget the past, endure or enjoy the present, and resign oneself to the future.

7. Life is reminiscent of a beautiful piece of music that enchants, that gives pleasure... but that does not last long.

8. Everything happens like a lightning bolt: good and bad last so little time that they deserve almost nothing; one should neither be encouraged nor angered.

30. Looking for recognition for good actions is almost to deserve ingratitude.

45. Love always subsists, whether it's happy or unfortunate.

46. The heart is made to love; it must love.

47. One is as one loves.

48. When esteem has caused love to be born, love is immortal.

49. One does not always love what one esteems, but one always esteems what one loves.

50. People are not made for pleasure, but pleasures are made for people.

97. The healthiest soul has sicknesses like the body, but its sicknesses are incurable.

3

The surprise could no longer surprise her, since she had intuited it from the air, from the croaking calls of the seagulls and the shameless way the tulips were offering up their leaves to be seen, without even a touch of a blush... And still, when she saw it, the surprise made her jump. A luxurious carriage, with glass panes in the windows instead of plain curtains, was waiting at the door of her house. A coachman in the driver's seat, a young lady, insignificant in her sheer gossipiness, on one side and, facing her, a woman who was looking at her. She had big hands, her nose was too long, she had plenty of chestnut-colored hair and her eyes were bulging, intense, a bit fishlike... As she was moving forward, Hélène kept her pace under control. First she breathed deeply, so that the air could get to her belly and let her avoid stifling, if I'm short of air it's because I'm coming from working, not like others who never worked a day in their lives, it's early morning and it's not as though I'm coming off a night's sleep, but rather from tending to my poor little woman, my ducky... Hélène reviewed her body mentally: she threw her shoulders back, not to let them give the impression that she couldn't cope with the weight of life, she let her bosom rise and stick out, proudly, in plain sight for anyone who was looking. Slyly, carefully, she wiped her hands on the back of her skirt, which was dark and didn't show anything. Whether or not the skirt showed things, she had her hands clean; she had just washed them in the basin that Zachariah had offered her; it wasn't cleanliness that was bothering her hands, but rather the need to move, for all of a sudden Hélène, feeling herself being looked at, felt uncomfortable all over her body and didn't know what to do with it. She stared at the lady in the carriage. Definitely she wasn't beautiful. She couldn't compare with her, even if she was ten or twelve years younger. And yet, those fish-eyes, ugly, bulging, with a fixed look… they had a certain attraction, like a mermaid in reverse, the body of a woman and the head of a fish, one would say they were the eyes of someone who had been submerged in the water and come back from it… One would say, and Hélène came forward more confidently when she realized that she had the words to name what she was seeing, that the eyes of the woman in the carriage had seen the sadness that is inherent in all the shades of white.

4

From the authentic *Moral Maxims*
of Queen Christina of Sweden
Selection from the First and the Second Hundred

First Hundred

52. Fools are made to be despised, in any state in which Fortune may place them.

64. There are men who are so arrogant about themselves that they inspire pity in others.

Second Hundred

5. Men learn in schools everything that should be forgotten.

6. It is as worthy of pride to know certain things as not to know others.

8. The sciences are no more than the pompous titles of human ignorance: one is not wiser because of knowing them.

9. Living well and dying well, that is the science of all sciences.

45. Great men have presentiments of their destiny that rarely confuse them.

5

Christina had arrived two days earlier at the port of Volendam, a little fishing village that had never welcomed such an impressive ship as the one that carried the former queen of Sweden. For she wanted to travel that way, alee of the comments, silently. And to get to Amsterdam, she first wanted to touch on an intermediate point, which would allow her to put in order her thoughts as a former queen, the very idea of not being queen, and, why not say so?, she also wanted Hélène to see her looking as good as possible, and not worn out from the crossing, for sea voyages, as she had made very few of them, always left her indisposed and upset. And it would be unfair to criticize her for this fit of vanity in someone who had always been so measured in the arts of elegance, because let she who is without sin cast the first stone, whether or not nature has granted us her favors, it's a rare human who doesn't primp and tidy up when about to see someone who has an effect on her guts. And that affecting of the guts is a complex concept, difficult to define, which those who haven't loved will never understand. For it's well known that the being who is in love has guts that are easily affected; the poor things become sensitive, and the sight or the sound of the voice of the beloved will produce vertigo, and the urge to roll like a ball and butterflies in the stomach, and desires to laugh foolishly, and a whole range of symptoms that, all put together, can put an end to the reputation of a worthy and serious person, for ever since falling in love she isn't what she used to be, now she commits unheard-of blunders, no matter how much she may try to hide having become the victim of such a feeling. But also, and this truly is a curiosity worthy of the attention of an internist, the person in love tends to experience feelings and sensations encountered when in the presence of someone who was, or is, close to the beloved. That's why mothers-in-law have such a bad reputation, and brothers- and sisters-in-law are either very much loved or sincerely detested, as if there were no intermediate feelings to have towards them, and, most especially, exes, just like those who still are loved, produce alterations in the central nervous system that would make you laugh at the treatises on neurology. And knowing, as Christina knew, that she was going to face the philosopher's only real ex, she was swept by a not very royal feeling, for she began to experience what the rest of us mortals who are not blue-blooded experience, which was a bit of fear, and embarrassment, and respect, and tenderness and jealousy, all mingled together as in preserves; if what she felt could have been put up in jars, she would have had enough and to spare for more years than she would live. With such notions of powdering her curls, softening the skin under her eyes and smelling of jasmine for her encounter with Hélène, it would have been normal to disembark in Egmond, which was the expected port for those coming from the North Sea, so much hers, as she had conquered much of it, but Egmond brought back dark memories for her, for it was there that the philosopher had begun to feel macabre premonitions or, as Christina would put it, presentiments of his fate that were not incorrect and, therefore, she preferred to seek a point on the other side of the coast of the Netherlands and, just for once, still in Stockholm, she raised her voice to demand that her wishes, no matter how unreasonable they might seem, should be treated as commands and immediately carried out. For she was right, and being right, they had to accept it, because wishes don't have to be reasonable either, for, in that case, they aren't wishes, they're reasons. And Christina, capricious for once, closed her eyes, which bulged out a little, like a fish's, and played with the map she was looking at, where the countries of northern Europe were shown, and, probably cheating just a little, because otherwise she could just as well have put her finger on some inland district, but without going so far as to read the place names, let her finger land wherever it liked. That finger could have landed on a couple of more northerly ports, better equipped to welcome the exalted ex-queen, but no, it landed here, and it remained fixed on that V with which the name began. "Volendam, I like that name… Vo… len… dam." "Your Majesty, please, that's not a place to accommodate someone of your rank…" "Dear Magnus, I have no rank now, neither queen nor vassal, I'm outside of all human categories. And, my dear fellow, remember not to call me *majesty*; you might be overheard by the followers of Carl Gustav, the king, and I don't think they'd like it." "Lady…" "Hush, didn't I say Volendam? Well, that's where I want to go." And that was all; poor Count Magnus couldn't cope; the status of royal lover had always been attributed to him; now with the change of roles of his dear Christina, who would drive the sanest man crazy, he had fallen on hard times and didn't know where he would go and hide when she went away. But that would be tomorrow and tomorrow doesn't exist yet today and therefore there's no point in worrying, for men of action like Magnus have to know how to dose themselves with their focus on the worries that each day brings. For now, Christina said it, and… no sooner said than done! And, in spite of not being well suited to someone of her rank, now so classless, the truth is that when such a whopping ship docked in such a nowhere little port, nothing happened, absolutely nothing; the sailors went on fishing, which was what they did, and there was nobody on the beach of fine sand to know who was getting off the ship or not getting off. And since the ambassadors had already prepared, and very well, the entire trip, Christina could give herself over at last to looking without being looked at. And she looked. And she liked what she looked at. She liked the immense flatlands covered with colors, as if an insane god had taken a notion to scatter his spoiled-child toys around; there were so many colors—Christina had never seen, living in a grand palace, such beauty. She wondered why and could come up with no better reason than that the Dutch gentlemen, merchants and conquerors, must have seen on the other side of the ocean the beauty of the tulips, the orchids, the lilies, and had busied themselves with planting them at home. And the queen lamented, though she no longer was one, because she had no names for that beauty, and found herself obliged to call them all simply *flowers*, and she decided that one of her first research projects, now that she was going to have so much free time for study, would consist of gaining a deeper knowledge of the things that arise from nature, for she knew little of this. And she noticed that she felt spiritual, and meticulous, and focused, and even a little mystical. And she looked at the change in her, with her inward eyes, and she was very pleased with it. As she traversed the miles, she became aware that the variety of the landscape was also seducing her: the byways lost themselves in polder after polder, and from time to time, a group of houses would appear. Since many of the districts she was seeing were below sea level, the struggle against the sea, she now understood, had left its mark on the history of this country. "Like my history," she thought. And she, who was Swedish, from a royal line of the people of the north, found herself in perfect harmony with the flooded land of North Holland. With only three weapons the people of that area had tamed the sea that lashed them: dykes, which held back the waters, windmills to drain them away, and canals to channel them. And a queen who no longer was one became aware that to contain her own personal sea she had constructed dykes and also windmills, and she only needed to lay out the canals of her soul. And, while she was thinking this, she could see very clearly a ship that was sailing tranquilly by in the distance.

6

From the authentic *Moral Maxims*
of Queen Christina of Sweden

Third Hundred

63. One mustn't believe anything until after having dared
to call it into doubt.

[Which sounds familiar, and one would say that the queen had
received some influence from outside… or inside? E. A.]

7

"Who are you? What do you want with me?"

With her voice noticeably altered, Hélène scolds, rebellious, proud, a little insolent. For a moment she had thought of fleeing, that the carriage must belong to Monsignor's officers: being a Protestant didn't give her the right to escape from the inquisitorial bonfire if her practices were accused of being black magic. But soon enough she thought that she wasn't going to hide, that she didn't even have anywhere to go, nor was she anybody without her books, her house, her cat, her plants in the windows, the fine cloths in the hutch, the smell of seeds from the Indies, so many things that she had been accumulating in the solitary years of her life.

"Do you speak French?" The voice seemed restrained, slightly cold, as if a glacier recently touched by the springtime had started to come down the mountainside. However, Hélène has no time to notice nuances, less attentive to the signals of the world than usual.

"Better than you do!"

And Christina smiles, for she isn't used to straightforwardness, and Hélène's rudeness, just because she was sincere, sounds like music to her. Nor, why try to hide it?, does she fail to notice Hélène's rounded, maternal, warm beauty; we already know that Christina pays close attention to erotic winds, no matter which direction they blow from. For the moment she's in control of the situation: the springtime is not so powerful as to light the flames of desire, for until not long ago she was a queen, and governed a state, and led an army, and one of the most important fleets in Europe, and she has a certain experience, well honed, in this business of imposing herself.

"Don't be afraid, Hélène. I've just come to return certain things that belong to you... and to give you news that will matter to you."

The woman who travels in the carriage speaks with authority, self-assured, competent. Hélène likes that; she's fed up with sugar-coating, wishy-washy people, oafs, people with no self-confidence, good-for-nothings, cowards, wimps, people who think one thing and do another, liars, half-baked reformers; she has been a maid, and seduced, and a mother without a man by her side, and a woman alone, without family networks that could protect her if she fell, without company, without money, without a reputation, for she was a disciple of white witches and now she's a midwife, a healer, a herbalist, and halfway a witch and therefore she only likes those who get to the point and she detests all concealment; she hates—she doesn't know the word but Christina would if she asked her for it—she hates dilettantes; of course Hélène, as she doesn't ask to borrow the word from her visitor, continues not knowing it, and the two of them continue not sharing that magical quest for the exact word. Not all these thoughts pass through rapidly; with so much explanation of the frozen scene it may seem that the dialogue was slow-paced, and it wasn't, it was quick and, to tell the truth, it went somewhat like this:

"Do you speak French?"

"Better than you do!"

"Don't be afraid, Hélène. I've just come to return certain

things that belong to you... and to give you news that will matter to you."

"Well, you're already doing it. Or do I have to give you a written invitation?"

"Since when is a foreigner treated this way? Aren't you going to offer me food and a place to sit down?"

"Your palate's not used to stews; seeing what you travel in, you've never eaten in a shack like this one."

"You still haven't invited me."

"Nor do I have any reason to; if it seems rude to you that I don't offer my house, the rudeness of the guest who invites herself into someone else's house is bigger; I'm not some servant who has to welcome any master... or mistress, for I'm not entirely clear as to who you are?"

Hélène turns away, her confidence in her strength reestablished; the air begins to smell damp again as always. She opens the wooden gate of the fence that surrounds the small patio and pushes open the door of the house, which yields easily, a sign that it was unlocked. From there, she turns back towards the carriage, and shouts loudly:

"Come on in, if you waaant!"

Christina is seeing a woman on her throne, for Hélène is like a queen, well treated by her neighbors, in the doorway of a house where every object has an owner; everything is where and how it is because she put it that way. Christina is seeing a beautiful, wise, secure, unintimidated woman, a woman in arms, for that's what women are called who never take up arms, for they themselves are the weapons, who's hugging a gorgeous angora cat. Three fat hens are running frantically around the patio. One of them has just half a crest; she must have lost the other half in a love-fight. Needless to say, the three hens are black, the cat meows, and Hélène is staring at the visitor, partly amused and partly defiant. It's plain that she's thinking: "Come in… if you dare." Without hesitation, Christina gets out of the carriage, with the help of her footman, and with barely a gesture indicates to those accompanying her that they should go away. They will probably get lost in Amsterdam, driving around blocks and waiting; they can't go very far so as to be in readiness for the queen's summons, pardon, Christina's, and they can't stay close by, because it might annoy her to see them in front of the place now that she's started visiting white witches, good grief, she was always strange but this goes beyond all imaginable limits.

Hélène is seeing a woman who's gotten smaller: fortune is capricious, and Christina had it all a few days ago; she had coins with her face on them, and monuments with her name on them, and statues, and thrones, and halls, and columns of the army with the mention of her visit engraved on them; now she's a woman who barely knows how to be one, a hermit, someone who renounced everything to seek goodness knows what, for sure to look for it until she gets fed up, because she never showed signs of moderation in managing her pleasures, did she? Hélène is seeing a woman who is definitely not graceful, with a fishlike look, a bit mannish, insecure, irascible, a woman who's always felt out of place, like a tree grafted in someone else's garden, in a place that isn't suited to her. Hélène is also seeing a woman who is wise, secure, unintimidated, a woman in arms, who are the ones who never take up arms, for they themselves are the weapons, and the extremely faithful chronicler of this history is sorry that she's repeating herself but there's nothing to be done about it, things are that way and that's the way they have to be told. Hélène sees a woman who's getting out of the carriage without hesitation, with confidence, but not arrogant, and who begins to walk, quite calmly, allowing the mud to soil the hems of her petticoats, her skirts, her fine shoes; she doesn't stop for minor details and black hens and cats don't worry her in the least. It's as though, if Satan himself crossed paths with her in the patio, she'd order him to go fry his fish somewhere else... and be quiet about it.

Hélène looks at the fine lady with a feeling of fellowship. Christina looks at this Amsterdam witch with an unexpected smile. The cat escapes from Hélène's arms with a mysterious meow, and the two women enter the house.

8

From the *Songs* of Christina of Sweden
[After she abdicated, Christina dedicated a good part of her
time to literature, moral philosophy, and the composition of
a philosophical work that specialists consider insignificant.
In this edition are included several examples of her works
in the popular style, like this little song that clumsily
emulates some of the European folk poetry of the time.
This is a rough draft that is kept in the library of Uppsala,
written in Christina's own hand. E. A.]

Sir, I was born a princess, I'm all too well aware,
in January I was born, my mother did me bear
with great rejoicing, sir, I'm all too well aware,
although she had an overplus of time, had time to spare.

And sir, I never had, I'm all too well aware
a skirt, a petticoat, a shoe, a hat to wear.
I never had a rock or shuttle, I'm too well aware—
it would have been so nice, but no, nothing was there.

If I was born a princess, sir, I'm all too well aware
it was for knowing how to look and learn, fill up the ware
with love and broth, good sir, I'm all too well aware
nor do I want another thing at all, nohow, nowhere.

Sir, I was born a princess, I'm all too well aware,
but easily could have been born a knight, all fair and square,
and I have never, sir, I'm all too well aware,
known when the time to speak was, when I should not dare.

9

If Christina were superficial, as they had taught her to be in the court where she was brought up, as was her little friend Eija-Liisa, without need of further examples, she would have been stunned on entering Hélène's house, because, no matter how comfortable the latter was with the way she lived and no matter how much she insisted that she didn't need anything, Christina was accustomed to another kind of plenty. A palace, obviously, has another sort of luxury and wealth, knick-knacks and rooms so that, no matter how little attention she paid to the decorations of Tre Kronor by comparison with what the stronghold of a queen deserved, her sight could not be totally insensitive to beautiful things. Despite considering it meritorious to despise anyone who cared only for items of value, it would be an error to despise anyone who loved what was beautiful, for what is beautiful is put there in order that it should be loved. But, as Christina had always taken great care to maintain her own criteria in the midst of a court that lectured her remorselessly, the differences of Hélène's house did not enter through her sight, they entered through her sense of smell. And in that respect Tre Kronor was trounced in the comparison, for it smelled of dampness, and of the horseshit that came in stuck to boots, and the lard that's used in the kitchen, and that dust that settled into the velvet two dynasties ago, and, in the best case, in the cleanest and tidiest chambers, Tre Kronor didn't stink… but it didn't smell of anything. And Hélène's house, small, plain, smelled of lemon and thyme, of mint, of green peppers, or marjoram, of linden, of quince, of transitory sorrows that can be mended, of mist, of mother-of-thyme, of wild roses, of nostalgia, of a fight over a girl in memory, of lemon balm, of fennel, of dill, of laughter that comes from the belly, of cares, of nice thick stew, of tarragon, of sorrel, of parsley, of old books, of new books, of ink, of wild strawberries, of licorice, of sea buckthorn, of very satisfied skin, well caressed and well licked, of nettle, of restharrow, of trefoil, it smelled of so very many things that they couldn't all be named, of valerian, of nasturtium, of marsh mint, to be explained, of lemon beebrush, of someone who had never come in, of pigweed, of bentgrass, that's how Hélène's house smelled. It had a certain sweetness that awakened the senses, of hellebore, of carnation, and elevated them to the highest degree of pleasure, of cinnamon, of millefoil, one couldn't hold back from plunging into the aroma, of elderberry, of mallow, of agrimony, and one was caught up in a kind of ecstasy, of coriander, of buckwheat, a wild sensation, of fennel, which closely resembled death... of gooseberry, of buckthorn, of sloe, the act initiated once again, of flax, of lovage, the act of sniffing, of course... what could she be thinking of?, of marigold, of borage, of dregs, there was nothing to be done but continue, of myrtle, of mistletoe, of verbena, and above all, of raspberries, until the end... and buuufff. How wonderful the body felt after entering the scent of Hélène's house!

And with that there was plenty for an honest lady, who didn't get involved with trifles or those amusements that work through the senses and stultify the mind, and she got to the point.

"My name is Christina, and until just recently I was the queen of Sweden."

"I already told you this was no place for you. Excuse me if I don't kneel, but I don't make a habit of doing that in my own house."

"I've never asked anybody to kneel for me; I'm not God, I'm simply a woman." Christina is no fool; she knows how to respond to the brazen woman she's facing.

"It's a good thing you cleared it up, you can't always tell by looking."

"Are you going to stop being rude?"

"Yes, my bad manners bother me a lot... sometimes they make me cry when there's a full moon. For the rest, who you are matters to me as much as whether you eat your soup with a fork. Are you going to stop talking down to me?"

Christina moves forward through the room. She doesn't sit down: she's been sitting for a long time, perhaps her whole life. She takes hold of a sprig of basil that's hanging from the roof beam and asks: "What's this?"

"It's basil. Its aromatic oil is highly valued, but I use it for sickness of the respiratory system... all right, now I understand... Maybe you want to learn the craft?"

Hélène's fine irony does not succeed in lighting the lamp of laughter in her guest; Christina has spent too much time sunk in sadness.

"No. I've come to talk quietly with you. Don't hurry, do whatever it is that you have to do."

"I'm not used to having such refined guests. If you want to eat, you'll have to help me. There's an apron, I don't like staining my clothes."

And Hélène, ready to get started, ties an apron around

her waist, and she ties the belt on Christina's; she lifts her arms like a child on whom they're putting a stiff petticoat, that kind that she sometimes wore for a dance. Hélène starts moving quickly: she puts a pot of water on the fire, she peels potatoes, she makes Christine get her hands into a dirty job, though not unworthy, and Christina, who's a worthy opponent, doesn't let herself be overwhelmed: she watches and does the same as Hélène, for little girl queens in winter palaces learn a lot by imitating those who know how to do things. Anyone who might observe through a peephole would be delighted to see two princesses in aprons making dinner, ready to share something, in spite of not knowing what. The air smells of poplar, of lotus, of the enchanter's nightshade which is also called St. Simon's wort, and above all... above all, sniff, sniff... of raspberries, doesn't it?

Suddenly, Hélène bursts out with all the power of the sea, which, even though it seems impossible, in some countries is higher than the land, and, being so, can do nothing but flood it.

"So you want to tell me that you took away my man."

"I didn't take him away; he was never yours."

Hélène stops stirring the stew, this onion's going to stick, it needs to be browned but not burned, that would give it a bitter taste, and fixes her eyes on Christina.

"That's true enough..."

And she goes on investigating the emanations from Christina's body, whether they, she and the philosopher, had been happy, if they'd desired each other, if they'd gotten to know their ways, if they'd visited those tiny paradises where sometimes the rafts of lovers run aground. For once, she, who's been quiet her whole life, Christina, the former queen of Sweden who today is cooking in the house of a witch in Amsterdam, a house that certainly does have a strong smell, of celandine, of laurel and agrimony, decides to speak:

"I loved him… but I didn't have time to let him know."

Hélène loves confessions, especially those about unlucky love, because of all the stories that can be told, unfulfilled loves, those that never came to be, with their promises never formulated, with their intense gazes scattered to the winds, with the brushing of fingertips with the entire soul bound up in them, those are the stories she likes best, for there are no written rules about taste, and where one would put in intense gymnastic activities, another, more romantic, prefers to favor conflict and turn love into an imaginative art. That day Amsterdam is more humid and sticky than ever; anyone who was in the place of the two princesses in aprons would feel a heaviness in the legs, an antsy sort of sensation climbing up to the thighs, a force that pulls the knees downwards; one feels the urge to sit down and sniffle for a little while, and remember those good happy times that are always the ones that once were, and, certainly, weren't as happy as one remembers. Thus it's not strange that Hélène, despite the strength she always has, today looks for a chair and sits down.

Christina hates confessions, in particular confessions about unlucky love, because they're all the same: when you've heard one, you've heard them all, because women always complain about the same things and then it's fine. And she's not going to let Hélène tell her her story, which must include concupiscent sessions that she doesn't even want to hear about, or maybe not, maybe so, don't forget that she had a daughter by him, but who knows, quite possibly one thing didn't lead to another, and besides, true love is dreamed, not consummated, she never saw a love last once it was satisfied, and in that respect she has plenty of experience; certainly Hélène, having conceived a daughter by the philosopher and being a few years older than she was, six, maybe eight, can't compare with her in the number or the variety of lovers enjoyed, all of which permits her to conclude that love is a feeling and nothing that has to do with the body. So that Hélène won't go getting sentimental, Christina decides to steal some time from silence:

"These papers are yours. Not long before he died, he made his final dispositions. He left no letters for you, but he did leave a bit of a diary and a piece of writing about a new language, both with your initials. On his deathbed he asked me to give them to you... I promised him and here I am..."

Hélène takes the papers that Christina is holding out to her. Since she has never known how to control her passions, right now the eyes through which she looks at the world, just like the country of Holland, are just about to be overflowed by the waters. Her lachrymal glands are producing tears, her lungs are expelling air, and her whole body is invaded by a profound sensation of sadness. The philosopher would like to describe it that way, and be surprised, how curious!, at the coincidence of a series of mechanical acts that we humans tend to interpret in a non-material way, as symptoms of grief, when crying is nothing more than the spilling of water through some diminutive canals that we have here, exactly here, and watch out, you're going to stick your finger in my eye. Probably that's the canal that Christina is lacking; she hasn't cried since on one occasion, she was still wearing knee socks, the rumors about her mother's honor were running through the palace like hares. But Hélène doesn't need to know the reasons; she's given over to the act of crying and she simply cries, with tears that come from her belly, like good laughter, from the belly where her guts are churning with the sensations of love lost. She cries thinking about how long it's been since she looked back over her life; she cries about life not having given her anything; she cries about not being able to forgive life for the lack of affection. It doesn't bother her at all to cry in front of Christina.

Christina, once she has handed over the papers, is left there with nothing to do. She has something else to say; she didn't make the trip just as an emissary—for that she had loyal and fast-moving servants available, who could have carried a piece of mail on horseback better than she could. She now just waits quietly because she knows that mourning has its own times.

Hélène, who, although she has read a lot, has lived very little, asks:

"What were his last words?"

Christina, who has loved a lot with her body and not much with her soul, understands her and quickly devises the lie:

"He muttered something about the little girl but... the last thing he said was your name."

10

From the *Moral Maxims* of Queen Christina of Sweden
Apocryphal series

1. Men think they are wise because they know how to pick up a stick to help themselves walk.

2. Men think they are wise because they know how to shake the fruit on the tree and make the ripe fruit fall.

3. Men think they are wise because they have established the measure for wisdom.

4. If anyone has mastered his science, it's the violets making essence.

5. Without all the teasing, lemons are the wise ones, making squeezings.

6. I always knew how little everything I was learning was worth; that is the key to all wisdom.

11

Of all the topics that the philosopher neglected to include on his agenda for *Philosophical Topics to Be Considered in the Next Twenty Years*, for there are those who affirm that he had such an agenda, the most relevant is time. It's not easy to explain how a mind that was so rational and enlightened, so exalted, so orderly, in a word so well set on his shoulders, could let so rich a topic escape him. But he did neglect it, for he was obsessed with the latest innovations of every moment and, in his fascination with technology, he missed something essential. Because time is, obviously, the topic. A strange substance, time, which converts curds into cheese, humble little blossoms into apples and teardrops into rainwater, once they have evaporated and been suitably filtered by the clouds. Physicists strive to demonstrate its existence or its non-existence, depending on the school, for in this as in everything it's all a matter of taste, and mathematicians sketch its curvature, and these efforts are useless, for no matter how these scientific labors may demonstrate the non-existence of time, we all know that time exists. Definitely. A plump little fellow in the cradle isn't the same as a man in full possession of his faculties, or as a little old man asking to be pampered, so that time, like so many other things, whether it exists or not, the fact is that it feels sorry for us and goes by at a reasonably slow pace, not so much so as to bore us, that's not what's going on, but knowing that it follows a trajectory that passes in front of us only once, at least it can let us try as many paths as we can! It would be something else, and something quite different, if time went in circles like a snail's shell and we could return to the starting point again and again, and be a gardener, and a poet, and a comic actor, and a cook and a monk before deciding what we really want to be. And by neglecting such a universal theme, which has all of us by the short hairs, so to speak, the philosopher didn't exactly cover himself with glory, precisely by refusing to concern himself with time; who can care about dioptrics and meteors and the rest of the trajectories of light and bodies who doesn't also care, and more so, about this question of change and anticipation, which, regrettably, always gets worse? And, since time is the measure of all things, whoever cooks is inevitably the king of philosophical systems. There is nothing so well suited to stimulating high-flown thought as a pot with nice hushed silent water that starts to boil and boil, one would say that the bubbles gabble with each other until they boil. Likewise there's no recipe that works without including the time, which is capable of making rich broth out of insipid water, dull flour into bread, or, if it's with eggs and milk, into cake. All that being said, it will be understood that two princesses in aprons, watching the clay pot where the potatoes are cooking, are two philosophers *in potentia,* for life is like that, a clay pot put on to heat up, and the sad thing is that we occupy the place of the potatoes. Therefore decisions must be made in a timely way, for if not you end up with mash, and that's not desirable for any self-respecting potato. And, seated in front of the hearth, with their hearts in mourning and a few urges to scratch each other's eyes out, watching the fire that licked at the pot and the boiling water, for the potatoes were already cooking by then, they exchanged their lives completely, and each one became the other during the time of the storytelling, and the two of them were one. And they began with time, and the customs of men which are perishable, and the necessity of finding a meaning for this damned life, for tell me, come on, what are we here for if not to suffer?, so that they ended up converting the humble shack at one edge of the Jewish quarter of Amsterdam into the most august hall of the university at the time of the philosophy lecture. And, without noticing it, without wishing it or being able to, they initiated the weighty rites of academic sessions. And, instead of "take out your Greek dictionaries," Hélène went on teaching Christina to cook, saying: "Get that jar from over there." And, instead of a bored response like "what page, sir?" the pupil of the lesson on time in modern philosophy was saying something like: "What do you keep in there?," and, in a Platonic dialogue, the professor would answer: "Herbs." And Christina would press her: "But what herbs?" And the doctor of philosophy, so regal, from the imposing lectern of her kitchen, with all the knowledge gained in the hard tests that selected her to be the teacher to impart wisdom on such an abstruse subject in the select university of life, recites, so everyone can hear her: "Winter savory, lavender, mother-of-thyme, marjoram, oregano, basil and thyme. Winter savory takes away the itch of old loves, lavender perfumes the air so that new loves can be found, mother-of-thyme leaves the memory clear, so as not to dwell on the experience of failures and appreciate life as if it hadn't been lived through, marjoram stimulates the appetites, oregano protects against evil omens, basil and thyme increase hope and produce sweet dreams and waking up peacefully." And the student, skeptical like all students, weary of having come there to obtain so little, impatient because the professor is focused on her own interests and her own cleverness, asks: "Is it really true that they have those properties?" And the learned woman, tossing a handful of chopped dried herbs into the potatoes, replies without looking at her: "As with everything in life, if it isn't true, it could well be."

12

From the *Songs* of Christina of Sweden
[Second version of the previous song, or the cow's return
to the millet. It's just as well that Einés recognizes that the
literary and philosophical work of this royal lady
is insignificant, because otherwise... She keeps on
wasting time with these things. M. V.]

My mother she bore me,
in the month of January,
tra-la-lee, tra-la-la,
in the month of January.

No money, no dowry,
no house or good name,
tra-la-lee, tra-la-la,
no house or good name.

While she blindfolded me,
she was teaching me too,
tra-la-lee, tra-la-la,
she was teaching me too.

You will be a princess,
a lady or sorceress,
tra-la-lee, tra-la-la,
a lady or sorceress.

You will not lead in war
nor will you make money,
tra-la-lee, tra-la-la,
nor will you make money.

In the long nights of moonshine
you will look at the sky,
tra-la-lee, tra-la-la,
you will look at the sky.

You will touch all the waters,
you will voyage in the smoke,
tra-la-lee, tra-la-la,
you will sing story-songs
round the campfire's flames.

13

That summer afternoon it was demonstrated, clearly and distinctly as was usually the case in those days, that to do philosophy the airs of a poet and fancy manners were superfluous, for with a pot on the fire and their skirts hitched up so that the warmth the sun provides could caress their legs, it was as if the two of them were seated, each in her own professorial chair in Paris, or Leiden, or Uppsala, for it's all the same. They ate potatoes and drank beer, cried their eyes out, got their sorrows off their chest, wove ideas. In a word, they philosophized.

14

At this stage of the encounter, all we know is that Hélène's house smells of so many different perfumes, all of them rough and unique, that evoking their aromas leads to an orgasm. It's true enough that we also know that the house is modest, that it has a patio with a gate and that Hélène usually leaves the door unlocked, an attitude suited to someone without attachments to material belongings, for whether we're poor or rich all of us have something that we wouldn't like to have taken away from us; that's not the point. It can be added now that Hélène's house is covered with pink tiles and has a Greek key in white, very much in the style that is seen now in the houses of the Netherlands, but there's no point in adding information, for we have enough with the fact that the basil is hanging from the roof-beam, probably with similar bunches of both wild and garden herbs. We also know that there's a hearth and pots, and aprons, and a hutch full of cloths, for cloths are very highly valued by the lady of the house, and above all there are books, many books. We know enough to imagine the setting in which they, of whom so much has been said, exchange their life stories, each one settled in her own chair, cheerfully, sadly, profoundly philosophizing. Surely, at some moment, the dialogue burst forth like a flash flood:

"I can't stop going over and over the matter in my mind… I'm sure that he wanted you to get your papers back, and that must mean something."

The one who's speaking is Christina, who falls silent to raise to her mouth a cup full of an infusion of black nightshade and raspberry leaves. The taste bothers her with its bitterness, because she's not used to it, because it's strong... and, notwithstanding, Christina dissimulates because, no one knows why, today she needs for Hélène to like her more than she's ever needed anyone to like her.

"Of course it means something... Everything in the world's a sign, for sure. Could he have wanted me to know about his death?"

"No, Hélène, there had to be more to it. I believe that at some point he thought about composing a universal language, even if he never came to do it. He must have thought you could still do it in his place."

"Not a chance... Why would I ruin my eyes and waste my energy on a job like that?"

"To show the world you can, that a humble woman can be redeemed from poverty by knowledge."

Hélène has a good laugh:

"I'm not so humble, nor was my father poor, nor has anything yet been invented to redeem women from original sin."

"Hélène, don't play the skeptic. A universal language would be the greatest discovery of our times. It would guarantee, for example, peace among countries. If those who governed countries understood each other better, they wouldn't get caught up in wars... Differences could be patched up in other ways..."

"Really? You would know; I haven't ever taken part in one. I thought wars were games of power, not fought for reasons."

Christina bites her lips. She remembers her urge to wage war when her own mother went off to Denmark for reasons of the bedroom, which are personal motives. She remembers her anger, the feeling that everyone shared a secret from which she had been excluded, and the thirst for revenge that built up in her chest until it made the Danes hated in her palace, in the narrow circle of Swedes who visit the queen, and she remembers also that the war cost the lives of many of her countrymen, of those whom she could call back then humble folk. Hélène continues her discourse:

"That only matters to the powerful. People are born and die without paying attention to those reasons: they bury the sons who never came to be, they plant, they harvest, and they sleep in their beds at night."

"You aren't like that. I informed myself well before coming. You're respected as a wise woman, you're in demand when there's a decision to be made, and they say you spend the day reading. You don't lead that monotonous life you describe…"

"Excuse me; I lead a life just like everybody else's. I'm tied up with my chores. I can't rebel, I always have to keep on, like the wheel of a mill that can't get out of its routine of turning, like the plough that kisses the furrow it just dug. Like you…"

"Like me? No, I've just cut the moorings that tied me to the ground."

"No, it just seems that way to you. We're the playthings of fate…"

"Playthings of fate?"

Christina, Queen of Sweden, who had called the fashionable philosopher to her bitterly cold court in the north, with the intention of having the very wise man educate her as was appropriate, did not believe in fate. She didn't believe in magical entities, or in supernatural powers, or in occult forces. She believed in neither the natural goodness of human beings nor in the purity of people. The truth is that Christina was pretty skeptical; there would be no other way of explaining that someone invested by divine grace with the power to guide and govern a state, to rule her subjects and even abuse them if she wanted to, would renounce such an advantageous condition to head off through that inhospitable world. Just as well. Because, if Christina did believe in fate, she would now be stunned on seeing that she, who had called the philosopher back then to listen to the central themes of his very scientific and innovative theory of the soul, had now traveled to Amsterdam, and had turned her hand to cooking potatoes with a beautiful white witch who, for certain, had slept with the only man she'd loved, and probably the only man she herself knew that she hadn't slept with, in order, on top of that, to go and receive from her, in an apron, lessons in philosophy. Sometimes life shows us some really unexpected paths! But she was stubborn, and she wasn't going to give up so quickly.

"And what do you say about the spread of knowledge? A language that served all countries would allow learned men to exchange their research, allow innovation and change to make an impact in a world that's too used to repetition… It would allow the knowledge that some have been accumulating for centuries to be transmitted, without doubts, to future generations."

"Yes, I thought of that once or twice, but… By any chance did the knowledge of the ancient Egyptians not come down to us, or the Greeks, without that marvelous invention? I don't think anything more is needed than the urge to know…"

"He wanted the papers to come to you again, therefore he wanted you to finish what you started at his side."

"He never knew what he wanted."

"He wanted you to continue your original work."

"He wanted to see himself reflected in a mirror with nobody alongside him."

"He thought of constructing an artificial language based on your outline, but he never found the right time to do it…"

"Or he wasn't up to doing it."

"Agreed, or he wasn't up to it… Probably, at the end of his life, he thought it was an attempt worthy of full praise and that you still had a chance of bringing it to pass, because back then he already knew that many were devoting themselves to seeking something of the sort… He thought that this was your time."

"On that we do agree, absolutely, this is the time to be Hélène."

But it didn't necessarily have to be that way either; it seems quite probable that they didn't talk, that they were fully satisfied with just putting up with each other, accepting each other, which was tantamount to accepting the fact that time had passed without their being able to conquer it. And on some occasions life offers us a stair where we can sit down with our enemy to have some black-nightshade and raspberry-leaf tea and, on such occasions, one must be at the philosophical level that fate demands of one and not get hung up on foolishness, and accept, and stop momentarily the windmill of thoughts so as simply to be there. Be there, nothing more, without asking for anything. Clear enough, it's one thing to say that and another to do it. The beauty of challenges lies in twisting the rules of what is written since the beginning of time, and for each person to write what seems best to her. And, applying this theme to this matter that concerns us, the lovely thing about the encounter lay in that two such different women in upbringing and fortune, in tastes, in interests, in preferences, in ways of dressing, and being, and boasting, should enjoy black nightshade with their spirits free; from so much pounding away in the same old yard, sometimes we begin to wonder whether or not we're on the right track in our lives, and we forget that we can twist it and mend it whenever we feel like it. And, for sure, if they remained silent, for certainly we will never know, the fact of having to speak to each other in French must have had something to do with it, this not being the natural language of communication for either of the two, and so, after all, Hélène Jans's idea about inventing a universal language seems to be quite well considered.

15

There are people who repeat all the time, before they're even asked any questions on the point, that they don't like goodbyes. No doubt these are timid, repressed, wretched people, crippled in spirit, who are afraid their humidity might escape through their eyes, trembling through their lips, anguish through their speech; who are afraid, in short, that those to whom they're saying goodbye will notice the effects of the absence on their face and, in order to obscure their feelings, say a hasty goodbye, which is not a goodbye or anything else, and nip in the bud any attempt to get close to them. Hermetic, that's the word to define such individuals, even though we've had the word shoved in our faces so much by fast-food joints, "look at this hermetically sealed container, it keeps the food perfectly fresh," that these days it seems to us like a good thing to be hermetic, when everybody knows that what's good is rusting, exchanging flows with nature, airing oneself out, getting rid of one's miasmas, sniffing other smells, soaking it all up, getting worn with use, getting wrinkled and... living, living like there's no tomorrow. Of course, neither Hélène nor Christina was one of the kind of strait-laced and standoffish people who are keeping themselves intact for the next life, if there is one; they always threw themselves into whatever came along, intensely, dedicated to living, consecrated to the very considerable task of spending themselves and not measuring themselves out in little doses, being as up in arms as they were, or as those people who watched them said they were, without even touching them. Therefore, when the twilight made their shadows look gigantic on the wall—one of them rounded and maternal, the other elongated, etiolated, a bit fishlike—Christina struck sail. And there was a flood of expressions in the goodbye: I take you by the hands and kiss your cheeks, mwah, mwah, just two pieces of advice, given in a motherly tone of voice, I'll put your handkerchief back in, it's sticking out of your sleeve, I'll put your hair back in, it's showing from under your headdress, what'll the neighbors say about us, thanks for coming, thanks for having me, don't forget to write, send me your new language, I'll know how to spread it around, I don't think I'll have the heart to do it, yes you will, no I won't, mwah, mwah, I'm bathing in your tears, I kiss your hands, take care of yourself, life's not the same outside of the palace, but you, if you need anything, whatever it may be, send me a message, I'll be here, who could have told him, my poor man, who could have told him that the two of us were going to be here, yoked to his shadow, he would say that there are no emotions other than those four basic ones that he established, poor fellow, a real shame that he didn't last longer, a real shame that he didn't dedicate himself to studying the passing of time instead of coming up with so many strange divisions, one more kiss, they're waiting for you, very happy to meet you and goodbye… goodbye.

A carriage in front of Hélène's patio could hardly contain the astonishment of a coachman and a gossipy young lady when they saw how Christina, Queen of the Swedes, the Goths and the Vandals, well, ex-queen to tell the truth, was coming out of the witch's house as happy as a little girl with new shoes, from where they had left her hours and hours ago, she's spending a lot of time there, I don't know if she had a spell put on her or what. It may be she came to ask for her help in getting pregnant; it wouldn't likely be for lack of trying that she didn't get pregnant, they say she's barren; that couldn't be it, what would she want children for now if she's not queen anymore? Well, if she has a male child she can demand the crown and it's hers, yes, no, do you see how they're talking to each other? The way they look at each other? There was more than words here, I tell you; for Christina, our lady, the boys were always as good as the girls, hush, what're you saying?, well, stuff and nonsense, yes, no, all of Stockholm knows that, well goodness, here we are all innocent, and I'm still not married, and if they find out in the court that I'm mixed up in these goings-on I'll be an old maid my whole life, no, you're never going to be short of suitors, with that ladylike walk and those gorgeous eyes, bah, the things you say…

And it's just as well that the two people in the coach ended up flirting with each other; they didn't notice certain effects of the goodbye, special effects without a doubt that cannot be avoided in a truthful chronicle like this one. When Christina, with one foot already in the carriage, turned her body and her head to look at Hélène for the last time, which amounts to the same thing as saying when Hélène waved from the gate before returning once and for all to the house to join the rest of her life, in that instant a tremor shook the hearts of every living thing in the area, the air crackled with electricity, the fur of the cats stood on end and the feathers of the hens fell out, charred, with a powerful stench of sulfur and carbon, dozens of flowers popped out of the earth, growing in an instant, the millet bloomed, the flax wept and the rye was pollinated, all out of season, and a cloud of stars bathed Amsterdam: all of nature, astute, uncontrollable, wild and little given to rational governance, was dedicating its best smile to a certain accord of two ladies.

16

At sunset on the 14th of April, 1655, a strange atmospheric phenomenon affected the city of Amsterdam and its environs. A cloud, probably toxic, invaded the town, the nearby countryside and the coast, impregnating everything with a powerful smell of raspberries. The most reputed astronomers speak of the passage of a comet, although it is not known which one, nor may it be supposed that the Dutch sky was on the route of the tailed stars, in any event, the comet would not explain many of the surprising effects that were experienced in the capital of the Low Countries, such as the streets being completely covered with flowers the next morning, the sea level dropping by two centimeters, the compasses ceasing to work, and a thunderbolt, accompanied by considerable electrical activity, discharging over the city without a single drop of rain. The most astonishing part is that the phenomenon affected the behavior of people beyond what was reasonable; thunderbolts tend to have magical consequences, but never had so great an effect been seen. Everything began when the children, from their cradles, pointed out with disquiet certain shadows on the windows, which ended up disconcerting their families. When they went out to show that there was nothing to fear, the mothers met up with each other in the patios and, gripped by an unusual urge to talk, left the pots of dinner unattended. Disposed to shout for them, the men went out after them, and in a few moments whole families could be seen happily frolicking, as if they had full bellies, which they did not, except of the scent of agrimony, breathing the evening air, which also smelled of mother-of-thyme, wild roses and above all of the aforementioned raspberries. More serious was the fact that the females of all species suddenly went into heat, and the males meowed, howled, lowed, crowed, whistled and wailed in rut on the rooftops. The women with nursing children lost their milk, and only those recovered it who dared to go to the mill for a whole week, for that truly is a load of grain. The people, from so much talking on the patio, ended up walking, in shirt sleeves just as they were, to the square, and there was a big party, with plenty of dancing and noise. And although no one in Amsterdam could sleep on the night of the comet, for that was what it was christened, in spite of the fact that no one knew which comet it was, a year from then there was nobody who remembered the incident. Perhaps it was witchcraft.

[From the *Very Truthful Chronicle of the City of Amsterdam, in which all the relevant events that have occurred there are related*, by a certain Raimar Grosenick, 1660, probably]

17

Letter from Christina of Sweden to Hélène Jans
Fontainebleau, June 19, 1655

My friend Hélène,

I write to you from Fontainebleau, in the brilliant and
courtly France that you have no need to get to know: it
is so frivolous and superficial that it would make you
shudder, even if, as is happening to me, you were unable
to resist its enchantment. I will not settle down here. For
now I'm having fun, because I'm a bit of exotica, a relic
that they like to exhibit in the salons full of fake counts,
fake dukes, rich clods who aspire to noble titles and nobles
of ancient lines who aspire to have the rich clods invite
them to dinner so they won't go hungry. You can believe
me: this is the most varied fauna I have ever observed. In
the midst of so many habitués of the salons, walking with
the former queen of Sweden immediately turns anybody
who introduces me into a rising stock in this powdered
society. Meanwhile, I enjoy what appearances can give
me, knowing full well that it's very little. Today I receive
an offer of marriage, and tomorrow they implore me to
intercede with two feuding families to smooth over their
differences and allow their children, who love each other,
to get married. No, this is not my environment. However,
there are a couple of matters regarding my estate that it's
in my best interest to leave all wrapped up, and, as soon
as they are, I'll leave for somewhere else, probably Rome.
I'm interested in speaking with the Pope and receiving his
blessing, and I think the tranquil peace of the Holy City
can serve as a refuge from the spiritual unrest that, more

and more strongly, troubles me. At the same time, I'll have leisure there to study. I want to finish the life of Alexander the Great that I started some time ago. Intellectual work tempts me more than ever because it offers me the possibility, no less interesting because it's hypothetical, that my life may at least make enough sense to lead to something finished, something that comes from me and has me as its cause. And I've always liked writing so much!

I cannot and do not wish to hide from you my preoccupation with the subject we spoke of in your house. For years the most learned men of all the nations of Europe have striven to find a means of universal communication. It's true that the greater part of them are flatterers who are trying in that way to satisfy the pride of the princes who support them, but the attempt is, in itself, a noble one. Ever since I left Stockholm my spiritual unrest, which I have already mentioned to you earlier, is greater, and that leads me to think that all human beings long for the same truth: to find a meaning for their life that can only be comprised in the mind of a Supreme Being. I believe that it is therefore totally senseless to think that the nature of that Supreme Being is a minor issue. A language with which all of us could communicate with each other would serve perfectly for the greater undertaking of identifying the similarities among the different faiths that people embrace. Therefore I review your effort every day, but I do not believe it is my business to improve it. You can do it. In fact, I believe that for this task you are the most suitable person: someone with an excellent philosophical training but not completely cut off from what simple folk do every day. In this era of discoveries we live in, wouldn't it be wonderful to obtain an instrument for the reason as considerable as a language that all the countries of the world could understand? More than fifty years ago a great man of learning, Francis Bacon, of whom you have doubtless heard tell, began to seek a language that would permit him to avoid the deficiencies of the idioms in which we usually express ourselves. Are you familiar with the five-line staffs that musicians use to write down their compositions? Think about them for a moment. With those symbols, what the mind of the composer hears is represented, independently of whatever language he may speak, because in that musical writing the capricious words of one language or another do not appear; rather, the idea is represented directly. Confronted with these demonstrations of human ingenuity, I find ample reason for admiration and excitement. Francis Bacon affirms that the peoples of the Orient write that way, representing ideas, and I think that's somewhat like what you were doing in your *lingua nova et universalis*. According to Bacon, one ought to start with any language, it doesn't matter which one, and establish a basic lexicon, which will be indispensable for all human beings, whatever their community of origin, their education or their preferences may be. Each word, next, will be made to correspond with a real character, a sign that will express it, independent of the label with which it is named in any language. I believe it is simply fantastic, and that the philosophical project of our mutual friend was parallel with this initiative. It would be a great shame if you, his best disciple, were to abandon such a project just because we do not have him with us… in body, for in spirit he really has remained among us. If I don't get over this nostalgia, I shall present myself in your pink and welcoming Amsterdam. Receive, meanwhile, all my affection:

Christina, Princess of Sweden

18

Letter from Hélène Jans to Christina of Sweden
Amsterdam, August 2, 1655

Dear Lady and friend,

It's plain to see that you grew up in a palace and that they fed you on unicorn's milk, because you're not settled down in this world. It's true that your visit was for me one of those rare treats that life gives us every now and then. I liked you, I liked sharing tales and memories, I liked feeling as many things as could fit into a single day, but it surprises me that you don't perceive, clearly and distinctly as our friend sought to do, the reality of the illusion. I neither wish to, nor can, nor should go forward with that intellectual project. I've already told you how my life has gone: the routine of a woman threatened by the powerful, always watched by the religious authorities, under harsh attack because of my knowledge. I have nothing to do with those learned men, comfortably ensconced in the court of a prince, and look, I don't want to offend you for anything in the world; you belong to the caste of those who support that salon wisdom, where thinkers keep themselves nice and cozy by caressing ears. That's not my role in life. They say that a rich Athenian who was walking along, on seeing the Cynic Diogenes crouched in a corner eating lentils, said to him: "Oh, Diogenes, if you knew better how to seek protection and weren't so sharp-tongued, you wouldn't have to eat lentils." It seems Diogenes, annoyed, answered him: "Oh, my friend, if you'd get used to the taste of lentils you wouldn't have to go around flattering powerful men." I'm free, free like Diogenes. And freedom is hard. I spend more time carrying water to the house than your dear friend spent studying. I can't allow myself amusements; I have to keep on. And in the shacks where those of us live who don't dwell in palaces, there's a time for everything, and God doesn't make a gift of time except to princes; around here, instead, death cuts down lives prematurely. I study a lot, but everything I study has the sole purpose of improving people's lives, saving them from the Dark Lady, comforting their bodies. Even though I would quite like to share many other moments with you, I have an unpleasant job to finish. True enough, at this time of year one must take very good care of the lungs, although in the lands where you are that's probably not such a big danger. But, since you seem nervous and ill-at-ease, I'm sending you with this letter a sack of strong scent. It's sweet flag, a swamp plant originating in India, although it's been grown around here for years. You'll smell its aroma from outside the sack, as wild as your friend here. Take it in a tisane and you'll notice how your appetites are stimulated, your digestion is aided and your nervous system is toned. May Fortune be with you. As always,

Hélène

P.S.: This Bacon fellow is a dolt, because, just by looking at one single language, he thinks he has enough to know everything. Thus he goes wrong from the outset, like one who, because on a certain occasion a hot poultice had cured his toothache, would use hot poultices for any ailment. I say this: if he starts with English or Latin, or any language whatsoever to select a basic vocabulary to put into real characters, there can be no certainty that that vocabulary is present in all the languages of men. If he takes the word "happy," just for example, and assigns it a real character, a little drawing, like (, soon he'll decide that "joyous" and "cheerful" and "contented" will have to be expressed in the same way. And he will be proceeding quite logically, because he's starting from a language in which "happy" and "joyous" and "cheerful" and "contented" are seen as equivalent. And if he came across a language where no such words existed? Or where such words were not identical and opposite to "sad," "disenchanted," "miserable," because it was recognized in that language that one can be contented and sad at the same time? What would that Bacon fellow do then? Sing? Tell that good gentleman that he's an impostor and what he's trying to do is put his own language in code and make it universal in use, and that he shouldn't get the wrong idea about us, that our mothers didn't raise any fools. With my best wishes,

Hélène, again

19

Letter from Christina of Sweden to Hélène Jans
Fontainebleau, November 30, 1655

My dearest Hélène,

Just as we were about to leave for Rome, I have received your letter, and I cannot resist answering it in a hurry and almost without giving it much thought, regardless of how sitting down to write to you may end up delaying our departure, and although my dear lady Rose harasses me with preparations that distract my mind from what I am writing. In fact, I can tranquilly permit myself this distraction since, of the small court that surrounds me in every move I make, two or three people are indispensable, people who are very fond of me, who try hard to understand the motivations that drive me, and the rest are nonentities whose opinion isn't worth a fig. Therefore, I'm writing. I'm writing to tell you that I'm taking the sweet flag, although I fear very much that, as far as my nervous ailments are concerned, nature knows of no extract or plant that can cure them. I value the sweet flag, more than for its virtues, because it comes from you, and with that its flavor does not seem bitter, nor will its effects ever be sufficiently welcome. I have also received with pleasure your diatribe, fair and sharp, like you, regarding Bacon; don't be thinking that such a personage has my support either. Still, as I see that the subject does not weary you, for that was what I feared, annoying you with matters that might seem absurd to you, I can't resist sending you a manuscript that I have just come across in my research. It has to do with the project of a certain Lodwick, also an Englishman, which at least around here is attracting a good deal of attention. You will tell me that it's bad, that you see a number of errors in it, and I concede it to you beforehand. But… you who are so ready to point out the cracks in the buildings of others, why don't you build your own? Is it perhaps that you don't dare? You know that you are loved by

Christina, Princess of Sweden

20

Letter from Hélène Jans to Christina of Sweden
[Which has greatly disconcerted historians and biographers
of the aforementioned queen, inasmuch as nowhere
can there be found a noble house called Jans,
nor any clue as to who this lady might be. E. A.]
Amsterdam, December 19, 1655

My lady and friend Christina:

Perhaps you think I'm some boy at a fair, one of those strong, impulsive men with nothing inside their heads, one of those you can get to do anything with a little needling? Perhaps you think it'll be enough to tell me that I'm not up to doing something to make me set out to prove that I am so? Well, you've got a splendid opinion of me. I'm very sorry to have contributed to that vision, but it doesn't match my nature or the functions appropriate to my sex. No, I will not compose a universal language, because when I tried to do it once, I was in love with someone, and doing that made up a part of the intellectual game of the seduction: showing that I knew something, improving myself. All that came to an end and, regardless of how much we may love times gone by, one of the consolations of getting older is that you depend less on the judgment of others and more on your own. I wouldn't recognize myself if I bent like a sapling in the wind, and the first time I was attacked I set about doing something that denies my self, for the development of such a language would be rather a part of the rational project of our friend, in which I no longer believe. I don't, however, want you to consider me proud or resentful, or to think that my refusal is a childish game, an exercise in stubborn insistence on ridiculous principles. Therefore I examined and reexamined the project of Lodwick's that you sent me, trying to let the beauty of well-constructed buildings, even with flaws, suffice for me, and hoping to be able to relax, telling you: there you have it, a beautiful building, enjoy it. However, it couldn't be; wishes are rarely granted, and of course, not on this occasion: I found it even more worthless than Bacon's proposal. To begin with, Lodwick commits the same mistake. These English gentlemen are quite sure that all parts of the world are just the way it looks in England, and they persist in dressing up as universal categories the ones they believe are essential, working from English. It seems to me that I'm seeing the Catholics, who are sure that the principle of life and the secret powers of good and evil have to be exactly as they think, not any other way. Definitely, these thinkers behave with languages like theologians with dogmas, and something smells bad to me in all that. At the same time, do you want to tell me what kind of memory one would have to have to use the language of that Mr. Lodwick? And, if all the projects that we have examined turn out to be so impracticable, couldn't it be that your learned men are devoting their efforts to something they shouldn't devote themselves to, being as it is far removed from nature and the essence of being human? I'm very afraid that I have insulted you; one of my virtues is this one of making everybody angry at me because I'm excessive and not very temperate, when I would like so much to have a place in your heart. May Fortune be with you, and my affection, in some way, reach you. As always,

Hélène

21

Throughout the seventeenth century, as the prestige of Latin was declining, various attempts to construct an international language were made. Although the appearance of the vernacular languages and their vindication had been a fact for some time, academic and religious circles conserved Latin as a language for mutual understanding. Still, philosophers such as Bacon or Comenius doubted the possibility that Latin could retain its function as a universal language and worked to develop some alternative. In fact, philosophical treatises begin in the seventeenth century to escape from a fossilized language, which was losing its usefulness for communication: Descartes publishes the *Discourse on Method* in 1637 in French, and Locke in 1690 his *Essay Concerning Human Understanding*. In the fad that circulates through Europe in this period, however, the goal is to establish correspondences among the lexicons of several already existing languages and an arbitrary code of signs. The written language is to represent concepts, and not sounds or words, so that it can be interpreted by the speakers of different languages. Their authors seek parallels in other codes, such as musical notation, Arabic numerals or the ideograms of the Orient. In this intellectual climate it was thought that such systems provided a representation of the corresponding concepts distinct from language. Francis Bacon, the first scholar who examined the subject in detail, called these conventional signs "real characters" in *The Advancement of Learning* (1605). Such a name underlines the supposed autonomy of the invention, which seeks to be a "real" support for the meaning, a means of communication unmediated by the differences among the various languages. Basically, a system of real characters functions like a multilingual dictionary, in which the words of different languages are made equivalent with a conventionally established sign. The process would consist of making an inventory of a presumably universal set of minimal units of meaning, along the lines of "mother," "house" or "table," and then devising a series of signs with which to represent universally the agreed-on meaning. Those signs would be the real characters.

The first difficulty that these new codes would have to contend with lies in the lack of consistency in what we call meaning in different languages. Even a physical reality such as color, which supposedly is a piece of sensory information, is always selected and manipulated culturally, since, no matter how astonishing it may seem, languages not only give colors distinct labels, they also recognize different colors. In this tribe green and blue are distinguished, but not in this other one; in this one it's inconceivable to be without the color pink and, by contrast, in another pink does not exist, although several shades of red do. There is no such thing as a reality that can be relied on in different codes: the codes construct reality. Moreover, and now in a purely practical sense, a universal language of this kind would present design difficulties because of needing to depend on a set of symbols that could be written with relative ease so that the errors of its users would not undermine a project developed with so much effort.

The projects of real characters were many, and of varied composition. In some cases letters of the Greek alphabet were used, with dots below and above, as in the project of Francis Lodwick published in 1647. In others, Arabic numerals are used as the foundation, a notation that possessed the advantage of not annoying the user with unfamiliar signs. Good examples of this approach are the project in English and French of Cave Beck (1657), based on the grammar of the classical languages; the proposal of Johann Becker (1661); or the *Polygraphia* of Athanasius Kircher (1663), which seeks to adapt the keys of ciphers for encoding secret messages for the construction of a universal language, open to everyone. These systems, however, are no more than amusements with which to encode messages in Latin. So simple a mechanism could not work, but it would continue to be dabbled in during the following years.

[Research notes of Einés Andrade, typed and collected in a red folder under the heading *Concerning the Universal Language Project of Hélène Jans*]

22

Letter from Hélène Jans to Christina of Sweden
Amsterdam, July 20, 1665

Esteemed Lady and friend,

The winter has ended, spring has departed and the summer is well along without my hearing anything from you. What could be keeping you in this persistent silence that worries me so much? Perhaps your body is ill from homesickness and your health as a woman of the north is troubled in those honey-sweet lands? I want to believe not: my vain heart suggests to me at once, when I think about the lack of mail from you, that if you were suffering from an illness you would let me know, for I'm not such a bad healer that you wouldn't rely on me when the hell of pain flares up. Thus I'm inclined to believe that a lover is keeping you busy, and I'm happy in that case, because solitude, my dear, should be owing to such sweet preoccupations; I will never tire of repeating how much we should enjoy ourselves in this brief life we live; most of the time we humans forget that we're only animals who, deluded regarding our own lot, steal a bit of spirit from the stars in order to dream that we last, and that we're doing something different from what an ant does on an August evening: carting food around before the first cold snap comes and puts an end to us. Truly I'm having dark thoughts today; perhaps I shouldn't have started the letter in this frame of mind. However, I have reasons to be that way: don't go thinking that I've gone and fallen in love like a young girl and I'm sinking in a glass of booze, it's nothing of the sort. In less than a week we buried the daughters of my neighbor women on either side, whom I love like sisters; you know what they say, and rightly so, those who live nearest are like family and dearest. Well, one of them passed away in childbirth, and the other from quartan fever. We weep for them both because they died and for the sake of the poor little things they leave behind: three boys, one of them, and the other a little girl scarcely more than a year old. A house without a mother is a ship without a rudder, and that's all I have to say. I weep for their passing and remember the day when it was my turn to say goodbye to my little girl. During the burial of the second of my neighbors, with the other death so fresh in our memories, people were remarking that the departed was only twenty-three, and I corrected them: that's not so very few years, there's no woman of twenty-three who's still looking her best, old age attacks women with its aches and pains from the cradle, and what can I say, I'm twice that age and I still have a few years left! I'm the same age that our friend was when the cold carried him off; we get more fragile all the time, and one day the wind blows and that's enough to whirl us away like a leaf... In short, my dear, you see that your Hélène must be better off than she says, since she's still letting all her strength out through her mouth: I write and write without stopping, and now I see how much ink I've wasted to tell you almost nothing, or to tell you only about painful things, which are mine. I have arthritis in my hands; it's an effort for me to write—everything I do is an effort; I don't attend births on my own anymore for fear that my hands won't work for me if I have to intervene and adjust the baby. My bones are getting heavier and I don't feel at my best. Therefore I turn to writing, even if I have to put gloves on my fingers so that I can hold the pen in the cold. I write more than ever, with the intention of recording what I've learned. My herbarium has grown spectacularly in these ten years since we saw each other: I now have more than a dozen folders with my notes on the values and medicinal uses of the herbs that can be found in Amsterdam, which must be about the same as the herbs of the whole world; every day more ships arrive with the essences of the Orient, plants from South Africa and the Americas. Indeed, along with this letter I'm sending you, so you can try it, a herb they brought from China years ago and that's enthralling people. It's called tea, and be cautious in consuming it: even though its aroma is intoxicating, and it tones and pleases the senses, it also sets the mind on a whirl and takes away sleep, which is the only natural restorative. Of course, once we wake up we have little memory of the repose, and it's best to pass the day with these small pleasures. Back to what we were talking about. I hope nothing happens to me without my having made arrangements for those who come after me, regarding everything that I have to arrange; if my father hadn't taught me, I wouldn't know anything now, so in order to maintain the necessary balance of the cosmos, I must pay my debts to my forebears by making sure to leave to those who come after me a knowledge of sufficient importance to justify my passage through the world. It's true that I haven't managed to create a progeny, but that doesn't mean anything. It amazes me when I see one of those rich clods strolling around Amsterdam, all puffed up, convinced that his children will inherit his fortune, for that's what people call the stacks of money gotten by evil means in far-off lands by exploiting others, a fortune that ensures that his children will be a pack of loafers. No, I don't understand that kind of inheritance. I'm talking about nature, about knowledge of the earth from which I come and which will cover me; for that it makes no difference whether the ones who suckle my knowledge are children of my womb or someone else's. It's nature that makes us sisters and ensures that we have the same interests: the interest that the sun will shine for us, that the moon will watch over us, the wind will push us along and the water will slake our thirst, noble interests, of knowing and being, for the rest, you know as well as I do, is worth nothing. I go back and reread what I am setting down for you, and I'm irritated with myself; what a sad discourse I'm sending you, with a yen to look back over my life and cry at the end about the lack of descendants of my own to whom I can leave the little I have! Receive the letter as an affectionate hug from this friend who loves you, and forget all the details that I go over in it. May fortune be propitious to you, as much as is wished by your

Hélène

23

Letter from Christina of Sweden
to the same Hélène Jans
Rome, August 22, 1666

My dearest Hélène,

I don't know how to ask your pardon for the way I've neglected you for so many months, but often life whips us forward under loads that are heavier than we can bear. I've been in Innsbruck, in Brussels, in Paris, from here to there, without my spirit, which is a lazy bee, managing to gather, from all the settings I pass through, even a little pollen to nourish myself. Why do I keep looking and looking and never find anything? I'm a flibbertigibbet, I let myself be carried along by those around me, and they turn me into a marionette who doesn't even know how to walk on her own. How I detest myself! And at the same time, my friend, if only you knew how much I envy you, who are a tree with your roots well established in the earth, sheltering those around you, secure in offering your branches to the wind, which will never destroy you... That's how I like to picture you, Hélène, like ballast, like a weighty being, I who am all lightness. It's true that I notice you're rather dejected, but it's not a decadent sadness, it's the sadness of mourning because of death, a sadness of those who have pure hearts. Definitely I ought to visit you, before our hair turns completely white and we look like a shadow of what we once were, incapable of attracting anything but flies. And since you ask me about lovers, there was something, though not pleasant. Good old Monaldeschi, after revealing to me all the miseries of lovelessness, ended up dying, and there was no shortage of people to blame me for his murder. Needless to say, in case it wasn't clear, I'm innocent... at least in this matter, although you know that just about anything can be proclaimed about me except innocence. Scandal surrounds my life: I'm used to that, but don't think I'm at all content with it. Let's turn, then, to more cheerful things; I believe that love was an invention to distract women from study, the context where we fully develop our capacities for attention, memory and effort. Everything you tell me about your herbarium stimulates my imagination and stirs up my desire to know. From your little house, all alone, from your daily experience as a worker, who reads and reflects, who commits herself and learns, you seems to be creating a great work, an up-to-date compendium regarding the utility of medicinal plants. Excellent. Do you realize that, if your effort were followed up by some other, we would be in a position to offer from this century to humanity to come a knowledge without equal? How much I would like to have something of the sort to justify my life. Or, at least, to be by your side and help you in the classification of extracts, plants, courses of treatment... I know that my insistence will annoy you, and it's true that I swore to myself years ago not to return to this subject that bothers you so much, but I believe that your search for botanical knowledge has many points of similarity to the search for a universal language. Now you want your personal experience with tisanes and drugs not to be lost and to become generally known, for it to be reviewed until it's established as a set of curative principles valid in all the world. And, in a similar way, in your tender youth, you were searching for a magnificent order to make an inventory of ideas and give them the names that would fit them best. The resemblance between the two projects is more than noticeable, don't you think? Why do I imagine you telling me no? Well, regarding that point, I can't resist keeping you informed. You probably know that a few years ago one George Dalgarno published a treatise in which he offered what he called the "first fully-developed universal language, solidly constructed according to philosophical principles." The author does not know, clearly, that his is not the first, but that's not his fault, is it? If you want to know more, he himself acknowledges the influence of Hobbes and Descartes on his treatise, in particular in logical and epistemological questions. The most select circles of Europe speak of him as a unique figure, ahead of his time, and lavish praise on the originality and brilliance of this inspiring project. Won't this spur you on to make your own work known? Doesn't it bother you that others carry off the fame that you deserve? If you don't do anything about it, your invention will be attributed to others. I know of your moral integrity, and I'm glad that you aren't motivated by presumption and lack of modesty, but isn't there justice in claiming as yours what is your own? Answer me soon so that the comfort your words always give me will reach me. Don't think that I'm pushing you like a piece of merchandise put on display; please understand that I only wish what, in my humble understanding, seems best. With my love,

Christina, Princess of Sweden

24

Letter from Hélène Jans to Christina of Sweden
Amsterdam, September 9, 1666

Dear lady and friend Christina,

I'm taking advantage of the fact that a certain bookseller
of my acquaintance is sending a mail packet to Rome to
send a quick response to your letter; it will not cover as
many points as I would like to discuss with you because
of the haste with which the person who's waiting for my
message must leave. I wasn't expecting your insistence:
at this stage of my life, more than anything, it makes me
laugh. Did you really imagine that a woman would raise
her hand and shout: "Over here, over here, I'm the one who
should get the honors!'"? Let all those Misters, Lodwicks or
Dalgarnos or whoever, enjoy their false glory as much as
they can; there never was a woman who was interested in
any fame except to hope that her adventures in bed wouldn't
be spread around. The new language was an amusement...
Must I say it again to make you believe me? Let them enjoy
making it, let them enjoy improving it, and above all let
them enjoy putting their names on the invention; none of
that is going to cost me any sleep. When I was starting out
in the craft, an old midwife taught me to use the forceps.
Most likely you, who live in a world different from mine,
don't know what I'm talking about. It's an instrument made
of two spoons crossed in the shape of an X. When a woman
has no strength left during the birth and can't push, we help
her with this sort of pincers, which grasps the head of the
baby so we can pull it out. They say that Hippocrates was

the first to attend a woman with a mechanism of this kind, but it was several generations of surgeons, and midwives, and dead women, and babies torn to pieces, who perfected these spoons which we now employ with great dexterity, many times achieving good results... and sometimes bad ones. Do you believe that anyone will put his or her name on such an invention? No, because nobody will be able to boast beforehand about its success. And, you know what? I think that the things that are important are, precisely, the ones where success is not ensured, like the forceps, or the gestures that no one sees, like the one of the person who sits and talks with a dying old man or wipes a child's nose. It doesn't interest women of my station in life to have our tombs honored when we're dead; it's better for our bodies to be caressed while we're alive. The only thing we aspire to is to remedy suffering, and make things better, and live well and be well. And my wishes, which are all good for one who esteems me so much, fly to you. Fortune always,

Hélène

25

The problems inherent in the systems of real characters, along with the desire to systematize language so as to achieve a logical and unambiguous means of communication, caused, towards the middle of the seventeenth century, the development of artificial languages to experience a turn towards philosophical postulates. By contrast with the effort at communication represented by the previous projects, the philosophers of the seventeenth century were not seeking a language in the usual sense, but rather a code that would reflect nature and its laws: a logical, rational system, free of irregularities and ambiguity, concise, clear, which would leave no room for errors. With this reformulation of objectives, the inventors of philosophical languages are aiming at accords with the new paradigms of the natural sciences: regularity, clarity, elimination of redundancies, harmony and elegance. On the one hand, languages seem to be ineffective tools for representing the universe; on the other, the symbolic system of mathematics, universally applicable, is held up as a model, with the idea of extending its axioms and deductive processes to the rest of knowledge. The quest for a supposedly universal language becomes at this point an intellectual problem of the first magnitude, since it demands a complete revisioning of the universe and its laws. History imputes the credit for encouraging this change of direction, which leads to the so-called philosophical languages, to

Descartes, although it seems that he had little directly to do with the matter. Simply, in a personal letter dated November 20, 1629, addressed to his friend Mersenne, the philosopher expresses his criticisms of a project of real characters devised by an unknown author. Descartes thought that such an artifice was impracticable, especially on account of the prodigious memory it demanded of its users and the consequent need to make continual use of the dictionary. This limitation would only be overcome, in his opinion, by following strict philosophical principles in the construction of the language, which would impose on concepts an order similar to the one that rules among numbers. If the arithmetical system could be constructed on the basis of a few figures, it would also be possible to symbolize thought exhaustively with a few signs. This idea would pass along to the projects of philosophical languages. A universal language requires, from then on, that philosophical truth be attained previously: in other words, it demands a knowledge of the world, of its categories and relationships. Despite the apparent simplicity of the argument, Descartes must have been quite skeptical regarding the possibility of constructing a language with these characteristics, because he never developed his proposal.

In any case, the difficulties no longer reside in assigning a real character to every possible notion, but rather in determining a reduced number of basic ideas. Once these simple concepts are identified and arranged in a hierarchical order, a rational analysis will permit them to be combined in order to express complex ideas. In the last phase, a limited number of characters would also be fixed, and exact correspondences of meaning would be established between the concepts and the characters that represent them. The totality of human knowledge would be perfectly encapsulated in such a code.

By a strange chance, Descartes' ideas flourished especially in the academic circles of London, where in the following years figures such as Seth Ward, professor of astronomy at Oxford, Thomas Urquhart, George Dalgarno and John Wilkins apply themselves to developing philosophical languages that not only attempt to symbolize the totality of concepts, but also to find a finite number of basic ideas. All these efforts included a summary of human knowledge and, in this respect, they go beyond preceding attempts: they no longer consist merely of the transcription of a language into convenient characters. On the other hand, inevitably, the classifications they employ convey a particular image of the world, the customary one of the West during the seventeenth century, and their authors do not recognize that other peoples would organize the world in a different manner. No matter how interesting they may be from the intellectual standpoint, none of the projects known as philosophical languages was at all capable of offering a means of universal communication.

[From the notes of Einés Andrade, who writes thesis chapters on the back of used pieces of paper, no doubt a very ecological approach but not very sensible, considering that what appears on the other side are some frankly horrible poems. Of all my disciples, she—or, as she would write it, s/he—is the one least likely to finish her/his thesis. M.V.]

26

Letter from Hélène Jans to Christina of Sweden
November 16, 1675

My dear Christina,

I received news through a third party that you're prostrated. I won't travel to meet you; the world's too big for a woman like me, who's scarcely ever left her house, but I implore the gods that your illness may not be serious, and I burn sandalwood incense with the intention of purifying myself so that my prayers will be heeded, and you will find yourself quickly restored to health. With the years the chronic ailments multiply and, not knowing which illness to tend to, we end up giving ourselves up entirely to the sickness that then gnaws at us and teases us. I believe that old age is the lack of illusions and that, at any age, we ought to live satisfied with just being here, which is plenty, and enjoying what each day brings us, which always turns out to be a lot, even if the day dawns steeped in cares, for those can't be avoided. If the two of us get through this winter that is menacing us, perhaps we should grant ourselves the happiness of a visit, an encounter that would reawaken our hankering to stay above the ground; there's more than enough time for resting below it. As I take for granted that you will accept my invitation and not make me leave my home, for the lares of my hearth are my protectors, your arrival will give me the chance to show you the work I've just finished. My book is complete. It consists of the herbarium, to which I've been adding a manual for women and a small portfolio on magical healing practices. I've had two copies made, one to give to Agnes, a girl I've taken into my house and who'll follow my trade. Haven't I told you about her recently? I attended her mother during her birth and, while the unfortunate thing was giving up the ghost, the little girl was whimpering about coming into this world—I believe that babies cry when they're born because of how heavy the air we breathe here is for them, so different from the light air of the maternal cloister. I loved her little face, like a newborn calf's, which made me go back in time and remember my Francine. Like the woman I am, I've always been intuitive, but for some time now my orientation towards the world has always come from the warmth that comes up from my chest and not from my head, and I believe more and more firmly that there exist occult forces that govern our lives. I know that you can believe me; therefore I'll tell you the story just as it went. While I was putting a shroud on the mother and washing the daughter, I felt in my belly the pains that women feel after giving birth. I took this sympathy with the pain of another as a sign that Fortune was sending the little girl to me, and I decided to adopt her as my own. From that moment on, Agnes has been with me, and she makes the weight of life more endurable. Now that she's a big girl, just turned nine, she's all ready to learn my trade; for that she needs as much guidance as I can leave for her. With my book all finished, all I have left to do is get her set up in life before I go away too. Do you see how this head of mine is starting to behave like an old pot? I waste all sorts of time explaining myself, I sew so much and so long that I end up losing the main thread of this piece of sewing, this letter. As I was saying to you above, once the herbarium was finished, and also the *Book of Women*, I gave them to a scribe so that he could make me two fair copies, with his strong young man's wrist. One is for Agnes, and the other's for you. I would like to hand it to you in person next April, which is the month for fulfilling love, and for us to laugh together at some of the remedies and tell each other our sorrows, because in telling them, even if it doesn't get rid of them, they are relieved a little, and one's spirit clears up like the sky after a summer cloudburst. And having said this, I now feel ready to say that that was my only reason for writing. I've had many disputes with you these past years; I can only believe in private efforts, in anonymous labors, and many times you wanted me to win a fame to which I never aspired. I hope you didn't misinterpret that; I always looked on your love for me with pleasure. But what do you want! I never wrote anything to gain recognition; that's a fatuity unworthy of a thinking person. If I wrote down my recipes, it was to help anyone they could do any good for and, in any case, so that they'd love me. I always was short of love; I lost the family I was born into very early, and I never got the love of our friend, and my little girl barely lasted the blink of an eye… And, because of the lack of everyday love, I was always looking for someone to love me; if I'm like anything, it's a cat next to the fireplace, you know that… And everything I wrote and wrote was more for the sake of your love and your pleasure than for anything else at all. Are you understanding me? I tell you, and I know I'm not mistaken, that in the coming years many will come along making revolutions in knowledge; most of them will stroll around, and become famous, and walk through gardens and rooms, as if time were given to them as a gift and it didn't have to be made productive. And other women in love will do the everyday work for these blowhards, and my sympathies, regardless of how learned and big-brained the men may be, are more for the women than for the men. You will see, I insist, in the coming years many inventors of things that already exist, scrupulous thinkers in need of someone to give them a prize or at least a few pats on the back. And certainly, it won't be uncommon for that someone to be a woman, even better if she's young and beautiful. Here's hoping April comes soon,

Hélène

27

In the Cartesian school, the German philosopher Gottfried Wilhelm von Leibniz (1646-1716) also considered the possibility of constructing a universal language and tried to attain that objective using all possible strategies. Initially he proposed the perfecting of a natural language, of German to be specific. Even if the history of linguistic ideas reduces it to a mere anecdote, it is at least curious to observe how intellectual figures as outstanding and influential as Leibniz can fall into the trap of their native language, and suppose that there exist languages better suited to the needs of universal interchange because of being closer to representing the world in its natural order, "just as one thinks." According to this vision, some languages would reveal the proper categories of the underlying grammar that must be present in all human languages by that mere fact, an idea that presupposes the privileging of some languages over others. This chauvinistic and naïve ideal of linguistic perfection can also be found in illustrious thinkers, who do not recognize the latent fallacy in considering that in their own mother tongue the categories should be just the way they think. Still, Leibniz must have had an inkling of some of this, because he soon abandoned the project of simplifying German to turn to other strategies. In different periods of his life he would construct artificial languages based on already existing languages, in order finally to suggest the deliberate abandonment of natural language in favor of a universal symbolic system. By resting on a solid logical base, he seeks to give the project the necessary coherence to deal with issues of understanding. Moreover, he is interested in simplicity, contriving to make it easy to learn and remember. On that basis Leibniz criticizes the preceding schemes, which in his opinion do not make a truly "philosophical" classification. The universal language that Leibniz seeks should not be limited to its communicative function, which in his opinion is superficial. More important are the representational, cognitive, judicial and heuristic functions. Leibniz wanted to construct a philosophical language adapted to expressing fundamental ideas as part of his dream that all nations would cooperate in the discovery of the secrets of nature and in the use of that knowledge to cause human beings to live in peace. His *characteristica universalis* would be an instrument of reason, an inferential mechanism that would allow any question to be elucidated or debate to be resolved: the contending parties would sit around a table and talk, and the clarity of ideas demanded by that universal language would dispel all erroneous conclusions. However, in order to be a universal language, this project would require a complete vocabulary and a grammar. Leibniz dedicated a great deal of time to analyzing all human ideas as a first step towards reducing them to "primitives" or simple concepts, attempting to compose a rational grammar based on the study of the grammars of natural languages, but he never managed to complete the task, and his universal language remained a project.

[From the notes of Einés Andrade. I must remind her that in research it's necessary to prune away tangential ideas and emphasize the essential. I would like to see a chapter of her thesis before the end of the trimester. I mean a real chapter and not one of these confused drafts. M.V.]

28

Letter from the German philosopher Leibniz
to Princess Sophia Charlotte
[Or, how Hélène Jans adds to her many trades that
of remarkable seer of self-fulfilling prophecies]
Berlin, April 4, 1700

My esteemed friend,

I receive with joy the news that your husband has just been proclaimed king, with the name Frederick I of Prussia. That presupposes that you will stop being Princess of Hanover, whom everyone was watching with misgivings, to become a queen. I wish with all my heart that you may overcome all the obstacles, that you may win the confidence of the electoral forces and turn your palace into the center of social life. You have the strength of mind and the spiritual values necessary to make Prussia a great power and to initiate an entire dynasty. You know that this humble philosopher loves you with a passion that goes beyond anything imaginable, and that I shall be at your service for whatever you may need. I hope, now that you are beginning the period of your greatest political glory, that you will not forget this servant of yours, who admires, beyond the beauty of your body, that which is distilled by your delicate soul. For the rest, I hope to meet with you soon to celebrate this auspicious occurrence and resume our most fertile conversations. Therefore today I shall not offer corrections of the commentaries on Plato that you sent me in your last missive. For that reason, and because I would like to fill this space, not only by bearing witness to you regarding my most sincere respect and my most absolute affection, but also by reminding you that the philosophical project I have been promoting for my whole life is now an objective that you find yourself in a position to support. As you know, I have been committed since my youth to achieving peace in Europe, the reunification of the Christian churches, the integration of the Occidental and Chinese religions and, especially, the expansion of science and civilization throughout the wide world. In order to attain these ends, it would be needful to adopt a single language. As you know, I have been familiar since childhood with Greek and Latin, in which I have written not a few hexameters, besides German, French and Tuscan, along with something of the grammar and the vision of the language of the Chinese people. With this arsenal I have applied myself several times to constructing a language valid for all nations. Speaking in all sincerity, as with you I am wont to behave, I must tell you that the schemes of Dalgarno and Wilkins, which became so famous and spread so rapidly through the courts of Europe, seem excessively arbitrary to me, which evidently keeps these gentlemen from devising a truly philosophical classification. I am certain, however, that the designing of a suitable language would contribute to bringing all nations to cooperate in the discovery of the secrets of nature, and in the use of that knowledge to cause human beings to live in peace. My *characteristica universalis*, which I will soon present to you in detail, will be an instrument of reason, an inferential mechanism that will permit the elucidation of any question or the resolution of any debate: the contending parties will sit around a table and talk, and the clarity of ideas demanded by that universal language will erase any errors that might intrude. Because my invention comprises the use of the entire reason, a judgment for controversies, an interpreter of ideas, a scale for measuring probabilities, a compass to guide us across the ocean of experiences, an inventory of things, a table of thoughts, a microscope to examine things present, a telescope to divine things absent, a general calculus, an innocent magic, a kabbalah that is not illusory, a system of writing that anyone can read in his own language and, finally, a language that can be learned in a few weeks and that soon will spread over the whole world [...].

[A letter found in Einés Andrade's portfolio. She, in her ignorance, which is always so bold, has dared to place in the margin, with a purple marker, the following incomprehensible message: "Blessed be all the princesses that have ever been in the world." If only she would stop playing detective and just write a talk for the upcoming conference on Rationalism! Definitely, I have to talk with her. I'm making a note on my planner: "Solve the Einés problem." M.V.]

IV

Einés Andrade

1

The night the little girl was born, everyone was watching, on the black-and-white television in a corner of the kitchen, how man had just made it to the Moon. Each of them stopped what she was doing, and the kitchen looked like the scene on the night after the day of creation, with homework half graded, dry clothing piled up in the basket, the book left right at the most interesting part and the erector set with the tower half built. Everything had been left hanging while they were looking, just for a second, that's all, at the television; there was no way they were going to miss a historic event like that one for the sake of dumb stuff: it had to be watched. It was a fact: man had made it to the Moon. Like in the science-fiction books, like in the sweet dreams of people in love, like in the fevered verbiage of the poets, man would one day live on the Moon and everybody would go there on weekend trips because it'll be like I told you, by the year 2000 everybody'll have a little spaceship parked by the door. It's true, for the time being, man needed a special suit, I suppose because of the low temperatures, and also a helmet; it was well known that the air on the Moon had to be unbreathable. Because if it were breathable, you tell me, come on, why wouldn't there be people on the Moon, and probably there are, are not, it was well known that people, just like us, with a head and two eyes and walking on two feet, with hands and a mouth and, in short, all the things people ought to have, like that, exactly, it was well known that there weren't going to be people on the Moon. But there could well be other forms of life: microscopic little critters, voracious monsters in unimaginable shapes, or even, how would you know if one of those craters they were looking at in the satellite picture wasn't a person with a different appearance, in this case looking like a crater; life doesn't have to be the same everywhere as it is here, it's absolutely stupid and silly to think things are only all right at home... And anybody who left the village would know that the world looked mighty different a few days down the road... so how're you going to expect people on the Moon to be exactly like here? Obviously, if they aren't the same as people, they won't be people, they'll be something else; to be a person there are certain limits, it's just like you don't call Fox a person, though that dog is as smart and sensitive as a hungry old hog, you wouldn't say he's a person because of that; it's hard to say for sure what a person is—if a kid's born with two heads you aren't going to say he's human, even if he's born from a woman. And they were all caught up in this, in front of the TV, though not mesmerized, they were anything but passive, eh? When, for example, the weekend news was broadcast, even Grandma Aniceta in her rocking chair would start spitting, it was a treat to see her, she had always been crusty and she still had enough wind to yell: "Down with National Catholicism! Long live the Republic!" And of course, since one is like the tit one sucks, all of them, starting out being shocked by what Grandma Aniceta came out with, ended up having a good laugh at it and adopting it as their own. That's how it became established that they had to spit at the repellent announcer on the Saturday night news, regardless of what she might be saying or not saying, and, while the beaters that were beating the eggs for the omelet were clacking away, the yells they were all letting fly could probably be heard all the way to Madrid: "Oh yeahhh!" "Because you say so, airhead! Worse than an airhead!! You don't know how to do anything but brush your hair, your head's just there for decoration!" And "nya-nya-nya-nya-nya," and after the "nya-nyas," one of them would stick her tongue out at the TV, another would put her thumbs on her temples and waggle the other four fingers rhythmically, like donkey's ears waving, and to top it off, there would always be one who would stand with her back to the TV and show her butt, contemptuously, to the poor lady who was quite far away, working, looking at a camera, unaware that she was the object of scorn and abuse. As I say, they were anything but passive. That night, however, the night when the little one was born, nothing like that happened; they were fascinated with the colonization of the Moon, certain that it would amount to no less than that.

That night, while they were watching Armstrong take a small step for a man which, however, was a giant leap for mankind, Olaia, the eldest of the younger generation, started thinking out loud about the world upside down, her favorite topic, because this business about Armstrong's step being giant for mankind remained to be seen, and besides, women were doing exactly the opposite of that Armstrong fellow: while he was stepping on the Moon, who knew how many women in the world were giving birth, and with that they were taking small steps for mankind, that's what they'd been seeing since woman was woman and not a she-ape, but for sure each of them was taking a big step for herself. And Olaia didn't know, while she was arguing so much and so well, that her youngest sister, Livia, was at that very moment, in the room at the end of the hall, taking a giant step for herself, which was a small one for mankind, even if one doesn't like to admit it. And while all this was going on, Carmiña, the middle sister, was busy talking back to the TV: "Well, I don't believe it. Ha, ha… well, I don't believe it." She was saying it to the TV because, while she was speaking, she was staring at the set and shaking her finger in the air as a sign of negation. They let her talk as much as she wanted, Carmiña was always like that, skeptical and grumpy, especially when she needed to get done ironing the sheets, the ones with the really stiff fabric, maybe it was Holland fabric, they say there's no place like Holland to buy top-quality cloth, well, the Dutch women must be very happy with their hutches nice and full of cloths! They all kept the Holland sheets on their beds from their grandmother's hope chest, they still hadn't had "terlenka" invade their house; soon "cellophane" would burst into their lives, "iron-on patches" to make jackets for books, "superglue" to stick everything together, and "Tupperware" to take food out of the house instead of casserole dishes. And Aunt Carmiña, for Carmiña, and Olaia too, were going to be aunts at that moment even if they didn't know it, because both of them were Livia's sisters, was ironing with great care, a little slowly, perhaps, relishing the activity as if the functioning of the cosmos depended on the smoothness of the things she was ironing. But after her tender care, the clothing looked like it was straight from the factory, that's what they used to say, "she irons so it's like straight from the factory," just like with Olaia, she made magnificent cream puffs, they used to say "she cooks like it's from a factory." Who knows where they got that cultural sense of an industrial factory, they who had only seen factories on television documentaries? And yet they always said that because factories were important and it was reasonable beyond a doubt, even the methodical doubt of Carmiña, that a factory would never make anything badly. True enough, Grandma Aniceta tried to explain from her rocker, to herself and to them, that factories were bastions of capitalism, swollen with dubious relationships of power, but they were too busy, always running back and forth, to take time for social analyses. As Carmiña used to say, let's suppose that if you're going to make three dozen cream puffs, you have to figure the dough for around forty or fifty, because some of them always turn out flat, or too soft, or too small, or simply, because the dough doesn't rise, or because a little bit sticks to the bottom of the pan. And you're not going to throw that away, that would be a crime. Just leave it in the bowl, and even laugh at it a little, it looks like Mario's bald head, that young fellow Olaia had once, yes, that guy from Castroforte, who was so dumb that we put banana peels down for him and he'd slip on them. But you're not going to laugh in a factory, much less about your sister's boyfriends, look, I'd rather be single than hanging on Mario's arm my whole life, no, that's not done, very serious gentlemen work in the factory, with white coats and brandishing thermometers, they measure everything, and not just because, but so everything will have the perfect conditions, "ideal," they say, and that's how they manufacture and why do you think they make *petit choux* and not cream puffs? First because in factories they always speak French or English, it wouldn't be right for everything they said to be understood. And second because they measure with special devices so the dough will have the ideal conditions, and there it is, presto, they all turn out exactly the same, like identical twins. And of course, even though Olaia made cream puffs that would knock your socks off, they weren't all that perfect, but almost, which is why they used to say "girl, they turned out like from a factory, real factory-made." And Carmiña, who didn't like cooking, and didn't try it, that's why she was a teacher in the national system, ironed with the perfection of a factory, with a black skillet without steam—she supplied the steam by taking a sip from a glass of water she had there on the table and blowing like an elephant in its Saturday night bath, and I've got that right when I say elephant because Aunt Carmiña, who was barely a meter and a half tall on a good day, must have weighed ninety or a hundred kilos. No one ever knew her exact weight; she had a *horror vacui* of scales. That "*horror vacui*" was a Latin expression, which probably wasn't very appropriate for the context of feminine weight, but Aunt Carmiña had seen it in one of the Encyclopedias that the Ministry sent to the school that she ran (that "ran" is a manner of speaking, really the students ran her, ran her ragged), entitled *What Children Want to Know*, and from then on she never said "fear" anymore, because from then on all her fears were *horrores vacui*. Well, that night when the little one was born Aunt Carmiña was doing her dampening by aspersion on the sheets while Armstrong was taking a step with his tiny foot that was insignificant for him although, in his opinion, of transcendent importance for all of mankind, old Armstrong can't have had a grandmother, and all of them entranced in front of the TV, and Aunt Carmiña was repeating "well, I don't believe it." It wasn't clear whether she didn't believe that part about the transcendent importance of the step or the ability of Armstrong to walk with that butt-heavy and humiliating suit they'd put on him, when the mother of all of them, Dona Carme, asked: "Carmiña, may I ask what you don't believe?" "Well, what else, Mama? I don't believe that what's-his-name made it to the Moon; it seems to me that it's all taped." "How do you mean, taped?" "Well, just like in the movies, with a set and décor... because, come on, why would the Moon be just like everyone imagines it? You, for example, the first time you see the sea you realize that it's not at all the way you thought, it's bigger and colder... right? Or the first time you go to a festival at night, you notice that walking at night has a certain magical something that you could never guess being at home in bed, right? And it's like that with everything. Well, if everything's different from how a person imagined it, how can the Moon be so much the same?... Huh? Well? Have a look, eh? Maybe you don't realize that he's not really walking. Hmmmm? Look there, you can even see on his helmet the reflection of the guy who's taping him with the camera. No, no, I don't believe in windmills... Ha... The Americans want us to believe they made it to the Moon. That's got to be because of Vietnam..." Carmiña never ran short when it was time to look for reasons. "Whyyyy?" "Because of the Vietnam War. For sure they lost or are about to lose. Mark my words..." And at that very moment, before anyone had to defend the honesty of American journalists—"They aren't going to go telling lies on TV, are they? Are they professionals, or what?"—at that very instant, they heard the cries of the little girl who, for the first time, noticed that in this world of ours the air weighs seven times more than on the Moon and therefore, I say, it's so hard to breathe when you have a problem, it seems that the air doesn't get in. And she, the little girl, had a serious problem in addition: adapting to the planet where she was going to live and where she had just landed, plop, from the dark maternal cloister, for there she had been free of the laws of universal gravitation, so natural to this planet. Alas, Carme the daughter and Carme the mother, or Carmiña and Dona Carme, if you prefer, were gobsmacked, this time for sure, because something that everybody (except Carmiña) could believe was that a man, especially if he's an American like Elvis Presley, can get to the Moon in a special well-organized capsule, and it was quite another to believe that a kitten got into the house, because those cries were something like the meowing of a cat, the women thought. Only Grandma Aniceta, who would spit at the priest when he was consecrating on the television, almost blind in her corner, knew with complete certainty that she had just become a great-grandmother. And just as she had followed with great interest, though she couldn't see it, Armstrong's stroll among those craters—"Hey, girl, tell me what you can see"—now she wriggled around in the rocking chair laughing her head off. "Oh, dearies, Livia's had a baby." "What nonsense a person can end up talking with age! Hush for a minute, we're just going to see what happens and then we'll bring you a nice cup of coffee, all right?" grumpily answered Carme, the mother, who had just turned into Carme, the grandma. And they all hurried down the hall to the girls' room, opened the door fearfully, and there she was. On the carpet, crouching, there was

Livia, sweaty, and with a puzzled look on her face. She had just pulled down her skirt and picked up the baby who had appeared between her thighs. "How strange! It doesn't even hurt…" The baby had just arrived in the world. It was a girl. Her mother, contradicting the Biblical curse, had not suffered in giving birth to her, although she hadn't enjoyed doing it either. She was pretty and precious as a treasure. She would be named Einés.

2

Concerning what Einés found when she looked
in the chest in the attic: many papers, very obscure ones,
which fixed for good her character as an impenitent seeker,
a sloppy researcher and a rebellious mind
From the secret papers of Hélène Jans: A spell for Camille

That same afternoon Camille, my neighbor, came looking for me. She wants to be loved by Johannes. I gave her the love-herbs in the right dosage but I couldn't give her the spell: Camille doesn't know how to read, and it's too long for her to learn it by heart. I'll say it in her place, although it's not as effective that way. Meanwhile, I'll write it here in case anyone should happen to need it: "Gigantic Hecate, you who protect women and shoot arrows, untamed, noble of birth, bearer of the torch, lady, listen, you who open the indestructible steel doors, guardian. You who open the earth, goddess of the crossroads, you who have visions that send forth flames, come to me, I invoke you along with the prematurely dead, who died without children, and place yourself over the head of Johannes and deprive him of sweet sleep. Let him not in any way join eyelid with eyelid, but rather, because of his loving preoccupation with Camille, may he suffer insomnia. If he is lying in the arms of another, may he reject her and place Camille in his heart, and, as soon as he leaves that woman, may he come to the doors of Camille's house, overcome by his desire for her love and her bed. And may he feel caught up in a powerful need for love, o Hecate, you of many names, propitious to women, protectress, you who walk in the flame, nourisher of everything, you who care for everything, make haste and act with all speed, for the night is growing cold." And this is to be done while burning Ethiopian cumin and the fat of a virgin she-goat, better if it's mottled. And be confident that it'll work, because with confidence in one's own strength, nothing is impossible, and for love to be attained, and achieved, and be fortunate, is not as complicated as they say: we're covered in skin and not lizard-scales, and skin must be there, I say, the better to feel what can be given to us, and to desire it again and again, for there's no true lover who wakes up sated in the morning.

3

It was one thing for the good women to be stunned by Livia's brazenness, and another quite different one to see how they reacted. They seemed like an army after the battle, all on fire to do something but not finding ammunition, or orders, or a chain of command, and when they couldn't find any of that or an enemy, but something had to be done, anything was better than standing around twiddling their thumbs. The most impetuous one, Carmiña, got ready to pick up the little girl, who, slippery as she still was, slipped out of her hands like a piece of soap and, slick as could be, slid all the way down the hall in the blink of an eye. It was lucky that Maruxa's cat, the neighbor's from next door, which had recently given birth, which accounted for the meowing they'd all been hearing, took her for another of her litter and settled down to lick her, because the truth is that the women didn't know how to deal with a newborn baby, with all its caul, and blood, and placenta, and the remains, in short, of the maternal entrails with which babies tend to be accompanied, and it was necessary to take care of her to turn her into a human being, one of those who look so comfortable in the cradle with their full little mouths and a pink cap with a pompom. With all their working and looking after themselves, they'd forgotten everything nature had granted them: they knew how to make cream puffs, and comment on television news, and iron, and correct division problems, and tell stories, and many other things, everything better than attending at births. If one of their forebears had lifted up her head and seen it, she wouldn't have believed it, but that's how it was and that's how it has to be told. And in this way the little girl entered life on Planet Earth, caressed by the raspy tongue of the neighbor's cat, which prepared her forever to be sensitive to the suffering of animals, besides leaving all her skin as soft as silk, except on her fingers, where the cat can't have gotten to, which were rough, dried out and cracked. And, even though Einés didn't realize it until she started to write her story, the prodigal maternalism of the cat gave her a personal seal: Einés could never be reserved and moderate, for from the first hour of her life, and ever after, she liked licking and warmth, the protection, in short, given by tenderness, and therefore she maintained an exuberant fondness for cats; it's said they don't recognize their owners, but they do recognize them, except when the owners don't deserve to be recognized and set apart from the undifferentiated crow, for cats have, just like Einés, who got it from them, a dreaming spirit and the urge to run around free. And so it was that Einés took on the knowledge of the cat, which knew how to provide as much as she needed, and just as well!, for Carmiña and Olaia had only ever seen babies in the women's section of magazines, for all their friends were single and virgins, needless to say. Even Dona Carme herself knew very little, because when she had given birth to the three of them, Grandma Aniceta had taken charge of doing whatever was necessary while she, propped up on pillows because it was so hard for her to sit up, sipped chicken broth through a straw which, when it's presented like that, is called "consommé" and is much more delicate, more appropriate for such occasions as the delivery of a baby. What Dona Carme did know, and she had no idea where she'd got it from, did she?, but she knew it by heart, was that what her daughter needed was an infusion of water pepper and cinquefoil, where in the world would she have gotten that from?, but she was sure about the good qualities of those herbs for new mothers, and also that it wasn't going to be so hard to get them, because even if there was no such thing in the store where they shopped, she thought she remembered something like that up in the attic, in the middle of a hundred strange things that they kept from an ancestor about whom they didn't know the slightest thing except that her name was Agnes, and that she was planning to go to America when she gave birth three months early and had to stay home. According to what had been passed down through whole generations, that ancestor who never did emigrate, as several of the women who came after her would do, had come a few years earlier from Holland, loaded down with a hutch in which she carried the fine sheets and the secrets of a white witch, for, in short... the fact is that in the chest upstairs there's a little sack, I don't know where I could know that from, I never stuck my hands in, the things of dead people give me the shivers, but it must be there, and while I go up I'm thinking about what I'm to say to this girl who's gone wrong on me...

While Dona Carme was going up to hide her discombobulation, Carmiña was like a crazy woman with the little girl; she'd always liked children so much! And look, her mother had devoted more money than usual to her studies, paying for her to become a teacher so she would have a way to support herself without getting married, since she had slated her to stay at home and take care of her in her old age. And Carmiña knew very well that that role was usually reserved for the youngest daughter in every family, but in this one, hers, that was impossible, because the littlest, Livia, today a mother, was a bit that way, a bit strange. In short, let's not say feeble-minded, or retarded, it wasn't that bad, but she was a little spacy; not completely clueless, but kind of thickheaded, naïve, childish, kind of odd, let's say, and of course, that worked just fine with marriage, that suited her "to a T," they all said. Who knows what they meant by that T, or if they simply figured that she'd be a docile wife, always contented and a bit out of it. On the other hand, Dona Carme thought, with those qualities Livia was not suited to looking after her even in old age, because having to take care of her own mother, Aniceta, who had been a formidable woman and now there she was, rocking in the rocking chair, had opened Dona Carme's eyes, once again simply Carme, who saw very well the troubles given by those who went gaga, and she judged, she who was pure resolve, that Livia would never be prepared and ready, as she herself was, according to what was fitting in that holy mission of honoring one's parents, especially when it was a matter of honoring her personally. In any event, Carmiña, being doubtfulness personified, seemed made for study, and Dona Carme, who was also a teacher, devoted time and effort to her training, so that the girl ended up as one of that generation of schoolteachers who at barely eighteen were out campaigning in the villages, putting up with cold, wiping noses and explaining things that were in the books that not even those who wrote the books understood, let alone when they were written in another language and therefore had something like a conversation with the Prime Minister, but there they said "Menister," because it was also very frequent, whether out of carelessness or as a joke, to say it that way. And Carmiña, designated to be the man of that house without men, with that sweet name, a name of Latin verse and holy mother, had to overcome her sorrow at the destiny imposed on her, and she cried every month over her bloodstained panties because, come on, so much pain, and so much filth, and so much discomfort that a woman has to put up with, and in the end… all that and never to have children, what a shame! However, since she didn't dare rebel against her mother, there was nothing for Carmiña to do but put up with her destiny with poor grace, getting her aggression out in any argument that came along and, not believing, she didn't even believe what was in the advertisements, which is saying something. In truth, rebelling against her mother, or not rebelling, I mean, was explicable, for Dona Carme was a matriarch of the old school; they say that her husband died with a smile on his lips at the thought that the eternal darkness was setting him free from enduring his wife, and perhaps his last words were: "I'm leaving her for you, allll of her for you," although this cannot be confirmed: people like to let their tongues wag, but, to be sure, even Dona Carme wouldn't have been surprised, the dead man had always had a mouth on him. To sum up, as soon as Carmiña saw the little girl, she felt that her sister, the little idiot, the innocent, the one with the out-of-it expression, had made a baby for her, and, happier than a cuckoo, she planted a pair of kisses on Livia's cheeks that almost did her in, because she could hardly stay up, crouched as she was on the carpet. Carmiña put her arms around her neck, put her to bed, washed her, pampered her and dressed her with all the maternal instinct she had always had inside, repressed, and now it was gushing out like an erupting volcano, or rather, like a glacier that was beginning to come down a mountainside after a thaw; comparisons of women with the behavior of nature deserve, most times, close attention, for a volcano's not the same as a glacier, nor Rosa the same as Lucía, no matter how much cameras insist on portraying all of us as if we were the same.

While Aniceta was rocking in her rocking chair, laughing her head off imagining the erotic escapades of her granddaughter, and Carme was rummaging in the hutch, and Livia was receiving the attentions of Carmiña, and Carmiña was discovering the hidden meaning of her existence in maternity by proxy as she imagined it, Olaia, standing in the doorway, was trying to make a rough sketch, following in this the advice read so often in magazines about women's work, "make a rough sketch so as not to get lost on this row of stitches, which is a little strange, you take a stitch to the right, make a knot, a pompom, one, two, three, four rows, a tiny stitch, knot," and if you don't make a sketch you'll get lost for sure, that's plain. Olaia's rough sketch included separating the baby from the cat, she couldn't deal with the two of them because they didn't want to separate after exchanging so much saliva, and next, chasing the cat away; that gesture didn't make those who saw it very happy, it was like throwing a wet-nurse out into the cold, and that's just not done, no matter how reasonable it may be. But Olaia was determined like that, because she knew how to play the piano and make cream puffs, and embroider like a nun of St. Clare, and make herself up without anyone noticing it, and show enough cleavage to please men's gaze without making it seem that she had any particular interest in erotic invitation. At the same time, Olaia knew how to revive a flagging conversation, keep up social relationships, get bored without anyone noticing, dance until she dropped and run a household, which is no small task, a house demands a mind with attention to detail, that's why patterns become so indispensable when you're at the tiller of this ship, the government of this country; for Olaia in her house was, as it seemed to her, the soul, while the others were something like the limbs. It never worried her in the slightest not to bring a dollar to the family treasury, anyone can make a dollar, the point is to be the soul and not some limb, a foot or a hand, they do the dirty work, not the spiritual work. In a word, from so much thinking of herself as indispensable, although destined to abandon the nest soon for the arms of an ideal husband, perfection personified, she governed the house until then like a general in command, at least when her mother let her; we would say that Dona Carme got the credit while Olaia did the work. And so then, it was Olaia who started doing what really had to be done, which was to find out how they could cope with this tense situation and such an important job; just exactly as if she were the boss of a business committee, she gathered them all in the room, with the mother and daughter, now clean and wrapped up, in the same bed, reconciling with each other after the fright they'd mutually given each other, in order to talk about the facts of life, for in that house without men such a thing had never been talked about. And there was an impossible obstacle, for Carmiña, as soon as they started talking about the Subject, for that's what they called talking about sex, they used to say "talking about the Subject," well, Carmiña in those solemn moments had an attack of nervous giggling, a bunny-laugh, just like steam escaping from a pressure-cooker on one side when the cover isn't on right and obviously you can't go on like that, she's like one of her pupils, and proud of it, eh?, yes, yes, I wanted to talk about honor, it makes me laugh, Mama, what am I going to do with her? Hush! After so many preambles nobody knew how to break the silence that ensued; silence is a fast-growing herb, it grows until it suffocates, especially if you're in a room full of women. The thing is that Livia, whom they were all looking at sidelong, wasn't saying anything, and she looked back at them with her eyes wide open, while old Aniceta flopped around in the rocking chair, singing in a reedy little voice: "I went off to the mill to grind, to the Barcelos mill," and Carme, Dona Carme, that mother so rigid and knowledgeable that they had, sat as if mute for a few moments, only to break down and cry, half hysterical, revealing what seemed to her to be the whole truth, to wit, that regarding love she knew only the name, that in her day these things were not talked about, and her Antón was a real man, one of those who never say what they're feeling. But since the exceptional situation in which they found themselves made it necessary, she was prepared to tell them something… such as it was, even though, definitely, she couldn't tell much about men, for so far as she knew, being the woman she was and more as a woman of education and reading, eh?, the matter of men was a topic still to be explored, a genuine *terra incognita* for science; they never let a word escape them about feelings and passions of the soul, much less during the execution of the Subject, so that she had done it with him, obviously, but what exactly she had done wasn't so very clear to her, it had all happened in a flash, she with her nightie pulled up, he'd pushed her down like that, somehow or other and for a few minutes, not many, she was feeling more like mares must feel when they've got a rider on top of them with his weight and his shoving than like the obscure object of desire that the novels of love told about, the kisses weren't burning, nor did their conjoined breaths make them faint, or anything, because that was a necessary action to have children, and that really was wanting! But enjoying, what you'd call enjoying, the Subject, she said very daintily, wrinkling her nose, only men like it, they're such brutes, that's well known. As is the fact that all decent women take advantage of that time to think about what they're going to serve for dinner the next day, and in the instant that the assault lasts everything is taken up with "I don't know, maybe lentils, oh, how nasty, or peas. Oh no, I didn't put them on to soak, better have rice, what? Are you done?"

The words of Dona Carme fell quite heavily on the room, producing a sense of discouragement and a more than considerable drop in amatory expectations. "Bleahh..." "Well, good grief, what a pain!! As much as I'd like to fool myself with enjoyment and experience an infinite ecstasy and..." "Girlll!" "Mama, that's the way it is, so that's the way it has to be said..." And Carmiña, always trying everyone's patience, blurted: "Well, I'd like for them to find my G-spot, they say it's the pleasure point that all of us have, and..." And right then Dona Carme had to step in: "If you all are like that, it doesn't surprise me that this has happened to us." When Livia managed to get a word in, for they weren't letting her talk, everybody knows that this one is a little naïve, yeah, yeah... she may be very naïve, but she knows more about it than Mama, chilllldddd! Things the way they are... when Livia managed to say something, I was saying, things really got so muddled up that even the one who invented this madhouse of a world wouldn't have understood them. Certainly Livia had been seen in the woodshed with Xanciño, the son of the pig-castrator, who had a face covered with acne and always wore his pants falling down. Still, they weren't doing anything wrong in the woodshed, sometimes it was equations and sometimes chemical formulas, not that those are good things, but they can't really have been what you'd call bad either, in the institute where they were both doing their fifth year of secondary school, with a more than deplorable academic record, those assignments were too habitual to think that they were what people were talking about when they said to them with silly looks on their faces: "And you two, you won't do anything bad? Huhh?" And, if she had to tell the whole truth, well of course she had to, we're never all right when you go keeping secrets, well, she'd never even seen any man the way she'd have to see him, if there is anything to see in men, at least dogs and horses did have something, and the latter for sure nice and big, and with a kind of red lance, not so many details, the rest of them aren't mothers! Poor Livia hadn't realized yet that at barely seventeen she had come to make up part of the category and class of mothers, which is a class made up of women who have known man, although the meaning of known here is hard to determine, in order to know man it's not enough to have seen him in more positions than the vertical, for, knowing that for women men are slippery, besides being inscrutable, begging your pardon, this business of knowing men is a well-nigh impossible task. And so, taking and talking, drinking chicken broth, she talks, she drinks, she drinks cinquefoil and water pepper, the hours went by and it was already late at night, Armstrong must have been all tucked up and sleeping in his space capsule, probably in a position different from the vertical, although not necessarily pleasurable, and in space everything's different, when they all found out. Livia finally said: "Unless it was that time…" and they all burst out: "What time?" For sure she's confessing now, and without any doubt that time was the time, that gentleman who was passing through, a traveling salesman or I don't know what… "Well, you all weren't at home. He wanted to see Mama, he was from the Ministry, or the Council, well, I don't know, he was from somewhere… He was there because of something with the school, I don't remember, he said everything really well, and he was so sure of himself, and I thought I had to invite him in, you know I never open the door for anybody, but this time I did. Grandma Aniceta was snoring in the rocking chair and I invited him to sit down and I went to make some raspberry tea, which I li-…" "Keep going!" "I'm going already. Well, the gentleman was really handsome, handsome as the devil…" "Keep going!" "I'm going already. I don't know how it was that we ended up on the carpet and he got on top of me, well, not on top, behind me, just like…" "Keep going!" "All right, all right, I'm going… The thing was that he was pushing a lot and I was a little scared, but with clothes on and everything, right? So I figured that way it wasn't a big deal and I didn't know what to say and…" "Keep going!" "Nothing, when he left I was all messy with him, with his smell on my legs… and higher up… And that's all. I thought he hadn't done anything…" When Livia finished her confession, Dona Carme wiped away a tear, Olaia said "son of a bitch" between her teeth, such a fine young lady had never said anything like that, and she went to cover up her sister, and Carmiña let fly with one of her clever remarks: "It's not so strange, just like Mama… and the Virgin Mary!… Don't look at me like that, none of them had a clue about any of it, right?"

4

Concerning what Einés found when she looked
in the chest in the attic
*Booklet of recipes for the Social Service, by Miss Olaia
Pereiro: Genuine factory-quality petit choux*

My sisters always say that I make cream puffs that are
out of this world. They really do turn out like factory-made
for me, and that's why I decided to write down the recipe
so that all of you, young women who, like me, are still
learning, may, when you found your own family, delight
your loved ones with these genuine delicacies. The dough
for cream puffs is easy to make and has multiple uses: in
cakes or doughnuts and in little Lyon-style pastries, which
allow a whole range of different fillings. The quantities I
give here are sufficient to prepare a dessert for six people.
First of all, pour into a pan one liter of water with 80
grams of cream or margarine, a half-teaspoon of salt and
another of sugar. Put it all on the heat and let it come to
a boil. Next, remove it from the heat and add 125 grams
of flour all at once. Stir vigorously until the dough comes
away from the sides and bottom of the pan. And here's a
little trick: you need to sift the flour first to get a lighter
and springier dough. Finally, add four eggs, one at a time,
not adding the second until the first is well incorporated
into the dough. And of course you know that for pastry
it's a must to reserve the freshest eggs available. Let the
paste rest for half an hour, and then you can put it in
the pastry bag and squeeze it out in little pastries on a
buttered baking sheet. Then put the baking sheet in the

oven, preheated to medium, for 35 or 40 minutes. When the time is up take the baking sheet out of the oven and let the shells cool. When they are cool, the time has come to split them in the middle and fill them with whipped cream, pastry cream, chocolate cream, angel's hair, or whatever you prefer. I always use meringue. To make it, you must beat the whites of two or three eggs very well with four tablespoons of white sugar, until you have a soft cream like a cloud but with a certain consistency, reminiscent of sea-foam and which pastry cooks call stiff peaks. Last, sift confectioner's sugar on top of them and arrange them on a pretty serving platter, covered with a cloth if you like. The good thing about cream puffs is that they are much like human beings: no two are the same. For those who love the French style, I will say that the varieties of presentation and tasting are many. They are called "profiteroles" when they are filled with a filling of vanilla or whipped cream and served with a hot chocolate sauce. Cream puffs filled with chocolate or pastry cream are called "éclairs." The Paris-Brest include sliced almonds in the dough, and, after baking, they are filled with a cream enriched with pralines. The most spectacular of the pastries made with cream puffs is the Saint-Honoré, a delicious cake consisting of a crown of cream puffs filled with pastry cream or whipped cream, stuck together with little threads of liquid caramel on a base of *pâte brisée*. The center is filled with pastry cream enhanced with a little cognac and thickened with a good meringue. No man can resist so much sweetness; therefore, being good pastry cooks will make you great conquerors—the way to a man's heart is through his stomach, or so they say. You can do anything, my daughters, except fry the cream-puff dough; in that case you have that nasty dessert, pure grease, so popular with tasteless folks, which people in Madrid love, they call them fritters. A young lady will make cream puffs, and with moderation, for even sweetness should not be overdone; therefore they should be given their natural name, cream puffs, without pretending to be a Frenchwoman, as some snobs do, saying "*petit choux*;" some people are just so clever that they make themselves hated.

5

The Livia incident, if that name may be given to the unexplained, to what never happened because it was never acknowledged as anything, had no consequences other than the birth of the little girl; in fact, not even the body of the mother had changed, and her waist continued to be, and had been during the nine months when she was carrying her, as slim as human anatomy allows. The Livia incident, if the mysterious may be called thus, what happens inside the body without asking the mind for explanations, did not have, I was saying, any consequences other than the birth of the little girl, for she was like that for a long time, being called "the little girl" for lack of agreement on a name to give her. There were partisans of following family tradition and calling her Carme, this time Carmelita or Carmela to avoid confusion, and there were also those who preferred for her to be called Branca, or Clara, or Alba, so that it would be quite clear to anyone that the honor of the virgins of the house had not been compromised by the matter, for they were all virgins there, even, practically speaking, Dona Carme, with her three births not meaning to do it. Or, if one has to be absolutely precise, they were all virgins except Great-Grandma Aniceta, who went wild with naughty songs that made the rest of them blush while she rocked back and forth in her rocking chair. Moreover, the question of the name was insignificant—they all had a dozen ways of addressing the little child: they called her "half almond" and "little bit" and "little rosebud," and, especially, "girl." And it could very well have stayed that way, with a whole series of manners in which she could be referred to, if the curate hadn't intervened, Don Fidel, what a bore, who showed up at yonder house, which was on the weavers' street, after crossing the bridge, and had to walk a long way from the church, to ask them questions about the way they were living and invite them to reflect on what they were planning to do with the little girl. Such nerve was unheard of, and on top of that from a man in a skirt; they listened to him going on and on and, with a wink, served him strawberry tea, and, open and chatty as they were, they told him all the details of a whole string of missteps and sins, so that Don Fidel left the house scandalized, and had to confess a hundred times the evil thoughts and the impure acts that he ended up committing because he couldn't get out of his mind the images that a pair of virgins and another pair of mothers who practically had never known a man had depicted for him with so much vividness regarding the pleasure they took in supposed sinful living; hot stuff like that was unheard of. All joking aside, even though good old Don Fidel was never the same again after drinking that strawberry tea, the little girl was baptized the next Sunday, in the outfit inherited from her mother, who had been the last of the previous generation, well washed and well dried in the sun to get rid of the smells of storage, a bit camphorous and musty, that it had; even though they didn't live in a city with canals, the climate was as humid as if they had built a house in the clouds; the valley they lived in, every morning from October to May, dawned in a fog as dense as petit-choux meringue, as proud as a modern bridal gown, as unreal as the sadness in all the shades of white. And for that day, the baptismal day, they all got out their Sunday heels and bought sheer stockings, not the beige ones they wore every day, except for Livia, who, once she remembered the incident that had made her a mother, never again took off her panty hose even to sleep, because at least panty hose allow the situation to be controlled, and in this she went along with several judges who in the following years decreed, like the sailors who took the philosopher to Stockholm, that bloomers or panty hose could not be removed except with feminine collaboration, that's plain, even with the possibility that she might change her mind, the woman was playing her part by undressing. So then, the little girl all starched, the women with heels and stockings, or panty hose that allowed control of masculine access, all went to the church. And there Don Fidel welcomed them, happy that his preaching had produced results, despite being a bit drowsy, for the wild dreams that were shaking him up didn't let him get a wink of sleep, and already during the Mass he couldn't concentrate and couldn't stop staring at those exceedingly chaste women, without being able to believe what they themselves had told him, and look, I can't question it, if I start doubting the confessions of sinners and imagining that they're all stories made up to drive me crazy, I'll have to talk to the bishop and take off for the missions. When Don Fidel, we were saying, during the Mass, a bit drowsy, asked Carmiña, who was the godmother, what the chubby little eight-month-old who was waiting all swaddled up on the font was going to be named, because it was high time the little girl was baptized, as those in attendance were saying, Carmiña held the little girl against her neck and allowed her, as she supported herself well, to hold her little hands out to the curate, have a good laugh, with a smile that came from her belly, while she herself, "ta-ta-ta," supplied the melody for the voice of her mother, who, from the bench on the side, said very seriously: "Einés Andrade." The curate was at the point of ripping off his cassock, his alb, and even his shirt, and hanging them up high: that was no name or anything like a name, but he controlled himself and, mouthy as he was, for before the seminary he had already been in the hands of his uncle, the Jesuit, who had taught him thoroughly to keep his emotions in check, said: "My dear, do you mean 'María-something'?" And Livia, whom they had all always thought was half-witted because she liked to look at the world at a pace different from the hurry that everyone else was in, answered very cleverly: "María nothing, Father, I'm enough of a María all by myself." And the curate swallowed the saliva that he tended to spew at the faces of his parishioners, and asked her very calmly: "And so what do you say her name is?" "Einés Andrade." And the curate stepped away a little to prevent everyone from hearing him, and said: "That Einés, isn't it a bit fancy? Shouldn't it be Inés?" "No, Einés is the right form," Livia replied, very sure of herself. "Very well then, she'll be Einés. "No, Father, she'll be Einés Andrade, since no man is going to acknowledge her as his, her aunts decided to give her a surname as a baptismal present. And since we always liked Pontedeume and the tower of the Andrades, that's the one they picked… So, Father, just like there are those named Ana Isabel or Luísa Fernanda, my little girl is going to be named Einés Andrade, and then she'll have my last name, which is Pereiro, as you already know." Don Fidel lifted his hands towards the sky and, with a look on his face that would make people feel sorry for him, said:

"I offer this prayer to you, o Lord, for with the three vows, and my commitment to the community, I already had enough to cope with, but to make me the only sane person in a parish of madmen, loons, nuts, crazies, neurotics, dreamers, fanatics, illuminati, fruitcakes, birdbrains and maniacs, that goes beyond the capacities of this poor sinner." Immediately afterwards, Don Fidel officiated at the baptism with all the rigor of a professional in the area and, without even waiting to take the collection from the cap that served him so well, once he had dispensed the sacrament, he took off, it's said to Peru, to enroll in the ranks of liberation theology, skeptical about Rome and its rites, liberated, hating the cassock, the tonsure and the dog-collar, dressed in blue jeans, in brotherhood with the rest of humanity and in the grips of a long-suppressed hunger for concupiscent passions, convinced, at last, that one must render unto the body what belongs to the body and put off the business of the soul for the last gasps, a moment at which one could get the greatest benefit from such an abstract and complicated concept.

6

Concerning what Einés found when she looked
in the chest in the attic
Poetical diary of Einés Andrade

Poem X

The mirror I look into sends back a stranger's face.
She—for that can't be me—
dances, smiles, shakes, looks at me.
The mirror I look into shows me her hair,
her hands, her urge to be
and she—for that can't be me—
is startled and surprised to be there naked.
I look at her laughing.
She doesn't know that she's just vanished
and that she'll never come again.

7

When Livia made her statement, she cited as the guilty party a man from outside, from the Ministry or some other place, so imprecisely that it would turn out to be impossible to recognize him or go and seek him. What's certain is that nobody that October afternoon saw a stranger walking along the weavers' street, let alone show up at the little house of the Pereiros, as all the neighbors called them. On the other hand, imagining a bureaucrat or a publisher's book representative as somebody, God pardon us for evil thoughts, capable of abusing a poor young thing in her own house was difficult and a bit of a stretch; it left room for doubt. The clean-thinking minds supposed therefore that Livia was covering for someone, Xanciño perhaps, or some other man she knew, and here the word had fewer naughty connotations than usual. But once her movements had been nosed into, and well nosed, the pertinent investigations made, once the matter had been rummaged through and studied from all imaginable angles, once the ancestral rites of shoving one's nose into other people's dens to look for ways of condemning other people's conduct had been carried out, nothing could be seen that made her seem suspect. It was strange, on the other hand, that she hadn't been affected, as the rape victim it was supposed she was; she never seemed bitter towards men, showed no fear or urge for justice; this invited the hypothesis that she didn't want to betray someone who had been warmly welcomed in her body. But she didn't show any symptoms of love either, of a crush or even a hankering, and even worse, she behaved in the following years like someone who had never enjoyed, participated in, or lived through a carnal experience of any kind. So everyone ended up convinced that some magical event had taken place that October afternoon; it was supposed that it was October because Einés was born in July, although she could also have been a seven-months-baby. And the nature and essence of Einés harked back, forever and ever, in the collective memory of her contemporaries, to an inexplicable event, one of those it's not wise to look at too closely. If Armstrong had set his feet on the Moon, it was no big deal that a woman should give birth without pain and conceive without masculine intervention, at least nothing clear-cut, they're shooting so many things into the atmosphere, an off-course sperm cell could just as well have gone where it wasn't expected, because to tell the truth, sperm cells are rarely given much of a welcome, poor things. That was a question of no importance; the really outstanding fact was that the little girl was born, and born healthy, and kind of pretty, and the mother matured because of being the main character of the drama; she swore to her sisters and even her very own mother Dona Carme that virginity was too heavy a load and they should all sleep with whoever seemed best to them and not be too long about it, for the body was made to be a body and not to be a spiritual reserve for nowhere, which left them all with their eyes wide open, her defense of free love, since she had started with maternity to be a formidable woman and had left behind forever the naïveté that had made her seem half-witted, because she had never been a fool.

For, with the incident that never happened, she became the first, including Dona Carme, to lose her virginity body and soul, except of course Great-Grandma Aniceta, for she had had the good luck to belong to that class of women who, instead of thinking about putting the lentils on to soak, think about how to keep sneaking out to the mill to keep rolling around for a lifetime, snuggled in with the warmth of good companionship.

8

Concerning what Einés found when she looked
in the chest in the attic
Poetical diary of Einés Andrade

Poem XI

Build a stone wall between us.
Make a house wall.
Construct a partition, a garden wall, a lattice, a fence.
Put in clay tiles, stones, hard cement, wood, steel.
Cover yourself up.
I'll turn the fences into doors,
the walls to windows,
I'll flow between the seams, the cracks, the fissures
        in the chimney
and, whenever you're not looking,
I'll filter into your dreams
and in your dreams tear all the barriers down
so you can't get away from me.

9

It might have been because man made it to the Moon, or because that summer when Einés was born a hot breeze blew that turned them all into pure sleep, but the fact is that, from then on, they were somewhat petrified and stopped being people of the normal kind; they exist, all in a row, and really they don't matter to anybody, look, go figure, how many of them die every day without attracting the attention of the rest of the world, only to acquire the renown of heroines of tragedy or mythology—of the women, in short, portrayed in art and turned into archetypes. Einés herself never behaved like a normal person. While all of them were arguing about the name to give the little rose, the little bit, the little girl, she climbed up to the attic, crawling on hands and knees, and she smelled something there that smelled of something burning, of mother-of-thyme, of wild rose, of cinnamon, of vanilla, of chocolate, of mint, of thyme, of horehound, of, in short, more smells than could be counted and beyond those recognizable by a baby still crawling around naked, above all, sniff sniff, the air smelled of raspberries. On the way back from the excursion, tippity tippity, on all fours, the little girl kept saying "Ag-nes, Ag-nes" or something like that. Her mother, perceiving a burst of light, an otherworldly something in the air, and it wasn't surprising that she noticed it with so much scent, and as sensitive as she was before that to unexpected and supernatural events, went up the stairs towards the attic. And there she encountered a cloud of rose and lilac, and also the open hutch, and some papers scattered on the floor. She quickly gathered them up and put them back, not without first noticing that there were, among other things that she didn't dare look at, because she didn't want to be in that magical place any longer than necessary, for prudence was acting on her, she realized, I was saying, that in there were the papers of the ancestor named Agnes, who had been, according to what she'd put in the notebook, the daughter or adopted daughter of a white witch of Amsterdam, one Hélène Jans, and she couldn't see anything else, she was a bundle of nerves. And she went back down the stairs as fast as she could and got to the kitchen panting and asked: "What kind of a name is Agnes?" And Carmiña, the most widely read, replied: "That's a French name. Here we say Inés." "Not Inés, Einés," corrected Olaia, who was the queen of precision. "Well, the little girl's going to be named Einés." And for a fact some magical power had watched over the house that afternoon because, for once, nobody had anything to jabber. Nevertheless, the matter of the name had still not been completely resolved; a day or two afterwards, Livia was to experience one of the most exciting moments of her life. This insignificant and almost half-witted girl had acquired great importance since the magical events, or just unexpected ones, had put her in the role of protagonist. She was folding clothes, because Livia, like so many women, was going to be caught folding clothes by almost all the important things in life, it seems that that never happens, but a woman spends many and decisive moments in the history of mankind folding clothes, not like Armstrong, they must give him his all dry and folded up just so in NASA. And her sisters came to her and started saying look, the little girl, if she's given the last name Pereiro, just like that, well, that's like saying that she didn't have a father and that's not… and another would interrupt, she means what's the point of having to explain to everybody about where she came from, and excuse me a moment for interrupting you, the first one rejoined, but she has nothing to hide, most of us didn't come to this world because we were called, but rather because it just happens, and please understand, it's not that we're ashamed of you, Livia, you're quite honorable, but sometimes children of unmarried girls… in short, why should she suffer for it, Livia got fed up with all the hors-d'oeuvres and ordered the main course: "What do you all have in mind?" Well, it had occurred to them that, as a second name, the little girl could have one that resembled a surname. "A surname as a given name?" A surname that sounded glorious and illustrious, it had to be a surname that was musical and pretty to hear, a noble surname, fitting and virile, look, in spite of everything that happened to you, men are a good thing, there are some who pay attention to the words spoken to them, and some as tender as cats, and affectionate, besides being intelligent and gentlemanly! And generous! Ad one after another, they recited the thousand names of the male… "Well, after all that defense, I feel like getting an operation and becoming a man," Livia retorted, that girl, ever since she became a mother she's become sharp as a tack, and they all shared a good laugh, belly-laughs, they ended up taking down the sheets and towels, still damp, they were really heavy like that, to wrap around themselves and wave around over their bodies, and the one who dropped the ball suffered the attacks of the others, they tickled and pinched. "So you want to be a man, do you?" "Yeahh, what about it?" and the tickling kept increasing until the victim begged for mercy, "no, I don't want to," a moment that another took advantage of to yell "I do, I want to be a maaan" and the other two hurled themselves on her. And the game continued until they were worn out, and the clotheslines were empty of towels and sheets; the battle ended then, and all of them lay panting on the patio in the middle of a heap of white laundry that would have to be washed again so that Mama wouldn't see the damage. And at that point Livia, with the little bit of voice she had left, gasped: "And what's the surname you all thought of for Einés?" "Andrade." "Andrade?" "Yes." And Carmiña, the educated one, who liked languages and etymologies, even if they were false ones, added important information: "It must mean 'man' in Greek." And Livia, "And what do we want the little girl to carry around something of men for?" "Well, because men say that we're talkative, trouble-making, suspicious, wishy-washy and timid… May the little girl be firm, calm, sincere, strong and bold like a man… we'll teach her the virtues of women, that's why we all have them." The choir fell to pieces laughing and, as we know, the little girl was named Einés Andrade.

10

Concerning what Einés found when she looked
in the chest in the attic
From the poetical (?) diary of Einés Andrade

My name is Einés Andrade. I'm one meter seventy-two tall and I weigh fifty-six kilos. I wear glasses. I like graph paper, place names, cheese, trees, Magritte's painting, cats, the color green, puzzles, swimming, cherry trees when they bloom, rummaging around in bookstores, shooting stars, Chinese movies, Humphrey Bogart movies, water, having time, Stockholm, wine, kisses, bursting out laughing until my stomach hurts, mist, computers, the poetry of Rilke and Sicart, jazz, thoroughly cleaning and organizing closets, conversations with sharp and fast repartee, strawberries, wind, utopia... I detest anecdotes where you had to be there, the pimples that sometimes come out on my face, rice pudding, men with moustaches, offhand opinions, clichés that get repeated until you end up thinking they're true, people who ask the second question before you've replied to the first one, plastic flowers, high-heeled shoes, pornography, chewing gum, weddings, first communions, traffic accidents, domestic violence, savage violence, hit songs, songs that can't be hummed, Christmas, eucalyptus trees, accepting what people say without wondering about it. Period; new paragraph.

I'm twenty-seven, the age of disillusionment; I've always heard it was a difficult age. I've spent five long years working on a doctoral thesis about Descartes, a seventeenth-century French philosopher I liked a lot when I was doing my coursework. Nowadays he has nothing to say to me. I don't believe that Descartes liked cats, which makes our relationship tenser. I'm white and heterosexual, although the hetero men persist in leaving me alone and bored. Up till now I've had, more or less seriously, three and a half boyfriends, and I don't plan to have any more. That doesn't mean I'm not in love, I am, although I won't tell even you, dear diary, who it is, it's better for no one to know, not even him; in any case it'd turn out badly for me, as always. Besides, it doesn't matter whether it turns out badly or well, the big thing about love is feeling it.

11

Einés was raised in a house that everybody called yonder house, because it was on the bank of the river across from the station, which was the hub of the town. She was raised amid more mothers than she needed and with no known father. But that didn't make her fearful of or resentful towards the opposite sex, let's not think that because it was a house of women men never entered there; the generation before hers was made up of women quite interesting enough for a whole regiment of men to hang around them. Whether that happened or not has nothing to do with this tale; it's not a matter of establishing what happened in yonder house, but rather of telling how Einés's story was intermingled, blended and interwoven with that of other women who preceded her. The fact is that she was raised in freedom, secure, with a warm full tummy, short pants that were called "minishorts" in those days and a ribbon on her head. And the most faithful chronicler of this history knows very well that minishorts, provocative and alternative as they were, don't go with wide ribbons, that really long kind that look like they've been ironed with a potato fork, but if that's the way it was, how else can one go about telling it? Besides the fact that in yonder house the majority of things didn't match and normal life, everyday life, got more and more full of contradictions, incoherencies, nonsense and mix-ups; in this it could be noted that the little house yonder was a real place and not the sickly invention of the mind of a poet. If one starts making things up, one might as well invent a nice orderly little world, neat and pretty, don't go inventing a chaos, if we want chaos we're well supplied by real life, we don't need to read about it. Returning to Einés, she showed herself from the beginning of her career to be a clever girl, loving reading and eating, rascally. She drove them all crazy, as well as those who visited the house, but she bewitched them with that charm of a little madcap, a freewheeler, a wild child, a witch. And as she was clever, they ended up pulling out her report cards and diplomas for anyone who stopped by, for any chance visitor ought to be amazed by Einés's progress, that's why she was the little darling of the house, and anyone who didn't want to give her some praise shouldn't go to yonder house, they never called for anyone so loutish, and that's that. As the years went by, Einés learned to swim, ride a scooter, enchant, to do cross stitch by spending a little time with Aunt Olaia, who got talkative when she was doing needlework, to make cream puffs even if she never tasted them, to listen, to go get herbs for a cold, to speak English and Swahili, when she hooked up with a cooperative young fellow in Africa, she learned so many things, and she did all of them so well that her mother and her aunts stopped having any objective in the world other than bragging about Einés's prowess. And she must have been quite a girl, because not even all that made her a fool. Regarding more hidden intimacies, Einés wasn't beautiful but, since she had a certain something, or two, there was no shortage of young fellows to follow her around; they obliged Livia to lecture her, for lectures, it's well known, are the job of mothers. "You have to be very careful, honey, we women of feeling don't have to do anything to get pregnant," for Livia had finally come to terms with her adventure through that myth of "feeling," according to which there are some people whose feelings overflow so much that everything they plant takes root, which for sure is very accurate for tasks in the garden but in this day and age nobody can believe in such a thing regarding human conception, or can someone? Einés herself had to say: "Maaaaama, don't be ridiculous." "I'm not being ridiculous, that's the way it is, you can walk by a man in the hall… and pow! That's all it takes." "Okay, okay, don't worry." And Aunt Carmiña horned in, agitated and curious: "And so in Santiago, don't boys go into girls' apartments?" And Einés couldn't resist and had to play. "Yes, they do, Auntie, but they go straight to the bedroom and never walk by each other in the hall, so I think there can't be any danger." And Einés laughed a wild laugh, which seemed to come from her belly, and made her pull her hair back; the older generation never liked to see the way Einés laughed, for on top of having a horse-laugh that was not very refined, inappropriate for a young lady like her, this girl was going to get wrinkles very early, she didn't show any moderation in her gestures. Livia used to say this to anybody, ever since the incident she had been too preoccupied with refinement, a *je ne sais quoi* like always being clean and impeccably turned out, which showed through in the intensity with which she devoted herself to crochet, specifically to that work with very fine yarn called "*frivolité*"—just as well that they used lots of nice French words but without paying attention to the original meaning of the words, for if they sat down and thought about what that "*frivolité*" meant they'd throw out their work just like that and start doing crosswords, which would be worse, and less artistic. However, since Livia had spent, when this conversation took place, twenty-odd years refining her skills in that *frivolité*, the house was already decorated. And that's considering that it was an old-fashioned house, with an abundance of rooms and built without measuring the millimeters, for while there are still bricks there's still energy. The curtains were covered with frivolities, the swags and the frames of the blinds, the TV set with its little doily, the armchairs, the bottles on the table at mealtimes and the water jug. The cats that Einés adopted from time to time had jackets of *frivolité*, the lampshades, the coasters, the place mats, the ashtray mats, the armrest mats and the everything mats were, obviously, of *frivolité*. And the strange part is that all that *frivolité* would go well in a lordly English house, not in that little "keeping-up-appearances" house, especially coming from the hands of a certain single mother who had never known a man, at least not with causal knowledge (ay! Is that what it's called now?), who spent the day, while she was making *frivolité*, listening to the music of Janis Joplin and Joan Baez, anyone who saw it wouldn't believe it, that with those musical tastes that *frivolité* didn't strike her as at all ridiculous, but, not being married, what could I do that would be as gratifying as those weekly arguments that I see in the marriages of my friends? Only *frivolité*. Besides, *frivolité* is so soothing! For in yonder house they looked closely at whether activities were soothing or exciting, and they appreciated the first kind above any other possibility. Decidedly, *frivolité* was soothing, at least as much as housecleaning. All of them, Einés included, liked thoroughly cleaning the windows and the floor, "it's really, really soothing," just like doing complicated manual tasks, from the *frivolité* or Camariñas lace to genuine knitting, woolen tapestries, or puzzles of eight thousand pieces, so that anyone would say they saw themselves as dangerous volcanoes, always about to erupt, volcanoes in need of a short course in relaxation techniques. Or not exactly... not like volcanoes, maybe like hurricanes, that's why crazy winds have women's names. Or, so as to achieve the exactitude required in a chronicle, they saw themselves as if they were glaciers which, with the first rays of the springtime sun, were beginning to melt and slide down the mountainside. But back to where we were, the recommendations of the mother-virgin-incautious woman to her daughter, who was no longer a virgin or incautious, as tends to happen in these cases. Einés had her own romantic problems, different from contraception, and hard to fix, even helping herself as she did with witchcraft. It all started with her incursion into the attic, not the one she made when she was seven or eight months old, for once they named her nobody remembered Einés's upstairs escapade again. But since emotions are treacherous, and it'll be just too bad if what motivated you once doesn't get you excited again, for we human beings are like that, always tripping over the same rock, it happened that when Einés was seven or eight years old, she read in a nature book that all creatures proceeded, in a long and exceedingly remote series, from others, and thus we humans came from monkeys, which in their turn came from a mammal similar to a rodent, which had fled to the trees from the ground, and earlier had learned to walk like a half-lizard from the time of its dwelling in the water, for we all came from the water, from those waters that definitely will not come again, so that it shouldn't be surprising that many humans still have fish-eyes, for our line comes from aquatic vertebrates, our line which is famous for that poppycock of distinguishing itself from the rest of the vertebrates by calling itself rational. When Einés had assimilated this information, she took it as literally as she had previously taken the creation of species one by one by divine mandate and, quick and rascally as she was, she asked if Great-Grandma Aniceta was a monkey. Great-Grandma Aniceta wasn't even offended, for she only gave importance to really important things, but Dona Carme grumbled a lot, and scowled, and clapped her hands to her head, and blessed all the saints and sang of the woes of this house, oh, my God, how are we educating this child. In consequence, Einés was punished, for Dona Carme was a creationist, or the next thing to it, and as such she believed that Adam had been molded out of clay and Eve made out of one of Adam's ribs, and point by point she believed everything that appeared in the Bible, for the concept of interpretation had not entered even remotely into her vocabulary. Thus Einés was punished by having to eat a dish of rice pudding, which makes one grow, and to reflect for a while in the attic, up there with the mice, let's see if you'll think a little next time before you get into it with your elders. And Einés, obedient, with white perlé socks with little pinholes, pin pin pin, and also a pompom or tassel hanging from the garters that held them to her legs, climbed every step of the stairs bawling her eyes out, for they had never punished her so severely, she'd only been in the attic in her mother's arms for a second; soon she was coughing with all the dust up there, that filthy attic where they kept everything that had come down to them from previous generations from the days of old, seemed like a world in miniature. Einés settled down in a corner, close to the stairway in case she had to hurry down in a fright; her eyes fell upon a large hutch, of chestnut, rather like a sailor's sea-chest, and she felt strangely attracted to it. She got up and went over there, and, as her steps advanced and she neared the hutch, as though hypnotized, the attic, damned attic, which always smelled of mold and damp, and of cat piss, and of mouse turds, and of bat's nests, and of fear, and of times gone by, and of dead people who are not dreaming of resurrection, and of passions now over and done with because the impassioned people are sleeping in their coffins, that same attic erupted in scents, it smelled of lemon and thyme, of India tea, of mint, of green pepper, of marjoram, of rainwater, of sighs, of eucalyptus, of sesame, of linden, of quince, of passing sorrows that can be fixed, of dew, of music, of mother-of-thyme, of wild rose, of homesickness, of the fight for a little girl in memory, of lemon balm, of fennel, of dill, of laughter that comes from the belly, of cares, of nice thick stew, of tarragon, of sorrel, of parsley, of that kiss you dreamed of and never dared to give him, of old books, of new books, of ink, of wild strawberry, of licorice, of sea buckthorn, of very satisfied skin, well caressed and well licked, of nettles, of restharrow, of clover, it smelled of so many things that Einés was frantic at not being able to name them, of pimpernel, of sheep's tongue, she didn't know how to recognize as many sensations as were crowding into her brain, of primrose, of valerian, of nasturtium, of peppermint, and it would have been impossible if she'd tried to explain, of lemon beebrush, of someone who had never heard anything of the sort, of knotweed, of bentgrass, of the way the attic smelled today. It had a certain sweetness that awakened the senses, of hogweed, of carnation, and elevated them to the highest degree of pleasure, of cinnamon, of millefoil, of cumin, and Einés couldn't stop plunging into the aroma, of elderberry, of hollyhock, of agrimony, and she was caught in a kind of ecstasy, of coriander, of buckwheat, of a wild sensation, of fennel, which resembled death closely... of gooseberry, of alder buckthorn, of sloe, one more time it awakens curiosity, of flax, of lovage, knowing that there was something in the chest that smelled of marigold, of borage, of lees, she couldn't stop, she realized that those aromas had been there waiting for her, with the deep smells of myrtle, of mistletoe, of verbena, to explain to her what her purpose in life was. When she managed to recover from the convulsion, she went sniff, sniff again, and that was her downfall, because from then on she would seek in the caresses of her lovers what she had felt in that moment through her nose, in spite of the sad outcomes that kept happening, of feeling passions with her body too and not just with her soul, for her body had never done anything bad to her such that she would have to repress it. And the fact is that, sniff sniff, stronger than any other sensory evidence, she had just been invaded by the incredible raspberry perfume of Hélène's house.

And that was the genuine act of knowing; Einés rummaged in the hutch, and rummaged, and rummaging, she found hundreds of things: love potions, so that love will be born and so that it will last, some of them very useful and interesting, remedies for treating the lungs and so that children will grow up nice and plump, recipes with which to make hand creams and heavily scented ointments, besides powders to dry tears and clear the vision, and unexpected things, such as fragments of diaries in French, moral writings by a certain Kristina or Christina, it wasn't always spelled the same way, and, the most astonishing, also there waiting for her were certain poems that she herself would write one day, they appeared there with titles and everything, and with notes as to how many lines and how many words they would have, even though the exact words hadn't been set down. And from that visit onward, Einés, who was a woman marked by mystery from her birth, who lived in a house of half-crazy and unreal-seeming women, who desperately loved tenderness and cats, was destined forever to write, and to practice with determination the very literary art of witchcraft, for so much information wasn't going to waste.

12

Concerning what Einés found when she looked
in the chest in the attic
The secret papers of Hélène Jans:
The occult powers of stones

In spite of being considered an art and invention of evil witches, the recognition of the powers hidden in stones can be very useful to anyone who may have ailments that can't be cured by other means. And although herbs, not stones, are the main thing in my science, I have a small catalogue which perhaps some other woman may wish to take further, and from here I encourage her and cheer her on, because good works go better if they're well finished. And here they are:

The *himeneira* is a stone colored red and green, which emits rays as if it were a mirror placed in full sun. It's said that it comes from Arabia but the people of that land hate it so much that they don't want it to set in rings, nor do they make use of it in any other way, although it's a beautiful stone; rather, they send it far away to be sold, in other lands where it's unknown, and where it's quickly bought because of its great beauty. Its virtue is such that anyone who carries it will forget everything he has to do, without anything coming properly to his mind while he has the stone with him, for which reason it's very useful for those who wish to practice evil arts, since with it they can leave anybody without a past, for he will never remember anything that's happened. But it has another virtue: women use it when they want to make their bodies look especially good, because, if they take its powder, moistening it with something wet, and put it in the vulva, those who are not virgins will be restored and, if they dust their skin with this powder, avoiding letting it enter the mouth and nose, this stone tightens them up considerably and prepares them in such a way that their lovers receive new pleasure with them.

The *marata* is one of the varieties of meerschaum. It is found, shaped like the moon, in the water near the shores of the land called Gallaecia, and it's brown in color. Mixed with a little wine and served as a drink, it alleviates dropsy and the ailments of the liver and spleen. When burned, it becomes a paste, good for the disease they call alopecia, when all the hair falls out of the head, and also the scabies that comes with dampness.

The *timbaino* is a yellow and green stone, like the eyes of certain persons, which has such virtue that whoever carries it is protected from all the diseases caused by melancholy, for it drives them away, strengthening the heart and making it glad. And it even has one more property, related to the previous one, for if a man looks at it every morning, it improves his eyesight, and comforts his spirit, and brings him joy.

The *fada das lagoas* is a stone of an intense blue that hypnotizes men and beasts. If such a stone, even a little one, is placed at the head of a man's bed, he will never be able to turn his eyes away from the first thing he sees in the morning, until this is taken out of his sight, or covered with a cloth or some other thing. You'll see from that that its application is very interesting in cases of surly and loutish lovers; you have only to appear before their eyes after putting it in the bed so that they won't be able to pay attention to anything but you.

Regarding the *tarmicón* I will say nothing, or almost nothing; it's a yellow stone which should be divided into small pieces that can be placed under the tongue; its only effect is similar to that of the herb called hops, and, since with this stone in his mouth the man sees that his amatory powers do not diminish or weaken, *tarmicón* should be used sparingly, for lascivious men would abuse women a great deal if they knew about it, and it will be better for women to administer it to their lovers who have proved deserving of maintaining in prolonged fashion such a good disposition to give unto the body that which is the body's.

13

That morning Einés was in the fellows' office at the School of Philosophy, seated in front of the computer again. She had a yellow pencil behind her ear, which already showed a bad attitude towards the work, because at the keyboard no pencils are needed at all, and, if you're going to take notes, you need paper, not a keyboard. Einés was thinking that even if she had all the *tarmicón* in the world, it would do her no good; she shouldn't give it to the one she would like, because for sure he'd use it with the other woman. Definitely Einés was gloomy and catty as never before, trying to work without concentrating, writing poems on the back of her notes regarding the recent proceedings of a conference on Rationalism in Philosophy, when she received that e-mail from her thesis director, the eminent professor, famous as a smooth talker and for his magnificent amatory availability, Miguel Valdés.

14

Concerning what Einés found when she looked
in the chest in the attic
Recovering our history. Published three times yearly,
May 1996: Aniceta Vilamelle

Aniceta Vilamelle was born in Pontecachelos on
October 22, 1898 to a seafaring family. Around the middle
of 1906, at eight years of age, she emigrated to Cuba
with her parents. Her father, who had found work as a
sailor in the Caribbean island, died a few months later
in a shipwreck. Her mother would have to fend for the
five children she already had, washing and ironing and,
from that day onwards, Aniceta would have to help her in
these labors and in supporting and caring for the family.
Still, she managed to complete her primary education in a
convent school in the Casablanca neighborhood in Havana,
attending evening classes. In 1915 she married Fernando
Botana, also a sailor and Galician immigrant. At the time
both of them participated actively in political struggles.
Between 1916 and 1918 Aniceta had three children: two
sons, Lois (1916) and Ramón (1918), and one daughter,
Carme (1917). These were hard years for Aniceta, who
endured the difficult economic situation, along with the
atmosphere of instability and political persecution of the
Machado government. In such a complicated situation,
Aniceta found herself one day helpless in the face of the
continual squandering of her husband, more addicted to
the taverns and the bordellos than to his family, and with
her three children she returned to Galicia. All traces of her
are lost for some time; probably she sought refuge in the

family home in Pontecachelos; but in 1926 she appears working in a well-known cannery in Vigo. Her experience in union battles and politics during her time in Cuba soon led to her being named as director of the Union of Cannery Workers, and to her carrying out committed and very active political work in the following years. Aniceta Vilamelle, a tireless negotiator, succeeded in getting the women in the cannery the same salary as the men. As she herself tells in an interview with the daily *Worker's World* of Madrid: "In those days, the owners argued that the pay of a worker included what the man needed for his own support and also his family's, while women were earning only to supplement, as they put it, to buy clothes to go to Mass... Those were difficult times... A man couldn't stand to bring home less money than his wife... so even the comrades in the unions were split into two camps... Nobody wanted to change that situation." In a struggle that can still be followed in the archives, the female cannery workers of that era succeeded in dignifying the role of female workers. They also insisted that the canners were transferring fish from some factories to others, defending themselves by saying that the profits were larger in some areas, when in reality the reason was only a mercantile strategy: the women of the smaller population centers were willing to work for less money, and indeed many of the milkmaids who came down from the villages to sell milk ended up staying to work in the canneries for a pittance. On the personal level, Aniceta raised her three children during those years with joy and dedication and she was said to have an occasional love affair in the business committees. In 1934 she formed a relationship with the union leader Camilo Bouzas, with whom she was to carry on a passionate romance. Beginning in 1935, Aniceta

Vilamelle won a certain amount of protection. She attended a workers' congress in Madrid and, in that same year, she was invited, along with Camilo, to travel to the Soviet Union to complete a course on Marxism-Leninism, but her advanced pregnancy prevented it. The military coup of 1936 caught her by surprise with an infant in arms, little Sabela, and in full union activity. Her sons were called into the ranks, where they would die before the end of the first year of the conflict. Aniceta and Camilo, persecuted on account of their union activities, fled to the hills, where they joined the Guerrilla Army of Galicia, which in the first months of the conflict, with few weapons and starving, succeeded in sabotaging some strategic Falangist sites in the area of Vigo. Their daughter Sabela had remained in the care of her older daughter, Carme, who at the time was already working as a teacher in Santo Estevo de Ribas de Sil. The rejection of her neighbors, hunger and lack of protection must have troubled poor Carme, and raising that sister who was almost a daughter became an excessive burden for her. Carme contracted scarlet fever and the little girl died in the epidemic in three days. It's said that a local witch, one of those healers and midwives who are still to be found in remote areas, attempted without success to help the little girl. With not much more than herbs and prayers, the witch, of whom nothing more was ever learned, barely saved Carme. It should be recalled that in times of poverty like those even the best of care often turns out to be fruitless. Meanwhile, nothing was known of the fugitives. Camilo managed to take ship for Cuba through Portugal. Aniceta was arrested and spent a year in prison in Vigo. When she succeeded in getting out through the mediation of the Cuban consul, she was not the same woman who went in. Having lost her sons—"My sons, nooo! So grown up, how they boasted of where they were going, we went through so much together, Lois and Ramón, bless you, and may the weight of the earth not be so heavy as to leave you without dreams, my boys"—having lost her daughter—"my little girl, I almost never saw you, they separated you from me, they had to bind up my breasts in the hills because the milk wouldn't stop coming, I longed so much to have you with me"—Aniceta had no desire to fight and no reason to do it. It was the year 1944 and her comrades in political activism were dead or in exile. But Carme, the daughter she had left, was a real survivor and wouldn't let her waste away. Without ideals, without convictions, without illusions, only linked to the earth by her love for Carme, Aniceta plunged into the everyday. She worked in the house as much as she could so that her daughter, married to Antón Pereiro, a drab and characterless little man, conforming with the new atmosphere, could raise her daughters. Aniceta found herself obliged to become invisible. While the little girls were growing up, she sat in the rocking chair to wait for death. According to anecdote, her granddaughters say that the day before she died, Aniceta Vilamelle, blind as she was, climbed up to the attic, rummaged among the skirts, and put a bundle of papers into a certain wooden chest the best she could. Nobody wanted to bother her with questions, but when it all came to an end, now back from the cemetery, they remembered that detail and went to see what she'd put in the hiding place. No sooner had they opened the chest than a deep and fragrant odor spread through the entire house, a mixture of strawberry, hawthorn and blackberries, or perhaps raspberries. In their grandmother's bundle were her membership card in the communist party and the love letters Camilo sent her to arrange meetings at the mill.

15

Hi, Einés, how're you doing? I'm just sending you a quick message; if there are typos, don't blame me, I'm at one of those damned computer terminals with an American keyboard. I've just read over your notes, and I think you've got a lot of material, plenty, but... maybe you could work on it a little. Talk with Esperanza Rocamonde; she's further along than you are and a really nice girl, she knows all the latest research methods. Please understand me: it's not that what you have isn't good, no—but it needs a different approach, a few adjustments, I believe, that would provide a certain consistent thread, because, when it comes right down to it, what's your hypothesis? What secondary hypotheses are you going to work on? What reinterpretations of the classics that justifies that your thesis can be supported? Please understand me: it's not that I'm against you, but we have to persuade a panel that what you say is worth something. I'll be here one more week; use the time to reflect on what I'm suggesting to you. If you need anything, you can call me on my cell (but be careful, it's really expensive) or communicate with me in this same way. As soon as I get back, I want us to talk, OK? Perhaps you need to start somewhere else, cut the extraneous stuff a bit and, above all, you have to have a clear idea of what you're trying to say. Everything's a little vague, much too vague for a doctoral dissertation. Hang in there, and tell everyone hello from me.

M. V.

16

Concerning what Einés found when she looked
in the chest in the attic
*Last letter of Christina of Sweden
to her dearest Hélène Jans*

My friend Hélène, now that you are no longer among
us and you're free at last from such cruel pains as the last
ones inflicted on you must have been, know, wherever
you may be, that your friend Christina has not abandoned
you. I used all the influence that I ever thought I had
to save you from the executioner. It couldn't be done. I
sought an audience with the King of France, the Prince
of Wales, the Prince-Elector of the Rhine Palatinates.
Even the Pope himself received my letters, because his
cardinals mocked my reprehensible conduct and denied
me an audience, leaving me to weep outside his doors in
Rome. It couldn't be done, for when the book of fate has
an ending written for us, no human power can change it.
And you are no longer among us. How empty and gray
this world is without you, without your enthusiasm, my
dear Hélène! I took so long to muster the courage to hold
myself up, and to hold the pen to write to you in noplace;
your body must now be mingled with the black humus,
nourishing the earth you loved so much, and your lips,
your hair, your hands, your breasts must now be giving
life to the herbs you loved so much, and your flesh must
be medicine, and your bones a miraculous remedy, and
everything must be holy and good... and I'm damned!
Damn me a hundred times, I can't manage to see the

good things you all shared in, and you've left me alone; my father went away, and my mother fled from me, and after them, every lover, every friend, they all go away and I can do nothing, you all leave my side and nothing remains… Now that nothing pleases me, nothing is to my taste, I can only console myself by imagining that I'm going back to meet with you in Amsterdam. If only we knew when we began to live the very brief times that our pleasures last, I don't know if we would want to come into this world; in all probability, if we were given the choice between not having been and being, you and I as well, my friend, would have asked not to have to make a choice. As I know something of this life, now that it's coming to an end, I can be certain that, if you reside and rest anywhere, you will want to know something about him through me. You will laugh with that wild laugh of yours when you learn that now, in death, our friend is an object of dispute among the ladies; since these girls never knew how cold and withdrawn he was with women, they can spend their nights dreaming of his caresses. Perhaps, Hélène, you've infiltrated me, since I'm no longer who I was, and I enjoy imagining the cutting curses you would hurl at these good ladies. Because there are three of them who call themselves Cartesians, or better put, there are three who most often call themselves that; today I'd say that there's no woman of the salon and culture who doesn't kneel before our friend, whom they name with their careful and elegant pronunciation "Monsieur Des-Caaartes." The three are friends and have much in common. All three are educated; they come from well-to-do families, and received instruction from the men in their house. The oldest is about the age of your Francine and is called Anne de la Vigne. She's the daughter of Louis XIII's court physician and the dean of the Paris School of Medicine. The second is Catherine Descartes, our friend's niece, Pierre's daughter, and she has the good sense to take advantage of the fortune and name of her father, councilor of the Parliament of Brittany. The third, about whom I know the least, is Marie Dupré, whom everyone calls "the Cartesian" more than any of the others, although I'm not familiar with any writings from which to infer what intellectual link she had with him. Perhaps the connection comes, rather, from an opinion expressed by this noble lady in some Parisian salon, for today they've all turned into genuine literary roundtables. So far as I know, she frequents the *chambre bleue* of Madame de Rambouillet, just as Catherine Descartes often puts in an appearance at the discussions of Madame de Sévigné. These women, both the visitors and the hostesses, have reputations as learned, which is good for the female gender, even though, if this herb goes on growing in such a way in the courts, it will end by being seriously pernicious for women as a group; it will suffice for one of them to get too puffed up, stumble in a matter of love or express a mistaken opinion, all these small defects being natural to all mortals, for the misogynists, who are so plentiful, to point a finger and exclaim: "How could you imagine that a wretched woman could have anything in her head besides lust and frivolity?" While that misstep does not occur, the *précieuses*, for that's what these learned women are called, insist on reading, on commenting on the most abstruse authors, and they even aspire to construct a map of the feelings, giving names to those that men never dreamed of naming. I suppose that the women hope from these salons to get access to the world of literature. I believe, however, that they're not just seeking the pleasure of interacting with men and perhaps that of arranging some relationship of gallantry. Since the universities, closed up in their dogmatism and the pride of men, reject with such hostility anything that contradicts the sacrosanct masters set up as such since antiquity, the cultivation of the mind is only going to happen in these princely salons, where new theories are commented upon, at the same time as their authors are welcomed and protected. You know as well as I do, dear Hélène, the attraction that these discussions can have for a woman, who will experience not only the possibility of talking and talking with her beloved, the best man in the world, but also that of eating the forbidden fruit, since all these subjects are specifically excluded from the instruction that's being permitted to women. Still, not only are new inventions reviewed; letters, beautiful language and delicate sentiments continue to be the principal interest of these salons. Therefore they're called *précieuses*, I imagine, because they prize, give value to, many things that until now lacked it, beginning perhaps with themselves... This is truly complex and not your idiom, Hélène. They, who are nonetheless your heirs, are not interested in the universality of knowledge; what they want is for everyone to know that they think, and think well. But there's something here that makes me mistrustful. With the cry "the mind has no sex," these women seem to distance themselves from their bodies, which seem to weigh on them, in order to initiate themselves into the pure and uncontaminated world of the soul. I don't know whether they aren't rather Neoplatonists, as the scholars say. I'm not sure, for death is stalking me, and I see nothing clearly and distinctly, but I remember you, so thoughtful and so definitely anchored in your woman's body... and I end up being suspicious of these intellectual females. I haven't said this yet. None of them has married, or had children, and I'm very much afraid that they have not known a man... How you would laugh if you were here... Hélène... how you would say that they're missing out on the best part of life... Just as well that we still have reading, right? How much I would like to believe that I'll soon be with you... and with him, again... and feel again what I once felt for both of you! Today, however, I realize more than ever that we will never again bathe in the same waters... of which the crossing, once and for all, my crossing, has already taken place.

Christina
P.S.

17

The e-mail message hit Einés like a bucket of cold water. Or not exactly—a bucket of cold water, though brusque and unexpected, tones and hydrates. No, so as not to leave it as a lame comparison, we ought to say that the message hit Einés as if somebody had spilled tomato sauce all over a brand-new white T-shirt. No, not that either, that would have a kind of clownish buffoonery that Miguel's message didn't have. The words of her thesis director, a brilliant, attractive man, clipped her wings, buried her alive in the garden, spat on her pages, left her drained, dried up and without ideas. It was hard to come up with an exact comparison, but Einés, who was not moderate or self-contained, and who didn't control her impulses more than was strictly necessary, who belonged to a breed of impetuous women, formidable women, and those are the ones against whom one should never take up arms, for when they fire they shoot out truths like fists and rose petals, insults and blessings, weeping and hugs, all mingled together. Einés felt angry, let down and a little betrayed. She, who had always been very studious, who had an undergraduate degree in philosophy and, interested by what was being done in the department, had stayed the summer after her fifth year to do a bachelor's thesis, and then to help a little old professor in the department with a conference presentation, and then as more or less a waitress in a symposium, and then as a research fellow and so, little by little, making herself indispensable, after all that Einés was one of those research assistants who might perhaps be professors on that day, always hypothetical and more and more distant, when the doctoral dissertation was finished. To finish it, for that's how it was expressed, finish the thesis, like someone who eats up all the soup; they never said "write the thesis" or "work on the thesis," but always "finish the thesis." It wasn't enough to start it or get to the middle, the undertaking had to be brought to an end, and a good end; well, with that in mind, as we were saying, Einés spent a lot of time reading biographies, reading complete works, reading encyclopedias, and recent publications, and dictionaries of authors, and dictionaries of philosophical terms, and proceedings of conferences, and many other papers, which among them would use up the forest reserves of the world with all the paper they stained, regarding a figure, a French philosopher of the seventeenth century, the century in which philosophy had become a science. That philosopher was a splendid mind, ahead of his time, fond of constructing automata, in love with new inventions, a man with his passions well controlled and locked away in his heart with seven keys, a man who had had a daughter out of wedlock and had not acknowledged her so that the affair wouldn't disrupt his career although he did love her tenderly, a rebel against the dictates of the philosophical tradition, someone who liked to stay in bed until the sun shone strongly, a convinced Catholic, a democrat who put his knowledge within the reach of those less fortunate, a writer of spirited letters, a man who was ugly, though always well dressed and perfumed, someone who didn't like cats, a man who had sinned with woman very few times, just once if his writings were to be believed, quite a few according to the sinful woman who surely knew better because of her personal interest, a philosopher famous in his lifetime who had been called by the queen of Sweden to explain to her the advances of science and write a ballet, a noteworthy thinker, a man who didn't consider it beneath him to exchange letters with women who read and thought, a fellow who, despite liking women who read, read very little. His name was René Descartes.

18

Concerning what Einés found when she looked
in the chest in the attic
From the Book of Women by Hélène Jans:
An infallible love-charm

I have a formula for love that always works, or almost
always, for the science of magic doesn't function with
exactitude; one has to let the story unfold and not take
it as finished before the beginning. But I've been told
that the formula works; I couldn't apply it and put it into
effect in my own person, because this is a spell for men.
Therefore perhaps it works, for we women allow ourselves
to be captured more willingly by amorous feelings. I can
assure those who try it that if they use this formula with
the women they love, these will truly stay with them
and will always be ardent and ready for them. You must
then, sir, write the name of the desired woman, and your
own, on an apple any way you like, provided that the
letters are clear and recognizable. You must know that
any man who wishes to inspire great love must write on
it himself and not entrust it to someone else to do in his
place. Then write this magical formula, which I give to
you in encoded language, with secret words: "*Eno de pari
qarqor qaratom pe loxenan peripoties mi daberan.*" Here
ends the love formula. Give the woman the apple and
make sure she eats it, and immediately without hesitation
she will do everything you want. Learned men say that
even if the woman just smells the apple, the man who has
given it to her will be loved with a very passionate love.

Those who lack confidence can make their luck grow by also giving the woman a bunch of vervain or verbena, which attracts the love of the desired person provided that one has thought about her while lying with another. And remember, man, when you use the aforementioned love-charm, that Love should be practiced with wisdom and knowledge, not merely with heat. I administer these formulas sparingly and with extreme caution, for they are not to be revealed to mediocre men, but rather to those who know and understand. The experience of love not only gives pleasure to the body: the woman who eats the apple, thought of and written on in that way for her, will gain deeper wisdom, and the man who watches her eat will never perceive life as empty or diffuse.

19

She hadn't been to her maternal home for quite some time; they hadn't cared for her last boyfriend. And we got that right with "last," huh?, because she wasn't planning to have any more boyfriends; she was done with men forever, although the reason for this radical and well-thought-out break with half of humanity had nothing to do with the displeasure of her mother, her grandmother and her aunts; rather, it was the fact that a man who was never going to be her boyfriend had established himself in her heart. For the rest, if her ancestors hadn't liked that other boyfriend, the last one, it was because when he got to the house he declared, pompously: "I like this…yes!… It's an authentic *locus amoenus*. It gives one a sense like 'no space, no time,'" for it would seem to him, a professor of Literary Theory, very charming to speak that way about the girl's house, but that's just not done, he treated us like a bunch of dimwits, and since we aren't "no space" here for him, let him go sleep in his aunt's house. With all this, Einés realized that they were getting jealous; for them she would never grow up, and what they wanted was for Einés to stop by the house and tell them things, so Carmiña could say that she didn't believe them, and Olaia, who had left yonder house to get married and had come back separated not many years later, could take an interest in her studies, with arcane questions to pass herself off as super-smart, even though she had got them all out of the famous encyclopedia *What Children Want to Know*. Mama, that is to say Livia, who was still a young and beautiful woman, looked at her in confusion and pushed her hair back from her face to kiss her and tell her: "That's how I like it, so people can see how pretty you look," with that unqualified praise of hers, the acceptance she showed in what she said about how her body looked. Einés was aware of how much she was loved in yonder house. At the same time, what they truly liked was for all of them to end up together at night in the room of now-dead Grandma Aniceta, may she rest in peace, with the bed turned into a stage, so as there, in embroidered nighties, to stay up until all hours doing reader's theater, like in the seventeenth century, with husbands entering through the door while lovers jump out the window, and of course, if the girl brought a boyfriend home we're not going to do it; this wasn't, not by a long shot, out of respect for Einés's amatory intimacy, but rather because they, single as they were, or almost, were not going to let themselves be seen in nighties by any man.

The fact is that Einés hadn't been to the maternal home for quite some time, probably too long, and on her arrival there was a genuine loving revolution: "Our girl's come home!" "Einés, honey, take off that jacket, it looks like a saddle blanket all wet like that." "Our girl's come home!" "I'm going to make some cream puffs." "What for? You know she doesn't like them." "What does that have to do with anything? Einés doesn't have to eat them, it's just so she'll know she's at home, the mind doesn't have any eyes to know where the body is, all it has are memories to orient itself." "Our girl's come home!" "Come and iron for a while, Einés, that way we can talk better, you know in this house a body's always overwhelmed with clothes…" "Our girl's come home!" "She's looking pretty, isn't she? And did that imbecile come with her?" "No, she came by herself." "Oh good!" "She came by herself? Why didn't you say so before? Oh goodie!"

In those familiar surroundings, warm, peaceful, welcoming, full of *frivolité* and adopted cats, of homework to be graded and steaming kitchen, with Janis Joplin howling loudly for her baby, with that urgency and determination they put into everything they did, it happened that the chest in the attic, as if it had been cooking over a slow fire for three hundred fifty years and now was finally coming to a boil, let a stream of pink smoke escape. The smell of that smoke, varied and deep, sensual, provocative, tempting, spread through yonder house and, going downriver, must have made it to the train station, for some drab traveler suddenly felt a crush and he didn't know on whom, and even the ticket-collector, with all the nastiness and military bearing that went with the job, all of a sudden felt his body to be so soft and spring-like that he took a notion to sit down in the tavern, on one of those really tall stools, with his feet dangling, to drink an orange soda pop. It must have been the smell of that smoke, musical, soothing, warm and slightly damp, that caused the ticket-collector, perched on his bar-stool, to dare to ask for a straw to suck up his drink slowly, and being a crusty gentleman and grumpy as an old badger, he put on a child's face and allowed the bubbles, very slowly, to go quietly up his nose. The girl was home, oh good! And the chest in the attic was all ready; its smoke, as soft and hot as a caress, smelled of many different aromas, especially of raspberries. In those surroundings, in short, so full of sensations of yonder house, which was called yonder because it was on the other side of the river or because the people who lived there had a certain otherworldliness about them, that's where Einés conceived her idea.

Concerning what Einés found when she looked
in the chest in the attic
*Report on Morality and Good Manners in the Social
Service regarding Miss Livia Pereiro*

Miss Livia Pereiro was expelled from the social service
in charge of the Feminine Section in this locale because,
as you can see for yourself, this piece of writing is not
appropriate for a decent woman. Asked in advance to
put together an article for our monthly newsletter on
the seasoning of stews, she showed up with this strange
composition in which cookery is mentioned only towards
the end, and indirectly, when through several pages its
author takes a perverse delight in a literary reflection, in
which will be noted, as is usual in these women of checkered
pasts, evil thoughts and a reprehensible tendency towards
voluptuousness, which is certainly well known in her, who
drags around with her the palpable proof of her repugnant
conduct: her natural daughter Einés Andrade. And, as I was
the one who decided to expel the said young lady from the
ranks of the Social Service, I am sending you the piece of
work so that you may judge for yourself the state of laxity
in which this young woman finds herself. One bad apple
spoils the basket. With my best regards:

María Isabel de las Heras
Director of the Feminine Section in this locale
May 1970

The finest minds call being in season the appropriate state of dampness of the earth for planting seeds; this state, plainly, is caused by the rain on the soil, although that way, suddenly, it reminds me of the description of the state in which women find themselves when waiting for their lovers, eh? However, this use of the word is uncommon; more usual is that of its derivative, we would say the symbolic sense, of the state of maturity or perfection of a thing that is developing, evolving or changing. Thus we say that a fruit is in season or, in a usage that is sometimes naughty, that such and such a moment is a good season for getting something done, indicating thus the most opportune time for carrying out an activity. But I don't want to get involved in the complications of grammarians, for I'm not fond of grammarians, and today I simply wanted to reflect on the well-known theme that there's a time for everything, and everything has its moment. There is a moment, this is well known, in which even a great enterprise, like love, is in season. And in such a moment lovers are sweet and lovey-dovey, their whole life slips away in smiles, and they laugh, they laugh so heartily that the laugh has to come from the belly, where else? For if it came from the brain, they would be more worried, most of the time, that others shouldn't notice their love and, if people in love are anything, they're imprudent; it's not that they want to show themselves, but rather that they don't give a damn if their guardian angels are crossing themselves, because certainly this business of being enchanted, with the soul held captive, leaping about, that business of finding ourselves in the middle of work, whether it be collecting herbs, or spreading clothes out to dry in the sun, that makes no difference, with a goofy smile, because we're remembering the talk we had, that business of the mind being stuck in a conversation is a gift that life gives us. It's said time is an arrow, always fired a little while ago, which runs forward and pulls us behind it, and most of the time by the hair. Well then, love makes one feel like time's arrow; it always flies facing forward; it stops and stays hanging in the air for a moment to give us a break, with a little time off, and therefore, no matter what one's age, when one falls in love, one regresses to adolescence, and feels once again a lump in the throat, one's tongue all tied, a fluttering in one's insides and an absolute sleepiness in the brain. And in spite of everything, people in love do their best work in a time apparently so ill suited to concentration; not everything glorious in human beings must be rational. The fact is that in those lucky moments love is in season and there's no scythe that should try to cut off its head, for Love is a small boy, naked, with wings, and it would be really wretched to do something like that to him for having played at surprising us. That visit we receive from the supreme idea of Love is worth more than anything, more therefore than the beloved being himself or herself; therefore when he just looks at me I feel like a bubble in boiling water, like an alembic on a low flame... Well, not just when he looks at me, but when he looks at me that way and says those things he knows how to say to me, which analyzed syntactically, with their clauses and sentences deconstructed, must consist of simple oral language, but to me it tastes like a butterfly's kiss, at dawn on the day of creation, like a warm bath with bubbles, like fresh-brewed coffee, like bread baked in a wood-burning oven, like wool socks, like candy, like moist lips, and, above all, like raspberries. Thus there's a moment, all curiosity and boldness, in which liking in interaction has become an obsession, in which the clock has stopped working, for surely we're winning minutes back from death in those balcony and window conversations, it's better to be separated by a ladder, a door, or a gate, for the conversation holds back leaps and slows them down to make them more delicious. In that moment, when the wind that blows pushes away the masks and gradually shows the faces just the way they are, the feeling is in season... To conclude, it's also seasoning, on the other hand, the flavor given to things to eat with different ingredients to make them agreeable to the palate. In this case it's adjusting foods with condiments that give them good flavor; it's always good when tastes aren't monotonous or life boring... but I don't have so much to say on this question of stews.

21

Hi, Miguel,

I know you're probably busy but I can't resist telling you that I've found the thread I needed for the thesis. You're not going to believe it... After all that looking and looking, I found it at home! Brace yourself, here it comes! I believe that Descartes is of no interest: rationalism has been studied from all possible angles in all possible versions. Please understand me: Descartes is a fascinating author but studying him is a road too much traveled. One can't say a single word that's new. You know only too well: not new, not old, there's nothing that can be said about these sacred cow authors without a hundred hyperspecialized scholars saying that you failed to understand such and such a word, that you should have cited Professor So-and-So, how dare you say this or that (what you say is the least of it), if you didn't read, for example, his compendium on music, which even if it's irrelevant, also said many things that, it so happened, they have studied and on which they are genuine authorities and with respect to the aforementioned compendium blah blah blah... And, ta-dah, ta-dah! Here comes my idea: his writings are of no interest... his life is interesting, for it's symbolic of the man of his time. He was a soldier, he wandered through the countries of Europe, a bit of a loafer, doing whatever he felt like, he shut himself up in Amsterdam to live off his father's estate and conceive works in which only he believed, for he was isolated from what was being done in his time... Were you aware of that? And there he has a daughter with a maid, a young woman named Hélène, Hélène Jans... Do you get it? To get access to Hélène, to her writings, to her thought, now that would be innovative, for she had to have influenced the philosopher in some way, and... You know, surely, how many famous philosophers, those studied by young folks in schools, had children with women of lower social status? A hundred. Look: Galileo seduced his best friend's wife; they had three children and he never married her. The servant who stayed with Leibniz the longest may have been a natural son he had as a young man. It's well known that Marx had an affair with a maid, when he was already married, because he took responsibility, at least partially, for the daughter... In short, I don't know why I'm getting myself all tangled up in all that, which is irrelevant. The point is that in the most recent biographies of Descartes it's stated with certainty that he kept up a correspondence with Hélène throughout the five years that his daughter lived. Maids who know how to read? That means something. Don't you think? She must have been a formidable woman, a woman who had to have an influence on him. I wouldn't be surprised if she were the one responsible for the changes and vacillations noticed in him in certain respects... I'm excited! What do you think? Proud of me? A hug, E. A.

22

Concerning what Einés found when she looked
in the chest in the attic
Einés begins the recipe book: Black nightshade
(*Solanum nigrum*)

The herb called *nightshade*, or *St. Marina's herb*, or *dog grapes* is an annual plant, brought over from America in the Dutch ships that, in the seventeenth century, transported everything of value that they found to the great European centers. In the lands of the American tropics the indigenous people used black nightshade as a vegetable and also as a medicinal substance for its emollient, anti-neuralgic and analgesic properties. Guided by this popular lore, Catholic missionaries collected it to include it in the vast catalogue of species that they would bring to their monasteries in Europe, and which can still be observed in the Hortus Botanicus in the city of Amsterdam, a place from which black nightshade spread all over Europe, judging by the varied names it is given in each country: *black solanum, devil's tomato, black morello, tomata borda, morelle noire,* or *schwarzer Nachtschatten*. The plant is of an intense green with ovate leaves with serrated edges, and flowers, borne in clusters, showing their corollas in the form of a five-pointed star. The fruit is a berry the size of a pea, and black in color, hence the name. It blooms, like everything else, beginning in the spring, and, as good flowers delight us by lasting, it remains beautiful until the beginning of autumn in vegetable gardens and places near homes, whether cultivated or not. It was a herb much used in Galician monasteries because the leaves have narcotic powers and could be applied as sedatives. Traditionally herbalists employed leaves of dog grape to prepare "the peaceful balm," a powerful analgesic made also with oregano, belladonna and poppies, which was applied by rubbing the injured area with a woolen cloth. The berries of black nightshade, calming and emollient, serve for making plasters with which to treat cracks in the skin, principally those that affect hands that do a great deal of work, or the breasts of women during lactation. Although its smell can be disagreeable because it contains certain active ingredients, the plant, despite its bad reputation, is not really toxic except when dry, that is, during a time when this kind of wild plant can no longer be eaten as a substitute for chard or spinach. Black nightshade has a mysterious quality, since, like good stories, it has the magical power to calm pain and, like all women, it has a bad reputation that in no way corresponds with what it does. Therefore, now that I have decided to join up with the initiatives that I have inherited from the women who came before me by putting together a herbarium in which I can gather together what I know of life, I wanted to begin with a plant as evocative as this one.

23

Good grief! Now how can I answer her? This girl is killing me… Let's see, let's see if something comes to my head if I just jump in… Hmmm. What kind of mess must she have got herself into to get so excited over this claptrap? A little slug of whisky, yes sir, that's just the ticket for thinking… Let's see, let's see what I can write to her. "My dear girl," whoa, none of that, she'll think I'm trying to get her into bed. Erase. "My dear," no, that sounds patronizing, and she's not the kind to let me get away with that! "Dear Einés, have you gone crazy?" No, no, not so direct. "Dear Einés: I'm in the airport and I can't go into detail now, but, as soon as I got your message, I wondered what could be going on with you." And after all I've thought about it, how can I still doubt that she must have been high, huh? A girl who's so obsessive, she must have been stuck on the thesis for five or six years and she hasn't come up with a chapter; now she ups and gets all worked up with this stuff. Let's see, try again, hmmm… "You seem a bit nervous and, to be totally sincere, I'm surprised by your excitement. I'll be in Barajas in a few hours and I'll stay in Madrid for just a couple of days. Then I can listen to that new idea in person, and we can take our time. At the moment I don't see very clearly where you're going with this." Let me see, I'll look it over: "Dear Einés, na-na-na-na… a bit nervous." Yes, yes, yes, that couldn't offend anybody… "Na-na-na… we can take our time, na-na-na-na… where you're going with this." Well, now to say goodbye. "A hug and see you soon. M.V."

24

Concerning what Einés found when she looked
in the chest in the attic
From the poetical diary of Einés Andrade

I'm twenty-seven years old. It's a difficult age, perhaps impossible. I do the same as when I was seven: study and try not to be stifled by the overwhelming personality of my family. I don't like the number twenty-seven. I'm the same age as Hélène was when she lost Francine, but I haven't yet experienced any of the grand emotions, the kind of profound feelings that can make you feel on your deathbed that you've lived, like love or motherhood or the sense that you can fly solo in life... I don't know what Mama and my aunts would say if they saw this, as if I didn't love them. I do, only with them am I sure that I've lived... Poor Hélène, so young and so old as she was on September 7, 1640. I'm also the same age as Christina of Vasa and Brandenburg on the day she abdicated and decided on something unthinkable in her circle of friends and acquaintances: to give up the enormous privilege of having been born a queen of a prosperous nation because of not wanting to make a concession in the insignificant detail of having children. I'm the same age as Christina and for me, as for her, springtime has bloomed twenty-seven times... And the springtime has bloomed so much before my very eyes and I haven't made a single important decision! Well, I swear never again to mention anyone's age for the rest of my life, never again to consider that time can be counted for people as if they were harvests.

I swear not to commit such an idiocy. Never. I'm twenty-seven years old. By this age some people have done a lot, others have done everything they're going to do in life because they'll never wake up again. Others of us at that age haven't done anything yet. I swear not to talk about age again, about how old you are, about how old you were when… I swear not to fill in forms with date of birth, never to say "he must be about your age" or "he's the age of your older brother," "she's my age," "he must be of your generation." I will not treat people as if they were vintages. I will use the word "age" for the final time. It will be to whisper, very quietly, that I am just the right age to become Einés.

25

Of the many ways that exist of inspiring love, one of the most powerful, most suggestive and most exciting is literary wooing. One could very well apply that term to the flame that is lit when one exchanges writings with another person. Of course, the initial spark is certainly supplied by the body with its clear signs, but the soul that writes feeds the flame to make it burn the way it should. Because the flame, as is well known, has to catch well and get close to good wood; the kind that just makes smoke is worthless, as is the kind that smells and crackles without burning: the fire must release heat, which is wood's way of giving itself; after having given joy to the sight, and provided shadows, after having been harvested and provided a place to support one's back in the middle of the journey, after having served as a motif for painters and poets, and after having been useful as a rest and solace for passersby, after having produced breathable air, ensured the life of the soil, given a home to the little animals of the field and a refuge to the birds, after having been postcard and food, the tree gives, finally, wood, and when it no longer has even wood left, the half-burned logs that are burned in the fireplace have a way of burning that makes a sound similar to the sighs of two embracing lovers who are exchanging their sorrows and caresses in that complicity that well-matched love gives. Of the many ways that there are of inspiring love, there exist some futile and superficial ones, which are those called love at first sight or getting struck by an arrow, a certain something, one doesn't know where it comes from or why, which as Queen Christina would say is a love that is constructed independently of the merits of the beloved person, and that can't be. Of the many ways there are of inspiring love there exist others that are those of people gone astray, those who had a jewel by their side but didn't see it, for the jewel was in plain sight, and was even accessible to the touch, but they, shielded with the armor of a beast, didn't see its virtue. Such falling in love is very friendly; it's born from observing the virtues of the soul and measuring them in their true dimensions, but what we would call burning, burning… it doesn't burn either. Of the many ways there are of inspiring love, one is very subtle and makes its appearance in sensitive and tender people, who are fond of writing and, for that very reason, when they read or when they write, put all their soul into it, so that the other person in question, seeing the soul bared, can get used to it and desire it, and having begun to desire the soul, may get a thought of that kind called wicked, though who knows why amorous and playful thoughts should be called wicked thoughts, which open the window of the imagination to let us intuit the way we would caress, not in general, like someone stroking velvet or the back of a cat, but rather the way we would caress precisely that one other person among all the people who have been in the world.

And all this is said here because correspondence is a dangerous thing. They know this well who decline to respond to letters, missives, Christmas cards or even e-mails: one begins by tossing out a handful of clichés and the recipe soon starts cooking by itself; sometimes one would say that there's a witch hidden in correspondence who's been keeping a pot on the fire for three hundred fifty years and if so, it's that witch who decides for a person and decides, for example, that one should start saying such interesting things that they draw the mind's eye of the other. And that other person can't help falling in surrender before so much beauty as is lavished on her or him in the message sent. Writing letters is making gifts with words, and words, if they are well chosen, and the soul is in the right season, can cure better than magical herbs; it's said that words prolong pleasure like aphrodisiacs and reduce pain like analgesics, for it's not for nothing that aphrodisiacs and analgesics are words as well. Definitely correspondence is a dangerous thing. We know it because of Eleonora of Brandenburg, the mother of Christina of Sweden, who didn't need to see the Danish king to guess that she needed his kisses as clouds need drops of water, that is, to maintain themselves without danger of dissipation. We know it because of Christina likewise, for with letters she managed to fascinate no less a person than René Descartes, a philosopher among philosophers, and that although she didn't write the letters personally, for with Chanut acting as intermediary they must have been somewhat weakened or, at least, it's certain that the intermediary didn't perfume them and write them in lovely calligraphy as he should have done. We know it also because of Hélène, who wrote back and forth for five years with the philosopher, after having slept with him for five more, without softening his heart or persuading him of how beautiful she was, both on the inside and on the outside, for the philosopher had chosen to stay only with the outside; well, to be exact, not with the outside outside, for Hélène took a bit of a risk showing him what was covered that evening in the Hortus Botanicus, for men, as is well known, like to go where they want and not where a woman wants to take them, regardless of how a practical lesson on the sensitive component of the soul shouldn't be something that might look bad. We know also, regarding the danger of correspondence, because of Christina, who managed, writing back and forth with Hélène, to mitigate the desire that the latter had initially provoked in her, and see Hélène with the eyes of the soul, just as she was: a thinker about daily life, like so many, convinced that philosophy ought to serve to free us all from the anguish that is caused by knowing that existence is short, irreversible, and specifically designed for our suffering, and that the only thing we can do to resist being swallowed up by the most absolute pain is to enjoy as much as we can. Finally, with so many cases in point, we know that correspondence is dangerous because it leaves traces of our lives, it leaves trails where we have passed, of how we loved and whom, so that this very truthful chronicle could not have been constructed if it weren't for the fact that we can rummage around and smell the correspondence of these characters, for the majority of them are pushing up daisies, except for Hélène, who is probably, if God is Omnipotent, pushing up mother-of-thyme and marjoram, cumin and, above all, herbs of love, because Hélène, just being evoked, makes us fall in love, she was so sensual and well set up.

But the artifice of history is as follows, and it could not be written in any other way. As women are generally compared with natural phenomena, poets tend to be a bit careless, and, since Rosa or Andrea, Luísa or Anthea, María or Beatriz are all the same to them, they insist that all of them, absolutely all, are the same. And, given that Einés was carrying on a correspondence with her thesis director, we could naïvely think that he is the object of her swoons, for we've all seen lot of movies and read lots of novels and, as a result, we know how stories are written. Or, if not, in case Professor Miguel Valdés, what a jerk that man is, not accepting the girl's hypothesis, that's not good either, were not the chosen one, this mysterious lover ought to show up any minute and let his face be seen in this truthful history. And there's no reason why. The heroines of stories can also have something to tell even if, like the heroes, they keep their private business to themselves; Einés could be in love with that man who just crossed the plaza with long strides. No, not that guy, he walks like he's too sure of himself. Maybe she's in love with the librarian who waits on her every morning, with such a darling smile, and hands her the books that she's just requested in writing through a hatch, perhaps. Maybe she's in love with that fellow who crossed rapidly last night in front of the car she was riding in without even seeing her, or the one who's looking alertly from the other side of the window, or the one who just congratulated her, mwah, mwah, on her presentation at that awful conference, or the one who didn't take a minute to make her a copy of the keys she just lost. In any case there's no reason it has to be the one with whom she's exchanging letters. He won't even have to show up in this truthful history, turning Einés into the girl in love, for the story of Einés's love, of that love she feels, is still to be written; this time, and for the history that interests us, it suffices to know that she, like Christina, like Hélène, is seeking the path to become herself... once and for all.

Concerning what Einés found when she looked
in the chest in the attic
Project book of Dona Carme de Pereiro

"Patchwork" is a kind of needlework, made by
combining fragments of different fabrics one has available
to compose a single piece, like certain books that are
made with fragments of diaries, letters and conversations
carried on by the characters. In all probability it was born,
patchwork I mean, with the objective of making use of
bits of scarce or highly valued materials to make practical
items, sewing together lengths of cloth of different widths,
textures and colors until new fabrics were obtained.
Historians tell, according to how they are represented
on the wall paintings in Thebes, that already in the sails
of the ships that plied the Nile in ancient Egypt one can
appreciate examples of this kind of work, with which the
ships could be identified as belonging to the same side.
With minimal differences, "patchwork" is attested in all
of north Africa, Turkestan, Persia, Syria, India and China,
and, beginning in the eleventh century, in Europe. Today
we can conjecture that pieces of cloth would have been
sewn into a fabric that served as a base with the idea of
renewing cloths that were worn or had holes in them.
Gradually they would come to have ornamental value,
and craftswomen would begin to cut out the patches in
different shapes and decorate the edges with threads and
raised embroidery. It's said that the Crusaders brought
these techniques back from Palestine, where they had been

fascinated by the colors and designs that the conquered Saracens had on their standards or the tents in which they camped. What is certain is that, upon arriving in Europe, patchwork began to be used for the most part for more peaceful purposes, especially for tapestries, bedclothes or ecclesiastical chasubles, since these techniques served to make compositions that were every bit the equal of those of painters. By combining two cloth covers with a thick, soft filling, women of the northern lands produced new fabrics to protect against the cold: eiderdowns for beds and also vests and warm leggings that were warm and also defended against the bites of animals, cuts and arrows. In the south, in Italy, in Portugal, in Toledo, artists let their imaginations soar and the techniques achieve noteworthy complexity: designs are outlined with ribbons with which reliefs are framed, or with baste stitching, gathered on the back through the stuffing. The work on fine white linen with patterns of gold thread and ribbons of different colors gives a particular finish to this technique. Now then, the true revolution comes about in the seventeenth century, when the stuffing of cloths of different weaves begins to be employed in doublets, pantaloons and petticoats, blankets, pieces of raw or embroidered silk. The techniques taken along by the colonists, especially by Dutch women, flourished in America to the point of being considered the most famous forms of popular art. These domestic craft pieces, made without preliminary designs, with scarce supplies of materials and in the harshest conditions of life, must have been considered a genuine luxury. The works of these craftswomen known as patchwork quilters were done by women who worked together, most of the time making the rounds from house to house so as to share the cost among themselves of the lamps with which they lighted their work or the firewood with which they warmed themselves, with the idea of making "friendship quilts," as they called these collective works made as a gift for a member of the community. Most of the time these were wedding quilts for the bride or "freedom blankets," which were given to males when they came of age. The arrival of the twentieth century put an end to the shortages of the past; material came to be available for everyone and, for the first time, people began to have machines at their disposal. In this way the need to create beautiful pieces of work at small expense, or to make warm and protective clothing with readily available material, disappeared. All work done by hand gave way to factory-made items. It's true that everything that comes from factories is beautiful, with such even stitches, so nicely finished, but I believe a certain something has been lost... I couldn't say what it is, but when I see quilts in the stores now I feel the way Rembrandt or Van Gogh would feel if they saw their paintings on folders, boxes, puzzles or T-shirts... I don't know, it's as if the magic had been lost... although, of course, you're not going to say that the things made at home are art, because they're not art, because we make them and we aren't artists, isn't that right?

27

Dear Einés,

Pardon me if in my previous message I seemed hasty or disrespectful regarding your work. You have to understand me. American universities are cricket cages, and, no matter how much this country boasts about its technology, it must be military technology, because to exchange e-mails with you I had to go to a computer lab where the lousiest students had access. I sound like a fascist, but the fact is that they would wear out the patience of the most experienced! As you know, they pay, and they do what they want. Here in Madrid things are different. Today I only had to hint at my need to get in touch with you for a colleague to offer me his office and his machine and... here I am. You see that I'm giving you the importance you deserve. Do you think you can accuse me of not being very interested in the progress of your research? No, nothing of the sort! I've always regarded you as someone quite special, with an artistic flair, but you have to understand that academic work has some requirements, requirements that we don't control, and I want you to adapt to them, just a little, enough so that your work, which, look here, even though I do agree with you on that point, has been going on for too long, won't end up being spoiled in the end. The fact is, I'm telling you the truth, you seem prepared to throw everything overboard, and that's not good for you or for me. What would you think about us speaking in person next week? Give me a summary in which you detail the change of objectives in outline form, and in the text you develop IN A REASONED MANNER why you're changing each of the points you plan to touch on. I can picture you wrinkling your nose and saying that I'm not listening to you. I am listening to you, Einés, but I don't want that fit of lunacy that's come over you, which sounds like third-rate feminism, to carry everything away... Damn! Still, I googled the name of that Hélène Jans and I applaud your strategy. It's interesting that you have the facts that anybody can find on the Internet, but that idea of rescuing her from oblivion... What oblivion? Can you tell me that? The good woman bore a child of Descartes', didn't she? Well, my congratulations to her, but... since when is that an academic achievement? I'm very much afraid that those historians who concentrate on private lives are driving you beginners crazy. We don't concern ourselves with writing biographies of outstanding and meritorious people. We do phil-o-so-phy, phil-o-so-phy... that means, young lady, that we are concerned with ideas, not people. M. V.

28

Concerning what Einés found when she looked
in the chest in the attic
Personal and private diary of Carmiña Pereiro

To finish this program at the normal university I still have to pass a class called Home Economics, which I hate, don't I? I don't think I'll ever be able to stand Dona Marián, the professor, with her fingernails painted red with the crescents in white at the top. Yuck, how horrible. This morning I was studying and I've got it all memorized: "The work of running a household is sufficient to fill a whole life if we do it with dedication, competence, professionalism and, therefore, with an impulse towards improvement." With an impulse towards improvement, it says... Ha, ha... I don't know how to carry out the cleaning of the toilet with an impulse towards improvement... I'd like to see Dona Marián scrubbing away with the toilet brush and those fingernails that say it all about her; she probably has an assistant for jobs like that, I reckon, for her job is the education of the national spirit. And, as far as I'm concerned, she should stay at home; I think she spends her life preaching that a woman's place is in the home and if there was an earthquake it wouldn't catch her inside, no sir. And memorize: "Attention to domestic tasks brings with it the purchase of all the items we need for the maintenance of the home, the preparation of meals, the care of clothing, washing dishes, attention to and care of children..." It's plain to see that for her the big thing is buying, she looks like a little market herself with all the charms and gewgaws she's got hanging all over her; if you turn over the handbag of any one of us what comes out is a handkerchief and, at most, a pencil or a lipstick. But hers... what doesn't she have! With her pillboxes, and her coin purses, and billfolds, and keyrings and carry-alls, and little cases that zip open to make a purse, and candy... and a hairband, and a pen and pencil case, and a chocolate, and three hair bands and a lapel pin she was given and that she only puts on when the director comes by, she must be the one who gave it to her and, I imagine, she doesn't like the confounded little pin at all, and two samples of perfumes, and a case and a spray, psshh, psshh, to sweeten the breath, and a piece of mint chewing gum... Well, to continue: "All the activities of the home can be organized and divided into lists with which, down to the minute, we can detail the most suitable day and time to carry out each of the domestic tasks." Down to the minute, huh? Let's hope we don't get our heads blown off with a bomb if we dust before we sweep, I know, yes, sweeping always stirs up dust... "There are three fundamental tasks that must be carried out by a woman in the house: cleaning (dusting, waxing the floor, windows, organizing and cleaning closets and chests, with special attention to the bathroom and the kitchen), care of clothing (which includes washing, sewing and ironing) and the preparation of meals (which includes cooking and serving). So that the woman may be able to make the best use of her working time and moments of leisure, she must organize and distribute her work in these three areas throughout the day, the month and the year." I love that, the woman organizing her inalienable functions throughout an eternity segmented into identical days, twins, so similar among themselves that you end up getting them confused and you never know any more if you see that neighbor from the third, what a handsome guy, on Thursdays and Fridays, in the end it makes no difference, for it's as though you're condemned for all eternity to roll along a big stone with the tip of your nose, and that's that!, what difference does it make if the man passes on Thursdays or Fridays, at ten after eight or twenty after eight, you're not going to see him pass in the middle of the series of gray days, not even by accident, that's not a woman's place; rather, it's making lists, so that everything can run smoothly like in space capsules in the future. What else does she say, can't leave anything out: "The home has to be an agreeable place, welcoming, to which the man will look forward to returning after the work done outside the house." Yes, that's all we need, there you are, trapped and locked in while he goes out, takes the air, sees other things, interacts with people and even on top of that he might not feel like coming back. Of course, why would he look forward to coming back, knowing that you were going to lock him into your grid of lists? Will the grid of lists also include "don't-step-on-the-rug, I've just cleaned it and I'm not scheduled to do that again for two weeks"? Will it include a "hi-honey-how-was-your-day-in-the-office," you see that in the movies all the time but you can't say that, of course, to husbands who don't come from an office, the wife of a miner, just for example, has enough to do to keep her husband from getting the whole living room dirty, upholstered in white which is the latest style, with that coal he's got stuck to his skin and ground in up to the whites of his eyes, how's he going to tell you how his day went? The best thing about the grid of lists includes the days when the couples do what they have to do, I mean that's what they're married for. Or could it be that they do that every day? I don't know… it seems like a lot for every day. Although with a guy like the neighbor from number three I'd be ready every day, even a couple of times a day, or even more, ehhh? Of course that probably can't be done so continually… Look at what I get to thinking about! "So that family life will be harmonious, the woman should be familiar with everything in the house; she ought to know where even the least and most insignificant details are located, and the function and utility they have in the home. As basic pieces of advice, these must be followed. In the first place, every object in the house must remain in its designated place, and every person will find the environment suitable for his well-being. In the second place, it's best that a moment at the end of the day should be devoted to going over what went right and also the errors of the day, because the order and good organization of a house brings many things with it. Always keep this motto in mind: 'Everything in its place and a place for everything.' Finally, it is advisable before retiring to prepare the clothing that is going to be worn first thing in the morning of the following day, and also the knapsack with the books of the children who go to school. Also, on the big shopping days it's advisable to cut back on cleaning as much as possible, whereas on the days of heavy cleaning the food should be prepared the night before, or else we will prepare a simple menu the same day." What a seductive life awaits us, like the vanes of a windmill, turning, turning, always the same, so organized, everything so well placed that it makes you sick, so perfect, so well brought up, with our minds so focused on these little things that don't matter to anybody... the worst part is preparing the kids' book bags, so if there were seven kids, there I'd be, preparing their little book bags, let's see... Can somebody tell me what destiny in life women have who aren't going to have children? What? Huh? What? Die of disgust? I definitely detest Dona Marián.

29

When Miguel called her "young lady" it was obvious
that he was annoyed, that he felt offended about something;
in fact, Miguel was a man with low self-esteem, that kind,
very common in university contexts, that needs a woman
in front of him, or underneath, or on top, for this matter of
positions is a very personal preference; it doesn't matter
where exactly the woman might be as long as she spends
the whole day saying: "Ooh, Miguel, you're so good at
this or that!" It was something positive for Einés finally to
get past the crisis, for her, for him and for the department;
she was a bright and affable young woman, very good
at teamwork, and he just couldn't figure out why she'd
got stuck in her thesis on Descartes; well, just thinking
about what she'd said to him in her last e-mail, Miguel,
he couldn't help it, he got the shivers: working on the
philosopher's life, what a joke! What was he going to do for
her if that wasn't philosophy? Einés was walking towards
the school, playing with an extremely long scarf, which
was dragging her along, or almost, and looking at herself
in every window she passed because she'd just gotten a
daring haircut, abandoning the long mane and showing up
with the hairstyle of a flapper from the twenties; it even
seemed as though any second she would break out into
a Charleston. Miguel was driving towards the school in
his car, nicely waxed but not at all expensive or showy,
for he still retained some principles from the hard-line
leftist principles in which he'd been educated, wearing a

very well-cut gray suit, a bit uncomfortable in the sleeves because the armhole was a little tight, but which, still and all, was his favorite suit because that defect, which hampered his movements so much, on the other hand made his arm muscles stand out, the ones he took good care of by swimming a kilometer three times a week; those clusters of sinew deserved to be taken care of because of the good results they got him with women. It's not that it was a bad haircut, but it made her feel insecure, because, as Livia used to say, whenever a woman cuts her hair it's because she's made up her mind to change direction in her love life, and, this being a proven and demonstrated truth, very much in keeping with the scientific method, she didn't want anything like that to be noticed, especially because she wasn't as sure about the new direction as the adage promised. It's not that he was some tinhorn Don Juan; the choice of the gray suit could also be viewed as a way of not giving in to the consumerist trends that were current; if you have a full suit, with trousers and jacket, all nice and shiny and of a good make, it doesn't make sense to throw it out because it's a little tight in the armhole, especially if that frames and sets off a part of your body that, what can you say!, isn't bad. Einés smiled insecurely when she looked at herself in the window of the University Document Center, which she had just passed on her left; it wasn't bad, she looked a little like Audrey Tautou, the one in that movie *Amélie*, or rather an everyday version of Audrey Hepburn. Miguel smiled insecurely, thinking about what women would imagine when they became aware of the muscular power of his arms, a bit like those of Kirk Douglas in *Spartacus*. Hmph! He hadn't set foot in a cinema for such a long time, although surely it hadn't been that long, it's

just that no other character came to mind. Einés entered
the Philosophy Building and stopped to talk with Dani and
with Fátima and Ánxela, who always went around together
like a pair of Siamese twins. Then she went into the bar
to have a cup of coffee and sat there at a table where a
group of friends, already assembled, were debating about
the possibilities of doing pop music in Galician, which
would fill a gap that's still not covered in the music scene.
Miguel greeted the custodian, the two women in charge
of the library, the head librarian, the department secretary,
three fifth-year students, and, somewhat comforted by
so much applause, he entered his office and turned on
the light. He scarcely had time to sit down and arrange
things a little, I'll have a look at the mail, even though I
looked at it at home an hour ago, I'm so obsessive!, when
there was a knock at the door. "Yesss!" His baritone voice,
well modulated, filled the air, and, from the other side of
the wall, a bit clumsy, stumbling first and making the thin
wooden panel of the door shake with her boots, an insecure
little voice said:

"Hi, Miguel, welcome back… Are you very busy now?"

She had an incredible haircut, woolen stockings with
colored stripes, like her gloves, which were about as
far from feminine as Miguel could imagine. She had,
however, a resolve in her look that he wasn't acquainted
with in her and, surprisingly, she had just rescued from
the bottom of a hutch an ancient sweetness, of a five-
year-old girl, of a mother, of a lover and girlfriend. She
was more Einés than ever.

Concerning what Einés found when she looked
in the chest in the attic
From the poetical diary of Einés Andrade

Poem XII

I have the strength to rebel
against this life.
I do.
And weep for the frightening past.
And to construct a house
on mountains in the Pacific,
the ice-fields of the Sahara,
the tropical jungle of Moscow,
the little plot of vegetables I planted in New York,
the asphalts of the forests,
on your face.

31

They'd been talking for nearly an hour. On Miguel's desk, piled high with books, Einés had built a cubbyhole from which she passed to him the material that supported her exposition. She resembled an employee of a technology company trying to persuade the directors, even if there was just one of them, of the need to attack the market from another angle. Or rather, the need not to attack the market, for Einés was not at all aggressive that day, though she was impetuous; she wasn't a whirlwind, a cyclone, a hurricane or a volcano, but rather she'd become a glacier at the beginning of spring, just in that moment when it starts melting, for glaciers are water and water must run and not remain petrified for an eternity, and so as soon as the heat moves in it falls down the mountainside to join up with the waters that are flowing, so that it never looks the same in any two moments, for in the end we will never bathe twice in the same water. The thing is that Miguel was listening so closely that he had forgotten to look at her cleavage; one would say that for once he had a woman in front of him and she had a mind, a soul if you like, not a body without a soul. Of course, so he wouldn't get disturbed by the body, Einés had made a point of wearing a shapeless sweater, in the "monk's-cowl" style with a long swan's tail which didn't let one even dream that she had a body underneath, although she did have one.

"The first thing," Einés was saying at that moment, "was the evidence of the artificial languages. Descartes changes his mind in a very short time. He reverses himself completely, and we know of no direct participation on his part in the development of any. We have the attempts that Mersenne had sent for his consideration, and they're so clumsy that it's impossible that he'd have changed his opinion on their account. So I started searching. Between 1635 and 1640, the time of Francine's life, Descartes is flourishing: he works constantly and everything is just the way he likes it. But ever since 1629, as soon as he settled down in Holland, the polished courtier he used to be undergoes a great change. One would say that he had somebody to impress. Since the love affair was known, for Francine was never a secret, I starting investigating that..."

"Silly romances. You'll deny it, but you women always like them."

"Of course. We women go crazy about what's inside... That's why you know so many female biographers, isn't that so?"

"I'm not following you, Einés..."

"Because speaking in first person, that's also a masculine privilege... no, please, let's not go down that road, we already know where the battle of the sexes leads and I haven't planned on sleeping with you."

"Nor have I suggested it... for now. And don't get your hopes up..."

"Seeing that you're taking the greatest interest in my research, I'll continue."

"Continue, please."

"In most of the biographies of Descartes it says that he had a daughter with a maid and that he loved her dearly. All very nice. Geneviève Rodis-Lewis has taught me what a rigorous and serious piece of work is in this sweet stuff of biographies. She tells, and tells very well, and later I was able to confirm it from other sources, that Descartes had a love affair with a young woman named Hélène Jans, but she specifies that she wasn't his maid; she served in the house where he was staying, which isn't the same thing. Probably when Descartes found out that Hélène was pregnant, he treated her very well, even if they didn't continue their romance. Of course Descartes acknowledged the little girl, but he didn't give her his surname. Doing that would have jeopardized his income in a period when he was living on handouts from his family, and they could still have forced him to marry some rich woman. I must confess to you that I didn't like that."

"Did you really want a romantic wedding in the seventeenth century?"

"I'm not stupid, nor as naïve as you think. Do you know what happened in that time period to maids who had a child by the master?"

"To be honest, no? Could they not make good matches?"

"They lost their job, their child, and their reputation. Nobody would hire them, and their own family rejected them. They were condemned, with few exceptions, to end up in prostitution."

"And Hélène Jans was an exception. Do you mind if I smoke?"

"No… Of course she was an exception, so her feelings towards Descartes couldn't have been class hatred or hatred of a seducer. Are you following me?"

"Vaguely."

"That's where it was left. Later I realized an important fact. During the time when the little girl was alive, Descartes was in the same house as the two of them for long stretches of time. When he wasn't, Descartes and Hélène exchanged letters."

"Love letters?"

"I couldn't read them, they haven't been preserved, but I don't think so. You don't see where I'm heading. Hélène was a woman who could write. In the seventeenth century, even in urban and well-to-do classes, just being able to write her name was the mark of culture for a woman. I mean, there were some who knew how to sign, and there were some who didn't. Writing letters shows a level of culture absolutely out of the ordinary in a woman of her class and her time!"

"Pardon me, Einés… I'm not seeing where you want to take me… but you know I'll go along with my eyes shut, it's all the same to me whether you want it in the country, on the beach, in the car…"

"Pay attention to me, please… and drop that game… Descartes is one of the targets of feminist thought. When he separated soul and body so utterly, with an intuition, moreover, that seems quite accurate to me, Descartes contributes to creating a support for the doctrines that the moralists of the church had spread and would go on spreading for centuries concerning women. For the man, very self-contained, is reserved the possibility of aspiring to a soul, which distinguishes him from animals. For the woman, who is all disordered desire, there's nothing but the body. Cartesianism, not Descartes, most likely, but definitely the edifice that he helped to found, confines women to a secondary place. If he had an exceptional lover, as is indicated by the simple fact that she could write, that ought to be salvaged for history. She could have been the one responsible for some changes in the philosopher's viewpoints, like the one concerning artificial languages."

"Maybe, maybe not."

"Yes, for now, yes. I'll come back to that later. Descartes, the unmarried father of a child to whom he never gave his name, was immortalized by his biographers and even by the painters of later eras, who never knew him, as a loving father, who was at Francine's bedside when she died. According to Rodis-Lewis, that's not true, and that part about what a loving father he was must be another myth, since a few months later both Descartes' father and his older sister died, the one who raised him, and he, when writing a letter to a friend, insists that in the last year he's lost two people he loved."

"So?"

"Two, not three. Are you following me? The death of his father and his sister were public events in his life. Including two people in the total and not three, the one left out inevitably has to be Francine."

"All right, Descartes wasn't a model father. Do you know, young lady, that you're introducing a modern concept into a historical investigation? Why don't you sit down and assess Aristotle's humanitarianism, since he owned slaves? Or Thomas Aquinas's misogyny, who never saw a woman at all? Don't you see that's mixing up categories?

"It only matters to the established power structure whether we do that kind of mixing, so we won't reinterpret its sacred cows."

"You sound a bit anarchistic.

"It's a family trait.

"Wonderful. Do you also practice free love?"

"Bleahh, you're getting on my last nerve."

32

Concerning what Einés found when she looked
in the chest in the attic
From the authentic Moral Maxims
of Queen Christina of Sweden: Twelfth Hundred

To conclude: This work is by one who neither desires nor regrets anything, and by one who does not impose anything on anyone.

33

At this stage in the conversation, Einés had already lost all hope of convincing Miguel. Probably just for that very reason, her expression began to be more resolute and freer: Einés was convincing herself.

"Look, Miguel, of course rumors circulated in Stockholm regarding the strange circumstances of Descartes' death. If they didn't become more long-lasting it was because at that exact moment Sweden had more important things to deal with. The queen was in a major struggle with the parliament, and she was resisting as well as she could the pressure from her advisors to get married and have a child."

"So then why didn't she have one?"

"How do I know why she didn't have one! Probably she didn't have a maternal instinct or… how do I know!"

"It's just that, ever since you've been fighting in the ranks of militant feminism, you have an answer for everything…"

"I'm going to let that wisecrack go, it's not funny. Christina was a free spirit and I've already told you that she must have been a lesbian."

"Didn't we agree that she was in love with Descartes?"

"You don't understand anything, do you?"

"No, I'm an old fogey, what do you expect?"

"Let me see, how can I explain it to you… The queen had girlfriends, several girlfriends, that's attested to in any halfway documented biography. What I believe is that with

Descartes there was something special... I'm not referring to anything concrete, all right? I don't have any proof..."

"I can see the headlines: 'Frigid princess finds her Prince Charming in the form of an ordinary philosopher.' As researchers we're going to cover ourselves in glory, aren't we? Einés, Einés... Are you playing games with me or what?"

"I've never spoken more seriously, and I certainly never realized until today how little you listen."

"I'm sitting here doing nothing except paying attention to a romance novel, and you say I'm not listening to you?"

"You're prejudging what I'm going to say..."

"Young lady, if I don't seem like an adequate director to you..."

"Yes, you do, Miguel, the best director I could have. Now may I speak?"

"I don't know if you're calming me down like a little kid, but for now we'll continue, to see where you get to. I think I still have ten grams of patience left."

"Well, snort them, because here I go. Instead of getting married, Christina named her cousin Carl Gustav as her heir and revealed to her inner circle her uneasiness about the situation of the throne; I believe that amounted to hinting at her desire to renounce the crown. She hadn't yet turned twenty-eight when she scandalized Europe by abdicating, converting to Catholicism and leaving Sweden on her way to Italy. No doubt Protestant orthodoxy was too rigid for the queen and her proclivities..."

"Her proclivities for girls?"

"You're being a bit slow. Just now I was considering rather that her intellectual curiosity was a proclivity."

"Curiosity is the first garment of Love," Miguel intoned with the dramatic recitative of an opera singer.

"Why do you say that?"

"I don't know. I read it somewhere and it popped into my head just now. Have I done something wrong, Miss Know-It-All?"

"No, it's that I've just written that…"

"In your thesis? It doesn't seem very appropriate."

"Not in the thesis… Forget it, it's not important. Perhaps Christina felt attracted by Descartes' peculiar religious disposition, although there's no evidence that he made any effort to convert her, no matter how widespread that opinion was among the Swedish courtiers. A historian I wasn't familiar with, one Hannah Skutnabb, suggests that a person as interested in the arts as Christina would feel better in the environment of Italy. The fact is that Christina only returned to Sweden on two occasions, to visit properties ceded to her for her maintenance, but her countrymen didn't like her presence. In Italy the most aristocratic circles considered making her Queen of Naples and even of Poland, although those schemes didn't go forward either. I don't believe she wanted it. Thus she settled down in Rome, and, with some travels to various places, she would die there thirty-five years after she left Stockholm behind."

Miguel lit a cigarette and broke the silence before it could become weighty. The atmosphere was intimate, strange in the world of research. All of a sudden it was evident that the distinguished professor was made of flesh and blood.

"That woman has bewitched you, hasn't she?"

"No, no, no! You see how you don't understand anything I'm saying? The one who bewitched me was Hélène and then it all came by itself: the love between Descartes and Christina, always so heavily criticized, the strange events of the philosopher's death, the fortunes of his theories, which grew and spread..."

Einés didn't smoke. It's not that she didn't like the taste of tobacco, that wasn't it. Recently she'd been doing yoga and she went out with a group of nature lovers who were very belligerent about those things. And also there was the possibility, not ignored just because it was remote, that one day he might kiss her. Einés wouldn't like it at all if he took that step and found her mouth tasting of tobacco. He didn't smoke. Since that afternoon would be taken up with the matter of the thesis and she wouldn't see him, with any luck, until the following morning, Einés stretched out her hand towards the pack of Ducados that Miguel had left on the desk and took one. She played with the lighter for a little while before lighting up. Right when the flame was licking at the end of the cigarette, she looked upward through her hair and murmured:

"I suppose if I told you that in the attic of my grandmother's house there's a hutch with manuscripts by these women, which allow me to have a different perspective from the one in official history as it's been told to us... if I told you all that, you wouldn't believe me." And Einés blew the smoke, provocatively, into his face.

"What are you saying? Are you crazy? Why would they be there?" Miguel, stunned, forgot to swallow the smoke expelled from her mouth, that is, he forgot to be himself.

"It's a long family story, I can't tell you the whole thing now. The fact is that the women of my family have always left a certain hutch to their daughters. It's not so strange.

Instead of a dowry, many women still do that, pass along the testimony of their memory with photos, with sheets, with old tablecloths, with discarded belongings that no one wants to get rid of. By a strange coincidence, as you would say, or by the action of magical forces, for one doesn't always see everything that exists, as Hélène would say, the chain of this particular hope chest has never broken up to me."

"Einés, you must be very ill. That can't be true."

"Like everything in life. If it isn't true, it very well could be."

Concerning what Einés found when she looked
in the chest in the attic
Proceedings against witchcraft in the Low Countries

A resident of Amsterdam, unmarried and more than sixty years old, named Hélène Jans, was brought before the general tribunal of the Low Countries in April 1676, after fourteen statements had been collected that accused her of very diverse charges. During the trial, where she was only sentenced to wear a rope around her neck, in addition to receiving a number of lashes, she elaborated on many of those statements with a certain insolence, insisting on giving half-replies. At the same time, she was vague in her explanation, and did not even bother to deny many of the other accusations. The prosecutor in charge of the case accused this healer, witch and sorceress of the following crimes:

First: She prescribed a curative consisting of the use of a ribbon that the same sick person was wearing.

Second: She boasted that an adopted daughter of hers, one Agnes Jans, had in her breasts a weapon with which she could make one man or a hundred lose all reason, if the said young woman so wished.

Third: She threatened with death the owners of some sheep which ate certain herbs from her garden, supposedly extremely valuable ones, when everyone knew that it was just a matter of some wretched black nightshade, of no value whatsoever. To the reply of the shepherds, who asked her what she could do against them, she declared that she would make them eat worms.

Fourth: She attempted to cure a woman by casting something into the palms of her hands and then ordering her to close them and not wash for nine days.

Fifth: She promised that she would make some stolen cloths appear and, as those whom she suspected of being the perpetrators of the theft would not admit it, she threatened them in a loud voice that she would force them to go with the cloths to the door of the church and make a wild wind blow that would lift up their skirts in the back, whether they liked it or not.

Sixth: She recommended to a woman that she recite a spell to attract a man.

Seventh: She made a chaste married woman inhale a certain magical herb so that she would bear a child without pain, in this way causing the incautious woman not to obey the Biblical curse of bearing children in pain. When this woman was asked if the fumigation with magical herbs had taken away her pain, she answered in the affirmative, and even added that with the remedies of the accused, a woman could have a child whenever she wished, happy and content to see it, with no worries except raising the child.

Eighth: She prescribed for another woman a conjuration with a flower of hers so that a beloved person would not go away from her.

Ninth: She had committed many other crimes.

"I'm going to tell you about another aspect of my research."

"Research, research... Well, let's settle for calling it a fishing trip."

"I didn't know you were so meticulous on matters of books, really. I thought you saved all your rigor for bedroom issues... No, don't interrupt, then I won't ever be able to tell you about this. In 1666, Descartes' remains were exhumed, put into a copper coffin, and taken to Paris to be buried in the church of Sainte-Geneviève-du-Mont. In the course of the French Revolution, they were dug up again, and were placed in the Pantheon dedicated to the eminent men of the nation. In 1819 the coffin was taken to Saint-Germain-des-Prés. Before they deposited it in its final resting place, they opened it for a routine check, and what do you think they found?"

"Worms?"

"Please be serious and listen to me."

"I'm doing that. Come on, I'm not a very imaginative guy... What could there be? What could there be?... Christina's panties?"

This time Einés couldn't keep from laughing. Miguel knew how to turn on the charm when he wanted to.

"I don't believe she wore them. In that era, dear director, the Dominicans prohibited the new invention of panties as indecent, and only window washers wore them."

"Hmmm, you know, that sounds like a good era to me."

"I'll go on with my story; I see that you're interested."

"Please continue!"

"They discovered that nothing more or less was missing except Descartes' head. Not long afterwards it showed up in a government auction in Sweden. Apparently the head was cut off the first time the remains were moved, because an inscription was found that read... Hold on, I've got a note card here, so I can be more exact... come on, come on, where are you? Here: 'The cranium of Descartes, taken in scrupulous care by Israel Hanstrom in the year 1666, on the occasion of the transfer of the body to France, and since then hidden in Sweden.' Whoever this Hanstrom was, he believed that the philosopher in some sense belonged to Sweden and should stay there. Probably it has something to do with a known Cartesian school that was formed in Stockholm around that time, I don't know... In 1878 the cranium was also returned to France and registered in the inventory of anatomical specimens in the Museum of Man in Paris. That means that the body and the head of Descartes are still separated by the waters of the Seine. Taking into account what we think nowadays about the relationship between mind and brain, the author of dualism is proving his theory in his own flesh..."

"You believe that the soul is in the head...?"

"Everybody believes that, right?"

"My dear girl, if you still think that, I believe you haven't had much sex, and it's been bad."

"Ha, ha... I'm not listening. In 1980 Eike Pies, a German scientist, was sorting the correspondence of his seventeenth-century ancestor Willem Piso in the archives of the University of Leiden in Holland. All of a sudden, he came across a letter written by Queen Christina's physician,

Johann van Wullen, to this Willem Piso, who was also a well-known physician. I have here the fragments of the letter that are of interest to us: 'As you know, several months ago Descartes arrived in Sweden to pay homage to Her Serene Majesty the Queen,' Van Wullen writes. 'Just now, at the fourth hour before dawn, this man has died... The queen wished to see this letter before I sent it to you. She wished to know what I wrote to my colleagues about the philosopher's death. She gave strict orders to avoid letting my letters fall into the hands of persons unknown.' Pies, another fool like me, interested in the history of private life, which is not philosophy, investigated. No, let me go on, Miguel, please... In good time it was announced that Descartes had died of pneumonia at the beginning of 1650; thus it was quite strange that no physician should have commented in writing to another colleague about the symptoms of such a common and sadly familiar disease. It is much stranger that the queen should have censored the correspondence of her physician. There was another possible explanation. Pneumonia begins with cold, trembling, fever and sharp pains in the chest, and the disease progresses with coughing, gasping and expectorations of a rust-red color. However, the court physician is describing a totally different set of symptoms to his Dutch colleague: 'During the first days he slept deeply. He did not eat, drink or take medicine. The third and fourth days he was agitated and did not sleep, still not eating or taking medication. On the fifth day I was called to his bedside but Descartes refused to receive treatment. As the unmistakable signs of death were advancing, I agreed with pleasure to keep my distance from the dying man. As he was going through the fifth and sixth days, he complained of dizziness, and on the eighth day of hiccups and black vomits. Then he had uneven breathing and a wandering gaze. On the ninth day all was lost. On the morning of the tenth day, his soul went to meet God.' Do you understand?"

"Of course! Our philosopher died of a disease other than pneumonia."

"Something more than that. This description of the progress of Descartes' final illness matches up better with the symptoms of acute arsenic poisoning than with the characteristics of pneumonia. If we can trust these indications, Descartes was the victim of a murder."

"So why don't you make a suspense movie instead of writing a thesis?"

"You know as well as I do that I'm onto something."

"Yesss! Obviously! Let's suppose that Descartes was murdered by the grammarians who hated him because of his enormous influence on the queen... What does that have to do with his work?"

"Who knows?... With what he said in the *Discourse* or the *Meditations*, nothing, obviously... but what do you say about how the story's been told? Christina was a great queen before he showed up in her life. His intrusion made her go down in history simply as a woman influenced by an ultra-Catholic philosopher. And what if things had been different? He could have been Christina's chosen one, the first philosopher-king or, at least, lover, and king in that way, just as so many women loved by kings have ruled throughout history..."

"I'll grant you that. So let's see, if Descartes hadn't died under strange circumstances, history would have been different. But I still don't see where you're trying to go with this and what it has to do with our work."

"Miguel, please, make an effort. Descartes, like Bacon and some others, ended up affirming one kind of explanation as good. They established what was research and what was not, what were the methods and procedures for doing research, what were the subjects, what kinds of influences there were. If the information I have about the life of Descartes' women could be proven, and I believe it can, many of those principles would fall. Hélène represents empiricism, attention to the great human questions, knowledge put into the service of human happiness and practical utility…"

Miguel interrupted her. For a moment his gaze revealed a juvenile interest:

"Hélène, no, your Hélène, who, for sure, is a fantasy."

"Not exactly a fantasy: a historical reconstruction, one that doesn't fit the canon… Hold on a moment. Christina, for her part, would be the rebellion against everything established, the person capable of putting any theory to the test because she was ready to turn her life around…"

"And who, according to your research," and Miguel, while he was saying the word "research," put air quotes around it, "devotes herself for years to convincing Hélène to publish an artificial language of dubious and deficient design…"

"Artificial languages were in vogue."

"It sounds like a weak argument, Einés, although I admit that I didn't know anything about this business of the languages…"

"It was the vogue, the invention par excellence of its time. All the thinkers of the seventeenth and eighteenth centuries composed at least one language, sometimes quite a few. And they all cite Descartes as a reference, when he is rather a skeptic…"

"Even so…"

"I forgot to tell you that all the inventors of artificial languages, absolutely all, are men. That has to be strange…"

"Why?"

"We women have a reputation as chatterboxes, as motormouths. If any invention should be associated with us, it ought to be a linguistic invention."

"It still sounds weak to me."

"What proves that I'm right is that Hélène's attempt never saw the light of day. It was a cursed invention because she couldn't be accepted in her time as an inventor. Everything she did was destined to disappear."

"That's practicing a ferocious reductionism. All the changes were produced because a few exceptional minds succeeded in modifying the way their contemporaries saw the world."

"That's a myth. The inventions of invisible people are unseen…"

"I don't know why you say that."

"When I was little, my aunt Carmiña used to say that by the year 2000 women wouldn't have breasts."

"Whaaat?"

"Yes. In the seventies unisex was the rage, and therefore, in her opinion, fashion would impose androgynous models."

"Something along these lines did happen…"

"Breasts would become something ugly and antiquated. The modern way would be to be flat. Those who were born with small breasts would win out…"

"And the others?"

"The others would get an operation. When she used to tell me that when I was little, I would declare solemnly that I would never do such a thing. Aunt Carmiña would answer me: 'Maybe,' and quickly say to me: 'And when you have a daughter, will you be prepared to condemn her to be different from everyone else? A kind of monster? And all because you insist on keeping your tits?'"

"You aunt's quite a sociologist…"

"Yes, besides being an artist, and many other things… The point is that she made me understand the difficulty of succeeding in having one's individual criteria respected. Therefore I'm going to write this story, even if it isn't philosophy, even if it seems improbable, even if Hélène and Christina, both of them, have lost their battle…"

Miguel gazed at her for a long time. In some way he seemed proud of his student:

"You're really going to write that, Einés?"

"I am."

36

Concerning what Einés put into the chest
in the attic at the end of the recipe book

I, Einés Andrade, composed this history for anyone
who may wish to read it. To weave it together, I chose
the fragments of lives that the hutch at home revealed to
me, which were not lives, only parts, and which I didn't
reproduce in their entirety, but only to the extent that
they could mark the thread along which all those women
passed before me, like in a piece of handicraft, like in a
patchwork quilt. At the time when I was writing, I realized
that I was rescuing the memory of the invisible women
who preceded me, and, moved by their spirit, sometimes
I invented, explored anecdotes, let myself be carried
along by the smoke of my imagination, and squeezed
the words as much as I could to extract the honey they
had inside and let them sweeten my mouth and make my
lips shine, to see if, with me adorned like that, he might
finally want to kiss me. When I wrote I failed in my
project. I'll never be a doctor of philosophy, and I truly
regret that, it would be a very vindicating position, in
which I could scintillate with my own brilliance, besides
dazzling attendees at conferences that were looking
for a specialist in metaphysics or ontology, raising the
standard for the female gender. Since I have to make a
living, I've just requested a loan. I'm going to establish
a herbalist's shop and make Hélène's scent spread out all
over the world, to see if we can erase once and for all the
stench of burnt flesh that still follows us around since her

death. To anyone who reads this, I would beg you not to reproach as lunacy, arrogance or presumptuous boasting that I, a woman, have criticized authors as subtle as the ones I mention, and skimp on eulogies of the great works of the consecrated thinkers. And let the reader bear in mind that they, the great authors, dared excessively to defame and censure the female sex without exception, and yet their works are not condemned for that reason, with people saying of them that they're the product of resentment. Especially, I beg to be pardoned for having had the self-assurance to exist, to cure, to stand, to think, to abdicate, to raise, to speak, to study, to evaporate from enclosures and escape, to suffer the deep feelings of love and maternity, to caress with words, to desire, to seduce. And in case Hélène, the wise woman, speaks through my mouth, I recommend to everyone that you get prettied up, take good care of yourselves, beautify your body, take care of your intentions and your words and enjoy pleasure as much as you can, for there will be occasion in the eternity that awaits us, being as we are earth, to return to the peaceful place from which we were freed by the chance that our father and mother happened to embrace. Make the most of the day, then, and take the reading with an infusion of raspberry, into which you should toss a pinch of black nightshade, a herb with black berries that is also called in some places wild tomato and in others dog grapes, which soothes pain, which is as much as we can do in this life, lull pain to sleep, and take advantage of having, like black nightshade, a bad reputation so as to make the nights of leisure last longer than the days of work. And let yourselves be seduced by words, because words, if they are well chosen and the soul is in the right season, are capable of prolonging pleasure like aphrodisiacs and soothing pain like analgesics, for there's a reason for which aphrodisiacs and analgesics are words too.

Compostela, March 3, 2005

Read more fiction in English from Small Stations Press:

Anxos Sumai, THAT'S HOW WHALES ARE BORN

A young woman, who has left Galicia to go and study marine biology in Mexico (Baja California), is recalled to Galicia when it is found out that her mother is very sick. Her aunt would like her to sign some papers agreeing to take over the family business and renouncing her Mexican studies and emotional ties that she has forged in her new life. However, returning to Galicia and renewing her family ties is not exactly what the woman wants. Her mother has shut herself in her room for the last year, and relations between them have always been strained. She received more affection from a nanny, Felisa, and better advice from her uncle, Cándido. There is also an older brother, Ramón, a larger-than-life figure who has left an indelible mark in the lives of those around him, and an absent father. Will the woman's visit to see her sick mother turn out to be permanent, and will it soothe any of the festering wounds in her psyche, wounds that she has buried beneath her marine studies and a relationship with her one-time tutor? *That's How Whales Are Born* is a return to our origins, a search into the usefulness of stirring up past memories and seeking reconciliation.

ISBN 978-954-384-073-1

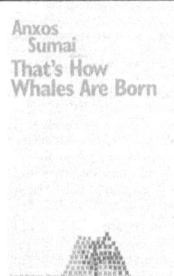

Xabier P. DoCampo,
THE BOOK OF IMAGINARY JOURNEYS
Inspired by Italo Calvino's Invisible Cities, *The Book of Imaginary Journeys*
by Xabier P. DoCampo follows in the tradition of great travel literature
that began with Homer's *Odyssey*. It purports to be the transcription of
two travel journals written by a certain X.B.R., in which the Traveller
gives as objective a description as he can of the cities and kingdoms
he visits. So it is he comes to a city you can only visit for three days
or where you cannot fall asleep, a city balanced on the fine point of a
diamond or rotating on a water wheel, a city whose inhabitants are
all tree-dwelling women or descended from birds, a city where the
tombstones are inscribed not with the names of the deceased but with
the titles of their favourite books, a city where money is only valid for
a year, where none of its inhabitants can go fishing because all the rods
have been turned into soldiers' lances, whose ministers are made to
wear nooses as a warning to stay clean... The Traveller records songs,
proverbs and remedies he hears along the way and describes some of
the people he meets – a woman who conducts imaginary orchestras,
a man who loves the earth so much he would like to plough it with
a pair of unicorns, another searching for a treasure guarded by seven
keys... Like translation, travel is a return to the source, the point of
departure. What the Traveller takes away from the experience is what
he has learned.
ISBN 978-954-384-063-2

Ledicia Costas, AN ANIMAL CALLED MIST

In *An Animal Called Mist*, a book of six short stories, the Galician author Ledicia Costas (Winner of the 2015 Spanish National Book Award) walks the tightrope between fiction and reality in a superb and sometimes shocking narrative. She bases herself on real events in and after the Second World War – the Siege of Leningrad, the sinking of the USS *Indianapolis*, the dropping of atomic bombs on Hiroshima and Nagasaki, the interrogation of Italian partisans by the Banda Koch, the sexual exploitation of women internees in Nazi concentration camps, the trials of high-ranking Nazi officials – and then recreates them, changing and inventing biographical details, giving free rein to her writer's imagination in order to produce a sequence of stories that look not so much at historical fact as at the essence of barbarism, the capacity of the human mind to conceive ways of torturing and tormenting fellow human beings. This is not a historical account of the Second World War – for that, the reader should consult works of history – but a book of fiction that focuses on the shadow projected by the events, their essence, the granulated content of their darkness. Ledicia Costas is one of Galicia's best-known writers who, in the tradition of writers such as Manuel Rivas and Agustín Fernández Paz, magnifies the voice of the persecuted in her narrative. *An Animal Called Mist* won the Losada Diéguez Prize for Literary Creation in 2016.

ISBN 978-954-384-062-5

Ana María Matute, THE FOOLISH CHILDREN

The Foolish Children contains twenty-one micro-fiction stories by Ana María Matute in Spanish and in English translation. The original was first published in Spain during Franco's dictatorship. It was rated by the Nobel laureate Camilo José Cela as "the most important work written in Spanish by a woman since the Countess Emilia Pardo Bazán." Ana María Matute, along with Camilo José Cela and Miguel Delibes, is widely considered one of Spain's most distinguished writers of fiction in the twentieth century. She was awarded the Spanish National Book Award twice and, in 2010, received the Spanish-speaking world's most prestigious literary award, the Cervantes.
ISBN 978-954-384-060-1

For an up-to-date list of our publications, please visit
www.smallstations.com